Human Seed

BY THE SAME AUTHOR

The Necessary Evil
Caresco, Superman
The Exploits of Professor Tornada (3 Vols.)
The Lynx (with Michel Corday)

André Couvreur

Human Seed

translated, annotated and introduced by
Brian Stableford

A Black Coat Press Book

ISBN 978-1-61227-880-3. First Printing. August 2019. Published by Black Coat Press, an imprint of Hollywood Comics.com, LLC, P.O. Box 17270, Encino, CA 91416. All rights reserved. Except for review purposes, no part of this book may be reproduced or transmitted in any form or by any means, electronic or mechanical, including photocopying, recording, or by any information storage and retrieval system, without permission in writing from the publisher. The stories and characters depicted in this novel are entirely fictional. Printed in the United States of America.

Introduction

La Graine by André Couvreur, here translated as *Human Seed*, was first published by Plon-Nourrit in May 1903. It was the second part of a projected trilogy of Naturalist novels collectively entitled *La Famille*, that began with *La Force du sang* (1902). It also became the intermediate point of another triptych, bracketed by *Le Mal nécessaire* (1899; tr. as *The Necessary Evil*)[1]—the first element of a Naturalist trilogy collectively entitled *Les Dangers sociaux*—and concluded with the futuristic utopian fantasy *Caresco surhomme ou Le Voyage en Eucrasie* (1904; tr. as *Caresco, Superman*)[2], linking those two very different novels by employing their central character, the brilliant but unscrupulous surgeon Caresco, as a minor character, and including a brief embryonic sketch of the utopia featured in the later novel. The trilogy to which *La Graine* belongs more intimately was eventually concluded, after the publication of *Caresco surhomme*, with *Le Fruit* (1907), the last of the author's earnest Naturalist novels; all of his later work, with the exception of two light-hearted satirical fantasies, belongs to the genre of *roman scientifique*.

The most obvious predecessor of *La Graine*, and the work that presumably inspired Couvreur to produce it, was Émile Zola's *Fécondité* (1899; tr. as *Fruitfulness*), the first volume of a projected quartet of novels of social commentary, *Les Quatre Évangiles* [The Four Gospels], only two of which were completed. Couvreur's novel takes up both the essential theme of *Fécondité* and its sermonizing mission, its deliberate attempt to provide contemporary humankind with a new gospel based on science rather than superstition. Unlike Zola, Couvreur was scientifically educated and he was a practicing

---

[1] Black Coat Press, ISBN 978-1-61227- 253-5.

[2] Black Coat Press, ISBN 978-1-61227-254-2.

physician, who had observed far more closely than the father of Naturalism the operations and consequences of human insemination in Parisian society and its underworld. His first trilogy had followed up its account of the license to kill tacitly granted to surgeons with elaborate examinations of the ongoing social disasters of syphilis and alcoholism—insistences inevitably recapitulated in *La Graine*.

Zola's original manifesto for Naturalism, most extensively elaborated in the essay *Le Roman expérimental* (1880), had claimed that the genre of fiction in question was essentially a scientific exercise, an inquiry into human nature to be carried out in the spirit of Comtean positivism, and his most extensive series of novels, *Les Rougon-Macquart* (1871-1893) attempted to illustrate the role played by flawed heredity in human affairs, in a disastrous series of physical and psychological stigmata handed down through the generations. One of Zola's followers, Édouard Rod, characterized his work as *roman scientifique* [scientific fiction], but that term had already been claimed as a description of Jules Verne's scientifically-informed travelogue fiction, and it was later adapted to apply to speculative fiction of the kind in which Couvreur specialized later in his career, so it is unsurprising that Zola always preferred his own term.

Couvreur was the most purist of all the later Naturalists in following up that quasi-positivistic aspect of Zola's manifesto and building on Zola's own precedents—much more so than "neo-Naturalists" of the ilk of Paul Bourget, who focused entirely on the psychology of their characters, detaching it in large measure from their physiology. Couvreur is insistent in rooting his psychological analyses very firmly in biology, especially in pathology, and in so doing he revealed very starkly the two key problems of that genre of fiction: the perishability of scientific insight and the penalty often involved in challenging popular moral judgments and prejudices.

Although Couvreur knew far more about contemporary science than Zola, and was therefore able to be more up-to-date and more elaborate in his analyses, he was nevertheless

6

dealing with a field of knowledge that was advancing very rapidly, and his insights were soon surpassed. Looking back from a viewpoint informed by the understanding we now have, Couvreur's science seems almost as rudimentary and as misguided as Zola's. That problem, however, could only become obvious in retrospect, and when the novel was first published, its effect paled into insignificance by comparison with the other; in his scathing attack on the alleged follies and evils of contemporary social morality, *La Graine* was one of the most shocking works of its era, and one that attempted more fervently than any other to push back the boundaries of the conventionally-unmentionable. It was soon flamboyantly outstripped in that ambition by *Caresco surhomme*, but it met exactly the same ironic fate: in attempting to shift the boundaries of the unmentionable, it became unmentionable itself, and was effectively eliminated from literary history.

Le Mal nécessaire had already touched on some of the issues raised in *La Graine*, but very tentatively. One of the greatest unmentionables of the day, contraception, is briefly discussed in the earlier novel, but very elliptically, as a bush mostly beaten around. *La Graine* not only features several characters who routinely practice contraception, but offers elaborate accounts of the methods they use and the reasonings behind their usage—accounts that might seem coy and oblique by today's standards, but were unusually detailed for their time. *Le Mal nécessaire* also mentions abortion, but does not come nearly as close to describing what the abortionists of the day actually did as the text of *La Graine* does, and the latter novel adds to that revelation an extremely gruesome description of the consequences of an abortion carried out with an unsterilized stylet. In 1903, it was an extremely shocking novel, even in liberal Paris.

Couvreur was not the first writer to venture on to that previously-forbidden ground. The employment of surgical operations as means of female sterilization, and hence of liberation from the consequences of libertinism, had been featured in Jane de La Vaudère's sensationalist novel *Les Demi-*

Sexes (1897; tr. as *The Demi-Sexes*), although La Vaudère had been very vague about the nature of the operation, apparently thinking that an "ovariotomy" could be carried out with the aid of a stylet introduced into the vagina, whereas *Le Mal nécessaire* was far more accurate in representing the necessary operation as a hysterectomy carried out with the aid of an abdominal incision, in which the equivocal Caresco becomes something of a specialist. *La Graine* does not labor the point unduly, but does reiterate it robustly.

Les Demi-Sexes had also pushed the envelope with its account of the role played by lesbianism in female libertinism—a hot topic of salon gossip at the time, although treated with considerable coyness in literary accounts, even in Catulle Mendès graphic horror story *Méphistophela* (1890; tr. as *Mephistophela*). *La Graine* takes up that theme too, offering a more elaborate account than either of the cited predecessors of the supposed sexual pathology of that phenomenon—an account typical of the ignorance of the day, but so far outdated now as to have become horribly offensive. Within the context of the 1903 novel, however, the treatment of that topic, like all the others addressed, is inevitably controlled by the fundamental philosophy of the novel's "gospel," explicitly represented therein as an "apostolate" on the part of its hero, Claude Fargeaud, an evolutionary botanist infected before birth with tuberculosis.

Although contemporary readers would undoubtedly have been most horrified by the author's handling of the superficial themes of contraception, abortion, "artificial fecundation" (i.e. artificial insemination) and lesbianism, all of those ideas are now commonplace, albeit still somewhat controversial, and the only shocking thing about them is that they were once considered so unmentionable as to be banished from public discussion. By contrast, the moral philosophy developed and advocated by Claude, and strongly approved by the novel's narrative voice, is still largely unmentionable, mostly dismissed without discussion as a matter that ought not even be considered, stuck with a label—"eugenics"—that it is sufficient to cite to produce a phobic reaction in many people.

Because of that phobic reaction, relatively few works of fiction have ever treated the topic of eugenic philosophy, and the scope of that philosophy has been left largely unexplored, although it is now bound to seem the most original and the most interesting aspect of the novel. André Couvreur would probably have been very surprised to learn that, a century after the publication of his crusading novel, contraception, abortion, artificial insemination and lesbian practices have all become matters of social routine in Western society, in spite of diehard disapproval on the part of certain sectors of that society, whose members have not yet despaired of their extirpation, but he would surely have been even more surprised to learn that the one confident prediction that he made about the future evolution of that society—that people would become more aware of a moral duty to consider the genetic quality of their offspring before indulging in reproduction—would not only have failed to come to fruition, but would have remained largely unthinkable.

By virtue of that residual unmentionability, and its consequent unthinkability, *La Graine* will seem to many contemporary readers to be a truly bizarre novel, not so much in putting forward the argument that it does, but in shaping the plot that illustrates and exemplifies the argument in question and contriving the denouement that arises out of that plot. Its representation of the decision that Claude Fargeaud eventually makes, and the motivation that leads him inexorably to make it, seems so alien to the denouements favored by the vast majority of modern works of fiction that it calls into question the very notion of a denouement. It is certainly more challenging than the far more conventional denouement provided for the flamboyantly imaginative *Caresco surhomme*. The reader might not sympathize with the denouement of *La Graine*—indeed, it is highly unlikely that very many readers could be found today who would be capable of sympathizing with it—

9

but that is the novel's true merit, its value as a challenge to established ideas, and a test of their rationality.

Although Couvreur did conclude the projected trilogy of which *La Graine* was designed to be a part, it is significant that he only did so belatedly, after first making a gigantic generic sidestep, and that after concluding his second Naturalist trilogy he abandoned that kind of narrative forever. There is a sense in which *La Graine* exhausted not only what he wanted to accomplish with the Zolaesque *roman expérimental*, but also exceeded what the genre, as defined by Zola's manifesto, was capable of achieving as a communicative endeavor. It was a novel that very few people wanted to read, or even to exist. In switching his attention to *roman scientifique* of a different kind, transforming his literary style (or stylet) as well as his themes, Couvreur was carrying out a further literary experiment, which also failed, in terms of receiving any significant sales or critic attention.

While he lived, André Couvreur remained an eccentric literary outsider, largely ignored, along with both of the genres to which he made crucial—or, at least, extreme—contributions, and the highly selective memory of literary history has done him, and those genres, few favors since, but at least, as a physician he could continue to save lives and credit himself with a certain social utility. Viewed objectively, however, from the standpoint of the twenty-first century, he can be seen, both as a Naturalist and as an author of speculative fiction, as a writer of bold imagination and considerable intelligence, so far ahead of his time in his thinking and invention that the world has not yet overtaken him. Although some contemporary readers will undoubtedly consider him a evil genius, the fact remains that he did have an unappreciated genius; his ideas are worthy of attention and reasoned reply, rather than being simply dismissed as too uncomfortable to be considered. *La Graine*, especially seen as part of an exotic triptych commenced with *Le Mal nécessaire* and concluded with *Caresco surhomme*, is a truly original work, and a crucial element of a unique and spectacular whole.

This translation was made from the London Library's copy of the 1903 Plon-Nourrit edition of *La Graine*.

Brian Stableford

HUMAN SEED

PART ONE

I

At the sudden crackling sound that departed from the al-most-extinct fire, Antonin Fargeaud, the father and old head of the family, raised his white-haired head momentarily, exhaust-ed by the fatigue and emotion of the night that had almost passed. From the armchair in which he was dozing he tried to distinguish the details of the closed room in the rapidly dissi-pating fulgurance of the fire, but his eyes, threatened by cata-racts, were poor, and his memory awoke with difficulty in a brain debilitated by the years, bitterness and disappointment.

One thing appeared in the gloom, however that prompted remembrance. On the whiteness of the bed where the invalid was sleeping painfully, his respiration punctuated by a few inarticulate groans, there was a bloodstain, a red splash that renewed the constriction of his heart. It evoked one of the most poignant shocks of his long life, already stirred by so much anguish.

The day before, his favorite son, Claude Fargeaud, brought back from Paris suffering, had been seized as soon as he arrived at the château by a hemoptysis so serious that it had required three hours to vanquish it: three hours of alarm, dur-ing which the urgency of Doctor Bouret, the physician from Rouen, had struggled in vain against the red flow emerging inexhaustibly from the livid mouth. Then, suddenly, as if the malady were weary of playing with so much resistant life, the red source had dried up and the young man, annihilated, with a feverish illumination in his cheeks had fallen into a heavy sleep, disturbed by a few groans, the unconscious plaints of having suffered so much and having so much still to suffer.

And he, the old father overwhelmed by the years, whose stiffened limbs required a gentler posture than the one he had, and who wished for a seat softer than the old wooden armchair that hurt his back, had remained there all night, in the heavy atmosphere charged with the emanations of ether, keeping watch on his child's curt respiration, trying to interpret the brief words that the latter murmured in his delirium.

At any rate, he was not alone in keeping that vigil. On a nearby sofa, one of Claude's childhood friends, a companion in thought, Raoul Fieux, had also put his affectionate devotion at the service of the invalid; but his courage had ceded to the imperious necessity of sleep, and since the moment when Claude had calmed down, he had been slumbering soundly, with all the lethargy of his thirty years and the need to pay with repose for the intense and powerful vigor that circulated in his veins, of which his blond and handsome Christ-like head, now lying on the back of the seat, revealed the youthfulness and the strength.

And that bloodstain soling the sheets, glimpsed in a flash of firelight, that human redness that no one had had the time to make disappear, dispelled the old man's daze, reanimating yesterday's drama, and the dread of a fatal denouement, now avoided, like a dagger-thrust tearing the veil of his torpor. He reproached himself for having succumbed to fatigue; he recalled the doctor's orders, the care to be taken not to allow the atmosphere to get cold. Although the day before, a beautiful bright June day radiant with precocious summer, had been warm, and although the dawn, still pale, filtering through a gap in the long curtains, promised imminent sunshine, the old Château de la Taquainerie, a vestige of feudal resistance, guarded the cold dampness of frost jealously in its stone carcass under the tall trees that dominated it, under the caress of fresh water that shivered at its flanks and protected it with a kind of natural rampart.

The old man straightened his tall frame, seized the little lamp whose light was almost dying, and raised it to the level of a thermometer hanging near the fireplace. Having observed the lowering of the temperature, he leaned toward a box of wood, took a log therefrom, and deposited it in the hearth, taking infinite care not to make any noise. Slight as his movement was, however, it awoke Raoul. Prompt in alarm, but less rapid in extracting himself from his heavy slumber, the young man had to stretch himself before recovering his senses. Finally, also returning to the reality of things, a little ashamed of having been a less vigilant guardian, he approached Antonin Fargeaud, who was finishing his task.

"Would you like me to help you, Monsieur? Do you need me?"

"No, I've finished."

"You should have alerted me," Raoul added. "I'm confused by the trouble you're taking..."

The old man made a gesture that excused a very legitimate lassitude; then, having consulted the clock, which was preparing to chime three, he said: "Go to bed, my friend...you're tired. At your age, one needs sleep. At mine, on the contrary, one sleeps little, for one knows that one can soon be compensated during the eternal night."

"I'm astonished to hear you talk like that, Monsieur Fargeaud. Have you lost your faith in a long life, in the twenty years of vigor that your strength reserves for you?"

"Yes," said the old man, sadly, "I've lost the faith. Since yesterday, everything is broken. Yesterday, I still had hope, I wanted to live, leaning on my old man's stick, and on my little Claude...alas, the poor fellow...! You see...!"

The desolation of his attitude indicated the bed where Claude was continuing a slumber disturbed by painful respiration. As Raoul was about to protest, he continued: "Yesterday, I was dreaming of grandchildren coming from him. That blossoming of young faces and clear gazes would have been an encouragement to subsist. The new sap departed from the branches would have come to render a little verdure to the exhausted trunk. Now, it's finished, quite finished..."

"You're wrong to be alarmed, Monsieur Fargeaud. Claude isn't so very ill. Numerous people have hemoptyses and subsequently engender fine children. Isn't Claude engaged, moreover, to the most reassuring of young women, to Henriette? Come on...you're being too pessimistic."

Antonin Fargeaud shook his head again, resumed his place in his armchair and drew the young man to a neighboring seat. Then, speaking in a low voice, for his solicitude for his son's repose did not quit him, he became communicative, he whispered his heart, he surrendered his haunting, the unique hope and the unique concern of his declining career; he unveiled his aspirations of old, his present failures, the disappointed illusions of a creator, of the custodian of his family, having maintained in his hands thus far the precious treasure of blood, and now seeing it escape suddenly, and spill into oblivion.

"My friend," he said, in a murmur that could not reach the ear of the invalid, "it's good of you to want to reassure me, but you'd strive to do so in vain. I'm not a physician, it's true; I don't have the science that examines and foresees...but unfortunately, I've been brought up in the school of experience; and I know that this accident that has befallen my son is the beginning of tuberculosis. I know because Emmeline, my second wife, of whom Claude was born, whose features he has preserved so faithfully—the great sea-blue eyes and the rosy complexion, so troubling in its false promise of vigor, and even the voice, through whose harmonies pass the hoarseness of a perpetual cough—commenced her phthisis in an identical fashion, with eruptions of blood, when I believed her valiant, the poor, ever-adored angel!"

Raoul was afflicted by that dejection. However, he protested again. "I tell you that Claude will be cured, Monsieur Fargeaud. Doctor Bouret affirms it, and he has no reason to disguise the truth from me. And then, have you no confidence in your other children? Hector has only to marry, and Madame Duverdon is very well..."

The old man hesitated momentarily before underlining with a negation the words addressed to him. The newly alimented hearth deployed a noisy and rapid effervescence, and by its glow, half-shadow and half-light, the physiognomy of the despairing man contracted. His thick white eyebrows came together, designing a cruel bar, and his eyes sketched briefly, with a flame as ardent and as fugitive as that of the logs, the sinister radiation of his past.

"Hector...! Rolande...! He said, in a voice so low that Raoul had to lean over in order to hear it. "Hector and Rolande...my two older children, continue my family, and prolong my lineage! You want to make me hope in them? You know them, however. And should one even hope? What fine progeniture, I ask you, could they reserve for me? It's said that children support hereditary flaws, and you ought to know, as a naturalist who has studied those particular subjects. It's said that creation is abominable enough to transmit to the descendants the deteriorations that blighted extinct generations, as if life were a ladder of misery going toward a gulf, a ladder that the race descends without being able to climb up again, or to stop. And you talk to me about Hector and Rolande!"

He fell silent again, and a new energy of the hearth, illuminating him from below, showed him to be grim, the crevices of his wrinkles accentuated, the gutters of shadow in his features hollowed out by the sketcher of old age, sinking dolorously into dryness of his mask, covered by the unkempt whiteness of his long beard. Without giving Raoul time to give evidence of his scientific knowledge and experience by certifying that ancestral decadence did not necessarily subsist, that it could be avoided or overcome by education, by the admixture of blood-lines, he continued his confidences precipitately, with bitter phrases, gestures and implications that expressed more than words.

He talked about his first marriage, to which he had been constrained by parents anxious to see him rich, his union with a woman whose hysteria had been carefully hidden from him, a hysteria that confined an epilepsy, attacks in which the unfortunate woman fell, her head striking the parquet, her eyes convulsed, her face atrocious, her lips soiled by red foam, in an improbable torsion of her entire being.

Yes, at twenty-five, that was the gift that had been made to him, and he had accepted it by virtue of ignorance, and also, a little, out of pity, the physician allowing him to hope that the neurosis in question might be tempered by marriage. The best moments were those in which he had only had to curb his head before his wife's changes of mood, before the whims of her prodigality or her suspicions, or before her amorous rages, her thirst for complicated voluptuousness, so untiring and so excessive that he had to stop, like those birds that are breathless from having loved too much.

And from that coupling, vitiated in its essence, his first two children were born, Hector first, now forty-five year old, whose childhood had been tormented by disquieting threats of meningitis, troubled by secret vices, and whose maturity was darkened by a exaggerated passion of women, a sensual bulimia that would drive him some day to commit some folly, if he were not guided to it by his pride, by ambitious whims that veiled an apparent eccentricity.

Thirteen years later—surprisingly, for his first wife had refused any other procreation—Rolande was born; and of her he scarcely dared speak. At twenty-two, after a youth unhinged by nerves, she had wanted a marriage with Julien Duverdon, a gentle honest and timid gentleman. She had wanted it abruptly, as she had wanted her toys and her clothes, doubtless in order to be more liberated. Later, while traveling with her husband, she had made a friend of Clara Boswett, an American woman older than her, almost aged, in spite of the make-up and the artifice of dyes, and who enjoyed a strange authority over her, dominating her with a troubling suggestion, never calling her anything but "darling."

"That was my first marriage," confessed the old man. "it was not happy, as you can imagine, and remarkable fruits could not be expected from it. My wife died not long after Rolande's birth; the devil has her soul!"

Again, the fire was animated redly, as if to support the malediction, and the old man appeared at that moment to become a kind of evil spirit himself, with the hostile flame of his eyes raised toward the ceiling. Already, however, that impression was modified, moderating and dissolving in the sweetness of other memories. And he unfurled the second phase of his life the same veridical impartiality with which the first had been exposed.

"The legal delays had scarcely elapsed," he said, "when I contracted a second union. This time, it was an idyll. Oh, what a charming, gentle and saintly creature Emmeline was! In any case, you've seen her, haven't you? You've known her, since she illuminated with her beauty and her grace the region that is your homeland. Emmeline! I had loved her for a long time and I believed that it was unnecessary to reflect on the bronchitis that had darkened her childhood, for she was apparently vigorous, she affirmed health. And then, I wanted a son worthy of me, a man to continue my race, to make me proud, in him, of all my past and all my future.

"The period of my engagement, the day of my marriage and the time that followed was a dazzle, something akin to a celestial enthusiasm, a bliss of adoration. I had resumed a new youth on contact with hers. In delivering myself to the ingenuousness of her transports, I ornamented myself with her virginity, her soul; I gave myself truly for the first time. She seemed to me so radiant of complexion that I forgot the coughs of her youth, and the death of her mother, extinguished by a malady of languor, I was told…a vague term about whose meaning I was wrong not to seek precision.

"You can, therefore, judge my joy—no, the word is inappropriate, there are no terms to explain what I felt—when, after the cries and sufferings of a long childbirth, I was presented with Claude, wrapped in lace, fresh, rosy, already intelligent, his eyes already open...her eyes, eyes as blue as waves irradiated by the sun! He laughed on seeing me…! I danced, my friend. I danced like savages around a prey! For that parcel of flesh really was my prey of tenderness, my prey of paternity, for which I had been lying in wait for twenty-five years. And in my delight, I imagined that I had finally perfected my masterpiece, built my true familial edifice on three friendly columns—had, in a word, subscribed to the holy obligations of the persistence of my blood.

"Twelve years later, the edifice collapsed. One of the columns crumbled, oscillated and fell. Emmeline spat blood, as Claude did today, and then died with the falling leaves, in autumn...and I remained alone with the child, alone with him, for you can imagine that his elders no longer counted; they had already manifested too clearly what they obtained from their mother...from the other..."

The old man's voice had taken on a higher pitch. Perhaps, too, the drama that he was evoking so dolorously had troubled the slumber of the invalid my means of a sort of telepathy, for the latter had turned over in his bed and was murmuring a vague appeal. Already, the father had got up, with an adolescent rapidity, and had approached the bed on tiptoe, his heart squeezed by the emotion he had just provoked. For a long moment he leaned over, monitoring his son's breathing.

"No, he's asleep," he said, resuming his place. "But how poorly he's breathing, poor fellow..."

"It's a matter of a few days. All that will sort itself out," Raoul affirmed.

Once again, Antonin Fargeaud did not share that confidence, and returned to his subject, as if hypnotized by its suggestion. While he spoke, Raoul was astonished by the wildness of his features, the mystic gleam that gave his eyes a disquieting hallucinatory fixity, directed toward the hearth, now in full activity.

"That child," he said, "that child! If you knew how I pampered him, once his mother had gone, how I cradled him with my dread, my solicitude! Well, yes, you do know, since you were his friend. You have seen me not quitting him with a single thought; summoning teachers here so that he would not be corrupted in class; you've seen me warming him when he was cold, brooding like a hen guarding her egg, a miser his treasure. But what you don't know is the frightful stirring of my heart when he coughed, my alarm when his temperature rose by a degree, my long waits in the antechambers of physicians, of all the physicians in Paris, and my emotion when I saw them, those impenetrable individuals leaning over his breast and listening to what was happening behind the ribs. But in sum, all went well; he grew up without too many hitches; he reached the age of twenty almost vigorous. It was then that I began to hate you."

"To hate me?" repeated Raoul, thinking that he had misheard.

"Hate. I could have strangled you on the day when Claude came to tell me that he wanted to follow your example and undertake studies in natural science with you. His tastes bore him toward serious abstractions, in any case, and your faith in the work was such an engaging example. I cursed you for a long time, my friend. But could I hate someone forever who loved my son?

"In vain I showed him the dangers of that career, unnecessary since he was rich; in vain I talked to him about the miasmas that float in laboratories, and which one respires; in vain I proved that his health required life in the fields, fresh air. He resisted my warnings, for he's headstrong, the child; he's stubborn, like his father, like his ancestors, all headstrong...

"He worked hard, he became a scientist. At twenty-three, like you, he was qualified, and savants noticed him. Last year he published his book on *The Amours of Plants*,[3] which made some noise, and which you are revising with him for a new edition. Well, this is the result! Look at his sheets; there is

---

[3] *Les Amours des plantes* is the title of the French translation of *The Loves of the Plants* (1799) by Erasmus Darwin; I have used a different translation of that title for what is obviously a different book, but the reference is not accidental.

blood on them, the blood of his bronchi. It's the malady that corrodes, the bacillus that devours...I know it, I've read the books, I've understood the images, and the little footnotes..."

The old man gazed more fixedly at the log fire, and in the phantasmagoria of the flames, he sought shapes soon dissipated, the evaporation of lives in gaps in the light, the symbolic destruction of phantoms dissolving into ash, red at first, then gray, and then black.

"Existence is stupid," he said, bitterly. "Why is that log blazing, why are we living, and why are we creating? The log blazes in giving its heat, we live and create squandering our energy, and afterwards, what remains? Dust and death...nothing!"

He repeated his final phrase in soliloquy; then he fell back into a hallucinated mutism, which floated dolorously in the bedroom while the fire slowly died down, collapsing into its scoria, and on the bed, Claude's halting respiration continued, oppressed and dying, like the breath of the hearth.

The obscure flight of the minutes was prolonged in the silence, amid the reek of potions charging the air with the sublimations of ether. The father maintained a fixed immobility. The night-light, which was sputtering, and the clock, which chimed, did not make him turn his head. He seemed a shadow among the shadows, pierced toward the ceiling by a golden radiation issuing through the crack in the curtains, bringing into the slumber of the room the suggestion of an exterior awakening.

Respectful of that calm, Raoul reflected. He revived his youth, spent in the verdant country in the environs of Rouen, silently ribboned by the capricious contours of the Seine. The son of a small landowner, now dead, he remembered his robust youth, vivified by running over the plain, by the pure air that followed in great gusts the natural current of populated wooded hills, the plastered walls of which delimited its fragmentation. Near the river, the country collapsed in white cliffs and broad stretches of clay all the way to the blond road that followed the sinuosity of the water. Behind the hills were the woods of Roumare and then fecund plains, dull in winter, damp with rain or snow, retaining in their entrails the promises of seeds. In summer, the plains awoke; life recommenced its cycle; muscular energies, the traction of beasts and plowshares animated the soil. Raoul followed the incessant labor; he saw sweat streaming over suntanned rustic skin, he heard the cries of animals, the oaths of herdsmen. The hunting season provoked the impetuosity of men and dogs and the flight of game through the furrows, throwing up dust. Everywhere, there was effort, productive effort in labor and effort even in destruction, and he admired it with all his atavism of a Norman laborer.

Above all he remembered the Fargeauds, whom he had not known in that epoch. Standing on a hill outside the village of Dieppedalle, the château was imposing, with its old thirteenth-century tower, alongside which, over the razed ruins, a heavy square building had been built in the last century.[4] That tower had traversed several seigneurial epics, and legends neglected by history persisted with the machicolations, barbicans and crenellations of its enormous carcass. A depth of fresh water made it a natural rampart. Once, a drawbridge thrown over that water had isolated the enclosure, but, felled during the Revolution, that drawbridge had been destroyed and replaced by an embankment, with the consequence that the water now stagnated. Restored several times, pierced with modern windows, the monstrous block gave the impression of a surly giant, still menacing, adapted to the fashion of the day

---

[4] This and another reference in which "le siècle dernier" [the last century] clearly refers to the eighteenth century, suggest that the story is set some years prior to its publication, and might have been written then; it is possible that an early draft was written before *Le Mal nécessaire* but could not be published then because of its highly controversial subject matter; however, datable references in the story establish that the final version begins in the year 1901, the story eventually extending into 1904.

in order to keep decent company with the rest of the habitation.

Raoul had been astonished by that enormity of stones, and from there his respect had reflected on to Antonin Fargeaud, the acquirer of the manor and a little surrounding land. So much mass and so much wealth dazzled him. The children of the first marriage, Hector and Rolande, passed over the sonorous roads on horseback, seemingly disdainful of the little vagabond dressed as a peasant. He feared them. Then came the death of Monsieur Fargeaud's second wife, with the impressive pomp of an unusual funeral, a black ceremonial spangled with silver, the chants of priests, the decoration of the catafalque, the heavy drag of the hearse that took the corpse to Rouen, and, in the first rank, a delicate child almost his own age, who was sobbing, his face in a handkerchief bordered with mourning.

The memory of that heir, consecrated to fortune and dolor, had remained vivid. He was surprised a few years later to see him grown, transformed, deprived of his silky curls, guiding an English carriage harnessed to a pony, with a young brunette by his side, whom he seemed already to be surrounding with a amorous solicitude. He learned that that was Henriette Divoir, the ward and niece of the château-owner.

One day, the carriage overturned in a rut, without any damage to its passengers. Raoul helped them to set the vehicle on its wheels again. The children's amity stemmed from that accident, Raoul was introduced into the château, and the three of them, Claude, Henriette and he, formed an amicable trio that the vacations reunited every year in inseparable games.

Then came the studies of adolescence. Raoul departed for a college in Rouen, while Claude, delivered to the zeal of private tutors, completed his education under his father's aegis. In the meantime, Henriette had been put into a convent; she drew therefrom the first seeds of a religious faith that her destiny did not necessitate, for at sixteen she was engaged to her cousin. She was impregnated with an obscure mysticism, while the two friends entered into brutal contact with life, penetrating into amphitheaters, fathoming the obscure causes of existence and those of death, the complicated mechanisms whose rhythms humankind obey in order to bloom and to disappear.

No study was more fecund in marvels, more disappointing in philosophy or more destined to slice sharply thorough the ideas transmitted by stupid social constraints, the prejudices of education and the embarrassments of faith. Thus, their conceptions matured and extended; thus they observed, reflected and exchanged the unexpectedness of their astonishments. And gradually, an entire flap of the veil was lifted over the light, a disturbing conviction that the truth had so far been restricted, enclosed in the narrow mesh of a stifling pedagogy.

Raoul, pushed toward Claude by a genuine affection, became anxious for the fate reserved for his friend's profound amour for the young woman who had just completed a pious education under the narrow direction of nuns. Could so much light, on the one hand, and so much darkness on the other, ensure happiness? Would the broad vision of the one and the paltry mirages of the other not lead, from the very beginning of the marriage, to surprises, frictions, and irritations destined to trouble subsequently the accord that two lovers in the flesh and the spirit would desire?

But in truth, that was already to take preoccupation with the future too far. A movement made by the invalid brought the thinker back to the contingency of events, to the dramatic hemoptysis of the day before, a warning so somber that one could wonder whether those moral anxieties would not collapse before the physical episode, and whether, in a few months, matter, resuming its domination over all eventuality, would not suppress the prognostication by annihilating the individual. For the illnesses experienced by Claude for some time—his loss of weight, all the precursory signs of a profound deterioration of his health—if they had not surprised their object, had disquieted Raoul to the point that he had recommended to his friend the therapeutics of repose and fresh air. It had required the appearance of the first drops of that red

25

blood to overcome Claude's indifference and bring him back to the paternal hearth, where he had collapsed as soon as he had entered, like a wounded animal.

At a movement made by the invalid, his two guardians ran forward. Claude asked for something to drink, and scarcely had the desire been expressed than his father handed him a bowl of milk augmented with a few drops of kirsch.

When his head, wearied by having lost so much fluid, had been delicately reposed on the pillow, the old man's voice, extraordinarily soft and sympathetic, interrogated: "Do you want to go to sleep again, my child?"

"No. Open the curtains."

A flood of gilded daylight penetrated from outside, with all the birdsong. Amid the foliage, almost level with the window, the star surged forth in an azure magnificence. Already, the hopping, joyful fluttering and fleeting intoxication of the birds was abruptly interposed upon the décor of the sky.

More light, more!" stammered Claude. "Oh, the sunlight, it's so good, the sunlight! And those birds, that life, that music!"

"Yes the sunlight, my boy. That's what will restore you. You're going to enjoy it for the full four months that you'll spend here with us, with Raoul—for I'm counting on Raoul staying—and with Henriette. Isn't that, for you, almost all that you need to be happy?" the old man concluded, in a tone that belied his anguish.

At the name of Henriette, Claude's physiognomy, which the abrupt irruption of sunlight had almost reanimated, suddenly darkened again, charged with melancholy. He shook his head slowly.

"Henriette! Your poor child! What will become of her?"

"What? What will become of her?" Antonin Fargeaud protested. "She'll become your wife when you've recovered."

"Do you think so, Father?"

There was such doubt in that question that the old man dared not reply to it. A false protestation would have been more dolorous for his son than silence. He contented himself,

26

therefore, with sitting down next to the bed, keeping in his stiff and wrinkled hands the hand of the invalid, overheated by fever.

Claude closed his eyes again, gripped by a touch of vertigo consequent on so much effort. Rings darkened the contour of his eyelids, above which the forehead, already creased by study and reflection, stood out, remarkably high and intelligent, surmounted by thick brown hair, a section of which fell over the right temple. The nose became thinner at the root, the lips were rather full, covered by a drooping moustache, to which a blood clot still adhered. The thinness of the clean-shaven square chin further emphasized its contour. All of that physiognomy suggested benevolence, moderated by a certain willfulness. If the eyelid had been raised, the blue gaze, too shiny with a gleam of fever, would have revealed the reflective studiousness and slight disillusionment that dominated that laborious brain. At the moment, the complexion, normally colored, especially over the cheekbones, was mat and dull, drained by excessive blood loss.

On considering that mask, so profoundly deteriorated, Antonin Fargeaud could not help encountering there the stigmata of tuberculosis that the malady of Emmeline, his second wife, had engraved so intensely in his memory. All the morbid heredity appeared in that faithful reproduction of a forehead, a nose and a mouth that he had adored. Even the long hand with the tapering fingers, the feverish hand that he was holding devotedly, revealed anguishing analogies in its structure, in the termination of the fingernails, curling at the extremity. Through the gap in the shirt he glimpsed the projection of the clavicles, the rectitude of the muscular fibers of the neck, fleshless, as if stretched, designing hollows behind which the rhythm of the arteries was transparent. The parted lips revealed the gracious sculpture of the perfect white teeth, exactly similar to Emmeline's. Yes, the unfortunate child was truly the son of the deceased. He had too much of her, to the point of having to depart, as she had.

A comparison could not fail to impose itself, between that scion of an exhausted race, the issue of a father already old and a mother touched by consumption, and the fried of iron, the prototype of strength destined to ensure the triumph of life, after having been engendered by the vigor of two healthy parents. With his ardently blond head, rendered astonishing by the contrast of dilated pupils, two centers of brown, living, bright, bold energy, flamboyant with a surprising youth, with the slenderness of his lightly flared nose, with his yellow full beard divided in the middle into two quivering points, that sun of the soil, from which scarcely a generation distanced him, gave the impression of a harmonious Christ, by whom Calvary had not been climbed. And his health also triumphed in the powerful squareness of his shoulders, the elegant litheness of his torso, planted delicately on the solidity of the legs.

Raoul Fieux thus presented, in spite of his serious expression, the attraction of a handsome male, the virile incarnation that accompanies unconsciously the curiosity of women, the secret desire of their amorousness. Passions that he had not had the whim of engendering, and of which he had great trouble disencumbering himself, affirmed his plastic supremacy. His person did not inspire languor, or emotion, or the flourishing of tender sentiment in the heart, but it transported with an esthetic enthusiasm, it emitted the fluid of a beautiful work of art, suggestive of appetite, virility and health.

In truth, the rectitude of the young man, his hostility to any expression of animality, and also his severe education and his precocious maturity in contact with his occupations, greatly attenuated his adolescent character of a young stallion propitious to the remaking of blood. The crease of his eyelids blurred the provocative glare of his eyes, the gracious cordiality of his lips enabled forgetfulness of the sensuality of the two bulbs bursting with health. It was necessary to strip away the covering acquired by calm and study to comprehend and admire the heroic robustness of the muscles and to sense the breath of creative generosity that he emitted, radiating with his gestures, his grave voice, his smile and the undulation of his beard. And although a night of near-insomnia next to the invalid had wearied him, he stood up again without fatigue and prompted once again the slightly jealous admiration of the old man.

But the father had to call a truce to his reflections, for the invalid, hearing a noise, had just opened his eyes again, and smiled at a delightful apparition. Henriette Divoir, his fiancée and cousin, Antonin Fargeaud's ward, was standing hesitantly on the threshold. On seeing the welcome that greeted her, she advanced.

She was exquisite, youthful in the splendor of her twenty years; she brought with her the balm of a bright morning, entering as the sunlight had entered a little while before. She was wearing a blue lawn dress, as light and spring-like as her advent, sufficiently tight-fitting to allow the divination of the eloquence of her torso and the curve of her hips, and short enough to allow the sight of an elegant foot clad in yellow leather. Her mat complexion was helmed by a brown torsade; her eyes had dark velvet reflections; her lips were lightly blurred by a down. The smile that she sketched as she approached the invalid put three good, joyous and piquant dimples in her cheeks and chin, while arching a mouth in which a nacreous row of teeth appeared.

Like Raoul, she could have seemed the expression of good health and exceptional vigor, for she was, for anyone who judged her in accordance with appearances, a beautiful work of carnal art modeled in a crucible of life and strength; but something humble and mystical contradicted the first impression that one might obtain from her. She did not draw from her person the advantages of seduction that she could have obtained therefrom. She walked with her head slightly bowed; her shoulders were a trifle folded, and her hands, cross in front of her waist, seemed disposed to join together for meditation. Her smile was almost confused, and belied the graciousness of her three dimples, the pure gleam of her eyes and the mat warmth of her cheeks. She conserved a kind of outer layer of religious decorum, and close to the earth as she was, in the splendor of her form, she drew away from it and approached the heavens in the attitude that she adopted.

She had taken the hand of the still-wonderstruck Claude, and spoke in a low voice:

"Are you better this morning? Did you have a good night? I wanted to stay with you and keep vigil, you know, but these villains didn't want it and sent me to bed."

With her finger she indicated the villains, the old man and Raoul, but without paying any attention to either of them. And she kept chatting, quietly and serenely, narrating a dream that she had had—for she had slept in spite of everything, vanquished by her great fatigue—but a good dream, entirely reassuring, which had shown her Claude clad in the robe of a saint, his head ringed by a luminous circle, accomplishing miraculous cures. She believed in dreams.

"Don't tire him, my dear Henriette," Raoul interrupted. "The doctor desires a great deal of calm around his patient."

She turned round, looked at the protester, who apologized with a gesture, and then blushed slightly.

"That's true, I forgot," she said. "I forgot that it's still early and that you need rest. I'll quit you; I'm going to mass. But from this morning on I want to stand guard by your side. I hope that won't be refused me, this time..."

She leaned toward her fiancé, as if for a confidence, and squeezed his hand, which she had not abandoned.

"I'll pray for you," she confessed—after which she withdrew.

The rustle of her dress was heard, brushing the doorjamb as she went though, and even after her departure, a perfume of freshness, youth and health persisted in the confined atmosphere, as if spring had come with her. Raoul marveled at that; but having turned to Claude, he saw his head fall back, almost unconscious, on the pillow, with a tear in the corner of his eye, by which Antonin Fargeaud was alarmed.

II

One of the ramparts of the Château de la Taquainerie, lowered to the level of the first floor, formed a kind of terrace whose circular base bathed in the water surrounding the domain, and the summit of which was bordered by a parapet of old stones, eroded by time in certain places and covered with moss and ivy in others. The soil of the terrace had not been macadamized, and plants sprouted there: an entire bizarre vegetation sown by the wind, of species unknown in the region, native to hot countries, which lived there stubbornly, by virtue of some miracle of resistance, in a climate hostile to their blooming.

An enormous oak dominated that languor. It was strong and powerful, having absorbed for its growth all the substance of the earth, while beneath it, the exotic population was crushed and confused, struggling wretchedly to survive in a tangle. Nevertheless, the virgin corner offered a charm that Antonin Fargeaud had insisted on conserving uncultivated. A short path, scarcely frayed in the enlacement of branches, led to the foot of the oak. There, a clearing was sketched, with an iron table circled by a rustic bench.

On warm summer days, the old man took pleasure in stationing himself in the shade of the large tree and reading philosophers, or in gazing at the landscape, the panorama of which fell, splendidly, down the abrupt declivity of cliffs eighty meters high, plunging, after intermittent white patches of chalk along capricious escarpments all the way to the blond road strewn with houses and factories, near to which the silky ribbon of the Seine snaked. At that location it circled an islet, the Île Sainte-Barbe. Beyond the river, the almost naked plain took flight, to end on the right at a distant denture of hills, while to the left, the décor of the city of Rouen unfurled, so picturesque with its sprinkling of spires and towers, so evocative of old legends, with its abundance of distant monuments.

In these days of effluvia, all of nature was ablaze and crackling. Insects buzzed under the stone, lizards wriggled under the moss and hid in the cracks. Sometimes, the stridor of a siren attracted the eye to the flight of a tug gliding under a plume of opaque smoke, before a trail of foam. From there, too, one saw at dusk the great red disk disappear in an apotheosis of concentric rings extending to infinity and persisting for a long time among the flight and accumulation of polychromatic clouds. An enchantment of colors burst forth thus, and the fluidity of the sky modified it marvelously until the belated hour when everything darkened or fell silent, in the solemnity of magical nights. Then there was the melancholy glimmer of the moon reflected in the silent lacquer of the river; there was the flutter of the constellations, the long unfurling of the Milky Way, the enormous spectacle of infinite space, illuminated powerfully enough to stupefy human pride and inspire the fecund embrace of lovers.

Henriette and Raoul, after a few hours spent at Claude's bedside—he had had just fallen asleep—had been brought by the hazard of their stroll to that terrace, which reminded them so much of the charming memories of childhood. In the three days since Claude had fallen ill they had both been living in a constant perplexity, in an anguish of seeing the hemoptysis renewed and carrying away their companion, drained to the last drop. Their anxiety had almost been confirmed, for during the second night, following a slightly more violent movement, the blood had sprung forth again with an astonishing abundance, in a red splash.

Twice Claude had fallen back on his bed in a faint, dying. But life had such roots in him that he had reopened his eyes almost immediately, astonished by the bustle around him. He strove by his attitude to embolden his fiancée and to reassure his father, whose face, at that moment if the drama, was animated by a singular brightness, combining suffering and alarm. Now, the danger seemed almost averted, and hope was reborn. The oft-consulted thermometer announced an almost normal temperature, alimentation was tolerated. The two friends had therefore quit the dolorous bedside, and submitting to an unconscious egotism, they were smiling at the beautiful June daylight, at the verdant panorama, and the pure oxygen, without forsaking the idea that in his turn, Claude might come to enjoy that visual celebration and that feast for the bronchi.

Henriette was the first to express that concern. She was leaning on the parapet, designating the horizon.

"Look, Raoul; when he's better, we'll bring him here. We'll install him in an armchair and we'll impregnate him with the splendid life that palpitates around us. This, I think, is the best of medicaments."

"You're right, Henriette. But when he will he be strong enough to be transported so far from his apartment?"

"You're saddening me, Raoul," she continued, sitting down on the rustic bench after having swept away a few leaves brought by the wind with the tip of her umbrella. "You're saddening me, because you're knowledgeable, and your opinion isn't mistaken. But in the final count, he will be cured, won't he?"

"Yes, he'll be cured," affirmed the young man, after a hesitation that did not escape the perspicacity of his interlocutor. Immediately, he added: "But it will take a long time, very long."

They fell silent. The sun had progressed, and its radiance was inconveniencing the young woman; she deployed her umbrella and leaned on the back of the seat. One divined rather than saw her breasts projecting behind the silk of her slightly loose mauve blouse. The melancholy of her eyes and the frown of her forehead went well with the subtle grace of her harmonious silhouette.

"What does time matter," she said, finally, "provided that we save him. We'll employ all our means for that: you, all the resources of your amity, and me, those of prayer. I have an unshakable faith in divine grace. I believe that destinies are modified under the action of celestial commiseration, when sad souls request its favor. I believe that begging God with all the force of a simple heart, influences his will as much as medical therapeutics favor the evolution of an illness. I don't want to deny the support of science, but you know very well, Raoul, that we only depend on God. And if his will is that Claude doesn't resist his malady, well..."

She suspended her sentence momentarily, in such a way that Raoul, before hearing the rest, could admire the charm of that virginal face, and the candor of those dark velvet eyes, filled with mystical reflections.

"...Well," she concluded, "I too will disappear. I'll go to prostrate myself before the Lord, and thank him by means of a lifelong servitude for the proof that he will have imposed upon me by separating me from Claude."

"You don't love your fiancé, then?" asked Raoul, stupefied by that abnegation.

"Yes! I love him...but is God not above everything?"

Her words evoked within her the austerity of cloisters, the cold rigidity of stone walls brushed by the pallor of recluses. Holy women, phantoms of life, passed by, clicking their rosaries. They were going to the chapel, and there, in the silence of the vaults, prayers rose up. They bowed down, sunk in solitude, before the great image of the crucifix, before the dolorous symbol of the Christ, lamentable in his fleshless suffering, in his bloody agony. Or else they were before the resplendent Lamb, ornamented with gold and dominated by the polychromatic stained glass window; there was the sacramental gesture of the officiant, the crimson embroidery of the holy stole, the slow elevation of the silvery pyx and the incantation of the incense succeeding the rhythm of the censer; there were also hymns intercut with murmurs, implorations, genuflections, an entire harmonious ritual of robes and white cornets.

What an intoxication she had once felt in humiliating herself thus, what an intoxication she would experience again! For, more that the sovereign capitation of her thoughts, a fascination of her senses attracted her to those practices concentrated around a symbol. Her eye took pleasure in superb sparkling, her ear heard canticles that were amorous; her nostrils respired inebriating perfumes; her fingers palpated sift fabrics and rare missals; her lips caught fire at the supreme contact of the host; all the vibrations of her nerves were thus confounded around the Christ, having their pretext in him. With the consequence that Henriette envisaged almost as a consolation the idea of losing Claude, the bliss of the reclusion that would keep her so far from the world, its cares and villainies, and transport her into an ether where her materialism, deflected from its natural destination, would find nevertheless an appeasement of the desires of the senses.

And by virtue of a logical association of ideas, Henriette's declaration had inspired in Raoul a similar order of reflections. He too saw her having, at twenty, thrown her youth and beauty at the feet of the divine creator, in a renunciation of terrestrial joys. But he saw her differently. She appeared to him to be subject to a grip, stifled by the impulses of nature. The initial exaltation having passed, her harmonious figure, her woman's womb, apt for fecundity, revolted against the imprisonment of the brown robe. The telling of the rosary enervated her hands, destined for the work of charm. The horizon, limited to high walls, had a narrowness that oppressed her and, by contrast, made her remember intoxicating rides in the country. The canticles rising toward the vault, and the incense escaping in opaline swirls from the cassolettes, reminded her of the song of the woods, the subtle aromas of flowers, lilac and orange-blossom respired in captivating disks. The adoration of the divine man was only a lure, the metamorphoses of the eternal need for amour that dominates all humanity, which is the primal movement of the creative instinct.

And Raoul followed those muffled vibrations, that constant struggle between the plethora of temperament and the artifice of will, between the shudders of the body and the discipline of the mind. He predicted weaknesses; he heard Henriette curse the approach and infiltration of the demon, when nature alone was rearing up within her, Was that succulent fruit of flesh destined to desiccate thus? Would the spring that wanted to run dry not overflow? Was not the disdain of so many faculties, although it was an homage to the great dream, a crime against life?

And seeing her so full of seductions, for the first time he had the inspiration that she was truly beautiful. Claude was a lucky man. How he would hasten to be cured, in order to profit from that beauty! He, Raoul, had never loved, had only ever wanted passing relief, in order to run off the excess of his sap. On the college benches where he was an external student, it is true, one was subject, as in the lycées of Paris, to the attractions of precocious vice, to the depravity that prowled the asphalt of the sidewalks contiguous with the university walls. But he had passed alongside the temptation without succumbing to it, in the great harmony that healthy nature alone possesses.

In the evening, the train took him home to his parents, and he worked on his impositions, or he wandered in the fields rich in crops, the woods cut by paths covered in moss in summer and crackling with leaves in winter. Sometimes, at harvest time, he lent a hand. All the health of the earth increased his moral health, the beautiful equilibrium of reason.

Later, his year of military service, similarly accomplished at Rouen, in the cavalry, had also kept him away from licentious centers. He had thus arrived in the laboratories of Paris as a vigorous ascetic, but with an unknown, unconscious asceticism that results from the normal play of life. At that time, his first amorous excursions had already disappointed him, and with the aid of labor, he had directed the efforts of his cerebration elsewhere.

However, although he had not desired women, he understood that Claude desired the most beautiful specimen of the species, Henriette. And it was her, precisely, who wanted to deprive herself of amour!

He was about to say that to her, to ask her whether, in offering herself one day to reclusion, she felt sufficiently sure of never deploring her sacrifice, when a familiar, antipathetic voice coming from an unseen person through the tangle of foliage, made him suspend his question. They listened with a certain hostility to the importunate person who was troubling their intimacy. Henriette, with a finger placed over her lips, signified her desire to remain invisible. But the voice came nearer, preceded by the crackle that footfalls made in parting the branches and treading on dry wood. The encounter was inevitable and they got ready to submit to it.

"Come this way, Mademoiselle Marthe. Come and admire this delightful corner and the splendid view that one has here. Take my hand, so I can guide you, for the path is scarcely frayed."

Almost at the same moment, a man of small stature, already stooped, clad with the contrived whimsy of the fashion of the day, with a broad jacket forming a sack in the back, a red waistcoat and narrow trousers, emerged into the open space. His thinness was emphasized by the accentuated bone-structure of his bilious face, whose elongated nose inclined toward a moustache tinted chestnut-brown, graying under the artifice of the dye. But the newcomer was most astonishing by virtue of the equivocal gleam in his mobile brown eyes. It was Hector, Antonin Fargeaud's elder son. He was leading by the wrist a young rosy blonde woman, admirable in her complexion in spite of her pretentious appearance and costume, who was allowing herself to be drawn without much resistance.

As they arrived before the talkers, Hector had a movement of chagrin and released his companion's hand. The latter was nonplussed, hesitant and confused, and in order to give herself countenance she began to pat the creases of her modest dress of gaudy percale. The talkers did not recognize her at first.

"It's you, my good Fieux," exclaimed Hector, recovering his self-assurance and hiding his irritation under the irony of his appellation. "I wasn't expecting to find you in this place, in the company of Henriette...do you know that this terrace is the refuge of lovers?"

"Is it for that reason." Raoul asked, "that you've brought Mademoiselle here?"

Hector avoided answering, and his attention turned to the embarrassed attitude of his companion, whom he finally introduced.

"Mademoiselle Marthe Servant, the daughter of Père Servant, Papa's farmer."

"I remember you very well, Mademoiselle," said Henriette. "We played together during our childhood."

"Indeed, Mademoiselle; but how changed we both are!"

In order to show off that transformation, which her costume emphasized too much, the daughter of peasants dissipated her momentary confusion, raised her face covered in rice powder, smoothed her impertinently coiffed hair, and then braced her breasts and hips. She had a petty air of assurance and provocation that reflected the high esteem in which she held her person.

Henriette had suspected long ago that she would find her again thus. Before life had parted them at an early age, she had already seen Marthe clad, in contrast to the creatures of the plain, in a garish skirt and apron, a luxury by means of which her rustic parents, who were very ambitious for her, estimated that they could differentiate her from her peers, bringing her closer to being bourgeois, and everything then announced the pretentiousness of her youth. The new observation was no less disagreeable than the old to the aristocratic young woman, who looked away and transported her gaze, by virtue of an invincible quest for similitude, to the accoutrement of Hector Fargeaud. The latter, sensing an implicit disapproval in Raoul's attitude, attempted to excuse his arrival in the place.

"Mademoiselle Servant has been sent to us by her father to obtain news of Claude. When she had acquitted her mission we were talking about the country that she no longer inhabits, for she's a schoolteacher in Lille...it is Lille, isn't it, Mademoiselle?...and then I told her that from the terrace, one can see the Servant farm, and as she doubted it, I brought her here."

He went to the parapet, designating in the direction of the fields a red dot in the green countryside, beyond the Seine.

"Look, Mademoiselle, do you see over there, on the hillside? That's the farm...that's where you've come from. You must have taken a long time, if you've made the journey on foot."

"It took a full hour, and I crossed the Seine by ferry, in order to avoid a detour," said the young woman, lowering her eyes, vexed that insistence that had been made of her mode of locomotion. She would have preferred to say that she had come in a carriage. But in order to palliate the effect of her confession, she added: "I'm very fond of walking. I so rarely have the chance to stroll in the open air!"

"Nevertheless," Hector persisted, "You must be tired, and I'll take you back by automobile, if you'll permit me to do so."

"Thank you, Monsieur, but I can return on foot without fatigue."

She was not telling the truth. Her excessively narrow ankle-boots, adopted out of coquetry, made her suffer horribly, and she had limped all along the road. She smiled however, without any apparent constraint, in order to show her teeth.

"No, no," said Hector, curtly. "I'm going that way. Accept a place; you'd give me pleasure."

The last phrase had been pronounced in a pleading tone, and the mobile eyes were charged with an avid covetousness. The schoolteacher did not dare to protest any longer, and contented herself with thanking him with a nod of the head. Henriette divined the annoyance of that acquiescence and she experienced less antipathy in consequence for the person who was about to be subjected to company that even she found repulsive. In addition, the inclination of the neck, revealing blonde hair overlaid by paler tresses, had a signification of delicacy and humble tenderness that pleased her, in spite of the rest of the person appearing to her to be too gaudy, affected and devoid of the modesty the she liked.

"You're a professor now?" she enquired.

"Yes, Mademoiselle."

"Are you happy?"

The schoolmistress hesitated to respond, and Henriette understood by her sudden melancholy that by persisting, she would become indiscreet. In any case, Marthe Servant, flattered by the term 'professor,' by which her petty employment had been ennobled, went on: "I certainly can't complain. Teaching is more distinguished isn't it, than staying on the farm…?"

"Why am I not your pupil?" Hector risked. He suspended his laughter, which revealed his unequal and well-groomed teeth.

Raoul, with an exclamation on his lips that he retained, looked at him. There was a great secret between them, a confidence entirely medical, relative to a physical avatar, the inevitable result of excessive indulgence and a frequentation of women of the basest prostitution. And if Hector stopped laughing, it was because Raoul would have been able to reproach him with having dangerous information to offer. But Henriette stood up and offered her hand to the schoolteacher.

"*Au revoir*, Mademoiselle, We must return to our invalid. Thank your father for his solicitude, and tell him that Claude's condition, while still being grave, is nevertheless improving."

She departed, followed by her companion.

As soon as they had disappeared, Hector took Marthe's hand again. Although not astonished, she pretended to defend herself a little. He led her as far as the stone parapet. Beneath them, the countryside unfurled its overheated regions. The gray vapors of the morning, condensed by the sunlight, persisted in the direction of the woods, limiting the horizon to a curtain of opaque warmth. He forced her to incline in order to look over, and to bend her waist, which he surrounded with a caress. She no longer resisted.

"There's Rouen to the left. You can see that it's microscopic from here. Even the Seine looks like a stream. Over there, almost in front of you, you'll recognize the Epinettes tavern. If you like, we can go too have supper there one evening, unless you'd prefer to have lunch there today. You'll see that it's amusing there. Is that agreed?"

His more-than-audacious hand had abandoned the contour of the waist and ventured over the hips, coarsely palpating the plenitude. This time, the young woman, anxious and troubled in her flesh, rebelled. She feared failing in the virtue of which she had made an obligation until the day she found a husband, an eventuality becoming increasingly improbable since, although she was beautiful and enviable in the rhythm of her body, soliciting masculine attention by her lush and alluring blondeness, she had reached the age of twenty-five without ever having been favored by any other propositions than those of amour in a private cabinet. She bumped into the eternal egotism of men continually. She suffered from it in her pride, but she was beginning to defend herself more limply. An abrupt sidestep removed her from Hector's caress.

"Finish, Monsieur. You're mistaken; I'm good. Is it because I'm poor and earn my living as a schoolteacher that you think you can lack respect for me?"

The gallant was amazed. He had not expected that resistance. Firmly convinced of his seductive qualities and habituated, on the other hand, never to encounter rebuffs on the part of the petrified peasant girls or young women whose favors were casual and bought for money, he was accustomed of measuring the virtue of women simply by the extent of his conceit. In addition, this one, judging by her attire, was similar enough to the prostitutes he cherished. Blinking his mobile eyes he stammered: "You're not going to make me believe that at your age…?"

"Am I so past it?"

"No, you're a springtime, but a springtime that must have, like this one, warmer days, with the ardor of summer! And to calm them, there's nothing better than a little amour, believe in my long experience…

"Oh, yes, you can't lack experience…you're 'fast,' you are!"

She started laughing, with a mocking little trill, fundamentally delighted that the peril was dissipating so amiably, and also delighted to have enameled her language with a few

41

argot expressions that she believed to be in good taste. Now she took pleasure in seeing her seducer rectify his moustache with the back of his thumb. Then with the aid of reflection, she was secretly flattered by having been distinguished by the seigneur of the domain, the son of the master, whose wealth and worldliness were legendary. It is true that there had been talk about his escapades, but they were reported with prudent implications, for reputations were tarnished by them. But was it not one of the forms of gentlemanly behavior, that fondness for skirts?"

"Come on," she said, "admit that you've committed a gaffe and let's not talk about it anymore. Another time, you'll be more circumspect."

"Let's remain friends, at least?" he said,

"So be it, friends."

And in order to retake a route that she did not know, she let him take the lead, accepting this time that he took her hand.

When they reached the perron of the château, she uttered a cry of admiration. The automobile was there, parked in the oblong space that the gravel described around a vast bed of geraniums. Delighted, she approached it. The machine's engine was concealed beneath a smart red carcass armored with copper bands that were fulgurant in the sunlight. It was shuddering at rest, its quivering exploding in the somersaults of an impatient animal, manifesting the intimate life of its mechanisms, and the energy ready to defy distance.

Hector smiled. The attraction of his machine was inevitable. He owed a great deal of good fortune to it; he was about to employ it to it prevail once again over the beautiful creature whose presence had awakened his desire so powerfully and checked his conceit. Again he was about make the charm of travel shine, to repeat the attractions of the Epinettes tavern, the delightful and cool excursion, twenty kilometers in the shade, that one could have before lunch, when the advent of his father, Antonin Fargeaud, arriving in the company of two men in blue blouses, caused him move away from his companion. He went to meet him, suddenly becoming timid.

In spite of his age, already mature, the peripeties of his indiscipline, and the audacity of his adventures, Hector still retained a sort of respect for his father mingled with dread. He was not sufficiently self-analytical to disentangle its nature, to discover its origin, but he sensed an acrimony in the old man's authority common to Rolande and himself, while Claude, the son of the second bed, benefited from all the preference of a partial affection. Hector, devoid of psychology, attributed that hostility to his own conduct, to a few differences of interest stimulated by his crass avarice and by his incredible stubbornness in forbidding him the two millions that his mother had left him, the disbursement of which he had demanded—a stubbornness so sordid that it made him live constantly in his father's hooks, either in the town house in Paris or in the château in Dieppedalle.

As he approached the old man he discovered once again the grim coldness of his gaze

"Bonjour, Father!"

"Bonjour!" growled the newcomer. "Where are you going in the company of little Marthe Servant? She's a good girl, that one...a worker...she earns her living as a teacher. I hope that you're not going to turn her away from the straight path...like so many others."

Hector became impatient. Lashed by the reproach, without responding, he went to the trunk of his vehicle, and took out a driver's helmet, which he put on. He was getting ready to climb in, abandoning Marthe, when his father, without any scruple about revealing his resentment in front of the servants accompanying him, called to him again in a curt voice.

"Where are you going? You're going to run around the country while your brother is ill? Your place is here, to wait until he's better or he dies. In any case, the machine needs a repair; Arthur has just informed me of it."

With a gesture he indicated the younger of the two workers, Arthur Grignon, the son of Père Grignon, the gardener and porter of the château, who was also beside him. There was such a close resemblance between the two men that if the fa-

43

ther had not been, at forty-eight, already worn out and white-haired, one would have taken them for two brothers. Another certainty of filiation was their equal passion for alcohol. A chronic ethylism shadowed their earthen cheeks with a identical hollowness, caused a redness of the nose and cheeks to stand out, excavated the eyes and imparted a similar feverish tremor to their fingers. The murderous heredity in question was clearly evident in Arthur.

The latter, having been cited, took a step forward, hitched up his blue trousers, which a dirty leather belt did not maintain sufficiently, and after expelling a jet of saliva, detailed the damage to the automobile.

"In fact, Monsieur Hector, the ignition is poorly regulated. It was crackling like fireworks on the way in. I engage you not to depart for a certain breakdown. Do I need to demonstrate that?"

He leaned over the machine, and Hector imitated him, no longer thinking about his excursion, or about Marthe, while Antonin Fargeaud resumed the interrupted conversation with the gardener.

"What were you saying, Grignon?"

"It's my wife, who's pregnant again," the man burped. "And you understand that it's costly, all those children So, I said to myself that perhaps an augmentation…"

"You can't have been paying attention," said the master, with a hint of scorn in his voice.

"What do you expect, M'sieur Fargeaud? I was drunk!"

The old man shrugged his shoulders. It was the same anthem he had heard repeated time and time again, the same misery of the peasant saturated with alcohol, losing all precaution reductive of the joy of amour, and in his brutality, conceiving, casting his seed to despair and ruination. Everywhere around him, in every cottage, there was the same inconvenience engendered by the same vice.

And Père Grignon, sometimes quavering, explained his situation: eighteen children arrived in twenty years, salaries that did not increase, the eldest, ingrates who no longer brought their pay and squandered it wantonly, and the land, with that, losing its value every day, with the result that the patch he possessed in order to grow and sell vegetables cost more labor than it rendered money, and all the other cruelties of fate, the kids' headaches, the midwife and the doctor to pay, and Mère Grignon always pregnant, no longer able to work, and all the tremors, the taxes, the brats to feed, to bring up, to educate—fortunately, it was necessary to say, out of eighteen children, eight had died of meningitis—and while he detailed his sinister weave of alcoholism, lust, childbirth, labor, malady and death, his entire brutal and inconsequential existence, Antonin Fargeaud, without listening any longer, reflected on the disastrous organization of life. the perpetual paradox of nature, creating families similar to Grignon's, beings born in evil for evil, with no strength to elevate against that unconscious pressure of instinct, without anything modifying that profusion, which, by its abundance, conducted the race to destruction.

And it was not only among humans; it was on every rung of the ladder of beings, every degree of organic classification. Whether one looked at the bottom, in the drop of stagnant water in which protozoa agitated, of which one could not say whether they were the end of animal evolution or the beginning of the vegetable kingdom, or one thought about the steppes, the deserts, the glaucous swarms of the sea, or even if one imagined the world unknown to the eye, the probable succession of the infinitely small that the most powerful microscopes could not reveal, everywhere there was unreflective insemination, the same stupid force of pullulating fecundity, producing, always producing, and sacrificing individual well-being to its will of persistence; arming the individual so defectively against vicissitudes and environments, that in the final count, the species, after being defeated, returned to oblivion.

And the old man's animosity against life, against creation, was all the more logical because he had been subjected to all its murderousness, and after a long period of illusion, he had come, by virtue of the illness of his son Claude, to see his family founder, in a fall all the more dolorous because it had been so long delayed. What a catastrophe! What a collapse! The first two manifestations of his virility had disappointed twice over. Hector was so debauched and perverted that he wondered whether it was really his blood that ran in his veins, his semen that had engendered him. Rolande, Madame Duverdon, was neurotic, unhinged and equivocal, so strange in her conduct that he preferred to forget her existence and was glad to know that she was far away, traveling, with the great veil of absence between them. Now, it was the third, the issue of another stock, the child of election and charm, who was subject to the universal law of destruction, whom tuberculosis was extending palely on his bed, after floods of blood had emptied him like a squeezed water-skin.

The rout, the incoherence of the world, the imbecility of creation: he was a victim of it in his thought, in his illusions, in his hopes, in his children, and in his heart. So, since everything was evil, since energy had no other end but dissolution, since to mark was to strike out and to commence was to finish, since a wasteful spirit presided over everything that hatched, everything that moved, why create? Would it not be better if the world came to an abrupt end: the abolition of origins; the neutral state; nonexistence; oblivion?

And in that ruination of his mirages, his aged thought was stubborn in not wanting to envisage anything but the inversion of things, straying into murder, into the rage of sacking everything. An escaped chicken approached, coming right up to his feet, with gracious gestures, to pick up a seed with its beak. That chicken was destroying a seed; tomorrow it would be destroyed in its turn, eaten. Monstrous cycle! Abominable inutility of lives resolving in massacre and immolation!

He was tempted to crush the bird under his heel, to obey the natural law, to kill. But two people were there, who were considering him. He passed his hand over his white head to chase away his evil intentions Then he granted Père Grignon his augmentation, and after having pinched Marthe's chin he dismissed her.

The beautiful young woman set forth along the hot road. Her stature evaporated health, but her excessively narrow footwear made her limp, and that inconvenience robbed her of her pride.

III

Claude emerged from a torpor that had kept him in the same position for two hours; the rhythm of his respiration now became even. A sensation of wellbeing saluted his awakening. He raised his eyelids slightly, and between his lashes he perceived his bedroom. He was astonished to find it so bright, the great curtains of yellow silk not having been lowered, and permitting on that afternoon dirtied by tempest, the access of a dull daylight, the obliquely reflected rays of which were silvered by a mirror before striking him in the face.

Gradually, his ideas, still blurred by sleep, became clearer. His situation appeared to him to be clearly favorable, and he was reassured. Flattened for a week by the hemoptysis, which had been reproduced again, he felt better now; the operation of his bronchi was accomplished smoothly, another blood had reformed in him, as if purified, and seemed to be flowing more freely in his veins. He no longer had a fever; he smiled.

He smiled because, among the familiar objects, two dear individuals were there, watching over him. First there was Henriette his fiancée. She was embroidering. Her brunette head, leaning over her work, revealed the opulence of her tresses, raised in a torsade, and the gracious notch of her nape rounded toward the tulle of the bodice, fastened at the top; finally, the pure contour of her profile, in which the nose was slightly turned up over the lips creased by the care of the labor. The chin, deployed by the inclination, protruded a little over a bosom whose still-delicate charm was dissimulated by fabric, but which marriage would enable to blossom.

The agility of her fingers was ingenious in the correction of the needlepoint, the harmony of the silken arabesques to which her imagination gave birth. But while she applied herself, her willfully modest pose, her intentionally discreet costume and, above all, her inexpressibly humble manner—that fashion of being always absorbed, amid the meager phenomena of life, by a supra-terrestrial abstraction, of floating in a celestial ideal, the ensemble of those small symptoms of a latent mysticism—deprived her of a certain beauty, only allowing her a grace, an almost plaintive grace that she could so easily have animated with corporeal radiance. A chrysalid enclosed in a cocoon of mysticism, she was a living contradiction.

Claude loved to see her thus. In that moment when the respite accorded by his illness allowed him once again to hope, he found Henriette in a disposition to bend toward sentimental amour, closer to him, more adequate to and more in conformity with his visions of the future.

Close by was Raoul Fieux. In him it was necessary to recognize the expression of strength and innate elegance. Placed facing him, he was radiant. His studiousness was betrayed by the fashion in which he was reading at the moment. Beneath his long blond hair, the tresses of which fell back naturally to frame the temples, the forehead was grave, the eyebrows brought together by reflection. The straight, almost translucent, nose was hooked toward the evaporation of the moustache, folded upwards by the habit of putting his fingers to it. Lower down, through the beard, lush and separated in the middle, one divined the square chin, suggestive of tenacity. The face of a fortunate Christ: Claude admired it, as he also admired the powerful hands and the solid wrists, vestiges of a land-working atavism. A native distinction gave grave to his gesture when he turned the page of the book.

What delicacy that hand also deployed, what finesse in execution of small tasks! Claude had appreciated its subtle skill during hours of communal study when, on the benches of the Sorbonne and then the Institut Pasteur, they had devoted themselves passionately to biological research, sowing entities on the transparency of gelatin, giving existence to animalcules and viruses transplanted into the favorable medium of culture broth.

What beautiful hours of ardent communion in vast thought! And how often, by virtue of remarks exchanged, the constant wonderment of discoveries, their two hearts had fraternized then, united more profoundly than by the sharing of pleasures or the commerce of interest! Yes, truly, in those moments of sacred labor, no light was worth as much as the one that came to them from the bright laboratory; no joy was comparable to that of moving the universe in crucibles of life! They felt, under the gray smock, more pompous than kings wearing diadems, on the wooden stool, more dominant and more sovereign than emperors sitting on golden thrones. They reigned over the world in serving science.

At other times, their masters sent them to visit hospitals in order to practice some analysis there. They followed the service of a celebrated physician. All of floundering humanity filed before them, revealed to their examination, with its inconsequence, its irreflection, its flaws and its vices. The most transcendent moralities, the most logical philosophical deductions, did not teach pity as well as those minutes spent in contact with suffering. They envisaged abysms in the despair of gazes; they surprised shame and anger, while the disillusioned voice of the professor rose, while hands palpated decay, and ears leaned over death-rattles.

The memory of those miseries once confronted caused Claude's hope, formerly so lively, reanimated by the cessation of his fever, to oscillate. Had he not become a clinical subject himself, now that auscultation could reveal the dilapidation of his lungs? He deduced therefrom the uncertainty of his compromised future. Healthier, he would perhaps be more distant from Henriette, but he would have had more audacity to hope for her as a wife. They would both have given a magnificent example of equilibrium, the mysticism of the one evaporating in the vigorous warmth of the other. Their two temperaments would have fused and Henriette would have profited from that accord.

Destiny had decided otherwise. Claude did not blame it; he merely tried to understand it, and found it disappointing.

The benevolence of which he had made a law, the work of which he had imposed the obligation on himself, the chastity that he had observed in the strictest measure obligations, in order to offer himself purely to his saintly fiancée: all those duties and virtues had no other end, then, and no other recompense, than to die at thirty, felled by a hereditary disease. Who was the guilty party in his birth? On whom was the responsibility incumbent? He was afraid of searching too hard for an answer.

In vain, the doctor, his father and Raoul strove to predict an imminent cure; in vain, a smile of tranquility would not quit his fiancée's lips, affirming the faith that she did not cease to retain in hm. Were not that confidence and that amenity merely the pious deception with which invalids were lulled, the humane lie of which he had so often made use himself with others? In any case, later, put back on his feet temporarily, he intended to go to Paris, to request a formal diagnosis of his condition from an expert.

As soon as he had made that resolution, the thought of his guardians, perhaps solicited obscurely by his own, escaped their tasks. One tore himself away from his reading, the other from her embroidery. Their gazes smiled at one another and then, with a common preoccupation, turned toward him.

"What!" exclaimed Raoul. "You're no longer asleep, and you didn't tell us?"

"I was watching you."

"You must have remarked," Henriette observed, "that we were very being good and very tranquil, in order not to trouble your slumber..."

"Yes, truly, both of you are for me what neither my brother nor my sister is...you're two adorable hearts that I bless. You lessen my pain singularly, and when you close my eyes..."

"Come on!" interrupted Raoul's voice. "Are you going to pose as a dead man now? You know your situation as well as I do; in a month you'll be rolling around the local roads on a bicycle...a velo, eh? Isn't that good? Yes, you'll be rolling around with Henriette and me, and in six months..."

He turned to the young woman, whose cheeks were blushing red, and added: "In six months, the march from *Lohengrin* will company your emergence from the sacristy in the church of Saint-Augustin, and when you place your feet on the steps of the peristyle, decked in red carpet, you'll have that superb square before your eyes, swarming with a dazzled crowd. Your nuptial carriage will come into it while you, huddled on the white satin of the coupé, will feel valiant, happy and fortunate—more so than any of your admirers, who will get out of the way of the horses.

"May your prediction come true!" murmured Claude, in a disillusioned tone imprinted with such melancholy that all three of them felt the suffering, and Raoul's joviality was extinguished like the sun eclipsed by the interposition of a cloud.

Henriette had stopped smiling. She seemed meditative. Raoul picked up his book again, and the invalid let his thoughts run on again.

Yes, why did he not have his friend's flourishing health? Why could his lungs, amply and harmoniously inflated, not defy the disease that was eroding their substance? What a radiant couple he would have been able to form with Henriette; what a broad task of perpetuity he would have been able to accomplish with her! Now, even cured, but spoiled in his essence, afflicted in full flight, wounded like a bird that a hunter has struck in the wing, would he ever dare to resume his impetus, to risk himself in the pompous and unsure path of creation, toward the distant region of dawns, so close to the sun, so close to life?

It was such a grave thing, to create, such a grave thing to charge innocents with hereditary misery! Many people, assuredly, did not worry about it, some by virtue of cupidity or amour, others by virtue of ignorance or thoughtlessness, ceding to the pressure of their ambitions, their lucre or their passions. Those people could not listen to voices that did not trouble their conscience. They inseminated brutally or blindly.

But would he, who knew, who could foresee, whose studies had enlightened the scruples of his pitying soul, ever dare?

And the minutes were passing thus, intercut by painful reflections, while Henriette continued her delicate work of embroidery and Raoul continued reading, in his fine vigorous serenity, turning the pages with his graceful gesture, his hand sometimes lifted instinctively to his beard in order to display the blond curve, when the noise of wheels screeched on the gravel outside, and a vehicle that approached, and then stopped, suspended the alarm of one and the occupations of the others. Henriette got up and went to move aside the curtain at the window

She recognized the travelers. "Here's Julien and Rolande, in the company of Clara Boswett."

"They've ended their voyage, then?" asked Claude, raising himself on to his elbow, with annoyance. "Is it my illness that has caused them to come back? That would truly be too much honor..."

He did not continue, for the door opened, and Rolande, his half-sister, entered like a gust of wind. Rather tall and very elegant beneath her overcoat, imperiously bearing a small, fine head on which the brunette hair undulated in an arrangement that the voyage had not disorganized, she had in common with her brother Hector their complexion and the mobility of their pale brown eyes. Her nose, slightly hooked by virtue of an eccentricity not without charm, rose appropriately, and a small blue vein circumscribed the troubling ring of her inferior eyelid. Although none of her features were regular, the mouth being wide and the chin slightly prominent, making the cheeks seem more concave, she offered, perhaps by reason of those very irregularities, a certain tormented grace, which was not belied by the bosom and the rest of the rather thin body, animated by tremors and continual shifts from one foot to the other. She approached Claude hastily and kissed him on the forehead.

"Well, you're not doing as badly as all that! You look superb! What is it that has been written to us, then, that you were exhausted by spitting blood? We've come back, as you can imagine! And poor Clara wanted to see Venice! That's our voyage spoiled now!"

Claude looked at her coldly, having withdrawn his hand, which she wanted to palpate, in order to evaluate its warmth.

"I'm very sorry that they've frightened you so much," he said, "but Papa, who always sees things in black, neglected to consult me on the subject of your return; otherwise, I certainly wouldn't have prevented Miss Boswett from visiting Venice.

"Oh, it's not to make a reproach to you," she said, suddenly milder, moved to pity by the invalid's thinness. The she added: "Clara and Julien would like to say bonjour. May they come in?"

"Introduce Julien. As for Miss Boswett, excuse me for not receiving her. I'm still suffering too much."

"That's all right; I'll keep her company," she said, dryly, offended that her brother did not accord more consideration to her friend.

She went to the entrance, called: "Julien!" in a slightly arrogant tone, and then disappeared in order to let through a colossus wearing a full graying beard, of debonair appearance, although his very delicate and soft blue eyes signified intelligent thought. And while Julien approached the invalid and shook his hand warmly, she returned to the vestibule where Clara Boswett, her intimate friend, was waiting impatiently amid the unloaded trunks.

Originally from New York, Rolande's friend amazed at first glance by virtue of the equivocal aspect of her attire. If a black cheviot wool skirt tightened around her stout hips, short enough to reveal the emergence of two solid and masculine feet, had not dressed the lower part of her body, one could, only considering hr upper body and head, have mistaken her for one of those fatigued adolescents emitted by the neurasthenic families of the nineteenth century.

Her flat chest left the bolero in which she was clad the rectitude of a man's jacket, with the plastron of a white shirt striped by a long red cravat, surmounted by a turned-down collars from which a stiff, sinewy neck escaped, as if extended my muscular cords. The apparent bone-structure of the face continued to belie the amplitude of the body. Very pronounced ridges of willful jaws were visible there, and the narrowness of the nose, whose broad nostrils palpitated nervously. At the external corner of the eyelids, which sheltered two green eyes, fine wrinkles separated, like claws engraved by pleasure, and each movement of the cheeks betrayed them more implacably. But above all, what one retained of her was the sensuality of the lower lip, protruding like a pomegranate bulb, heightened by make-up, while the upper lip was small and dry, almost absent.

There was also the ruddy mahogany color of the short-cropped frizzy hair, dyed with henna, brought down over the forehead and coiffed with a boater. And in the same way that she did not appear to have a definite sex, she had no age. The slackness of her features accused her of the forty-five years of an exhausted woman; their   alertness, their attention to ap-pearing gracious, stiffening them and lighting up the eyes, rendered her the youth of a plump and vicious gamin. As a woman, she was ugly; as an adolescent she was indistinct; androgynous, she was disturbing in the equivocation of her entire person.

On seeing Rolande reappear, her impatience dissipated and she became almost pretty. With the very particular charm of a vibrant voice with an exotic accent, she welcomed her friend

"Darling, I was waiting for you to take me to your broth-er…but I don't want to; I'd rather go and unpack my trunks with you…"

"Yes, we'll see Claude later. He's very weary…"

"Rather say, darling, that he doesn't want to see me. Me neither, anyhow. Everything to do with men doesn't interest me. It's so ugly, truly, a man, ill in bed, dressed in a night-shirt, isn't it, darling?"

She uttered a nasty little laugh, filled with rancor for the sex that she abhorred, while she passed her arm around

Rolande's waist and drew her toward the marble stairway, whose magnificent banisters, with wrought iron arabesques, were guarded by two fire-breathing dragons. She was going up, in order to take possession of her apartment, in Rolande's company, when a little soubrette, very crumpled, crowned by a vapor of blonde hair, arrived and named her.

"Pardon me, Mademoiselle Boswett, don't you recognize me? I'm Rose, the chambermaid that Mademoiselle hired before her voyage."

"Yes, I remember you very well. You received my letter?"

"And I arrived his morning in order to commence my service with Mademoiselle."

Clara thanked her with a nod of the head; then, placing her foot on the first step, she gave Rolande her appreciation of the domestic. She found her pretty; she admired in a loud voice the suppleness of her figure, and the little white apron that, passed over her shoulders in an overlap of iron-smoothed ribbons, rendered her sweet enough to eat.

They disappeared at a turning of the stairway. Then Louis, the valet de chambre of the house, stout and powerful, with a shaved chin and separated side-whiskers, before sending up the trunks, abandoned his ceremonial gravity in order to address a wink to Rose followed by a filthy gesture that defined strangely the sympathy of the two young women.

For his part, Julien Duverdon, after having received Claude's amities, turned to Raoul and Henriette, whom Rolande had scarcely noticed. He apologized for his wife's incorrection, attributing it to the care of a rapid reinstallation. Their voyage having been cut short by a fortunately unnecessary return, they were counting on not departing again. And sensing questions coming, in order to avoid them, he talked abundantly, with a loquacity that was not customary to him, behind which lurked a disenchantment, the annoyance of submitting in a servile manner to the caprices of the disordered woman whom he adored, and by whom he knew that he was disdained. While he expressed himself, his entire person revealed the contrast between his soul and his body, the tenderness of his timid and faint heart beating within a Herculean torso, his humility of a faithful hound, his disabused melancholy dissimulated by the force of his broad, bald, graying head, behind the simultaneously naïve and intelligent astonishment of his blue eyes,

"Yes," he said, with a customary reserve of gestures, in order not to be too expansive, "we've seen Rome. It's very beautiful, that city so fecund in traditions, with its Porta del Popolo and its Vias, and its Quirinal, its Vatican and its other palaces. And Saint Peter's, of course. There are also museums full of marvels, and I would gladly have visited them...unfortunately, Miss Boswett doesn't like museums, with the consequence that I didn't see them. Miss Boswett wanted an audience with the Pope. I had to spend my time taking steps, writing to the ambassador, going to see the Secretary of State, and I finally had the letter in my pocket when the news arrived that recalled us to your side, my dear Claude."

He had turned toward Raoul and had noticed the slightly scornful smile with which the young man welcomed his confidences of the voyage, his confession of a foreign authority implanted in the household, acting on the wife and paralyzing the husband. He blushed, not in shame, but in believing himself to be suspected of the wound by which he was tortured, for as in children, his face easily betrayed the emotions that were upsetting him. He went on: "I think that we're going to spend some time here, until you're fully recovered. Then we'll probably go to my château in Lorraine to hunt..."

"You hunt now, then?" asked Claude, surprised to discover new tastes in him.

"No, not me," he replied, blushing again. "Not me...but Miss Boswett has the truly original intention of having a wild boar hunt in which there are only huntresses... Ah, that makes you smile! What do you expect? One can't do what one wants with women..."

The last phrase, emitted at hazard, but involuntarily summarizing his situation with regard to Rolande, scarcely rendered him his aplomb, for, gripped by a sense of having spoken inconsiderately, he stammered a few more words and then shut up.

Claude took advantage of that presence, which would ensure a guard at his beside, to beg Raoul to take Henriette for a walk.

"Please, go out, go to take the air for an hour. Julien will stay with me, won't you, Julien?"

After a little resistance, the young people rendered to his desire. The weather was damp and the wind was whipping up little showers of refreshing water, so dense that the Seine, in the distance could no longer be perceived. In order to walk, under a large impermeable cloak, Henriette was obliged to take her cavalier's arm. Laughing at the slaps that her capeline gave him, she showed her pretty teeth, the healthy and nacreous adornment of jewel-case rendered rosy by walking.

He felt strong, supple and vibrant, ardent to go forth against the rain and sustain the young woman's arm against his breast.

They both rejoiced in being warmly side by side, united against the anger of the tempest, which. whistling and exasperating, was already bending the tall trees, making the tall poplars of the park creak. The downpour increased and the water from the sky filled their eyes and mouths, provoking joyful exclamations.

In reality, it was an unconscious egotism that was dilating them, a *joie de vivre* crammed with youth and health, while back there, in the closed room, two dolors were facing one another, one physical and the other moral, both so acutely sensed, so painful to be near a little while ago, that they experienced a pleasure in distracting themselves from it, in struggling against the angry wind...

IV

Having arrived at the turning of the road, in front of the wide open door of the farm, sustained by two cross-beams and protected by the inclination of a thatch roof dirtied by time, Hector Fargeaud leaned gently on the pedal to tighten the brake, and the automobile, lacquered in red with an armature of polished copper that played with the sunlight, came gently to a halt, while continuing to palpitate like a beast harassed by running. Hector descended from the vehicle, awkwardly and addressed the mechanic who was accompanying him, the son of Père Grignon.

"It's understood, Arthur, that you don't budge. The brats are insupportable here, they might damage something."

He indicated a group of filthy children that the appearance of the machine had amassed. Clad in rags, with bare legs and feet, their faces smeared with dirt, they were already swarming around the vehicle. Hector beat the air with an impatient gesture, trying to drive them away, but as they only took one step back, he left Arthur the care of opposing their approach, and went into the farm. He had deliberately neglected to remove his protective dust-mask, with the consequence that, with the droop of his moustaches and the animal skin that he had judged it opportune to put on, although it was warm, he had the appearance of a carnival marionette.

The Servant farm was vast, filled with the odor of dung and animals. Sheds for the plows extended to the right, a low cowshed surmounted by dark grain-lofts occupied the background, while a rudimentary habitation rose up to the left, the upper floor of which pierced by small oval skylights, was the roof. Englobed by those buildings, circumscribed by a brick platform, the dung-heap was festering, half-solid and half-liquid, made of a mass of animal straw, faces and household waste, marinating in the rain of the recent downpours. A legion of chickens, ducks and geese, paddling and pecking, hoping and glad to be alive, were extracting their nourishment from it. Almost manure itself, so viscous and turbid with organic matter was its water, the trough displayed its glaucous sheet near the cowshed. The end of a recently-renewed wall delimited it, and from all of that an intense life was disengaged, the noisy and greedy activity of the soil, of animal-breeding, the communal effort of animals and people united there around the stinking mass, in the frame of the rustic buildings.

Near an open cellar, from which effluvia of sour milk were escaping, a strong girl in rags was beating butter in a sonorous churn, a kind of horizontal barrel traversed by an axle armed with perforated paddles. From the back, her accoutrement did not differentiate her greatly from the livestock. Her red hair was scattered, nothing could be seen of her but her solid rump and the vigorous movement of her arms, successively distended and then brought back toward the torso, lifted up at every rotation of the handle that she was turning her short skirt of blue cloth, under which extended a bare, astonishingly slender ankle, going astray in large clicking clogs. That was Julia the farm-girl, a bastard.

"Hey there, Julia!"

She turned round, laughing in advance, for he had just administered a vigorous slap on the buttock, and she thought she had received it from Douvard, the deputy schoolteacher, a big fellow who had already tried several times to knock her over, without succeeding, for, being much stronger than him, it was she who had felled him. But her laughter suddenly froze when she perceived the strange individual, the werewolf who, with his frog's eyes, was watching her bewilderment, delighted by her alarm.

"Holy Virgin, that's new!"

Hector took off his mask, and then she was entirely jovial, guffawing, letting go of her churn and running to the house to inform Mademoiselle Marthe.

"Come and see, Mademoiselle...an acrobat!"

The young woman, very smart in a bright summer dress, further decorated at the neck by a red velvet ribbon, emerged from the humble farmhouse. But the effect of the surprise for which Hector was hoping on account of his accoutrement was spoiled, because other people came into the farm. It was a couple who, after having left their carriage outside, approached arm in arm, the monsieur, with precautions of infinite solicitude, sustaining the lady, who seemed to be in pain and walking with difficulty.

Hector, who had turned round, recognized rich country neighbors, the Fortins, a childless household of which the wife, always afflicted by a mysterious malady of the generative organs, spent almost all her life in the country, the physicians having prescribed distance from fêtes, rest and fresh air. Having bared his head and taken off his mask again, which he had replaced for Marthe, he went toward them and saluted them cheerfully. He had taken, and he conserved in his own, the diaphanous hand of Madame Fortin; and the latter smiled with a suspicious embarrassment, for Hector had once courted her, fruitlessly, when she had not long been married to her husband, whom she adored.

Marthe, a little impressed by the arrival of that elevated society, confused by receiving them in the rudimentary habitation that revealed the modest situation of her parents, nevertheless advanced to meet them. She hoped secretly that Père and Mère Servant, in the fields for the moment, would delay their return and permit her to greet the strangers without the disturbance and embarrassment of their rustic presence.

"To what do I owe the honor of your visit, Madame and Messieurs?" she asked, giving her voice the most correct and more gracious inflection, like a young woman who knew fine etiquette.

"My wife is a little fatigued by an excursion in a carriage," Monsieur Fortin explained. "She asks your permission to rest for a moment in your home, and would gladly accept a cup of milk."

"With the greatest of pleasure. Come in!"

And, turning to the farm-girl, whose eyes were wide, she was glad to command her: "Quickly, Julia…take two pots and go in search of milk for Madame and cider for the Messieurs."

She escorted them to the threshold of the dwelling, apologized for the poverty of the abode, gracious and very attentive

"I'm not always here, you understand…and then, my parents let things go, caring little about the elegance of their interior."

When they had come in, she regretted again only having wicker chairs to offer them. In Lille—yes, in Lille—she had genteel furniture, with an armchair in crushed velvet, whereas here, there was rural simplicity in everything, in all its lack of comfort.

"Be assured, Mademoiselle, that we will be very content," protested Monsieur Fortin, gently sitting his wife down.

Then it was Hector who talked. In order to legitimate his presence he recounted that he had me to interrogate Père Servant regarding the probabilities of the game, notably the success of the coveys of grouse. But the mobility of his pale brown eyes, going to Marthe, snaking over the promising contours of the pretty girl's breasts and the hips, signified something else so clearly that the latter blushed deeply, slightly flattered at the same time.

And the reception passed cordially, without a hitch. Julia had brought glasses, milk and then cider, when Marthe's assurance was suddenly covered in chagrin. She had, in fact, seen the old folk arrive, her father and mother, already worn-out and stooped. The man was dressed as a laborer, in a smock and baggy trousers, his face bristling with white hairs whose growth the razor had respected for a week, dragging in his callused, knotty hands, after mowing, a loaded wheelbarrow covered in herbage. Her mother, with a benevolent little face, withered and striped with wrinkles, like an old apple, bore in the tan of her complexion the reflection of the earthenware tiles of her kitchen, and the influence of the stove, where, hanging from the pot-hook, vast slabs of meat were smoking.

The old couple came in, and there were further ceremonies, the ordering of another pitcher of cider, of which Julia went in quest, clogs clicking and rump expansive, plunging into a kind of trap-door that gave access to the cellar.

Now that they were all at table, after having clinked their glasses, Père Servant, wiping his lips with the back of his hand, broached the eternal question of the land on which he lived, the crops that were promising, especially the wheat, growing thickly, favored by the early rain and the subsequent dryness, which the sun would soon gild, with the result that the harvest would be a fortnight in advance.

Very sure of the question that obsessed him, which impelled him every morning to open his window in order to interrogate the sky, and in the evening, when he laid his weary body down in the coarse sheets, to lie awake with the last glimmer of thought, and very amorous of the glebe that he had courted more than his wife, as if it had been his, shifting it and shoveling it, inseminating it with broad gestures, decorating it with the rectilinear strips of the plow, in a confused attachment of peasant atavism, he predicted with near certainty the fate of the crops and the caprices of the old mistress whose womb never wearied of being fecundated. And he deplored the fact that that love of the soil was becoming rare among the new generations, the young folk being attracted to the city because the salaries there were more remunerative, the labor less hard, and perhaps also because machines were replacing arms, the land no longer having need of manual effort, being labored at present almost mechanically, almost by itself.

"Is it for that reason that you only have one daughter, and you've had her educated and sent to the city?" asked Monsieur Fortin, expecting a response very different from the one he received.

"Yes, it's for that reason," affirmed the man, with a positivity that surprised is interrogator, "and I certainly don't regret it. She's so dainty, the demoiselle, and so good with it that she's worth ten. Oh, she gives us a great deal of contentment!"

All gazes, fixing on the young woman, confirmed the fellow's opinion. Marthe, however, was chagrined that the eulogy did not come from higher up. She coughed as she adjusted the ribbon securing her hair over her blonde and firm flesh. In fact, she was "the demoiselle," but did her father need to underline it so precisely, in a tone that seemed to indicate the sacrifices that had been made for her?

"It's for that reason," the old man went on, "that I've only had one daughter. Oh, it the land had belonged to me, if I hadn't been working for others, I don't say; sons would have served my purpose very well; they would have helped me...but, you understand, I had no desire to work all my life to die of hunger in my old age. Can you see me like Grignon, the gardener at Monsieur Fargeaud's château? He's been married for eighteen years and his wife has had a kid every year...and now it appears that there's a nineteenth on the way. It's true that they drink, those fellows. So, what happens? Misery at home, and, with the aid of eau-de-vie, that becomes permanent! Anatole, the eldest, is a soldier, because he can't do any better, and Arthur, the second, who was a gas-lighter, had had the luck to be hired as a chauffeur by Monsieur Hector here. Alphonsine, the third, wanted to go into service in Paris and she became a lost girl, a good-for-nothing...and the others—oh, the others!—how they live! No, me, I'm more cunning. When I saw that it was a girl I said to my wife: 'Let's stop!'—and that hasn't prevented us from loving one another, has it, Mother?"

The old woman, who was partially deaf, shook her head regardless, with confidence. Monsieur Fortin listened with amazement to that discourse exposing the logic of egotistical precautions that, contracted by the bourgeoisie, were now reaching the peasantry. Père Servant took that logic to the extreme, and his life, so valiant in labor, so curbed over the glebe, so desirous of fecundity in the soil, had been, for his own creation, a grim parsimony, in a measure that approached heroism, since it caused the avoidance of the embrace dear to men of the fields and reduced the customary pleasure of amour. Perhaps it was one of the consequences of the civilization and education that were spreading everywhere, from the cities to the most obscure corners of the countryside, that hesitation before familial responsibilities, that reflection, now common in alcoves and hovels, deflecting semen from its true destination to its use for pleasure, leading instinct to bankruptcy.

Monsieur Fortin rediscovered in Père Servant's confession the arguments of rich landowners, those who limited themselves to a single child in order to accumulate the ancestral fortune on his head, to make of him a well-to-do heir who was protected from division. Was it truly to that shameful conclusion that capital led? Had civilization and social ameliorations led to subjective interest? And he, who desired so much to have a family, whose procreation had been annihilated at the outset of his marriage by Madame Fortin's mysterious malady, could not help experiencing a slight sentiment of indignation against the cunning peasant, a miser of his semen as of his écus. He certainly did not want to punish him, but what destination would his savings have if Marthe disappeared one day? He exchanged a sad gaze with his wife, which said a great deal about their common disappointment, for the same reflections had assailed Madame Fortin's thought.

But Julia, the farm-girl, emerged from the trap-door again and brought another pitcher. Full, firm and powerful, in spite of the elegance of her wrists and ankles, the delicacy of her features and her ruddy complexion, she went from glass to glass, filling them to the rim. Her gesture, accomplished by a round and sun-tanned arm, enunciated the glory of the marmoreal body, the perfection of lines that her twenty years still conserved impeccably, but which carelessness, negligence and pregnancies would later allow to deteriorate.

In passing, she brushed with her lifted skirt those she served, and her movement gave off an acidulated odor of human animality. A clumsiness that caused her to make a glass overflow provoked a deployment of her fleshy cleavage, and a white flash of her teeth in healthy laughter. Père Servant

65

scolded her, and then, when she had gone away, he profited from her disappearance to recount her story, in order to draw a moral from it favorable to his egotism, for he had understood Monsieur Fortin's mute reprobation.

"It's like that Julia," he said. "She's a bastard. For us, certainly, she renders us services. She has a heart for work; she gets up at four o'clock in the morning, and all day long until eight o'clock in the evening she doesn't stop. She's better than a machine, and without ever one word louder than another, too. Yes, there aren't two like her. So I pay her well; I give her twenty francs a month. But for her, Monsieur, would you believe that it's very fortunate, that position. Would she have done better not to be born? Her mother, La Choupe, a beggar-woman had fourteen children by anyone at all, for she's never been married, and not one of her children resembles another. Yes, Monsieur, with anyone who wanted...of the fourteenth, she died. Julia, it's believed she's from a sub-officer in the dragoons, then on detachment in Rouen, who had such a sentiment for La Choupe that he left his post to come to find her again...and one day, having been caught by a chief, he fought and was put before a court martial, which put an end to their frequentation...

"Well, Julia, would you believe that she's favored on earth? Sometimes, I can see clearly that it's no, when she looks at my daughter, so pretty and so well dressed, while she beats butter and milks the cows. Then I understand that she's suffering. The other day, I saw her weeping. Well, anyway, I ask all of you: if I too had had fourteen children, what would Marthe be doing at this moment? She'd be beating butter and milking cows like Julia instead of being here, a demoiselle schoolmistress on leave, drinking cider with you! Isn't that true?"

And those two words, *demoiselle* and *schoolmistress*, inflated his mouth, taking on as they passed through the gaps of his toothless maxilla, a character of respectful devotion, of idolatry, common to peasants for their wealth, for their crops gilded by the splendor of the sun, for their grain-lofts crammed to the rafters with the August hay. The shifting of soil, the tracing of furrows, the cares of a long servitude, had their end, their apotheosis, in that beautiful young woman, the unique crop of the household, in which all familial force was educed and concentrated. Their pride was to have brought her up, nourished and educated her like bourgeois girls, to have spared her heavy manual labor, to have kept her away from the cowpats and the dung-heap. So much sacrifice and effort however, were not attracting Marthe's gratitude for the moment. Wounded in her vanity because so much insistence was being put on her humble origin before this good society, aggravated and apprehensive, she tormented the substance of her red velvet ribbon, coquettishly disposed over the milky surge of her blonde cleavage.

But again, Monsieur Fortin resumed speaking. He, so desirous of progeniture, to whom nature refused procreation, whose fortune would eventually be dispersed between the hands of distant cousins, could not understand or admit that restriction of the family. In addition, he confessed that a chauvinistic preoccupation accompanied that anxiety of depopulation: a terror of seeing neighboring nations increase and grow rich in human produce while the land of France decreased, in spite of its wealth, in spite of its colonies, so extensive and rich in resources, where people could be born and subsist generously.

He concluded, tapping the farmer's thigh: "Fortunately, Père Servant, fortunately for our fatherland, not everyone thinks like you...we'd soon be reduced to annihilation."

But the man raised to his interlocutor a cold gaze, as metallic as the silver coins in his savings. Irony made him blink his eyelids.

"The fatherland, war! The children who depart and never come back! Another song the newspapers sing. The soil is being depopulated and it's necessary to make citizens! It's easy for journalists who make money, and it's easy for you, Monsieur Fortin, who are rich. Your means permit you to have children and to offer them a great deal. When one comes, you have a physician to bring it into the world, midwives to care for your lady, a big cradle with frills and ribbons to lay your kid in. And yet, the rich also restrict themselves, in order not to scatter their fortune. But what about the poor, Monsieur…what about me? The midwife costs twenty francs and twenty francs, for me, is probably like a thousand francs for you…and also, it's necessary to earn them Then again, the work doesn't wait; Mother has her tasks to do, and I don't have too much of her to help me, to supervise the men. And then, once they've come into the world, it's necessary to dress children, to nourish them…and all that to send them abroad, where fevers and bullets kill them? No, that's not justice! And if I die before they're grown, who will look after them? I know full well that there are good people like you, charitable to the poor…but one wearies, in the end, of always giving."

He swallowed a swig of cider and his tongue, with a dry click, applauded the pleasure that the acidic aliment gave him. Putting down his glass he concluded: "No, personally, I didn't have the means to have many children."

The discussion came to an end, for Madame Fortin had just risen to her feet. Her pretty face had suddenly been altered by a intimate suffering, so painful that she compressed her side with the flat of her hand. Sensing the advent of a crisis already experienced many times before, she wanted to go home before the pain exploded entirely, in order to go to bed and receive care. She was still gracious, striving to smile, thanking the people who had welcomed her; but her husband was already alarmed. He was very familiar with those preludes to a relapse that was about to lay his wife low for days and necessitate applications of ice and injections of morphine.

He reproached himself loudly for having exposed her to the jolts of the carriage, an imprudence of which it was impossible to foresee the consequences, with that obscure illness that the most celebrated physicians had difficulty diagnosing. And shaken by anguish, stammering words of idolatry and anguish, he had seized her by the waist, sustaining her with all his fibers, encouraging her to reach the victoria that would soon transport her home, helping her to make, with a halting step, the short journey to the door, enabling her to avoid bumping into asperities in the brickwork. But scarcely had the poor woman taken a few steps than she collapsed, uttering a cry. A lividity hollowed out her features, droplets of cold sweat, issued from her forehead, mingled with the tears that she could no longer hold back. Then Monsieur Fortin, tottering with dolor, tried to take her in his arms, but he was tremulous, slack, vanquished by his tenderness. He only had the strength to stop her falling to the ground.

Julia saw that and was moved to pity. Having suspended her work, mouth open and eyes widened by an unusual spectacle of weakness and affliction, in her rustic and solid pose, she really dominated the collapsed woman and the people who were leaning over the invalid, wasting time in van consultations. Slowly, reflection saw the light within her, inspired her unkempt red head, and gave her confidence in the solidity of her agrarian muscles, in the service she could render. Then, suddenly decisive, she moved away the meager and flabby Hector, who was talking about going for help, with the back of her hand.

"Wait! Let me do it!"

Already, without the shadow of an effort or a contraction of her ruddy face. she had picked up the sick woman, taken her in her arms, and, with the facility with which she would have lifted a bale of hay, she transported her all the way to the vehicle. The human burden did not weigh upon her breast, the full and round outline of her firm hindquarters did not buckle under the coarse skirt. She went through the doorway, advanced gloriously toward the carriage, her clogs clicking and her breasts high. As she hoisted herself up on the footstep, Monsieur Fortin, who had followed her, noticed her remarkably structured leg emerging naked from the crude footwear and launching, white and gracious, above an admirably-sculpted ankle.

"*Sapristi!* You made a handful of her!" he said, finally reassured on seeing his poor wife installed.

He tried to put a hundred sous in her hand, and when she refused, stupefied by the size of the tip, he turned to Père Servant,

"Will you permit Julia to accompany us to my house? When we arrive she can render us the same service in getting Madame Fortin down easily, for I don't think that any of my domestics could do it as vigorously.

The farmer had scarcely agreed than the beautiful young woman had climbed on to the seat next to the coachman, content to break by means of that excursion the monotony of her animal life, her perpetual servitude of a beast of burden. The coachman touched the horses; she turned round several times toward her employers, laughing, and amid the dist that the wheels stirred up, her high-perched rump and broad back was seen to draw away and then disappear into the sun, along with the suntanned nape surmounted by the red mass of tangled hair.

"She's a brave girl, who doesn't flinch before the work," Père Servant granted her, by way of a eulogy. Turning toward Hector Fargeaud, who was getting ready to step into his automobile, he saw him deep in conversation in a low voice with his daughter. Having approached, he heard the gentleman say, conceitedly, that he had once been very fond of Madame Fortin, but that he had disdained her because she did not have, like Marthe, the fine promise of health and beauty. And Père Servant felt very proud to see his "demoiselle" so appreciated by the heir to the château.

V

At a rather weary pace, Antonin Fargeaud completed the daily tour of his park that he made every afternoon after the siesta. After a few cold days the weather was fine again, and from the gate overlooking a vast stretch of woodland down below, a capriciously cut out horizon was outlined sharply in a fluid sky. That perspective was diversified by the one that animated the other flank of the domain. It gave an impression of calm, repose, enigma and death. It caused Hamlet's doubt, to be or not to be, to quiver, and the old man, in looking at it— or, rather, suspecting it, for his weak eyesight could scarcely perceive it—concluded on the second part of the problem: not to be.

And yet what attractions there were in that corner of nature brushed with infinitely varied colorations, how much charm in that shady vastness, where the vegetations took on new hues with every change of season, from the most cheerful greens of spring to the most melancholy heliotropes of winter, passing through the gold of autumn: an entire gamut of expressive tonalities. But the disillusioned man passed by; of those marvels he only wanted to conceive the infinity that was beyond, the inexplicable, incommensurable, enigmatic extent in which everything is confounded, lost and annihilated. He scorned pompous evocations of nights, misty mornings, flamboyant middays and evenings of apotheosis, for having once admired them too much.

Fatigued by his walk, accompanied dolorously by the creaking of his old joints, he was about to retake the path leading straight to the château, when suddenly, sonorities of brass, the blast of a trumpet and the apparition of a mail-coach coming in a straight line along the dusty road held him immobile where he stood. What could be happening? The road that the carriage was traveling was part of his domain and had no other terminus than the gate of the park.

Now he could perceive more clearly the uniform dress of the six piebald horses, disposed in pairs, the first pair mounted by two postillions costumed in green, booted in yellow and whose trousers and coats were extraordinarily braided with gold and splashed with red. The body of the coach appeared more distinctly, all silvered, with the benches of the platform garnished with an amphitheater of bright costumes and polychromatic umbrellas. In front of them, on the seat, a sumptuous stout coachman was cracking his whip; behind, in the same livery, upright and lofty, two trumpeters were making their instruments glisten in the sunlight.

It's doubtless a band of acrobats, thought the old man, *who have mistaken the road.*

He was already preparing to put the strange equipage on the right path when it made an expert half-turn, and then stopped dead, the carriage door facing the gate. The joyous appeals of women, in chorus, demanded the door. And as no one came to open it, the mild clean-shaven face of a man of fifty, ornamented by a yellow panama hat, appeared at the window of the coupé and ordered in a high-pitched voice: "Valets, sound!"

Again the trumpets were raised and the fury of brass spoke, finally drawing Mère Grignon from her house. She came, complaining of the weight of her nineteenth child, staggering a little from drunkenness. Then, first the panama, and then the glabrous face, and a little thickset, broad-backed, rounded body low on the legs emerged successively from the vehicle, clad almost to the heels in a severe black frock-coat with a multicolored rosette in the buttonhole, in which red dominated to the extent of effacing the other colors. From the notch of the breast to the heart-shaped waistcoat flattened over the abdomen, a large white ruffle was deployed, folded and vaporous, which surmounted a high collar holding the stiff neck, ornamented by a white cravat with two turns knotted in the fashion of 1830. The ensemble had an aspect that was both solemn and comical, and also slightly disquieting because of

72

the metallic gleam of the gray eyes and the absence of lips from the face.

The little man, so debonair in appearance, so well-furnished in the abdomen, sheathed in black and adorned with white, arriving, sickly and sumptuous in the simplicity of his manner and the gaudiness of his vehicle, had the appearance of another age. Scarcely was he on his feet than cries saluted him. The ladies, from the height of the banquettes, unleashed an entire guttural vocabulary of the Parisian faubourgs,

"Say, Uncle, will you be long?"

"Aren't you going to let us down, Uncle?"

"What an idea you had, bringing us here!"

"And then planting us here!"

"Hey, get on with it, poussah!" clamored a younger voice.

"Mademoiselles, I remind you of the proprieties!" observed an old lady enthroned on the last banquette, which she alone occupied.

But the little man was undisturbed. Graciously, he blew a kiss to the entire swarm of pretty young women; then with an unctuous gesture that blessed and prayed at the same time, he moderated their impatience with a few words of his high-pitched voice, lisping with Italian exoticism, pronouncing *u* as *ou* and stressing the penultimate syllables.

"My little doves, my darlings, ten minutes of calm, I beg you. You have, in any case, everything you need to distract and refresh you: a handsome boy to kiss you and pour champagne to delight your mucus membranes. I even believe that the servants must have prepared the elements of a lunch. There. a hundred paces away, is a clump of trees whose thick shade will be beneficial to you. Go, my little lambs! Rest, eat, drink and kiss. In the meantime, I shall work, for science and for humanity!"

A new exclamation of joy drowned out his words, and there was an immediate flutter of bright dresses, a tumble down the footsteps of six young women, characterized by differences in the color of their flesh and their hair, but identical in brazen make-up. The only man in the society, a robust fellow of twenty-five with curly brown hair, his torso clasped by an aubergine jacket, helped them to descend, naming them successively.

"Come on, Carmen!" he said to a tall, stiff, slim brunette impregnated with warm Spanish blood, whose temples were bloodied by two large clusters of geraniums.

Then, receiving a small, pale, slender blonde: "Let me help you, Mascotte!"

And, passing on to a third, plump, with shiny mahogany-red hair, whose nose plunged toward the mouth like an eagle's beak: "Have no fear Sarah!"

The fourth one hesitated, inclining the gracious and delicate profile of a Murillo virgin, embarrassed by her skirt. He convinced her: "Jump, Marquisette, I have you!"

Then came the fifth; she was a tall natural beauty, hieratic, with a gilded torsade with Venetian glints. Fearful, she uttered a roulade of little cries, extending long arms; he reassured her: "Lean on me, Mignon!"

And finally it was the urn of the sixth, a curly-haired African whose face was summarized by a flat nose and a broad grin, exploding in astonishingly white teeth. "Your turn, Bamboula, my flour!"

When they were all on the ground there was no longer anyone on the imperial but the stout old lady, of very distinguished appearance, and in order to transfer her, the young man became respectful, calling her "Maman" and lending her the support of his muscles.

And all of them, after having received his aid, thanked him politely. "You're a darling, my little Cyrano...," while Cyrano, content and bold, without the appearance of having made an effort, convinced of his royalty, like a cock in a henhouse, led them to the nearby clump of trees. He had taken two of them by the waist, and was followed by the gaudy crew of domestics carrying picnic baskets.

Then the stout and glabrous little man of 1830, seeing his orders executed, returned with a satisfied expression to the open gate and prepared to enter. He did not appear to pay any heed to Mère Grignon, whose astonishment pierced the fog of her drunkenness, but Antonin Fargeaud, emerging from the corner that hid him from the visitor's eyes, came forward.

"Pardon me, Monsieur, what do you desire?"

The dwarf sketched a slightly protective smile with his thin lips. Nevertheless, he took off his panama, showing a strange bald cranium, as if peeled, lumpy, diabolically kneaded. He lisped: "Is this not the Château de la Taquainerie, the property of Monsieur Fargeaud?"

"Indeed, Monsieur. What do you want with Monsieur Fargeaud?"

"With him, personally, nothing at all. It's to his son, Claude Fargeaud, that I wish to speak. I'm Professor Domesta."

He put a certain emphatic importance into declaring his name. And as the old man remained nonplussed, and expressed by his attitude that he did not know the name, thus invoked as a Sesame opening all doors, he added: "You don't know Professor Domesta, doctor of the University of Rome? Then I can classify you: you're not a scientist!"

From the deep pocket of his frock-coat, which he had just opened, taking care not to disturb the creases of his ruffle, he took a vast crocodile-skin portfolio stuffed with papers, unfolded it and extended a card edged with gold, on which, under the name that he had just pronounced, after a long series of honorary titles, his social rationale, his function in humanity was summarized in bright red letters by the two words: *Artificial fecundation.*[5]

---

[5] Although anecdotal reports of human artificial insemination go back to the fifteenth century, and the first report of an experiment is dated to 1770, the first disciplined experimentation was reported in *Clinical Notes on Uterine Surgery* (1863) by James Marion Sims, a highly controversial figure who employed slaves as experimental subjects. Couvreur would also have been familiar with a sensationalist novel published in

And while Antoine Fargeaud, surprised, turned the card over and brought it close to his weak eyes, the little man commenced his patter in a reedy tone in strange contrast to the plump and pale animality of his face.

"Professor Domesta, doctor of the University of Rome. Former physician specially attached to the chapel of Pope Pius IX in 1870, Commander of the Nicham Imtiaz in 1880 for having given children to the Sultan, castrated during a war, then Chevalier of the Portuguese Order of Our Lady of the Conception, for having rendered identical services to Prince Gaetan; and obliged, after so many honors, in consequence of political disgrace, to come and seek refuge in the great and liberal country of France, where, in Paris, an independent professor of artificial fecundation, I am finally realizing and fulfilling the veritable aspirations of my laborious existence by practicing and teaching all physicians my marvelous method. Thanks to it, Signor, every man, while remaining chaste and sparing the productive resources with which the Eternal has endowed him, can nevertheless have children as sturdy and as endowed with vigor, health and beauty as you or me, Signor...yes, Signor! My consultations are three times a week, on Monday, Wednesday and Friday, from two o'clock to four, and it's necessary that I practice in the city...but at present, I'm on vacation in Canteleu, where I have a country house, not far from this château...but to whom do I have the honor of speaking?"

"I am Claude Fargeaud's father."

"Illustriousness! You're his father! I admire you, Signor, for having given birth to the author of *The Amours of Plants!* By the Madonna! This is a fine day for me!"

France in 1884, *Le Faiseur des hommes*, by Yveling Rambaud and Jean-Louis Dubut de Laforest, in which the procedure is employed at the behest of a wife, unknown to the husband. Rambaud was a journalist and Dubut de Laforest a prolific popular novelist; neither had any medical expertise.

The panama hat had inclined even more respectfully; now it was almost at ground level. As the sun was hot, however, the little man put it back on his head and smiled again. Now, the château-owner remembered that he had, in fact, frequently read the name of Domesta in newspaper headlines, which a trial for the illegal practice of medicine had rendered famous, whom interviews and even polemics on the subject of his practices had raised on the platform of shady notoriety for the contemplation of the amused and easily-duped idle crowd of Paris.

And although convicted several times, the man continued nevertheless his inseminations and his controversy, alimenting the publicity of the newspapers in order to make the gong of advertisement resonate, stupefying the thought of the capital by means of the documented display of a false science, attracting clients as a bird-catcher lures skylarks with the glare of a false sun, in a dazzle of implausible luxury. His silvery landau appeared in the Bois, at sporting solemnities, at the doors of the great theaters, harnessed to four horses, with gold-braided grooms and powdered footmen, such as are seen in London; it was garnished with three pretty women accumulated on the front banquette, while the master occupied the back, modest and serious, with the handsome Cyrano by his side.

Legends circulated on his account, still distant from the truth. People wondered about the role of his female colleagues, whispered about the eccentricities of his town house, and told tales about his gypsy orchestra, calming the impatience of clients in his waiting rooms during the hours of his consultations. Worthy of tempting the pencil of an artist, the caricaturist Sem had sketched him; he animated three pages of his album. And the wily Domesta had understood the utility of his bewildering manifestations. They bore fruit in the mind of the public. It was necessary to strike hard, to throw pepper in the eyes, to have his detractors and his incense-burners. And he had succeeded, for his charlatanism only left, after a time, the memory of a notoriety, of an individual who, whether good or evil—no one knew—had generated talk. He imposed his name, with the question mark that publicity designs. He allowed to brood, under the still-warm ashes, the advertising ever ready to spring forth, and the public remembered, if not a glare, at least a smoky plume of startling glory.

Antonin Fargeaud was astonished to find that man, so decried by some and so lauded by others, so small, so gla-brous, so fat, of an appearance so negative, in spite of his frock-coat and his ruffle and his 1830 collar.

"Yes, I remember now," he said. "You are, in fact, quite famous."

And in his hostility to the legend of repopulation, in his hatred of everything that was creation and all those who fa-vored it, the old man was about to throw him out, when a sud-den idea modified his intentions: the desire to distract Claude, who, feeling better, had just gone out for the first time. This extraordinary burlesque specimen, having arrived in the ex-traordinary cortege that he had seen a few moments ago, would certainly amuse his son. He softened the grim expres-sion of his face and began to smile.

"You do me a great honor, Monsieur le professeur, in coming to my home. I know your work and it interests me. In what way can I be agreeable to you? You've come to see my son, you said? I'll take you to him."

Then he addressed Mère Grignon, who, after reclosing the gate, was leaning against a tree, her head nodding. "Well, what are you waiting for?"

Domesta had observed the bewildered gaze of the wom-an and the instability of her equilibrium.

"This is your concierge," he said. "I shall also deal with her. She seems to be in the vines of the Lord, and I won't get much out of her today. At the moment I'm drawing up a report to the global academy of new medicine, and I'd like to include in it the results of an investigation of fecundity in the lower classes of society, notably on the physical, moral, social, eco-nomic and political causes that impel poor people to have many children. I've heard it said in the locale that your conci-erge has had eighteen, and it seems to me that a nineteenth is on the horizon of her maternity. It's a fine result, although I haven't had anything to do with it! That's a subject of observation. But what a pity, Signor, truly, that the poor woman is drunk!"

"Monsieur le professeur," said Antonin Fargeaud, "that woman, who is part-brute, and whom I conserve out of pity, could not respond to you even if she were not drunk. But I can inform you and give you the arguments that she has repeated many times when I have interrogated her on the subject. She has a great many children, she has told me, because making them is her only pleasure; because her husband, a drunkard like her, is unable to restrict his appetites; because both of them, driven by alcohol, make love without reflection; because allowing herself to become pregnant does not complicate her existence and because, in that world, a female gives birth like a bitch; and because, finally, of her eighteen children, save for the oldest, who are well, eight have died of meningitis and the others are nourished partly by public charity and in larger part by me—a generosity for which I reproach myself increasingly..."

"It is necessary never to regret the good one does, Signor."

"It isn't good, it's bad."

"How can you say that!" protested the little man, raising his arms in the air. "What ideal is more noble than favoring creation? All my life—an apostolate, Signor!—has had that goal...and may Heaven strike me down if I don't give you proof of it, instantly. Look, Signor!"

He rummaged hastily in the flaps of his long frock-coat, which was bulging in the rear. First he took out a sort of vast gilded set of compasses, traversed in the middle by a mobile curvilinear hook, engraved with figures, like those geometers use. He waved it in the air.

"Look, Signor. This osteopelvimacromimeter, with which I measure the bones of a woman's pelvis, is my own invention, and it is marvelous. Yes, Signor, marvelous to have thought of it. Does not genius often result from the execution of a very tiny thought, something trivial? Have statues not be raised to Pasteur because he had the idea of cultures? It's simple, however. Well, this will have a statue erected to me, in time, like Pasteur!"

He placed the compasses against his abdomen, deployed them, making the hook creak, and dug the points into the fabric of his garment, in such a way as to delimit the width of the hips. It was quite difficult, because his paunch got in the way and his arms were too short for the task.

"I can read in your eyes that you understand me, Signor. With this instrument, no pelvic floor can deceive me, no measurement can escape me. Three movements, click, click, click, and I can tell the woman who is consulting me veridically: "You can have children" or "Your bones are too narrow to have them." It's simple, but it's necessary to have genius to think of it! That's not all."

He plunged once again into the depths of his garment, whose reserves seemed inexhaustible. He took out another instrument, gold this time, which had the structure of a small telescope, fitted with a perpendicular handle at the axis of the tool. By pressing the handle, two valves with the form of a duck's beak opened in the tube. What made it eccentric, however, was the ornamentation of the sculpted hilt, in pale green and lunar yellow, of a naked man and woman embracing one another. Domesta brandished the object of intimate examination radiantly. His lipless mouth widened, uncovering the alignment of yellow teeth.

"Do you see, Signor? I illuminate the tube with electricity. Isn't that ingenious? It's pretty too, and dainty, this art nouveau speculum, a veritable showcase exhibit, by the Madonna! I shall bequeath it to the Louvre Museum after my death. In any case, I like artists and I patronize the arts. Isn't fecundation an art that is too new, a science too disdained? As I told you, I have made it an apostolate. Do you understand now, Signor that I cannot permit anyone to pronounce before me such a blasphemy against the holy law of nature!

Antonin Fargeaud was no longer smiling. Domesta's last words had just reawakened his obsession, the inutility of creation, the crime of engendering beings condemned in advance to a miserable life; and he deduced therefrom the extreme, the annihilation of everything, the suppression of the human world. And under the weight of his reflections, his forehead suddenly subsided; his face filled with an immense melancholy, which the strange visitor noticed, and which he attributed to his own provocation.

"Signor, I've spoken to you brutally; only blame my love of life, and pardon me. And since you're gracious enough to take me to your son, I'm yours."

He replaced his instruments in his pocket; then, abruptly smoothing his long frock-coat with a movement of his two hands, he adjusted its rectitude. With a slight flick of a finger he expelled a few grains of dust deposited by the journey on his ruffle. His gray eyes measured the depth of the park and the vault of the trees, a gap in which revealed the old tower and the mass of the manor. In an admiring fashion, his lips protruded a little further, and he admitted: "You have a very pretty property, Signor; this park is admirable!"

"You can make a tour of it after having seen my son," said the castellan, indicating with a gesture the avenue of plane-trees that they had to follow.

"I'd accept gladly, if I were not awaited by my companions."

"Yes, your family…your nieces, your sister…I could invite them…"

"No, no," protested the Italian, swiftly. "Leave them where they are. They'll be patient, the darlings. They have what they need to charm their wait. And then, Signor, they've seen many others!"

Without further explanation, with an enigmatic smile that had just reentered his lips, Domesta followed Antonin Fargeaud. As silence weighed upon him and volubility was an inexhaustible secretion in him, he expanded in speech, like a stream hat nothing can dam. They advanced toward the château. The fat man talked about his profession, his method, his therapeutic successes, his trials. He defended himself against the calumnies with which, out of rivalry, the syndicate of physicians had tried to blacken him. In his high-pitched, lisping language, filled with images and protestations, supported by philosophical and religious ideas, he lauded life, and the sovereign joy of giving it. His plump little hand fluttered with his speech, underlining is principal propositions, blessing them in priestly fashion. His pear-shaped, contented and monastic abdomen, had a tidal ebb and flow beneath his frock-coat with every step he took. But Antonin Fargeaud was no longer listening, and hastened his pace in order to bring that toy to his son sooner.

Finally, they reached the verdant lawn protected from the heat by the principal body of the edifice, which the sunlight, already in decline, was shaving obliquely. There, the guests of the château, Raoul Fieux and Henriette, and Julien Duverdon next to Miss Boswett, were sitting and chatting around Claude, who was extended in a rocking-chair with a plaid blanket over his legs. Rolande was absent and Hector, stretched out on the grass, was asleep, enveloped in his animal skin, his head in a leather helmet.

"Don't get up," said Domesta, observing the astonishment in their gazes; and he added: "I admire the château, and I'm looking for the genius that inhabits it."

Holding his panama very low, he bowed in a circular fashion, and inspected with an expert eye, like a horse-dealer evaluating fillies, the two women, Henriette and Clara, sitting near the invalid, sprightly in the brightness of their summer dresses. A slight gesture of astonishment, which he could not repress, underlined the unexpected encounter with the American. The latter responded with an identical amazement. But the shock of their reciprocal surprise passed unperceived, because Antonin Fargeaud was introducing him to Claude.

"Monsieur le professeur Domesta, of whom you have certainly heard mention."

"Well, well," Claude could not help pronouncing in a low voice, considering the eccentric and celebrated individual curiously, whom Sem's satirical album had rendered picturesque to such a point that the memory remained implacably engraved in his mind. At that moment, perceiving him for the first time, he recognized him via the artist's whimsy.

Antonin Fargeaud completed the introduction: "My son, Claude Fargeaud."

"It's you, it's you," clamored Domesta, putting his little monastic hands together, as if suffocated by admiration, "who are the author of *The Amours of Plants*?"

"It's me, indeed."

The panama hat, which had rejoined the little man's shiny cranium, was briskly seized, and shaved the ground again.

"Signor, I say to you that you are a grandmaster! Yes, yes, don't protest! You are a grandmaster! Your book is my bedside reading. I go to sleep over it. I seize it when I wake up. It enthuses me. How could it be otherwise? You do with plants what I do with humans. We are destined to understand one another. Shake my hand…clasp it! You're giving me good warmth!"

Claude allowed him to seize the hand, without any confidence in that overflow of enthusiasm, although he was slightly flattered, deep down, to know that his work was known, even by this charlatan. The violent movement with which the little man had communicated his sympathy provoked a slight cough, and Domesta became anxious.

"But what do I hear? What do I see? You're coughing! You're lying down! Blood of Christ! Are you ill? Science has need of you! I shall become your brother!"

"You're very good, but I'm receiving admirable care from a physician from Rouen," Claude said, a trifle dryly, irritated by that sudden explosion of devotion.

Domesta did not seem to have noticed the invalid's impatience. Now he had turned toward the ladies, and it was to them that he addressed his speech, his advertisement, which he

83

never neglected to sow in new milieux, every time fortune furnished him with an opportunity, with the hope of a future harvest, and in any case with the certainty that the strangeness of his doctrines would achieve the success of curiosity that aids renown so powerfully.

"For Mesdames, Claude Fargeaud is a veritable genius! I and he...he and I, I ought to say...are side by side on the same route. With different methods, we fecundate artificially. And do you know, Mesdames, what artificial fecundation is? No, you don't? I'll explain it to you..."

He had a finger in the air in order to commence his demonstration, and was already rummaging in his coat with the other in order to take out his instruments, when Antonin Fargeaud came swiftly to whisper a few words in his ear.

"Monsieur there's a young woman present!"

"Good, good...I understand! It's necessary to respect the modesty of young women. A young woman is delicate and charming, a rosebud that hasn't yet opened...the pistil of the flower devoid of pollen..."

His thin lips smiled. Then, turning to Julien and Clara, the latter disdainfully aristocratic, looking at him with an arrogant fixity, he added: "That will be for another time. Now, I'll retire. But I shall come back," he said to Claude, "And we'll be able to talk science."

He lowered his panama again with a flourish, without disturbing the dignity of his frock-coat or the creases of his ruff. Then he pivoted on his heels. He was withdrawing alone, without being astonished that Antonin Fargeaud did not take the trouble to accompany him, when Hector, who had woken up, interested by the little man's bizarrerie, got up and joined him.

"Permit me to show you out, Doctor."

Two minutes of travel having almost made them friends, Domesta, in a surge of familiarity to which his habitual observation of humans, their curiosities and their neuroses, had convinced him that he could abandon himself, had taken his companion's arm and fluted and lisped the confidence that he had been prevented from making a short while ago before Henriette.

Sometimes suspending his march in order to give his discourse a more communicative importance, and sometime hastening it, as if to follow the surge of his speech, he recounted his doctrines, his method, his sacrifices to science, his austerity, his interest—not complete, by the Madonna!—and his love of life, which had become such a suggestion and such a care of his nights and his long days that he had made it a sort of religion, of which he was the high priest, a worship of which he was the supreme officiant.

"The newspapers reproach me for making people pay very dear, but do you know what the Holy Father receives per year? I know; I've lived near him. Millions, Signor! Well, I'm the Pope of artificial fecundation!"

The pitch of his voice becoming higher, warmer and more communicative, with a fury of gestures and interjections, he narrated his entirely apostolic fashion of bringing the seed all the way to the intimate regions of fecundation, after having blessed it, baptized with a sign of the cross, in order that the good God would protect it, in order that if, by chance the seed died, it would not be lost to heaven. And that without dolor, without peril—"the syringe sterilized, yes, Signor, sterilized in the autoclave!"

And since he had been exercising, since, with the aid of nature, he had been creating, how much joy he had dispensed, how much gratitude he had acquired! Parents, overflowing with gratitude, had come to dispose treasures at his feet, to thank him for having brought happiness and noise to the sad and silent hearth: children little, charming vigorous and tender, brunette, blond, and even red-haired—"yes, Signor, even redheads!"—children of the syringe had come to throw themselves into his arms as if those sweet innocents had sensed that he was the one who had aided their existence, and they seemed to thank him with their gazes, with their stammering and their smiles.

In conclusion, he said: "I'm a benefactor even more than a scientist."

They had arrived at the gate of the park. Hector was surprised to hear, departing from a clump of trees, a sort of chant brayed by women's voices, a vague canticle of prayer, the words of which, emitted by untrained organs, reached his eardrums indistinctly

"It's my nieces, singing my music," Domesta pronounced, by way of explanation, smiling with his thin lips. The little man's chest swelled, his throat tightened, and a few shrill cries escaped therefrom, like the barking of a fox. Immediately, a clamor of joy resounded. The whinnying of women, the stampede of bright costumes, spread out in his direction, with the African woman Bamboula at the head, because she had longer legs and more muscles closer to the wild state.

"Aren't they nice, the little kittens?"

"Oh, joker, joker!" exclaimed Hector, clapping him on the shoulder when he had distinguished the creatures that were approaching.

And, in fact, those ladies, as soon as they arrived, threw their arms around Hector's neck. He recognized them all, he named them all. The boss, Madame Eulalie, "Maman," who was the last to arrive, breathing hard and leaning on Cyrano's arm, shook his hand, not without distinction And Hector laughed, recalling their delicate charms, pinching their chins, delighted, exultant at the good fortune that brought a entire seraglio thus to the gate of the familial domain, the inmates of a brothel sited in Paris, signaled to the attention of passers-by by a red lantern enclosing a large number. He had spent exquisite evenings there, welcomed and fêted, even although he paid rather meanly and did not always settle up, because he was funny, amusing and chatty, because he interested the inmates and had a consideration for Madame mingled with affectionate deference.

"Oh, joker, joker!"

But Domesta shaken again by Hector's clap on the back, protested. While the swarm of creatures resumed their places on the coach, always with Cyrano's aid, and the trumpeters raised the instruments again, ready to clamor the return and the impassive coachman and the braided grooms picked up their reins, he drew Hector toward him and took hold of a button of his fur coat.

"You're mistaken, Signor; I swear to you that you're mistaken. I'm chaste, ascetic, and these women simply serve for my experiments...they're my guinea-pigs!" And as he did not understand: "You've head mention of laboratory experiments Signor? One makes use for experimentation of various animals—dogs and rodents—and those animals are known as guinea-pigs. Well, I do my work scientifically. Conclude, Signor!"

Before introducing himself into a coupé, he doffed his panama.

"Come to see me. I live two leagues from here, at Canteleu, on the edge of this forest, in a flowery Eden. I'll explain to you. Come to see me. Grazia, Signor."

His rotundity disappeared into the box. The trumpeters raised their instruments hieratically, which caught the sunlight. There was a retreat, mingled with the sound of little bells; then everything, the horses, the gold braid, the silver coach, the skirts and umbrellas of the woman, and even the glabrous face of Domesta, leaning out of the window, disappeared into the sun."

When Hector had drawn away to escort Domesta, Clara Boswett, with an enervated movement, straightened her arrogant bust and her curly little head of imprecise signification, where two broadly etched rings below her eyes betrayed recent pleasures. Then, addressing Julien Duverdon, she declared: "He's grotesque!"

"Yes, unfortunately," replied Claude, who was thoughtful.

"Why unfortunately?" asked the American "Is there anything more improper than what he practices, if I understood correctly what I read in the newspapers during his trials?"

She looked at Henriette, but the young woman, after having been asked by Claude, had just got up in order to take a short walk in the park in the company of Raoul, and the two of them, a charming couple, disappeared in the radiance of their beauty and their grace. Claude followed them with his gaze, momentarily saddened, with a hint of regret and envy.

"Yes," the American went on, "is there anything more improper than that vulgar manipulation? I'm very glad that my dear Rolande wasn't here, for her absence will have spared her one sickening more..."

As she pronounced the last words she launched her effrontery at Julien, who started to blush, sensing the thrust go straight to his heart, the direct allusion to his misfortune, as a husband whose wife had found him repugnant as soon as the first night of their marriage. A confidante of Rolande's rancors since an equivocal amity, contracted while traveling two years ago, had united the two young women strangely, Clara, in her hatred of men and her rancor against everything concerning the abhorred sex, never failed, every time an opportunity presented itself, to deliver a spiteful thrust of the claw that signified her victory, with an audacity all the bolder because the man did not respond, remaining weak and disabled before her cruelty.

This time, however, she was very surprised to observe an expression of revolt igniting Julien's gaze and drawing his taurean neck into the broadness of his shoulders, as if he were about to draw it out in order to thrust with his head. But it was only a sketch of rebellion, quickly paralyzed by his timidity. The bald cranium and graying beard of the husband turned toward Claude, whose slightly weary and somewhat disillusioned voice protested:

"Don't you agree with me, Julien? Isn't it unfortunate that artificial fecundation has thus far only been the prerogative of charlatans? Physicians could occupy themselves with it usefully...and the children, arriving in disunited households, would be attached to the heart of certain women isolated by sterility...or deflected from their duty or their veritable affections by indefinable passions..."

Julien, having turned toward Claude, experienced a veritable illumination on hearing him speak. He suddenly reflected, and his thought perceived the future, going as far as envisaging Rolande's maternity and the evidence of the unity of the household returning to joy, confidence and tenderness.

"Oh, you think that a child...," he stammered, without finishing.

Clara had risen to her feet, because her friend had just appeared. She ran to meet her, and seized her by the waist. Her androgynous red hair leaned toward the young woman's ear. Both of them started to laugh, with an enervated mockery so evident that Julien and Claude understood that they were taking about amour and the child.

"My dear," said the invalid, in a voice rendered more vibrant by anger, pointing with the end of his cane at the disappearing foreigner, "You're no more a man than that woman is a woman. You have no courage, you're neutered. You can't, therefore, arm yourself with a whip in order to thrash Rolande, and a broom with which to sweep that bitch into the gutter. And you love your wife!"

"It's because I love her that I'm so impotent," replied the colossus, with an intonation that betrayed his distress. "It's because I'm conscious that there's a good deal of my fault in her withdrawal. You see, I've been clumsy with Rolande...I've wounded her in her fragile and nervous flesh. You don't know all that. That's why I persist in remaining so weak before her, before her caprices, even the most abominable, that of having introduced that foreigner into my home. That's why, in order not to lose her entirely, I allow her to transfer to her the tenderness that is destined for me..."

He stopped, blushing, fearing having said too much. But Claude, who felt that he was on the slope of a confidence, and desirous of knowing in depth the dilapidation of that heart, encouraged him to speak.

"Go on, speak. I sense that you'd feel relief in enabling me to penetrate your misfortune. Speak, my dear. The petty miseries of life are sufficiently familiar to me for me not to be astonished by what you've just told me, and what I've divined..."

With an elegant gesture that was particular to him, Julien caressed and tapered the rectangle of his graying beard; then, in a low voice, while his mild blue eyes addressed the tall trees in the park, he said:

"Yes, I've only had one ambition since I reached the virile age: to love a woman, to marry her and to have children. All my life, all my aspirations have been concentrated on those three wishes. In order to realize them, in order to present me to them with all the purity of my heart and my senses, in order to be worthy of the woman on whom my choice would eventually be fixed, I repressed sternly the nascent penchants that always traverse the sentimentality of young people; better still, I never yielded to the solicitations of my virile instinct, and I remained chaste, and virginal...you'll find me ridiculous."

"No," Claude affirmed. "Heroism is never ridiculous."

"It was then," Julien went on, "that Rolande appeared to me. "You remember, it was at the 'Friends of Science' ball, at which you were present..."

"I remember it perfectly."

"I can't describe to you the dazzlement she provoked in me. It would require, to translate those impressions, the most beautiful music with the most beautiful verses. I was maddened by her. She seemed to me to realize, in the charm of her face, the harmony of her person, the sound of her voice, and her proud stride, in sum, in everything that emanated from her, what the poets sing about woman. I had myself introduced, I danced with her, awkwardly moreover, since I tore a flap of her dress...but even the mocking laughter with which she greeted my clumsiness was a new hook for my wonderment.

She furthered the deception, because she read my depths and understood my nascent passion.

"Then there was the long period of my uncertainty, my torments, my alternations of hope and discouragement. She didn't love me. On the day when I was about to disappear, to seek forgetfulness in the changing panoramas of voyages, abruptly, she decided. Why did she put her little hand in mine? Why did she pronounce the yes that confounded me? Doubtless because I was weak, because she sensed that I was resolved to sacrifice everything to her whims. Our engagement was the most delightful period of my life. And yet, I always sensed her distance. She was elsewhere; I was convinced of it. When I talked to her about love, she laughed; when I talked to her about children, she frowned. But I wanted happiness with her, I was blind; I thought that marriage would change her dispositions, and that she would be transformed like so many other women who, unenthusiastic before the wedding, are subsequently smitten.

"I arrived at that event, and I'm ashamed to confess my conduct, Claude...the first evening...I had, however, promised myself a great deal of sweetness, a great deal of delicacy...the first evening, I made her suffer; and she wasn't able to suffer, poor child; she was afraid of the pain...oh, what I saw then in her lovely eyes, the revolt that widened them, while she was alarmed by my violence...and the scream that the tearing caused her to utter...!"

He stopped, still distressed by the memory. He had put his head in his hands. Claude remained silent.

"Such is the origin of her aversion for me. Since that moment, an abyss has separated us. My slightest further attempts have run into a cold rage. Furthermore, I've sensed that she has transported to all men the disgust that I've provoked in her. Then, during our voyage, capricious and whimsical, she used with her husband procedures of authority that one doesn't even use with domestics; I, following her like a slave, and, in spite of everything, still blessing my misfortune, which per-

91

mitted me to accompany her, to respire her perfume, to hear her voice, sometimes to touch her hand...

"Yes, we traveled, and one day, she encountered that Clara Boswett, and imposed her on me...at first, I didn't know..."

He interrogated himself again, and blushed, vanquished by the colossal effort of his confession.

"So there it is; the guilty party is me, as much as her. It's me, for not having known that woman, or rather, not having penetrated sufficiently her neurosis before acceding to it."

He shut up. He waited for a consolation that Claude, understanding the need for it, hastened to give him.

"Certainly, my dear Julien, that's regrettable. You haven't understood your wife. But as for accusing yourself of being the ferment of the dissent that separates you from Rolande, as for incriminating your violence, that's taking your responsibility too far. The first act of amour, the taking possession of a wife by her husband, is always a dolorous ordeal; there are, however, few examples of the wounded individual retaining rancor for it. Often, the effect produced is exactly opposite: the wma appreciates confusedly the person who has just dominated her and the strength by which he has overcome her...she has a little of the humility of a dog that loves when it has been beaten. She bows her head before the more powerful, and that is the expression of human weakness. Later, when she takes pleasure herself in that communion, her reversion has no limits. Yes, blame your inexperience, but above all blame your wife's nature, so weak before pain..."

"What can I do? My God, what can I do to bring her back to me? What is the remedy?"

"I told you just now...a child."

"Make her suffer again? I no longer have the audacity; and then, she'd resist me..."

"You could seek Domesta's aid," Claude concluded, by way of a joke, while his proposition awoke in Julien's mind an entire world of new suggestions,

The two friends came back. They brought fruits for Claude. The husband took advantage of that to get up and go to look in the direction of the path that the charlatan had taken in company with Hector; but the road was empty. He only perceived, under the vault of the tallest plane trees, already blurred by the declining daylight, the silhouette of a radiant couple.

Raoul and Henriette were walking slowly, conversing. They were almost equal in height, and the sunlight, skimming the roofs, had just aureoled their beauty and their harmony in an apotheosis of crimson radiance.

"You're doing much better, my dear monsieur," said Doctor Bouret, taking his ear away from Claude's chest, which he had just ausculated minutely.

His white head straightened over the strength of broad shoulders. It allowed the sight of the honest physiognomy of the physician, such as one encounters in the old practitioners of a difficult profession. The separated side-whiskers framed the rectitude of a straight neck broadly opened over the throat. The dark and bushy eyebrows, frowning reflectively, shielded the benevolence of two bright eyes that labor had not aged.

Grouped around the scientist, confident in his good sense, looking out for the diagnosis in the play of his physiognomy, Antoine Fargeaud, Henriette and Raoul were there, the invalid's three supports, his three consolers. The doctor's words and his contented smile relieved their anxiety. They rejoiced. A gaze of religious solicitude, after having posed on Claude, was exchanged between Henriette and Raoul, and it transmitted, like a telepathic fluid, the tenderness that they experienced for the young man. In mobilizing it on him, it seemed that the tenderness in question added a new link to their own affection. That consultation, which affirmed Claude's amelioration, rendered them strong too. Henriette's upper body, liberated from a restraint, appeared to Raoul to be more harmonious, more disengaged from her mystical attitude. The prominence of the breasts under the fabric of her blouse was evident. For her part, Henriette estimated that Raoul, distracted from his constraint and straightening his torso was taller and more significant of vigor. Their eyes, while they applauded Claude's improvement, could not hide their reciprocal admiration.

"You're making great progress," the doctor's voice went on. "But don't go thinking that you're cured. Any imprudence might reanimate your illness. You'll need care for a long time."

"Come on, Doctor," said Claude replacing the clothing that it had been necessary to remove in order to be examined, "tell me the truth; you owe me that, and I know that you're a man of great conscience. Do I have tuberculosis?"

Before responding to such a brutal question, destined to engage so completely the tranquility of his patent, the doctor looked for a long time at the man who had asked it. He judged him to be mentally strong, exempt from all the nervous weaknesses that often determined him to hide his impressions from others. Above all, he saw him so magnificently surrounded by characters apt to aid him in his care that he believed that he did not need to hide the gravity of the illness in order to obtain the cure.

"I do indeed owe you the truth, because you're an intelligent man, and because, in knowing it, you'll be more convinced of an amelioration first and a cure subsequently. Yes, you have tuberculosis. You've shown all the classical signs, and your expectoration, which I've examined, contains the bacillus. The very localization of your lesions confirms my opinion of a hereditary tuberculosis...besides which, I cared for your mother..."

He turned toward Antonin Fargeaud in order to seek approval for his diagnosis, but the old man, having fallen into a chair, his two fists clenched, remained insensible to that mute interrogation. A hallucination took him away, kept him distant from what was being said now.

The doctor went on: "You have been, like many others, who have been no worse for it, engendered by a father who, although quite well, was already too old to create, and a mother whose tuberculosis caused her to die at thirty. You might have escaped the poor heredity, but circumstances, and perhaps also a few imprudences, opposed it. However, you ought to be able to cure yourself. It will take you a year, perhaps two, to succeed in that. I believe it to be more useful than medicaments to inform you of your condition. The true cure consists of good air and good nourishment. You should not lack that. The rest is superfluous. One more piece of advice. Your cure will be slow. You will be the objective of a thousand solicitations coming from strangers and even from yourself. Mistrust them. Mistrust, above all, unworthy exploiters of supposed new therapies, those that we worthy fellows call metallotherapy—which is to say, the art of curing by means of metal...the metal in question being the money of clients..."

"Thank you, doctor," replied Claude, firmly, shaking his hand.

The honest man had sat down, and in order to close his consultation he drew up a hasty prescription. His large hand ran over the paper, and his bushy eyebrows shifted while he reread his recommendations.

"Here, my dear monsieur, is the superfluous. Hurry up and make use of it while it is still active...tomorrow, perhaps, something else might have been found..."

He laughed frankly, parting his side-whiskers, and Claude was impregnated by his good humor. Henriette and Raoul were also moved by the pity that transpierced his pleasantries. They all went out in order to escort him back to his carriage, stationed before the perron. They had forgotten Père Fargeaud, who, left alone, collapsed in his armchair, conserved the same fixed, hallucinated attitude, a stranger to the reality of events.

The modest rig was waiting at the door. It was a cabriolet, high on its wheels, the raised hood of which provided protection from the ardor of the sun. A red border ran along the concentric shelves and extended along the shafts, parallel to the flanks of a young horse whose large blinks, coated with polished leather hooded the head. Under the hood, a domestic wearing a waxed leather helmet was waiting patiently, with a child with a healthy ruddy complexion.

"Is that your son?" Claude asked, when the child saluted him without any embarrassment.

"That's my Benjamin...my sixth..."

"Six!"

"Yes, six. I ought to have eight, but malady stole two of them from me. Perhaps you remember the nasty influenza that decimated the region ten years ago?"

His bushy eyebrows arched under the sadness of the forehead. The piercing remembrance of the disease carrying away two of the jewels of his familial collection effaced two radii of his heart, traversing him like a dagger-thrust.

He went on: "For a quarter of a century, I've had a child every three years. I wanted them to be handsome and strong, so that's why I spaced them out, I also wanted to let my wife rest, to give her time to recover her strength for a new maternity. Isn't it logical and charitable not to demand too much excessively exhausting labor from nature? So, every three years, I acquired an heir. The first two are physicians. One is installed in Paris, the other will soon come to relieve me of the burden of my clientele, already too heavy for my weary shoulders. Then I had a daughter, now married to an engineer who departed for the Congo to construct a railway. She's already a mother twice over. Then another daughter—two out of six— engaged to a young student at the École Normale supérieure, who will be a professor. The fifth is finishing his rhetoric, with difficulty, and as he has remarkable dispositions for music, he wants to enter the Conservatoire to study harmony...I won't stand in his way, esteeming that one only does well what one loves... As for this one, my Benjamin, if he doesn't manifest another taste, I'm disposed to make him the most fortunate of the six; I'll give him a domain and he'll be a peasant! He'll savor, in contact with the old soil, the joys of my ancestors, the great sensations that one experiences in watching the sun rise, in predicting the weather and inhaling the healthy aromas that earth freshly moved by the plowshare emits. I'll unburden him of all the prejudices that civilization accumulates, the theories and narrowness in my mind and those of his brothers and sisters. He'll rediscover the simplicity of tastes, the joyous candor of living, the frank quietude of which cities deprive us. Yes, he'll be the happiest...he'll be a peasant!"

Was he mistaken in his prognosis of happiness, the old laborer who, in spite of fatigue, in spite of ingratitude, had been paid with so many glorious satisfactions and so many secret recompenses? Claude would not have been able to affirm the truth or the error. But at that moment, he admired sincerely the white head of the physician and the black bush of his eyebrows, and his grave harmony of an incomparable and obscure benefactor. His legs had accomplished so many excursions to attend to the sick, his back was in pain because of the jolts of the cabriolet, his hands had plunged into horrors, bandaged wounds, aided births, relieved agonies; his brain had ruminated the care of multiple prescriptions. He had gone to trouble for others, for strangers, for his own family, in order to enable the fine crop of children to grow which, in its turn, would yield seed that would be disseminated throughout the region, engendering strength and thought. Had the superb evolution of that cycle not compensated him adequately, now that he was about to complete the curve?

"You must have worked hard, Doctor, to improve everyone's destiny?"

"Yes, I've worked; but isn't work a joy, when it's accompanied by health? I've raised my children well. To my daughters I've given, as well as a small dowry, a physique not badly tucked up and all the moral prerogatives of a wife, so they didn't have to wait too long for a husband; the first was settled at twenty-one, the second is betrothed at nineteen. To my sons I've bequeathed an education, a taste for study and the principles of honesty...what more do you want? Capital? What would the capital be worth in twenty years? Who won't have to work for a living in that epoch?"

He stopped for a moment. He became more somber in passing on to another order of ideas.

"When, in the space of a fortnight, I lost my two little ones, it seemed to me that a great void had been created, which nothing could fill. It was a crop destroyed. I had a desire to recommence. I like large families. I think that everyone ought to have as many children as the wife is capable of bearing, as long as the social conditions don't oppose their blossoming and their wellbeing. But I was already old. I was fifty. Furthermore, I had contracted a bronchitis in that era that fatigued me greatly I reflected then that a man of that age, ill and demoralized, no longer has the right to create, that he can no longer ensure to those he would engender, the integrity of health, the preoccupations of education, the material and intellectual capital that he owes to is descendants. So I abstained. I contented myself with my six. The gaps caused by death have been filled in by the satisfactions that the survivors have given me. And Benjamin has remained my Benjamin...isn't that so, Benjamin?"

"Yes, Papa," replied the boy, who was listening seriously and seemed to be assimilating that noble lesson in life."

"As for my wife," continued Doctor Bouret, "and as for me, we're now tranquil. Our savings will procure us a little more ease, of which our children will inherit the surplus, If I die before the time, they'll permit Madame Bouret to continue the education of my last-born modestly. In addition, the Medical Mutuality, of which I'm a member—solidarity thus comprised, you see, Monsieur Claude, is the future; it will preside over the fate of every citizen.—will give me a pension of three thousand six hundred francs a year. That will permit me to spread a little more butter on my bread and give presents to my children every new year.

"One day, therefore, I'll have the leisure to take my staff and go and watch the plants in my garden grow. In winter, I'll read some Latin text by lamplight, or accounts of voyages. The chronicles of my newspapers will inform me of the evolution and the success of the sciences; the theater critics and a few good novels will satisfy my taste for dreaming. In the meantime, I'll still give a few consultations. And when my eyes are tired, when my excessively weary legs refuse me long walks, I'll think about my grandchildren. I'll follow their efforts in life, and I'll gaze, in the future, at the evolution of my lineage, and in the past, at the furrow I've traced...and in order to go to sleep definitively, to lie down in the tomb next to my wife—oh, we'd like to go at the same time, and our only worry is thinking that one of us might disappear before the other!—well, for that final journey, I'll have six children to accompany me with their grateful thoughts. What more do you want, Monsieur Claude? And you, Raoul? And you, Mademoiselle Henriette? To accomplish one's life soundly and to retire with a clear conscience, isn't that the most beautiful of human destinies"

He already had his foot on the carriage. He shook hands, made a few more recommendations, and saluted with an affectionate gesture and a twitch of his bushy eyebrows. His tall hat with a flat brim, tilted backwards on his white crown of hair, seemed to put an aureole on his head of honest simplicity. Then he took the reins from the hands of his domestic, and touched the horse with a caress of the whip. The cabriolet moved off; its wheels squealed on the gravel; its jolts took away, with the old-fashioned quivering of screeching springs, the energy, labor and beneficence of forty years of a loving and virtuous life. A last ray of sunlight reddened the leather plate of one of the blinkers; then the rig turned and plunged under the vault of the plane trees.

"A worthy man," murmured Raoul.

"A good father," insisted Claude, looking at Henriette, who was pensive.

They went back inside. The drawing room seemed empty, and yet the father was still fixed there, huddled in his chair. A melancholy descended from the windows, which a little shadow was already powdering with its ash, rebounding on them after having brushed objects. The high stone fireplace, where entire tree-trunks could have blazed, the gallery of sculpted wood framing the greenish silver of mirrors and the profound seats, the armchairs equipped with large arms that seemed able to close in order to embrace, everything, in the declining twilight, at that vague hour when the palpitations of the world slows down before going to sleep in waves of silence, was impregnated with majesty, confounded in a harmony of sad calm. Then, as Henriette had gone to fetch a light,

Claude's voice rose up, a little weary and disillusioned, shaken at intervals by the effort of a dry cough that the young man strove in vain to suppress:

"I venerate that Doctor Bouret. He's a worthy man and a good servant of life. He has given it all that he could, with moderation, method and dignity. He didn't want either irreflective fecundity, nor the egotism that restricts the family. When he created, he thought at the same time about his wife, the collaborator in his work of perpetuity, and of the children that are its fruits. He spared the former and let her rest every time before demanding a new effort of maternity. He assured the latter of the finest resources of health and reason. He's a sage. If everyone behaved with the same discernment and the same probity, the earth would be fortunate, a great equilibrium would level all happiness…"

His language was a reproach addressed to the father he believed to be absent. That plaint was his plaint. But he shivered, because the shadow had just moved in a corner. Antonin Fargeaud stood up and advanced toward him. In that declining hour when the old man's sight was even more uncertain, his progress was groping and oscillating. He emerged into the dying light of the window, and his hollow voice protested bitterly.

"Happiness! Why pronounce that word? Happiness is a myth! Who ever attains it? Is it that Doctor Bouret? Get away! He works, he tires himself out, he deludes himself. He's seen children die twice. Do you know what it's like to see the flesh of one's flesh go like that? No, you don't know. He's suffered that, and perhaps a further catastrophe will take away a third tomorrow. Then he'll spend ten more years until the tomb, bandaging a new mourning. And you talk about happiness? No, are we not always menaced by some new gesture of Fatality? What can our mind foresee against the stone that falls from a roof and fells us? The world is full of stones that menace us. Creation is stupid…nothingness is preferable. One lives in order to suffer and to die."

He sat down again, and fell back into blackness. Claude made no response, for a word would have made him sob. His father was advancing toward an increasing folly of neutrality, and he knew that he, Claude, was the cause of it.

He reflected. What was really the cause? Would he not be able to throw back on the old man all the responsibility for present situation? Who, then, had created the seed of evil that was tearing his heart? Who had created it?

He did not want to think about it any longer. He sensed a dull rancor coming, which it would have been too cruel even to allow it to be suspected.

Night had fallen completely now. The invalid's silence, after the coughing that had just tormented him, harmonized meekly with the calm of the darkness. All three of them remained motionless in their armchairs, only listening to their reflections. The sound of the siren of a tug on the nearby river, colliding with the escarpment of the valley, was reverberated like a long plaint, a dolorous echo of the life that was dying away outside.

Henriette reappeared. She was carrying a lamp, the spilling light of which provoked a common evolution of ideas. Turning toward her fiancé, she saw him lying back in his chair. He was watching her coming like a dolorous radiation, all the distress of his heart upsetting his physiognomy.

"It's necessary to go and rest, Claude," she said, in her melodious voice.

And as he did not move and made no reply, she went to touch his shoulder; the placement of her hand made him shiver.

"Don't be sad, Claude. You heard what Doctor Bouret said…good humor is part of the treatment. Remember that he affirmed that you'd be cured…"

"What's the point?"

"Claude, you'll cause me pain…"

At that argument he stood up, his back stooped, and headed toward the vestibule, which he had to traverse in order to regain his apartment.

Hector came back in at the same moment. Returning from Paris by automobile, he was still dressed in his animal skin, gray with the dust of the roads. His nose plunged toward his black chin.

"Bonjour, little one," he said. "I've come from Paris. I'm exhausted. What a trip!"

After disappearing for two days without having given notice of his return, he had an air of conceited satisfaction that did not escape his younger brother. He hardly took the time to shake his hand, and did not even enquire about his health. He threw his fur tunic to Arthur, the driver, and went upstairs wearily. He was in haste to get back to his bedroom.

When he had reached it he lit the lamp and cast a victorious gaze over the walls, garnished with a multitude of photographs of women. From floor to ceiling they invaded and radiated. One sensed that they were simultaneously his dominatrices and his victims; they were his reason for living. Some of them were in color; some of them were nudes; some had costumes more immodest than nudity. Some of their postures, arms raised and backs arched, affirmed the pride of a part of their body or strove to conceal defects. Actresses and chorus girls draped in peplums, pretty napes surmounted by smooth coiffures or vaporous tresses tinted with henna, breasts emerging from rigid corsets, bright or somber leotards revealed the contours of hips and legs, gracious enlacements of arms, couplings of figures, pretty laughter expanding over cruel teeth, Hector appreciated all of them in their portraits, and remembered them all.

Vice radiated from their accentuated mouths, ran through the undulations of their hair, was emitted by their eyes, darkened by make-up, flowed over their full shoulders, and descended with the folds of garments toward the projection of rumps. Also apparently candid were the frail masks distinguished by the fall of black tresses covering the ears and wrapping around the nape. To calculate their number would have been difficult, there were so many. But with the punctiliousness of a scribe, Hector had catalogued them. When he had a doubt about one of them, when the act had not been sufficiently notorious for him to have retained a memory of it, he raised the lamp to the level of the photograph and deciphered in the margin the broad rounded handwriting that named them, as well as the theater at which they had appeared or the brothel in which they were boarders. Then, under the designation came a number, a serial number.

There were known names, prestigious names that were displayed in lights every evening and ornamented the multi-colored posters of café-concerts. There were others, affectedly pretentious abbreviations, attributable to the inferior gallantry, and others even paltrier, more remote in anonymous forgetfulness. All were mingled together in accordance with his satisfied desire, the sole trace of which consisted of these portraits, all side by side in a final equality of display, from the frills of great courtesans to the dirty skirts of streetwalkers. One of the latter, characterized by abundant golden hair surmounting a flat and bestial face, had become famous since in consequence of a crime.

Hector turned the light toward another wall and his pride increased. There, set apart, were the young women, the feeble flesh of which wily matrons negotiated the virginity several times over. He had believed it until the day when one of them, among the most recent, had caused him to contract syphilis. He looked for a long time at that astonishingly sickly physiognomy, which he had surrounded with a black frame. Long favored by an incredible immunity, he owed to her the malady that had polluted his blood. She went back two years. A respite in the sexual prodigality of debauchery had doubtless been demanded by the physician since, following the black flame, there were only a dozen portraits at the most continuing the series. For a moment, he was hypnotized by her; then, with a great sweep of his gaze, he returned to the ensemble.

Decanters of sterile amour, mercantile flesh, stranglers of virile energy and fecundity, some were still continuing their lucrative trade under the sun of the great city; others had already disappeared into old age or the tomb; whether they were perfumed courtesans covered in jewelry or low prostitutes with dirty and rancid underwear, they were hostile to childbirth. He admired them, he venerated them. He had squandered his original capital with them in hysterical fantasies, but he did not regret that voluptuous scattering. He imbibed their presence, their smiles, their nudities and the recall of their practices as if he were still inhaling the perfume of their alcoves or the acidity of their squalor. He forgot the stings of disappointments of sensibility, miscalculations of money and failures of vanity only to remember the pleasure, and to salute them as collaborators. The fluttering of his eyes fixed on each of them, evoking each embrace, reanimating each past enjoyment with a almost tender excitement.

"Oh, the sluts, the sluts!" he sighed, in a kind of grateful homage.

Now he had a new print for his dossier of amour. He had brought it back from Paris. He took out of his portfolio a recent portrait, and before cataloguing the serial number and aligning it in his collection, he considered at length the swollen face with the atonal eyes, the curl of the short-cropped hair surmounting a flaccid nudity of tranquil and laborious vice. In truth, the esthetics of that conquest would have been despicable, if she had not manifested her professional conscience scrupulously. She had a high price, at which he had been obliged to regulate her favors, the obol demanded before the act, of five louis—a dolorous figure—but she had compensated him royally. He pinned her up.

Then, going to a kind of strong-box, he activated a secret catch. From among the deeds and bonds, he brought out a large ledger, which he put down on a table within reach of a writing-desk. He opened it and turned the pages furrowed by columns and charged with figures mathematically divided by the year and the month. They were his full animal accounts, regulated and ordered, his sexual archives. He turned the pages proudly. Having reached the last, he inscribed the debit, with the date: five louis. On the credit side, which was divided into several columns, he first noted the serial number of the portrait he had just fixed to the wall, 1,030; then the level of satisfaction, 18; then, in another column, that of orgasms, 5— which, added to a previous calculation, produced a total of 7,006, the quotient of twenty-seven years and three months of amorous practice.

Then, utterly radiant, he thought about changing his clothes and washing himself.

VII

In the meadow fully adorned with verdure, the picnic was finishing noisily, in a superb décor. In the rear, the old feudal ruin, of which two enormous sections of wall still existed, looming up like reefs at sea, steep peaks in the azure plain, quivering with sunlit joy. In front, there was the valley of the invisible river, with the slope of the hill that overhung a rocky fall from a vertiginous height.

Clamors rose up regarding everything and nothing, demanding victuals. They increased at the pop of the first champagne cork, awkwardly removed by Louis, the Fargeauds' valet de chambre, who was serving in the company of Rose, Clara Boswett's new soubrette.

The impetuous foam of the liquid had spilled over the lawn blouse of Madame de Berge, a rich young widow, a country neighbor invited by the Fortins. The latter, surprised in her flirtation with Hector, uttered a cry of fright that echoed the pleasure of the guests. Small, stiff and dark, immeasurably nervous, she had already got up rapidly with the aid of her cavalier, in order to wipe away the inopportune invasion, when Monsieur Fortin reassured her: "Have no fear, cousin, champagne doesn't stain..."

Then, always gracious, loving and mild, Monsieur Fortin caressed his wife with a smile; she was languidly extended on a folding armchair that he had taken care to bring. He saw her, with contentment, intoxicated by the general joy. Placed next to Claude, their two sufferings were side by side; stretched out like him and similarly covered by a plaid, she seemed to be revived by the pure open air, and her lips and cheeks were impregnated with an artificial glow of health.

"I'm enjoying myself, I'm enjoying myself," she said, in reply to her husband's mute question, nodding her head to give more weight to her affirmation.

But she had affirmed her joy too quickly. The piercing menace of the next day stabbed her loins, and she had to put her hand to her side in order to suppress its pangs. She turned to Claude and looked at him. Their common misery set them apart from the communal overflow. She was grateful to him for the compassion that his blue eyes expressed. However, Claude had already turned his head and his gaze went with a little impatience to interrogate the wall of old stones behind which Henriette and Raoul had already been concealed for five minutes—preparing a surprise, they had said. Soon, he settled down again, for they both reappeared, sprightly and gracious, triumphant in their flourishing vigor, one carrying a cooking-pan and the other a colander.

"Here's the surprise," shouted Raoul, from a distance. "They're potatoes sliced by Henriette and fried by me. You're about to taste, Mesdames et Messieurs, the exquisite result of our collaboration. Who wants fries? All hot, all boiling!"

Plates were held out, with mad gestures. The occasional cooks, making a tour, went to serve each guest. Raoul held the pan while the young woman, armed with her colander, plunged into the fat, still sizzling, and drew out the little squares of potato, roasted, gilded and ripping, and distributed them, having sprinkled them with salt. Their joyful and expansive distribution made a circle. Having arrived at Claude, Henriette suspended Raoul's offer.

"Not, not him. The doctor has forbidden it. You know, Claude, that you ought not to eat fried food."

"That's true, you're right," said the young man, withdrawing his plate.

And with a hint of bitterness, he saw them draw away from him and recommence the division. More than ever, amid everyone's pleasure, he felt isolated. To laugh like the others would have provoked a coughing fit; to move about would have threatened him with suffocation; to lie down on the grass would have had repercussions for the delicacy of his bronchi. As a precaution, in case he was chilly in summer, he had to cover his thin legs with a plaid, keep quiet and huddle up. The physician, while reassuring him, had nevertheless traced above his head a dolorous question mark, about which he could not stop thinking. For a time doubtless longer than anyone had dared to predict, he was going to be denied all the joys of movement and energy. And still, the troubling question of fatality, the why of destiny, assailed him.

Why was wellbeing divided so unequally; why was his share, after having seemed at first to be complete, restricted so brutally now? Yes, why? A fugitive animosity darkened again the affection that he had for his father and the tender remembrance with which he surrounded the memory of his mother. Did he not owe to those cherished individuals, however, the transmission of the disease that set him apart from the life of others, which removed him from their pleasures, from their enthusiasm, from their effusions? Could his shoulders support, and with what difficulty, the hereditary burden of a marriage accomplished in conditions of defective health?

He was afraid of finding a grave responsibility in his creators, and he no longer wanted to think about it; he told himself that those thoughts were unworthy and acrimonious, provoked by a momentary chagrin. He could not and must not linger over them. His mother was dead, a victim herself of a morbid transmission, and that holy memory ought to remain intact. As for his father, he was suffering enough in all the fibers of his being only to be charged with irreflection, perhaps only of ignorance. The old man had betrayed his intimate despair often enough, his renunciation of all kinds of enjoyment. He was concentrated on the cares of the invalid, abolishing himself before them. No, it was not those beloved figures that it was necessary to blame, but blind fatality, stupid creation.

At least one supreme and delightful consolation remained to Claude. He was gazing at its object at that moment; he saw it in motion in the person of his fiancée, who was coming and going, busily, laughing, gracious and chaste, continuing her light-hearted offer of fried potatoes. Animation had stripped away her veil of mysticism; she was new, and none of the women present had her splendor: not the disquieting, equivocal, masculine Clara; nor Madame de Berge, to whom Hector's conversation was nevertheless giving a certain renewal of rosy youthfulness; nor Madame Fortin whose languid grace was reanimated by pleasure, like a flower already withered, revivified by a breath of fresh air. Joy rendered all of them desirable at that moment, enjoyment gave a charm to all of them, causing unsuspected attractions to emerge, but none of them had, like Henriette, the beautiful flame of youth and health, the limpidity of a new spring untainted by any impurity.

She had just leaned over, and while Hector had turned his head toward his neighbor, with a gesture of adorable mischief, she had thrown a handful of salt into his champagne glass. As she inclined, she allowed the suppleness of her body to be divined, the vigor of her virgin breasts and the gracious curve of her hips, which molded her almost-clinging cycling skirt, while her stockings revealed the fine prolongation of the ankle and the foot, both imprisoned in yellow leather ankle-boots. And when she got up from having accomplished her prank, her face was bursting with gaiety, emphasized by the purity of her white teeth and the piquant grace of the three dimples hollowed out in the cheeks and chin by wholehearted laughter.

Claude admired her; Claude fed on her gaiety. But suddenly, by a reversion of thought, he became immensely sad. Was not the new appearance of his beloved, the modification of Henriette, suddenly blossoming in an innocent joke, unveiling everything that he suspected of being behind her veil of abstraction, inspired by a prognostication contrary to the one that he wished? Would she ever warm his hearth, that dear joyful child; would she ever be its radiation?

The antagonism of the Faith that had continued, since her emergence from the convent, to exercise itself upon her, to enlace her in the toils of a vague sentimentality for the great Enigma, which, too frequently, suddenly suspended her laughter, restricted the physical pleasures of her being in order to render her anxious about a mystical problem, and made her envisage the afterlife piously, had thus far brought their two weaknesses—Henriette's mental languor and Claude's physical debility—closer together. Was that antagonism, so reassuring for the invalid only yesterday, not destined to fade away?

It derived, at the most, from a particular impressionability to the suggestion of the cloister; it resulted from a sensual psychosis contracted from adoring Christ's mask of suffering, seeing the candles of the altar, hearing the sounds of the organ and respiring the perfumes of incense. It would disappear, expelled and annihilated by the more certain exigencies of nature, by the need to love something other than a symbol, to submit to other, more real, passions. Claude could no longer hope for its persistence nor count on it for Henriette's generous abandonment of her heart, as yet incompletely delivered.

In spite of the amicable solicitude with which she surrounded him, in spite of the tender devotion that she manifested in caring for him, he took account instinctively of the day when the ditch hollowed out by faith would be filled it by nature, and on that day, his fiancée would be lost to him. It was sufficient to see the overflow of animation, movement and joyful exuberance with which she was agitating at that moment to be convinced of the proximity of that moment.

All those reflections Claude expressed rather confusedly, but their uncertainty and their threat was emphasized more particularly by the spectacle that he had before his eyes. While believing in Henriette's loyalty, while admitting that it was the first time that she seemed to have acquired an appetite for society and amusement, he suffered nevertheless from not having been invited to share her joy, either by a wink or a smile. He suffered even more when, after a fit of hilarity provoked by Hector's grimace as he threw away his polluted champagne, he saw her go to sit down next to Raoul in order to nibble the last fried potatoes.

Then, more intensely, as the fulguration of a flash of lightning illuminating the opacity of the night gives everything the importance of relief and shows the proximal abysms, at the sight of the radiant couple so insouciantly occupied in eating food that was forbidden to him, Claude sensed how long he would still be separated from those inferior participations, which are nevertheless the currency of conjugal felicity, the small change of duel egotism, the slim dividends that shore up communal wellbeing.

For as long as his illness lasted, for as long as obscure parasites were eating away the substance of his lungs and the fire was devouring his throat, for as long as he was obliged to curb his head before that cruelty of fate, his conscience would prevent him from asking that pure young woman for an abandonment that would be a sacrifice, and from making her promises that would be lures. Above all, the great consequence of marriage, the supreme goal of union, the child that would consecrate its magnificence, he would be obliged to refuse her. He rejected the idea of creating as he had been created, the responsibility of enabling to blossom a being deprived of the health necessary to wellbeing. And that future, which he had never envisaged so bleakly, appeared to him now in all its melancholy, in all its alarm—and it wrung his heart.

And as if hazard were striving to render his conviction more ardent, as if it wanted to particularize an example to strengthen the sincerity of his reflections, he saw Madame Fortin's mute interrogation addressed to his suffering. She seemed to have understood what he had just thought; she seemed to be stirring identical cares, Seeing other people enjoying themselves so much fatigued her. Languidly, she turned toward Claude her pretty face, crumpled and undermined after the reaction of the open air, betraying her secret tortures more intently. A little furtive smile, consecutive to a glance toward her husband, expressed her disillusionment.

"Aren't they crazy, Monsieur Claude? How they're enjoying themselves! One only truly understands the intoxication of health on the day when one can no longer laugh...or eat fried potatoes!"

"You neither, Madame?"

"Me neither...we can sympathize in our privations. However, what causes me the most chagrin, Monsieur Claude, is not those petty sacrifices to greed, or the movements that are refused to me, or even the constant threats that I sense here in my side. No, that's nothing. The affection of my husband, so good, so tender and so devoted, compensates me amply for that. But what I suffer from beyond all expression is thinking that I might have children playing around me, in my care, and to be deprived of it. That, you see, is too painful. In order to have just one, I'd give half my life, I'd gladly multiply my dolors tenfold. And my husband desires it as much as I do; he knows that a baby would make me happy."

"You have no hope, then?"

"You'll understand, Monsieur Claude, that I haven't failed to consult many physicians...perhaps too many, for their opinions have been contradictory. Some have affirmed a definite sterility; others have allowed me to hope that with time and care, I might one day obtain a pregnancy. Doctor Bouret, who is occupied with you at present, is of that opinion."

"I have great confidence in him," Claude confessed.

"Me too...but at length, one gets tired of waiting. Then, without the approval of Monsieur Bouret, who was hostile to that step, I solicited a consultation with Doctor Caresco. Do you know Doctor Caresco, the surgeon?

"Ah! You've been to see Caresco!"

An entire legend of bloody deeds, consecrated by publicity, passed through Claude's mind. The prestigious name that floated above surprising cures as well as abominable deaths: Caresco, the fanatical cutter, with a hand so rapid that instantaneous photography could barely follow its movement; Caresco, the stirrer of throbbing flesh and advertising, whose unfathomable ambition had traced through the country and the world a red route bristling with glorious summits and hollowed out by frightful abysses; Caresco, whose audacity, dexterity and insouciance had sown life and annihilation with the

113

same lack of conscience, under the glorification of some and the hatred of others.

"You've been to see Caresco?" Claude repeated.

"Yes, on the advice of one of his colleagues, who affirmed to Monsieur Fortin and me that he's the only surgeon capable of curing me. At first Monsieur Fortin resisted...he'd heard so much ill spoken of that scientist that he was afraid of the consultation. Oh, Monsieur Claude, society is very malevolent! I've never encountered such a superior man! And so marvelously seconded by the good sisters! Out there is the heart of the Bois de Vincennes, he has an operating theater installed with an exceptional cleanliness and surgical luxury. We went there. When we went in, an amiable nun, Sister Cunegonde, received us. She embraced me, and that welcome from a woman devoted to the good God and to the sick already had something truly encouraging about it...

"As the doctor was occupied, in order to give us patience, she gave us a tour of the house. I've never seen anything as cheerful and as neat, No noise, either...the patients, surrounded by foliage, rest in an immense peace. I would have liked to be installed immediately, without going home, as Sister Cunegonde invited me to do. Eventually, the doctor received us. You can't imagine his study; it's an assembly of marvels, bronzes and paintings, gifts owed to the gratitude of those he has saved. Immediately, I was seduced, and my husband too.

"After having examined me—oh, not for long, scarcely a minute, he's so habituated to it—he declared that he could cure me in a fortnight, and affirmed the possibility of children. 'A simple scratch will be sufficient,' he said to us. We accepted immediately. I'm going into his clinic tomorrow. I bless him!"

"Wait another fortnight to bless him!" Claude could not help exclaiming, so prompt did the decision of the Fortin household seem to him, and its enthusiasm premature.

But Madame Fortin made no reply. Her eyes, illuminated by the certainty of an imminent fecundity, were following the peripeties of a hand-to-hand contest that had just been engaged between Hector and Madame de Berge. A challenge issued by the young widow, who doubted the musculature of her cavalier, had lit the fuse, and now they were at grips like fairground wrestlers and prolonging with a manifest pleasure the overheated contact of their two clinging bodies, to the great interest of the company, either shocked or amused.

A treachery on the part of the woman defeated the man. The mouth of the female contestant had seized Hector's hand and bit it deeply enough to draw blood, with the consequence that the latter, surprised by the pain, all resistance abolished, let himself drop and allowed his shoulders to touch the ground.

"He touched! He touched!" proclaimed Madame de Berge.

Hector got up, vexed. The high opinion that he had of his strength could not permit him to consent to a defeat, even one so innocent.

"Damn it, you bit me! If you believe that I was still thinking of defending myself..."

"Poor thing! Give me your wound so that I can bandage it," said the widow, offering her lips to suck up the blood of the wound

The freedom from constraint of the picnic excused all liberties. Hector, tamed again, was already holding out his hand when the intervention of Claude, who had suddenly risen to his feet and run to him, suspended his movement. The young man placed himself deliberately between the two wrestlers, and his gaze, directed at the wounded man, reminded him of a recent confidence and signified to him amply the imprudence that he was about to commit, the contamination that the bloody kiss was capable of provoking—at least, he believed so.

"No," said Hector, withdrawing his hand. "Claude's right; they aren't appropriate games..."

In the madcap joyousness of the moment, that incident passed unperceived. The pleasantries resumed their fervor. Ice

115

cream was consumed while crunching biscuits. Hector had made peace and replaced himself next to his adversary, who, red from her combat, was blowing into her cheeks. Raoul and Henriette, seeing her crimson face, smiled. Claude also returned to his place, seized by a slight cough provoked by the rapidity of his movement. That excited Madame Fortin's pity.

"You seem better, though, Monsieur Claude," she said, to hide the expression of a commiserative thought that her expression might have betrayed.

"I am better," the young man replied, "but I shouldn't have come out today. But then...I wanted to come with Henriette..."

"When are you getting married?"

Claude raised a disillusioned hand, which answered more clearly than his voice, and in order to change the subject, asked for information about Madame de Berge, whom he scarcely knew, and on whose account he had nevertheless heard scabrous adventures recounted. While confirming the possibility of that, she could be seen at present redder and more exuberant, engaged with Hector in a conversation that was doubtless very spicy, for in spite of her complaisance in listening to lewdness, she occasionally feigned a revolt, and, in order to punish her interlocutor, applied little thrusts of her fan to his fingers, which the other, ever conceited, accepted as a tribute to his triumphant virility.

"Madame de Berge!" said Madame Fortin. "We don't really know her..."

"But it's you who have brought her."

"Indeed. She's even related to us by marriage, having married one of our cousins two years ago, but since her widowhood she's neglected us greatly. We found her again by chance, occupying a property in our neighborhood, near Maronne. We thought we ought to invite her today, to show her that we don't bear her a grudge for her indifference."

"She seems to be supporting her widowhood valiantly."

"Yes, I believe that she's scattered her crepe right and left. What do you expect? She's young, and seems not to be deprived of temperament."

"Why doesn't she remarry, in that case?"

"She claims that a first ordeal was sufficient. And then, she doesn't want children. Can you imagine that?"

No, that was not conceivable for either of the interlocutors. and Claude, who attained a philosophical attitude more tranquilly, and was not, like Madame Fortin, haunted by a sentimental obsession with progeniture, and who, superior to instinctive motives, understood the function of the producer in life, the obligation that nature imposes of beings, after having received an ancestral legacy of persistence, to transmit it to descendants in perpetuating the race and prolonging it through time and space, became indignant at the recoil before a sacred law of that determination, deliberately admitted by certain creatures to sacrifice duty to their egotism and their pleasures.

He recalled the honest physician Bouret; he heard his words again. Certainly, a man endowed with reflection can, in a certain measure, in order to ameliorate the subsistence of his family, not follow blindly the example that the animal and vegetable kingdoms give. Often, in fact, that pause in creative impetuosity demanded by social encumbrance, by human plethora, is a necessity, a wise and useful precaution. But ought one to push the consequence as far as integral refusal, to the point of the rarefaction of families? Should one, like the widow who was flirting with Hector, deliberately avoid any union because a new marriage would have exposed her to having children?

He knew what a wealth of sexual instinct the young widow possessed and how nature had allotted her more appetite for reproduction than another, and he found her avoidance even more abominable. Married young to a feeble man, Madame de Berge had, from the first nights of her marriage, organized an entire debauchery of the alcove, a overstimulation of untiring nerves, soliciting pleasure without respite, demanding of her husband an incessant heroism, a constant retreat from

117

paternity that left him, after the embrace, annihilated by sensuality, panting from having been deflected from its goal. She did not want children, she cried, in full intoxication, and the obliging man had always obeyed—with the result that after two years, she had emptied and destroyed him, and it had only required a slight illness to finish him off definitively, in order to return to oblivion what he had striven to obtain in their intercourse.

Since then, immediately after the last spadeful of earth had been thrown on to the coffin, while the mourning-carriage was taking her back to the empty domicile, the male had become her thought, her hypnosis. Her morbid rage was on the lookout for incessant satisfaction, while avoiding the generative consequences. There was a jugglery of every sensuality, an equilibrium between her senses and her fear, an ardent hysteria limited to cold strategic calculations. She subordinated her slightest actions to it. She sought equivocation in the most chaste reading. She leafed through novels to race to the pages which allowed a rapprochement to be suspected, and weighed upon them. She collected obscene photographs, and the slightest manifestations of current life provoked her frenzy. Her numerous lovers, with whom she toyed with a marvelous cunning, shared the maddening work of the defunct husband.

A few hitches occurred nevertheless; several times she was obliged to send weeks in bed, blaming improbable stomach aches, which she had treated by a midwife, after having dismissed her usual physician. A month later she got up again, ran to rendezvous, knotted new intrigues, went to supper, came back to the domicile late, or did not come back at all. Except for the domestics, however, no one suspected her debauchery, so clever was she in hiding it. Now she was enticing Hector, a man of forty-five, prudent and wily, a savant lover probably destined to augment the number of those she trailed behind her perfumed skirts.

Claude, in his generosity was indignant at that positivism, so brazenly aimed at the avoidance of children, accepting the lust of the senses passively and refusing creative duties.

Was not that disdain for natural forces comparable to the un-exploited wealth of a field, to the rusting of a precious mecha-nism or the unemployment of an industrial machine designed to contribute to the comfort of all, to universal wellbeing?

To create, to make life, to prolong the species, was an obligation so superior that the genius of the world had preced-ed its execution with intoxicating transports, but vile and hate-ful were those who, in the universal effort, after having ac-cepted the pleasure, avoided the responsibility.

The young man's gaze then went to Rolande, his half-sister. A surge of shame turned his cheeks crimson, mingling with the vesperal fever whose customary frissons he sensed going against the current of his vein and planting warm tints above his cheekbones. Rolande had just lain down on the grass next to Miss Boswett. She had taken her hand and was squeez-ing it. Her husband, Julien, wounded by the signification of that testimony of amity, kept apart, timid and anxious, his tau-rean neck withdrawn into his powerful shoulders. However, little sparks illuminated his eyes at times, directed toward the red hair of the American.

At that spectacle, Claude, after the anger, no longer had anything but pity. The case was pathological; it would have been necessary to care for those lovers as others were treated for mental aberrations. Their amity was the most notorious expression of a decadent race, its fluid exhausted, weary of normal functions, carried away by inversion. Whereas in Madame de Berge the seed was diverted from its route or de-stroyed in the first manifestations of its work, here, in that morbid coupling, it was no longer even to be feared, it pro-duced horror. Amour was resolved in unisexual dupery, in-complete, deviant and maddening deceptions, leading to an inevitable cerebral consumption, which was already evident in the eccentricities and mental anxieties of the foreigner horri-fied by semen. And there were men who took pleasure in those vices, in order to seek the spur of their virility. What insanity, then, also tormented them?

But a soft voice made the thinker tremble. The presence of Henriette drove those demented images far away. Healthy nature radiated with her appearance.

"It's necessary to go back, Claude. You know that the doctor has forbidden you to stay outside for more than four hours.

"Thank you for reminding me, my dear Henriette. Please have someone inform the coachman."

"I'll go myself. Anyway, I'll come with you."

He looked at her, so pretty, so brown, still so sprightly in her innocent pleasure. In spite of the care she took to hide the evidence, her attitude, returned to humility and devotion, betrayed the irritation of the obligation to company her fiancé while the others continued their excursion gaily in a noisy procession of horses, carriages, automobiles and bicycles. Perhaps for the first time, extracting herself from the decent reserve of daughters of God, she had savored the movement of society and vacation, the joy of pedaling next to Raoul, the slight difficulty of renouncing the end of the party. Claude, with a hint of disappointment, understood the obscure combat.

"No, Henriette, no; I want you to stay and amuse yourself. I'll go back alone. Believe me, you so rarely have the opportunity for a little gaiety that I'd reproach myself for making you lose it..."

"Do you think so?" she said, uncertainly. But immediately, the determination of duty got the upper hand again, and she added, firmly: "I don't want to quit you, Claude."

"Let's go, then."

He got up, took the arm that she extended, and after saluting the Fortins, they both drew away. When they were in the carriage, the horse set off at a trot, and laughter accompanied their departure. They turned round and saw Hector recommencing his wrestling match with Madame de Berge. A circle had formed around them. The sunlight put a dusty haze over the valley that they were skirting. Claude felt the sad charm of that festival coronation powerfully.

VIII

Claude raised his head, momentarily inclined over the microscope, and before calling his two companions in laborious solitude he watched them in action for a minute.

Alongside him, Raoul, clad in a laboratory smock of coarse gray fabric similar to his own, was cutting up a leaf that he had slid into the fissure of a piece of elder-wood, in order to study its anatomy. Armed with a trenchant razor, he was running the blade perpendicular to the axis of the leaf. Without getting impatient, he had recommenced the same operation twenty or thirty times.

Finally, having succeeded in obtaining a sufficiently transparent slice, he slipped it gently between two plates of glass, disposed them in the field of the microscope and, guided by a reflective prism shining at the summit of his magnifying apparatus, he traced on paper the fibers of the tissue, concentrically spread out in a sheaf of fine stripes. All of his attention was applied to that task.

Claude remarked the finesse of the tawny beard when he curved his face at the brass armature of the instrument, and the power of the musculature of the fingers, so astonishingly utilized in the delicacy of a task that would have demanded the hand of a fay.

How complete he was, that man so obstinate in his work; how marvelously the equilibrium of his body, built to sustain heroic struggles, lent itself to the functions of his brain! For it was him who had encouraged Claude to transform his still-insufficient book on *The Amours of Plants* into a more extensive publication destined to mark his place in science, to serve for the discoveries of others. He had taken up the book again, he had magnified his personal visions; he had augmented the scope of its big ideas, the fruits of his delicate manipulations.

Thanks to him, Claude would leave behind a work. And seeing him so patient, so resolute, so dogged, so methodical and so harmonious, he could not retain his admiration and expressed it aloud.

"Raoul, truly, you never cease to astonish me! How many times have I seen you recommence your cut? Thirty times, perhaps, without jibbing. You confound me, with your organization, so sure in the service of a vast thought. Isn't that so, Henriette?"

Henriette turned round, as if surprised by the question. She had heard the eulogy that her fiancé had made, but did not want to appear to attach any importance to it. However, it caused her a secret pleasure that Raoul's superiority was recognized, without her fathoming the nature of that satisfaction.

Standing in front of an easel occupying a corner of the laboratory, she nodded her head and then resumed painting. Clad for that labor in a sort of white surah peplum, the turquoise decorations of which attenuated its uniformity, with a palette in her hand, she was painting a head of the Virgin destined to ornament the walls of the château's chapel. She mixed the colors and her arm precipitated the resultant mauve hue with little strokes of an active brush.

Sometimes, she took a step back. She measured the success of her work, squinting; then, advancing again, she recommenced, correcting a shade, and ended up with a long and satisfied exhalation. Her smock fitted her admirably; after having espoused the harmonious torso it tapered over the impeccable arc of the hips and fell all the way to the feet, solid in light shoes.

The mauve of the canvas, reflecting on the artist, softened the animation of her cheeks, warmed by the labor, covering a section of her face with neutral tones, rising as far as the delicate arabesque of the ear, which was surmounted, brightly, by the glaze of smooth hair, gathered in the Greek fashion. By contrast, the graciously rounded chin announced the force of a firm throat imprisoned by the collar of the smock.

Claude admired her again, so beautiful, so lucid, so radiant in her simplicity.

And around them there was the sacred calm of the laboratory, built under the eaves of the château: an etheric tranquility, a serenity of blue sky in which they seemed to be living, so much infinity purity did the great bay window, five meters broad, pour into it.

The valley of the Seine, which it overlooked, was invisible. In order to attach them to the world there was nothing but the very simple furniture in white lacquered wood, and the long shiny table covered with a multitude of flasks and instruments appropriate to the study of botany: pipettes, microscopes, scalpels, herbals, and an entire enigma of scientific utensils, were complicated gears destined to aid the perception of human faculties.

Claude, who was resuming contact with them for the first time in a month, rejoiced in that display, which promised profound joys and efforts having their formula and their goal in the transcendental knowledge of vegetal organisms. Vibrant with a renewal of health that accorded him once again the favor of his cherished studies, he called out again.

"Raoul! Henriette! Come and see what a transformation I've achieved in my infusoria, in an hour in the incubator at thirty degrees. Come and see! It's incredible, the potency of life when it's favored by certain milieux. Oh, our book, Raoul, will be nicely documented.

The young people ran in response to his appeal and leaned over the microscope in turn. Claude explained to his fiancée the changes operated on beings so minuscule, so infimal, that the eye could no suspect them in a drop of water, that they did not even trouble its transparency, and that one ingested them all the time without suspecting their presence. A temporary warming, an hour's sojourn in a temperature more elevated than normal, had sufficed to give them an intensity of action and reproduction so impetuous that soon, in order to live, they would be forced to eat one another.

Henriette watched the little creatures, magnified three hundred times by the magic of lenses. She knew all that; several times during previous vacations, under Clause's teaching, she had already fathomed certain evolutions of vegetal life. Her mind, rapidly initiated, had glimpsed the fecundation of animalcules and plants, their couplings and their amours, without her holy conception of superior forces being tainted in any fashion, not the candor of her celestial flights. But what dominated her at the moment, in that peculiar spectacle of infusoria agitating confusedly in a drop of water imprisoned by a plate of glass, was a repulsion for that somber swarming, for that suspect development of beings that one could swallow, invisibly, in a crystal glass.

"What! Those horrors!"

Claude laughed. And as she came to place her hand on the table in order to lean on it, and look again, he took it in his own, and then started to explain that the world was full of those vibrions, that human tissues contained a infinite number of them, that they were often indispensable to the functioning of organs and the chemistry of fermentations. But above all, he saw the symbol of creation in that obscure bustle, in that pullulation of the incubator. They manifested the energy and the stubbornness of nature, profiting from all the circumstances furnished by environments and elements, even abusing them in order to endanger incessantly, and not to let the flame of life go out that kept vigil in the most infimal corners of the universe.

Whether one looked down toward the species intermediary between the animal kingdom or the vegetable kingdom, or, looking higher up, one followed the scale of animal perfection, or whether thought focused on humans, the most complete and most harmonious being, everywhere in the slightest rudiments as in the most sumptuous forms, the implacable destiny of beings was manifest, which was to serve transition, to fabricate seed and to collaborate before disappearing in the formidable and incessant hatching. And everything, joy and sadness, pleasure and suffering, instinct and palliation, movement and repose, was confounded in a task of perpetuation, everything collaborated in the sovereign action of renewal.

The precaution of survival was so infinite that as soon as beings were annihilated, reduced to the state of inert matter, they still had their reason for having lived in their disintegration, in furnishing fodder to those that were hatching. Thus, life originated from death, and reciprocally, in such a way that the world was a perpetual cycle, a colossal gyration of individuals employed in being born, creating and then dying, in order to ensure the eternal repetition of life.

Henriette listened to her fiancé's speech with a certain surprise. She learned nothing new, for Claude had already furnished those elements of instruction many times, but she was astonished to see him drawing such broad philosophical consequences from it, astonished that the spectacle of universal life could surge forth from a drop of water. Those conceptions distanced her from the concrete horizons of religious morality, limited to the narrow mysticism of the convent, to the minutiae of innocent practices, to the confused adoration of the superior Being. However, that God existed and the world depended on him. Why was Claude neglecting to invoke him? Was that God not all of nature, since he was everywhere, since he presided over everything, even the fruitful union of men and women?

But in wanting to go too deep, she went astray, and as Claude looked at her she felt a slight shame in thinking that she ought one day to collaborate in the work of life, via the amour of her fiancé. Embarrassed, believing that her reflections had been divined, she turned toward Raul; he was looking at her too, with a singular intensity in his physiognomy. Then she blushed more deeply.

Raoul was astonished by the modesty thus betrayed by the young woman's cheeks. It was the first time that he had surprised the enigmatic manifestation. In their inevitable conversations about the energy and the evolution of germinations, before a young woman who had been the inseparable companion of their labors, their perceptions has seemed limited thus far to the pure domain of general science, and no idea susceptible of having personal implications had been emitted.

In addition, Henriette had always shown herself to be so limited to the play of her pious abstractions, so haloed by chastity, that it seemed that the radiations of sexual life would never triumph over her candor or pierce the aura of grave purity that surrounded her.

And Raoul was alarmed by Claude's language, the philosophy of which had just made an initial impact on Henriette's innocence. The disapproving mime of his physiognomy tried to communicate that to his friend, expressing a mute plea to halt that troubling excursion into a realm of ideas that ought not to invade the blank soul of a child.

But Claude did not want to understand. He had seen the young woman blush; he had divined, in that manifestation of her modesty, a new testimony of her mysticism. He therefore continued, as if Henriette had been absent, as if they were merely two erudite individuals elaborating the great work of science in the peace of the laboratory.

"Yes," he said, "It's the only thing we ought to admire, the concern of fecundity, so complete and so sincere, that nature has given to the senses of vegetables as well as to animals and provided with the instincts of pleasure, in order that both will obey it—with the result that amour, the generative attraction, dominates everything. Neither the humblest plant not the lightest gnat, nor the bird whose vertiginous wings swirl through the air, nor carnivores, nor humans, escape its exigencies. From the cold poles to the torrid equator, that instinct reigns. It reigns over polar bears and desert lions, over the inhabitants of a cottage as well as the moss that covers its roof. It reigns even in excrements. It is the primal law; it is necessary to cast the seed and to receive it in order to create, in order to reproduce. And in its will to perpetuate, nature gives birth to seeds with a surprising prodigality and incoherence. Millions and millions of them are lost; inundations destroy them, epidemics ravage them, fire consumes them. But what does it matter? Nature produces billions and billions, such a formidable plethora that if they all developed, none could live. That is doubtless why it cares so little for the individual, always sacrificed, since it has so many admirable resources to produce more individuals."

Claude paused momentarily in order to coordinate his ideas. Launched on his favorite track, he could not stop his momentum. Henriette had sat down a wooden stool. Her body leaning on the table, and her head maintained by two fingers of her pretty long hand, she was listening like a disciple and fixing on the orator all the serous softness of hr dark velvet eyes.

He continued.

"And in humans! Oh, in humans that's where nature shows itself even more disorderly and paradoxical. In them, it has developed to the supreme degree qualities of order, taste and intellect of which the rudiments are scarcely suspected in the other beings of creation. The original affinities, already certain but confused, in plants, brutal in animals, it has ornamented for them with a superb mantle of special sentiments, which hide the fundamental ground of amour, which permit them to accomplish it like a proud function. The brain veils with a sumptuous decor of mental beauties that which the mechanism of the senses comports basely, and in order to render the creative duty more attractive, it multiplies a hundred-fold the intensity of the joys and dolors that it attaches to it...

"It seems, then, that humans, provided with such a intellectual prerogative, capable of reflecting, of sensing the importance of the treasure of perpetuity, ought to engender more respectfully, to surround themselves with all the mental and physical guarantees that would ensure the integrity of their products...

"Well, no! Humans are as inconsequential as plants and animals; all their superior gifts are lost when instinct drives them; the radiant mantle, they take off, they throw it in the mud; its décor is consumed in the fire of animality; they become brutes spurred by passion; they disseminate their seed bestially, confiding it to fields unworthy of cultivation when it is not squandered or goes astray; and if, by chance, it is sown in good earth, it is because hazard has played a part and served as its most precious auxiliary..."

A small effort of hollow coughing suspended his discourse again. Stopped at the end of a sentence, Claude recovered a notion of the contingency of things. He sensed that, carried away by his subject, he had gone too far in his explanations, that he had brushed with too many images the real candor of his fiancée, and he repented almost immediately of not having moderated his enthusiasm.

Henriette, who had listened at first to the lesson with her ordinary meditative attitude, her brunette head still sustained by her two fingers, had suddenly straightened up, under the empire of a new suggestion . She now had a gaze of particular significance, which, passing successively from Claude to Raoul, caressed the former with a long commiseration, while it shone as if fixed itself on the latter, with a singular gleam, quivering with an undissimulated admiration.

The invalid understood that, with the suppleness special to women, his fiancée had been appropriated to those who found in his presence the morality of that instructive eloquence; and the result of it was immediate, since she was rejecting the weakness of Claude and adopting the strength of Raoul. At the same time, she sighed; at the same time, she delivered herself to an embrace. Her bosom projected, gloriously, her nostrils palpitated. She shook off her mysticism. She took a step toward Raoul; and an apotheosis of the sun accomplishing its gyration surrounded her with a golden frame in coupling in a illumination the vigor of the man and the grace of the young woman.

And it was a tableau of admirable equilibrium, by which Claude was saddened, for it gave him the conviction that in those two beings there were the two complimentary virtue of life, power on the one side and tenderness on the other. He would never be able to harmonize as remarkably, with his hollow cheeks and his stooped back. In spite of the illusions that he loved to make for himself, his most beautiful future would have to remain, for a long time yet, until his cure, one of the withered trunks incapable of putting down clinging roots and radiating by means of its sap as far as the growth of new buds.

Henriette! O chaste splendor! What a burning procrastination he had in his heart now, what an anguishing uncertainty agitated his conscience. What would become of his amour for the beautiful young woman, of his engagement so sumptuously declared and so lamentably continued? Yes, a frightful casuistry surged forth in confrontation with his enchanting dream and his holy aspirations; and the stir of doubts would prevent him henceforth from demanding of her the sublime work of amour, since he could only offer her a compromised semen, of which vitiated fruits would be the harvest.

And while he envisaged the future so somberly, as if to corroborate his desolation, a voice rose up at the back of the laboratory that made them turn their heads. Antonin Fargeaud, the father, who had come in without them hearing him; he had kept quiet at first, listening to his son's diatribe. Now he responded to it; nothing visibly moved in his physiognomy except his long white beard, moving with his words, while the rest of his body was upright, inert and stiff; the eyes, opalized by cataracts, had a distant, lost and absent expression, seemingly looking into the void and drawing inspiration therefrom.

"You talk about living, creating—truly, what's the point?"

"It's you, Father," said Claude, with great respect, offering him a stool. "Sit down."

But the old man refused with a gesture and continued in the same low voice, his torso straight, fixed and prophetic.

"And you praise life! And you admire the fecundating power of nature! Insensate! You don't see, then, the destiny of everything that hatches? Look, then, interrogate the soul of beings. Just think! The tree that astonishes you by the majesty of its trunk, do you know what battles it has had to deliver in order to subsist? Do you know what assaults it has had to endure? Everywhere, it has suffered. Its roots are attacked by species that hide in the soil; its bark and its wood are eroded by beings that establish their dwellings there and metamorphose there; its leaves are devoured by minuscule herbivores, lacerated by multitudinous insects; finally, to complete the kill, birds aliment themselves on its buds. And when the tempest passes, the colossus cracks and breaks!

"Everywhere, everywhere, I tell you, there is suffering and destruction! Animals gorge themselves on living prey and make war without respite. Under the green water of the oceans, incessant dramas agitate, fish kill one another, mollusks devour one another, and ignoble tentacles of gelatin are arms that extend toward victims and enlace them in order to drink their blood...

"And among humans, oh, among humans it's even worse! When the powerful aren't destroying the humble, when society isn't crushing them under its oppressive heel, it's disease that lies in wait for the innocent, frightens him and annihilates him. Oh, yes, admire nature, thank it for its prodigality, Claude, and you, Henriette, render thanks to your God. Personally, I acclaim nothingness!"

Henriette greeted the old man's blasphemy with a signs of the cross surreptitiously traced on her forehead, but Claude was moved in his heart. He understood the despair that had been embittering his father for some time, and had determined such a disturbance in his poor old head that he was now pushing his bitterness to the extreme, cursing life in a kind of madness, leveling everything to his paternal disappointment. Nevertheless, he tried to protest.

"No, Father, don't. You'll diminish your example, so virtuous and so careful of the interests of your children. Those words are unworthy of your good heart. You know very well that there are fortunate people in the world."

"I'm not one of them... and neither are my children...what do the rest matter to me?"

Claude had taken him by the arm and guided him toward a seat. A tenderness gripped him for that long white beard and those eyes veiled by leucomas, now almost blind, perhaps by virtue of having admired his preferred son too much.

"Rest, Father."

They remained silent. The old man, sitting down next to the table, had encountered Henriette's hand and, after having conserved it in his own momentarily, he drew the young woman to him, placing her in the light.

"How beautiful you are, my child! How tall you are! I don't have long any more to see you, for my sight is getting weaker every day, and I don't want to deliver it to the surgeons, who might end up destroying me completely. Come on, then! Come closer...closer still, so that I can engrave your features in my memory...for you're the only star that attaches me to my night, now, since it's you who'll make Claude's happiness when he's cured."

She smiled graciously, in order that he might also conserve the memory of her tenderness. However, she observed: "Why, my father, did you pronounce such nasty words just now?"

"Be generous, my daughter...I forgot to think of you."

She pardoned him with a kiss on the forehead. Then, entirely content, she led him to her painting, and obliged him to lean very close to the canvas, in order for him to admire the gracious contour and pretty colors of the Virgin she had depicted. And before him, she picked up her palette and added a few more touches, while Raoul and Claude returned to their work—with the consequence that, for an hour, as before the problem addressed by Claude, a charming and mild intimacy of toil returned, a profound and laborious peace. The old man was sitting next to the young woman and he remained grave, listening to her paint.

Then there was a medley of voices, dominated by a falsetto, and footsteps climbing the stone stairway giving access to the laboratory, and four men came in, Hector guiding Professor Domesta and, behind them, Monsieur Duverdon and Monsieur Fortin, the last-named having come to obtain some information from Claude, his expression anxious and irritated.

As soon as they appeared, Henriette slipped away, carrying her canvas in one hand and guiding the old man, who was fleeing his elder son, with the other.

Immediately, the room filled up with the shrill lisps and reedy sonorities of the little Italian.

"How are you, *illustrissime*? By the Madonna, you're as velvety as a face by Rubens! I've come to bring you news and talk science with you."

"And I've permitted myself to accompany our illustrious professor," added Hector, releasing the epithet in a tone half-jocular and half-serious, caressing the foreigner like a tributary gift, for he could not grasp the sly intentions of his language. Domesta straightened with a certain pride, his abdomen bulbous under the amplitude of is frock-coat, tapped his ruffle, which was soiled by a few grains of tobacco, and then sponged his bumpy cranium with a lace handkerchief, and, playing with his panama as if it were a fan, he exposed the purpose of his visit again, without losing the gaze of Julien Duverdon, who had been following him since he arrived as if he had a special interest in listening to him and understanding him.

"I've come today expressly to discuss a point in your book, Signor. It does so much good to the heart of a scientist..."

"Not today," Claude cut in, coldly. "Today, I'm really too tired to listen to you."

Then, without paying any more heed to his interlocutor, he turned to Monsieur Fortin, who was waiting with a question on his lips.

"How is Madame Fortin?"

"Not well...not well at all...she's still suffering, and it's with regard to her that I wanted to ask you a question. But..."

His mime finished the sentence and indicated the importunate presence of the poussah, before whom he did not care to take his step. Subtly, the other surprised the signification.

"You can talk before me," he said, in a protective tone. "I'm bound by professional secrecy."

And as Raoul and Claude smiled, Monsieur Fortin became more confident and confessed the goal of his visit

"Oh, in any case, what I have to discuss with you isn't a big secret. I wanted to know Monsieur Claude's opinion regarding Doctor Caresco, the surgeon. We went to consult him recently and he's promised to cure my wife in a fortnight. She ought to have gone into his clinic already...she insists that I take her there, but I'm hesitant. An operation might have such major consequences. And then, that delay of a fortnight seems so improbable to me, so unhoped-for that I wanted to know, via your intermediary, the opinion of the scientific word of that man's worth."

"Caresco!" fluted the Italian, who had not been asked. "Caresco! I know him. He's a remarkable man, but he's a charlatan."

There was no way to resist; the appreciation of the strange individual provoked further hilarity on the part of Raoul and Claude. In fact, Caresco beat the big drum, like Domesta but at least he had an incontestable scientific value. It was piquant that the naivety of the Parisian public allowing itself to be caught by the lure of identical methods of publicity, permitted the fecundator to appreciate the surgeon with an appearance of verity. And Monsieur Fortin, who did not know the little man, widened his eyes in surprise.

In addition, the latter, without waiting to be asked to explain himself more fully, with the exotic aplomb that imposes itself so brazenly on our credulity, commenced a dissertation on Caresco. He did it with such twists of personality that he arrived almost immediately at talking about himself, explaining his theories and the nature of his practices, which he had not dared to do during his first conversation with Claude because of the presence of Henriette

"There are, Signor, two great scientists in Paris, one French and one Italian, Caresco and me..."

And the little man with the asexual face perorated, pivoted on his heels, smoothed his frock-coat, played with his ruffle and his panama, with an exuberance rich in gestures, emitting his discourse from his strange lipless mouth, devoid of a beard, underlining it with impetuous frowns of his peeled eyebrows, replaced by a streak in black pencil.

Yes, the two great men were Caresco and him. However, their methods, like their results, differed as much as shadow and sunlight. Both were interested in the same area, the female organs of generation, the mysterious lair in which the first human manifestations were elaborated; but while the surgeon was a destroyer, he, by contrast, was a conserver—more than that, a producer.

Bring to Caresco one of those poor women undermined by damage to the abdomen? He took his knife, and crack! He removed the trouble with a prodigious mastery, certainly, with a twist of the scalpel that provoked the admiring clamors of the spectators who were always present at his feats of prestidigitation. On the contrary, bring the same patient to him, Domesta? Oh, things would happen very differently. To begin with, there were never any spectators; that was his rule, as well as a means of not divulging his methods. No, everything remained between the patient, the husband and him. Then, he treated the woman medically, scientifically. When he had cured her, it was then that his apostolate truly commenced, and that the grave and sovereign beauty of his work as a sower was deployed. No more scalpel, no more blood, no more chloroform, no more drama: a simple syringe and a cup of semen—"Both sterilized, sterilized, Signori!"—and then, click! A little thrust of the piston, a jet of seed, a tampon, and the woman had no more to do than to depart, in a carriage or on foot, preferably in a carriage. But how beautiful, noble and glorious she was as she retired, in the certainty of her imminent maternity!

While saying that he had taken his instruments from his pocket and displayed them in front of Julien Duverdon.

"Isn't my method more honest, more worthy of the fine renown of conservative science, more hostile to the depopulation that is undermining our country—yes, undermining it, signori!—and less costly, too, much less costly! For while Caresco demands crazy prices. I'm affordable to all purses..."

And having made that little remark in passing, with the air of an apostle who is able to detach himself from any motive of interest, he resumed proclaiming pompously the philosophy of his generative role as a scientific disposer of life, the clysterian hieraticism of which had something majestic about it, stripped of the ridicule that the genius of Molière had extended over Diaforus. Was that gesture, in sum, not that which nature demanded of the male, with the exception that he accomplished it with chastity and scientific rigor?

More and more loquacious and emphatic, small, rotund and pale, with his apostolic attitude of a priest, smoothing his frock-coat, his laic soutane, respectful of the creases of his ruffle and the disposition of his 1830 collar, in his reedy and singing voice, which lisped and swelled, he lauded the improbable activity of the minuscule spermatozoa, little worms with big heads, human tadpoles of a sort, launched by him in profusion, accomplishing their route in the secret organs thanks to their movements and also to the aid of vibratory cilia: "The vibratory cilia, those supporters of fecundation...yes, Signori, veritable supporters...bringing the male to the female with their little arms fixed in the mucus, endowed with a perpetual agitation!"

And as he said that, his arms made a rotary movement, in order to give his documentation a more convincing importance, and he seemed himself to be an enormous and suspect vibrion. Thus, the spermatozoa accomplished a dark, crazy journey through the anfranctuosities of the uterus, and the first of them arrived at the goal imposed by creation, at the ovule, in order to fall upon it, to penetrate it—"as the horn of a bull penetrates the breast of a horse, truly, Signori!"—and, once having succeeded, to install itself and imprison itself there in a delirious communion, in order to perpetuate there "the one who, tomorrow, will be your brother, your son, your wife or yourself...for it is from that Signori, that you issued!"

135

And those elements, which he had read in specialist books, and which he only knew imperfectly, although they were the foundation of his fortune and his fame, he narrated with a conviction and an abundance of graphic details destined to dazzle the meager intelligence of dupes running to the banging of the gong, those who were hypnotized by the luxury of his carriages and the improbable excess of his equivocal sumptuousness.

And this time, again, he was not speaking in the desert. Julien Duverdon was attached prodigiously to his voice, to his gestures, to the golden instrument, to the sculpted hilt that he raised religiously like a pyx. Hector listened too, interested by those questions, which reawakened his unhealthy passion for women. Letting his fugitive eyes flutter, secretly fascinated by the legend that the little man was gilding, he still conserved the amused memory of the brothel that Domesta was entertaining at that moment in his luxurious country house, and which the poussah made, he had said, his field of study.

Raoul, irritated, had turned his back and resumed his task of vegetal slicing. Claude, having drawn Monsieur Fortin into a corner, was informing him about Caresco, a remarkable operator indeed, a prestidigitator of the scalpel who had accomplished miraculous cures, but of dubious moral sense; in sum, a man that it was necessary to fear, to whom one only ought to confide a bloody intervention after having had the opportunity appreciated by others.

"At least, that is what is said, my dear Monsieur Fortin. Myself, you know, I'm unfamiliar with the question, and there might be a good deal of jealousy in those accounts..."

A carillon announcing the meal interrupted them. Monsieur Fortin thanked Claude warmly, although the conversation had rendered him perplexed. Followed by Domesta, who, sniffing a client in him, no longer wanted to quit him and offered to take him in his phaeton and drop him of on the way, since their properties were almost neighbors, he started down the tortuous stairway that led to the second floor. Then there was also the descent of two sets of stone steps, all along the

136

admirable wrought iron banisters, and the arrival in the high vestibule guarded by two fire-breathing dragons.

The Italian, rendered more humble by the majesty of the place, calculated its amplitude. He appreciated the genius of the builders of the previous century in having shifted, disposed and raised up so many gigantic materials. The cold flagstones of red sandstone and the flight of the two marble columns supporting the arch evoked, fugitively, with a frisson, a memory of elsewhere, the mosaics and magnificence of other palaces he had known out there in the Orient, during years of misery and servitude; and instinctively, moved by a reflex of old habits, he curbed his torso and sketched a forward extension of the hands as he traversed the vestibule.

Outside the door, waiting for them, were two women silhouetted against the light, whom they did not recognize at first. On was coquettishly dressed, her neck decorated with a cherry red scarf, bare-headed, revealing, in the gap in her bodice, low-cut in the center, an area of blonde and iridescent flesh. She was standing slightly in advance, manifesting her intention not to allow herself to be confused with the second person, her servant. The latter, of rustic appearance, clad in a short skirt and having taken off her clogs, was carrying a basket of eggs. Of the former, only the city-dweller silhouette could be distinguished, the agreeable design of the figure, disciplined by a corset, and the movements of the upper body, willfully thrust forward. Of the latter, further back in the light, the red scatter of hair could be seen, like a halo, and the rustic attitude, embarrassed by having penetrated into such a beautiful place. When they approached, however as the visitors bowed, they finally placed them.

"Mademoiselle Servant!" exclaimed Hector, joyful at that advent, of which he believed himself to be the motive.

He went to take her hand, and held it for a long time in his own, observing with pleasure that the young schoolteacher did not resist the significant pressure of his fingers, and that the blush invading her cheeks was even more a kind of proud

137

satisfaction than a confusion at being so amiably distinguished by the château-dweller.

"What good wind brings you to the château, my charming demoiselle?"

"The pleasure of bringing fresh eggs for Monsieur Claude personally."

"Is that really the only motive?"

She did not reply, turned toward Julia, the servant, and said in an imperative tone that she was not sorry to employ before such distinguished company: "Approach, Julia; present your eggs to Monsieur Claude."

Hesitantly, with less frankness than usual, the farm girl took a few steps and held out her basket.

"Here they are!"

"They're fresh today, and I collected them myself," Marthe avowed, striving to dissipate by the graciousness of her offer the familiar tone of the servant.

"Please thank your father, Mademoiselle."

Julia withdrew to the side. Decidedly, she had a motive for sadness, since she was not laughing. Monsieur Fortin, who had been able to appreciate the complaisance and good humor of the young woman, was intrigued by that. He remembered her disinterest on the day when she had rendered him the service of transporting Madame Fortin and accompanying her to her home afterwards. Had she not refused the hundred sous with which he wanted to gratify the vigor of her arms? While the others chatted and surrounded Marthe, he approached her.

"Hello, Julia! Is something wrong!"

The countrywoman turned toward him, rubbing her hands together, astonished to be distinguished. The red scatter of her hair and the broad arch of her back, the extraordinary slenderness of her neck gilded by the open air and the aristocratic finesse of her wrists and ankles, that ensemble of strength and hereditary grace so abnormal in a peasant, a bastard of the streets, surprised the questioner again. He saw again, with a warm surge of blood, the leg that he had glimpsed when she climbed into the carriage in order to deposit Madame Fortin therein. In addition, she emitted a healthy odor of human animality, the rising aroma of which impressed the male and troubled the chaste reserve that his wife's condition imposed upon him.

"It's not that there's anything wrong, but I've had words with my master."

"Really, words?"

Monsieur Fortin begged her to explain. Then she recounted her deep chagrin, the event that had upset her rudimentary psychology That morning, Douvard, the deputy schoolteacher who had been courting her for a long time, had come while she was doing the laundry in a barn and had tried to throw her to the ground; but she had resisted. With a wet cloth she was holding in her hand she had slapped the face of the violator, with such force that, in order to console the poor repentant young man she had drawn him to the straw, where they had both sat down, chatting very politely, even kissing, but without taking the marks of sympathy any further than those simple familiarities, for she had decided to remain sage until marriage, neglecting the example of her mother, whom a first fault had thrown into the gutter.

Unfortunately, the arrival of Père Servant had disturbed that feast of chaste intimacy on the warm and soft straw of the barn. The master, doubtless a little jealous—did one ever know, with these old men?—had thrown out the amorous young man and agonized the young woman with a volley of insults, reproaching her for idleness, for no longer earning her keep. How could he say that! She put so much heart into her work, got up with the dawn and went to bed well after dusk, in order to toil and sweat and use up all her strength in the service of two miserly old people and a young woman who put on airs because she was a schoolmistress!

Then, outraged, not tolerating such unmerited reproaches, she had riposted, she had had words, grave words, since she had threatened to quit the farm. Oh, if Douvard wanted…! She found him pleasant, Douvard, not pretentious; but he was selfish, like all men; he sought her for pleasure, but he refused her marriage…but she would have been very loving, very devoted…

Monsieur Fortin listened to those naïve laments, devoid of acrimony, as one listens to a distant, foreign story, which might, however, become yours if the whim took you to have a little active pity. He divested her of her rags, he covered her with a coquetry of fresh frills. Then he admired her, so full of health, so alive, so radiant in her rustic humility, and so tempting also, as one gazes at a ripe fruit that is forbidden to you, the scarlet seduction of which surpasses the border of the path, and which one would only have to reach out a hand to pluck, to bite into it without any great sacrilege and without remorse.

To what did she seem destined, in fact, the beautiful girl, in her laborious poverty, in her obscure splendor, if not to tempt the passing fancy of a Douvard, or someone else, without either the schoolteacher or the other caring about the seeds that they were about to sow and the childbirth that might follow, any more than the passers-by, an entire line of good-for-nothings, vagabonds wandering the roads, had cared about shoving her mother over the edge of the ditch and impregnating her? Was she not condemned by social negligence to support the burden of the hereditary fall, in a perpetuity of abandonment and shame?

And yet, she defended herself. Did not her obstinate honesty, that determination of a self-respect at odds with the mechanism of instincts, in resolving herself to the conception of marriage, distinguish her from facile brutes, her peers? Whence had she drawn that instigation? Did she owe it to paternal atavism, to the hereditary predominance of the sub-officer of dragoons who had loved the prostitute and who had deposited in her fertile womb the seed of a moral intention at the same time as he had specialized those aristocratic forms, that graciously sculpted ankle beneath the coarse fabric of woolen stockings, and the arch of the lower back, supple and powerful, of which no corset modified the curve?

And while she continued her anthem of humble revolt, and her voice, without the help of gestures, discouraged in advance, expressed the simplicity of her hopes, Monsieur Fortin admired again her complexion, furnished by the sun, dotted with red patches, and her crimson mouth, in which her fresh teeth sparkled, and the tawny aureole of scattered hair, with undisciplined locks that emerged behind and in front of her white bonnet. He was impregnated by her; he inhaled her aroma of human animality, rising in teasing effluvia, in sexual gusts. An obscure stir of covetousness assailed him: an awakening of instincts dormant by virtue of long abstinence, and the imprecise idea that he might obtain from that child what Madame Fortin's poor health refused him. But he hastened to suppress the suggestion, for he adored his wife, in spite of the impossibility of their caresses, in spite of her sterility.

"Come on; console yourself my child, all this will sort itself out."

"No, I'm going to quit the farm."

"Where will you go?"

"To your house, if you wish, M'sieur Fortin. I have solid arms, to care for your lady..."

"Let's see...yes...one day, in fact, if you're without a place...come to find me."

Content and reassured, Julia patted down her skirt violently, and resumed laughing.

Monsieur Fortin returned to the Fargeauds and took his leave of them, for the second bell announcing the meal had just rung. Louis, the domestic, and Rose, the chambermaid, came running, very animated, very urgent in their lateness, and opened the door of the dining room, where a table set with several places was visible.

Marthe Servant set forth on foot, followed at a distance by Julia. Hector accompanied her coquettish and pretentious retreat with his gaze. Then Monsieur Fortin's and Domesta's carriages moved off, drawing away simultaneously and making the gravel screech. The professor's phaeton was mauve this time, with yellow trimmings; the coachman's brandenburg fasteners emphasized the dark green Prussian blue of the more discreet livery. Those eccentric hues were lost in the distance.

141

Raoul and Henriette, who had lingered to watch them disappear before going into the dining room, smiled in a happy mockery that continued during the meal, devoured avidly, next to Claude, who nibbled his food without enthusiasm.

IX

June came to an end, and Claude's health was sufficiently ameliorated for Doctor Bouret to authorize a few short walks in the park at dusk. After the evening meal, therefore, he and Raoul went out in the languid twilight, which gave the mildness of a solemn blur to all the contours. It was the hour when, beyond the plains and the hills, the sky and the earth were wedded in a grayness of infinite melancholy scarcely striped by broad mauve streaks, and that calm visual harmony was combined with the last sounds: the distant peal of an angelus, the cry of a pastor and the ripple of the stream of fresh water that wound around the château; a grave, troubling concert of dying breaths that would soon fall sleep religiously in the definitive fall of night.

The two friends were wandering at random. Without speaking, Claude had taken Raoul's arm. Henriette, having some embroidery to finish for the chapel, which she was decorating with her active faith, had abstained from accompanying them. The absence of the young woman, the usual companion of their walks, did not seem to have any repercussion on their joy in wandering slowly in the warm dusk, perfumed by the scents offered by the plants. A sort of unavowed embarrassment, provoked by Henriette's presence for some time, without them taking account of it and without them suspecting its nature, had even flown away, and they only experienced the customary contentment of their long amity, in being alone and making their thoughts correspond without expressing them.

A bend in the path brought them to the main gate. The dwelling of the Grignons, the concierges and gardeners of the château, stood out in the gloom, with two spires sticking up into the azure of the evening. The windows seemed to be more brightly illuminated than usual. They were about to turn away when the movement and unusual noise coming from the interior invited them to extend their walk that far. The entire family was braying a drinking song.

"They're drunk this evening," Raoul remarked.

"A gaiety of which I pay the expense," replied Claude. "Père Grignon came this afternoon to inform me of the return of Anatole, his eldest son, who is a corporal in the marine infantry, reengaged to the profit of his second brother, who is returning from campaign in China, where the maladies and the bullets have spared him. He held out his hand in order to celebrate the soldier's colonial medal and I gave him twenty francs. They're drinking them at present..."

And Claude, looking through the ground-floor window, from which the light and the noise were coming, perceived the spectacle of the end of a feast. The family was seated around the untidy table, the father and the mother occupying the middle, and then the children in order of age. Anatole had taken off his tunic, and with his torso only covered by his coarse cotton shirt, his neck surrounded by his knotted regulation cravat and his kepi tilted over his ear, he seemed relaxed and satisfied. After him came Arthur, the driver, still wearing a leather jacket stained with grease. Then there were seven other children, three girls and four boys, aged between eighteen and two with variable intervals, death having scythed down eight at the dawn of life. The feast was lacking Alphonsine, the eldest daughter, whom his generosity would also have fortified. She was rarely seen since, having departed for Paris under the pretext of going into service, she had thrown her dishcloth into the nettles during the first months of her sojourn in order to fall into prostitution.

What was most surprising, however, what characterized that disorderly joy, was the same air of heavy bestiality in all of them, from the white-haired parents to the smallest brats, asleep at the table. Alcohol, the great killer, hollowed out their features similarly, caused the cheekbones to protrude colorfully, making the eyes of the older ones wander with an indescribable brutishness and sealing those of the younger ones leadenly. For they were all drunk on eau-de-vie; those who were stammering had received their ration like the others. Around the rabbit stew that was trailing on the table, the glasses still contained the fiery toxicity obtained from distilling the local vintage. The mother, whose belly, devoid of a corset, protruded at the level of the table, had just started laughing stupidly on seeing her man stand up, tottering and quavering an obscene song to the tune of a hymn, the chorus of which the whole family repeated, beating the rhythm with spoons on the edge of their plates.

Around the table, in spite of the elegance of the building's exterior, there was the sickening décor of a neglected interior: dirty walls, rickety cradles a greasy wooden sideboard cluttered confusedly with vases, dusters and a comb—all the disorder and abandonment of a hearth that had never been maintained by the careful hand of a housekeeper or warmed by any familial solicitude. The untidy dwelling was as unsteady as those who inhabited it.

"Come on, let's go!" said Claude, trying to draw Raoul away. "That spectacle sickens me. I don't know why my father keeps such people!"

But they had been perceived from inside, and Anatole and Arthur, the least dazed by drunkenness, surged forward on to the doorstep to beg them to come in. And when they refused, offering the pretext of the late hour, the drunkards persisted, attaching themselves to their heels. Anatole, especially, put a disrespectful stubbornness into prolonging his invitation. Belching and unsteady, he had seized Claude's sleeve and was tugging it.

"Come on, Messieurs…take a glass with us…it will give Father pleasure…we're worthy people, good servants…."

"No thank you, not this evening," said Raoul, trying to move them aside. But they would not let go. They marched behind the young men, slightly sobered up by the pure air and the fresh emanations of the foliage, which rose to their brains in odorous gusts, temporarily extinguishing the alcoholic flamboyance. Claude was obliged to stop in order to listen to them.

Then Anatole started recounting his recent campaign, the movements of the expeditionary corps sent to China to join the troops of other powers and punish the boxers, the yellow men who had sacked the legations and murdered the Europeans.[6] Oh, it had been an amusing voyage, and without great dangers, in spite of the fatigues. First, five thousand leagues at sea, five thousand leagues of dancing and pitching over the great waves, being parked on deck furbishing weapons, idly, making jokes. It gave one a small idea of humanity, all that water and all that depth!

Crossing the equator it was hot and one sweated. Many died of dysentery. They disembarked at Takou, unpacked all the kit, and marched into a bare country bristling with little horned houses that looked like children's toys. Then the Chinese appeared, like little lemons with all the juice squeezed out, dressed like women, with long, thick, black hair twisted in a braid. How they had killed them, good God! How they had massacred them! How they had ravaged and sacked their dwellings! They knew they were ferocious, and knocked them over for pleasure. Anyway, they died without too much alarm, so cruel themselves in their customs as torturers that they seemed astonished that they weren't tortured. And so numerous too, pullulating, that when one was killed, ten came back.

Already, in Takou, a French shell had exploded in the fort and blown up a powder-store. It was a magnificent spectacle, when they penetrated into the breached enclosure and they saw everything topsy-turvy, twisted and annihilated, and the little dying grimaces that they nailed with a thrust of a bayonet and which went tranquilly, fatalistically, yellow in the red blood. And then Tien-Tsin, and then Tong-Tcheou! Battles, a frenzy of murder that became so banal, so facile, that the Rus-

---

[6] The multinational forces sent to put down the so-called "Boxer rebellion" departed in the summer of 1900, the first objective of the so-called Seymour Expedition being the town that Anatole calls Tien-Tsin, now known as Tianjin, and then proceeding to Tong-Tcheou (Tongzhou) in June of that year.

sians, in order to make a diversion and not to use up the bullets, organized the great drowning in the Pei-Ho river, precipitating into the water an innumerable corps of livid little warriors, perhaps ten thousand, no one knew.

Oh, that was truly funny! To amuse themselves the cossacks knotted the little lemons together by their long pigtails and pushed them in the water. They were left to splash, to disappear, then reappear, finally to sink into water, stirring up eddies with their death-throes. And nothing was as hilarious as that long file corpses drifting away, belly up, stiff in the supreme contracture of their thin little limbs, conserving in the annihilation of their features the supreme indifference of their death—that immense, interminable file of floating androgynes dragged by the current all the way to the sea, where the fish must have feasted on the crows' leavings. They fled, they died, but what did it matter for life? There were so many of them, those little lemon-men dressed as women…!

"Enough! Enough!" murmured Claude, with a horror of hearing affirmed what he already knew, and above all hearing it repeated by one of the murderers of those abominable massacres.

Surprised by those words and the tone that criticized what made him glorious elsewhere, the corporal tried to protest. Was it not the eternal law of war, that savage killing? Were not hecatombs accomplished everywhere and at all times, even among civilized people, with a similar ferocity? Oh, if the Chinese had come here, many others would have been seen, tortures more atrocious and more barbaric. And in his ferocious common sense, which was not numbed by drunkenness, he repeated the common obligation, the evident necessity of struggles, until humans were transformed and reached an understanding for the triumph of good. It was necessary to be cruel, to be the strongest, in order to enable the supremacy of the fatherland one served. Didn't the English employ explosive bullets?

"Anyway, Monsieur Claude," he concluded, with a nasty smile, "do they count, colored skins? When a Chinaman disappears, ten more are found the next day. It's true that the whites have helped the yellows rudely. They were rather tempting, the Chinese women with bizarrely cleft eyes! At twelve one might have take them for gilded marble status. What do you expect? It was pleasure on the cheap, of the unexpected, of the new, and one took advantage of it. I'm sure that more than one Frenchman could recognize his work in a little lemon less yellow..."

Claude and Raoul had hastened their steps, and Anatole and Arthur, hiccupping, solicited by the next gulp of alcohol, finally left them and returned to their house. Rid of their importunate company, the two friends slowed down, all the more so because Claude had just been seized by a small coughing fit, a consequence the effort of his flight.

The darkness was now complete; the last indecisive contours were effaced; the insects had folded their wings beneath their golden elytra. They took the path that led to the terrace of the château. But beneath that shadow, in its shelter, the life that went to sleep for some awoke for others. The two botanists surprised confused and mingled noises, a tender concert in which the nocturnal plants were animated, sacrificing obscure creations to the eternal exigency. From them came an incomparable sweetness, soft and penetrating gusts of perfume; one might have thought that a secret incense-burner was disseminating aromas magically to celebrate their clandestine weddings. It was an odorous fête, borne by a warn zephyr, of discreet kisses, the sensual communion of sweet peas, jasmine and honeysuckle.

They respired the embalmed advent ardently, as if to dissipate the human pestilence that the soldier's conversation had evoked. And yet, Claude could not help returning to his primary obsession, of all that the information of history had of the disappointing and the barbaric. He gripped Raoul's arm more forcefully and raised his voice, his speech often betrayed by the weakness of his breath.

"Oh, those horrors, those destructions, those crimes! That soldier drunk on killing! Don't you find it abominable that one can still, in our epoch, recount such atrocities cheerfully, and excuse them by the necessity of social defense?"

Raoul smiled internally. In his fine indifferent complexion, he did not linger over such pity. He was not, like Claude, drawn by the misery of ill health to bring everything back to charitable considerations, to evaluate the suffering of others in accordance with the quotient of his own affliction.

"Bah! That's life!"

"Yes, that's life; but why is life thus? Why doesn't the force that presides over the world equilibrate happiness and misery? Why so many smiles for some and so many tears for others? Why doesn't the intelligence with which humans are so magnificently endowed bend and moderate the brutal instinct that immediately gets the upper hand, runs riot and triumphs, as soon as destruction is possible?"

He stopped, his mind veering toward another path. Then he said: "Destruction...and creation also! The sowing of seed is no less inconsequent that the gesture the cuts yellow throats. Anatole has sown life with the same carelessness as he had destroyed it. Yes, is not scattering his semen with the same caprices of lust, delivering himself to the fecundation and no longer caring afterwards, as culpable as killing?"

The ideas were still swirling. He connected the facts; he appropriated the contingency to his personal philosophy.

"It's the most magnificent thing in the world: human semen. All future energies are resolved therein. Genius slumbers within it, ready to manifest itself when it hatches out. In its more or less fortunate distribution, the fate of those who will be constructed in our image, who will think, love and suffer like us, who are our brothers in humanity, is decided in advance, prepared and organized. For its conservation, for its development, for its employment, nature has be so careful, so prodigiously far-sighted, that it creates it infinitely every day, and in a drop of seed embryonic life pullulates, as numerously as particles of light vibrate up there in the fluid sky on beautiful nights. It might be lost, it might be destroyed; there will always be too many riches in that inexhaustible treasure.

"For its dissemination, too, in order that it might spread, a man does not even experience an effort; in order that he might even find it a pleasure, nature has created amour and sensuality, and delivering its seed is the supreme transport. But by a paradox, as if weary, or rather, as if concentrated on its eternal and identical task of always generating, nature's foresight stops there, and for the individual conceived it has no concern. It does not care that it is born at hazard, that it grows in accordance with its destiny, that it subsists as it can, that it eats, drinks, suffers, laughs, exists and dies. Yes, it does not care. It has another task in which it employs its activity, since it is manufacturing seed and yet more seed...

"Well, what do men do, humans who can think, men whose intelligence ought to meditate on the incoherence of the great creator? Are they ever seen to think of repairing the insouciance of matter, if resisting phenomena, of placing their seed better? Do they ever conceive the responsibility they are assuming toward the being that they are about to engender, who will resemble them, who will bear their original imprint, to whom they will bequeath instincts for growth, for subsistence and for creating in their turn, and nerves in order to feel suffering or joy? Are they ever seen to worry about it? Can they be taught—is it even possible?—to preoccupy themselves with it? No, a man caresses, a man enjoys, and he limits everything to the narrow measure of his egotistical and brutal satisfaction."

He stopped, for his voice had dried up from taking for so long, and again a hoarseness tore his throat. And that little cough of alarm, gravely commenced, terminated in a final broken shrillness, declared with more eloquence than words the truth of the plaint that he addressed to the generality, but which was confirmed so opportunely by his own particular case. Was it not because of the ignorance or unconsciousness of his father, Antonin Fargeaud, in having inseminated a woman suffering from tuberculosis, that he, Claude, found himself the soiled fruit of a union vitiated from the outset And he was obliged to stop momentarily, for the formidable future rose up before his eyes, frightening in its culpability and ruination. His hand, shaken by a tremor, clenched on Raoul's arm.

They had now reached the end of the pathway, in the vicinity of the terrace, and, as they quit the shadow of the leafy vault, the sky appeared to them in a resplendent sumptuousness of mauve or blue-tinted vacillations traversed by the spangled silver streak of the Milky Way, while to the right, the half-risen moon emerged from the château and ran a bright metallic varnish over the slate of a turret. In the background, under their feet, twenty-five meters away, they sensed the black decline of the ground falling away toward the Seine, whose curves were shining with flickering flames that the current extinguished and ignited by turns. And on the other side of the river, the plane took flight, all the way to the distant hills plumed with woods, which the light inundated, and which seemed to be curly tresses fleeing all the way to the blue vault of the sky and the powdery sumptuousness of the stars.

"Come on," said Claude, finally. "Let's go sit down for a moment before that enchantment. Do I know whether my eyes will be able to contemplate it again next year?"

"Oh, Claude! My dear Claude, can you think that?"

"Alas, yes I can. Beneath my feigned indifference, you see, many ideas are colliding, and a great deal of bitterness is causing me anguish. To think that I might perhaps go, and that all those splendors of the sky will be lost to me! To think, above all, that I shall leave the person that I love inexpressibly, Henriette, of whose saintly communion I've dreamed, of whom I wanted children..."

His voice betrayed him again. But it was no longer fatigue, this time, that cracked its timbre, nor the cough that paralyzed its emission. It was a profound, absolute dolor departed from the heart, rising to choke him, casting over his throat the heavy burden of intimate distress.

"Children!" he went on. "I aspired to that magnificence. My race surviving and being retempered in the generosity of another blood! An eternity of myself awakening and animation, and the atavistic chain unbroken! I had immensity behind

151

me, immensity in front of me, and more directly, clasping a wife in my arms. I held beneath my kisses a entire field of fecundity, and also my field of happiness. But even if I were cured, even if the physicians assured me that my lips could no longer be a source of disease, even if they aid to me: 'Create!' would I dare to launch myself into such an unknown, to risk becoming, for my progeny, what my father was for me: an unconscious executioner."

Raoul had listened to the beginning of that diatribe with a certain impatience. Why could he not hear his friend talk about marriage without experiencing a hint of bitterness? Was it because, in fact, he no longer recognized that Claude had a right still to hope for a delightful creature like Henriette, a hope that he divined still vibrant beneath his apparent restrictions? Was it because he had unconsciously established the comparison between his vigorous person and the debility of the invalid, estimating that nature would be better served by the former than the latter? He hastened to reject those two reasons; but he could not help, under the suggestion of the night, sensing the thought of the young woman stirring his nerves, as Claude also sensed it, differently.

They had reached the terrace now and installed themselves on the rustic bench where, in broad daylight, the admirable panorama unfurled of the valley that night transformed into an encasement illuminated by the oblique radiation of the moon, the full disk of which was so powerful that all things conserved their relief, as if exaggerated and brought nearer.

They gazed. To the left, remote in the décor, the minuscule silhouettes of the houses of Rouen were dotted, dominated by a few monuments whose roofs striped the blue of the azure with black. The lunar intensity was such that the street lighting, visible in obscure weather, could not be distinguished. Ahead, the sinuous meanders of the river snaked, speckled with silver, an entire movement, an entire luminous course, darkened in places by the emergence of large islets populated by birch trees, and which then resumed, only to dissipate in turning around a hill. That was another caprice of

festoons, bordered by a lacework of woods, now more perceptible, more aureoled with azure, married at their summit with
the serenity of the palpitating sky.

They respired. At their feet, more abundantly, more de-
lightfully, the plants, exotic plants brought to that soil by the
hazard of the winds, and autochthonous plants, honeysuckle,
jasmine and sweet peas, under the enormous spread of the
dormant oak, swung their perfumed censers, saluting the
warmth of the night and the splendor of the languid star with
suave exhalations.

The plants were making love, they were secretly enlac-
ing, or they were confiding the richness of their odorous pollen to the zephyr, kissing it with their fecundating atoms. They
were making love, they were creating, in an unparalleled fête,
in an expansion of their meager organs. And coming from the
blue disk and from the great veil of azure dotted with the dist
of worlds, and the profound outpouring of the earth, and the
shiny river, and the limpid woods of the hills, and the air and
the light, a great current of amour and reproduction passed by,
noisy with a concert made of a thousand indistinct harmonies,
of infinitesimal clamors united in a song of tenderness, a fecundating hosanna of plants, insects, animals and human: the
universal rut. And both of them recognized the soul of seeds in
that soft uninterrupted rumor, in that perfumed breath: the soul
of seeds, the unfathomable activity of creation, the awakening
of eternity.

In a fashion quite different from his ordinary reveries,
Claude was subjected intensely to the voluptuous appeal of
nature. Whether he gazed at the shine extended by the moon
over the surface of the river, or his eyes went further to collide
with the enigma of the woods populating the hillside and envisage the blue-tinted transparency of the sky, it was into those
fluids that he would have liked to take his fiancée, to sustain
her in the warm water, to lift her up into the space dusted with
diamantine stars, and draw her into the unknown, higher, ever
higher, into the fusion of the immensity.

How marvelous it would be, once having reached the azure ether, to receive, as a tribute from the distant Earth, the generative exhalations, the perfumes of pollen and the light of worlds, and marvelous also to sense voluptuous rising, enveloping and intoxicating; the marvel of murmuring the prayer of amour that the zephyr said, of singing in unison the canticle that vibrated in the celestial waves! Oh, the sacred delirium of mingling his voice with that great harmony of the night, in order to invite Henriette to share the firmamental embrace, to pant, and to sense her panting at the same time, with the unanimous kiss!

Could he, alas? For merely in thinking about it, his excessively rapid heart transmitted pulsations to his lungs that strangled and stifled them. A dry cough ripped his throat with tones so sharp that they seemed to be clamors of despair, strangely tragic in the calm splendor of the night. He stood up, walked, and stretched his muscles, wanting air, health and life. And when, finally calmed down, he sat down again, he perceived, fusing in the atmosphere, the dazzling plume, immediately extinguished, of a shooting star.

He raised his hand toward its flight.

"Look at that meteor. It's a foreign body that has touched our atmosphere. It has come from an unknown world, it has no right to stay. It fades away, after having smiled luminously that the world that perhaps it wanted to inhabit. That meteor is my symbol. I'm a stranger, like that bolide fusing in an apotheosis of rapid flames. Like it, I've brushed happiness; I've been burned by it... I can't stay; I have to pass on. I ought not to leave traces after me..."

"Claude, it this the moment to be saddened, when you're doing better, when you're going to be cured?" Raoul observed, with a calmness that belied the acuity of his impressions.

Immediately, however, he was convinced that all reflection was futile, that it would augment a sadness that refused to allow itself to be persuaded. In any case, he too was obedient to other suggestions. Like his friend, he was imperiously sensitive to the amorous appeal of the night. But whereas in

Claude the possibility of the work of creation seemed something remote, almost set aside by the other problem of disappointing consequences, the child compromised as soon as the dawn, while it drifted into a vertigo of imagination as vast as the eternal cycle of the race, in Raoul, by contrast, the need for love sprang from his vigorous constitution, become immediate when subjected to the voluptuous attraction of the provocative flowering. Aureoled by a delicate sentimentality in the aristocratic scion, by contrast, the evocation inspired in the son of peasants, the Apollo of the glebe, a purely material effect.

Thus, Raoul appropriated every manifestation of the elements to his desire. For him, the stars lit up as the eyes of an ardent woman light up; for him, the perfumes of the flowers had a carnal suavity; for him, the confused noises of the world were agonizing in sighs of intoxication and the caress of the wind brushed him like a breath of supreme sensuality.

How profound the intoxication would have been of taking his part in those fertile joys with which the soil was quivering dully in its lascivious womb, and to draw a virgin there, on to the rustic bench, and clasp her in his arms, and then, after a gesture that would cast all veils away, to lay her down on the ground stirred with the toil of generation, on the quivering mosses and flowers, and demand from her the supreme initiation into that divine work, and to obtain, in kisses, tears and cries, the primal act of universal fecundation.

And he had to defend himself against the Form, for the person that he saw seduced and gasping was the one he must not see, the one whom the presence of Claude, so dear to his fraternity, commanded him to reject dolorously.

He expelled her. But involuntarily, in spite of his fear of a treason against their integral amity, she came back more luminous still. And it was in Henriette's eyes that he saw the flame of the stars; it was her that he drew, impeccable in harmonious virginal maturity; it was her whose warm breath he respired, breathless for the next kiss; it was her that he laid down on the moss and odorous flowers, magnificently, in his pride as a brutal and victorious male.

155

Suddenly, he shivered. A hand, which was not his friend's hand, had just been placed on his own, which he was holding extended along the bench. And the pressure of a delicate and moist flesh was prolonged, doubtless involuntarily, thanks to the obscurity that the great oak spread in that place, for Henriette, having arrived unperceived, believed that she was holding Claude's hand.

On being subject to the delectable contact, as warm and perfumed as the shadow, without daring to withdraw his arm because he had not drawn it away quickly enough, because he was quivering with pleasure, and perhaps because he felt the other hand, mistaken in the destination of its caress, was obtaining in that possession a pleasure equal to his own, provoked by a similar enervation coming from the seductive night.

Finally, when, frightened by what he was allowing to happen, he recovered consciousness of his duty and withdrew from the embrace, a little stifled murmur confided Henriette's surprise to him. But almost immediately, the calm and religious voice of the young woman rose up.

"It's necessary to come back inside, Claude. I heard you cough...you might get cold."

And at the moment when they were about to depart, she addressed Raoul: "Are you coming too?"

"In a little while; let me respire for a moment longer," the young man replied, which was not the real reason for not wanting to accompany her; for in the depths of his heart, he was experiencing shame for the thoughts he had just had, like a treason toward the loyalty of his friend, a profanation of the candor of the fiancée. But, his flesh still seething, as he gazed at the immensity of the landscape bathed in light, he found the smile of the stars less palpitating, the zephyr less caressing, the water of the river less silvery and the enigmas of the woods in which the flowers were fecundating one another less tempting, for the luminous vision that such beautiful things rendered him had just disappeared into the park, on the arm of his friend.

X

The midday meal had just finished. Limply extended in rocking chairs concentrically disposed in the shadow of the tall plane trees protecting the lawn, the guests of the château wee according their digestion a eupeptic respite. Next to Antonin Fargeaud, who, his eyes no longer aiding him, was awkwardly cutting the pages of a large book recently received, the title of which he was concealing carefully, Claude had gone to sleep, after casting off the excessively warm plaid. He was breathing smoothly, but to judge by the appearance of his pink-tinted cheeks, there was no doubt that the disease was continuing its slow evolution within him.

Then there was the inseparable couple, Clara and Rolande, clad in a similar fashion: a short white skirt and a red surah blouse with a straight collar. Julien, the husband, was staring at them almost timidly at that moment, with a weary constraint.

A little further away, in her grave and silent purity, Henriette was designing in needlepoint the silk arabesques of an altar-cloth. If, at times, she raised her head, it was to dart a glance at Claude and to smile with a reassured expression. She avoided looking at Raoul, who was, in any case, reading a newspaper

One might have thought that an equal tranquility of the heart disposed the attitudes and leveled the contented appearance of those seven people sitting quietly in the shade. The reverie or slumber of some seemed as natural and as calm as the labor or reading of others. However, a less superficial observation of their manner would have revealed in all of them symptoms of unavowed anxieties.

Claude twitched in his sleep; anguish pursued him even in his slumber; a light sweat on his temples betrayed the persistence of his malaise. As he separated the pages of his book, the old man seemed to be avid to know its contents; he was agitating the concern of wondering by whom he could have it read to him. Ordinarily, the calm voice of Henriette rendered him the service of communicating the thought of writers to him; he did not think that there could be any question of that this time, the book being nothing other than a treatise on Malthusian philosophy.

Further away, Rolande and Clara, with a sharp exchange of glances, were reanimating their vice, and Julien Duverdon, who had grasped the intention, was blushing behind his graying beard, his fine Herculean head withdrawn piteously into the squareness of his shoulders.

But the gravest and the most contained emotion was agitating behind the cold reserve of Raoul and Henriette. The remembrance of their involuntary caress, the pleasure they had obtained from prolonging it for a few seconds under the solicitation of the beautiful amorous night, and the unexpected treason that had resulted from it, one for his friend and the other for her fiancé, plunged them into a kind of regret mingled with a delectable remembrance. They no longer dared look at one another. Raoul was following the lines of his newspaper, but his mind was escaping, going much further than the large pages of print, running toward the rhythms of an unavowed tenderness. Henriette's hand was enervated beneath the needlepoint. She had pricked herself several times. The dolor she felt had reminded her of the suffering of the other; the red blood that dotted her finger, which she had sucked up with her lips, reanimated the dramatic spectacle of the blood of a hemoptysis poured forth by the other, to whom she owed it, and wanted to love. The, she impregnated herself with Claude.

The deceit of attitudes and the lures of appearances, sprawling in rocking chairs, were dominant, therefore, on that warm afternoon. Hector Fargeaud dissipated them suddenly by arriving noisily. The automobile, screeching over the gravel, expelling a pestilence of gasoline, caused the heads to turn, relaxed the anguish momentarily and awoke the sleeper. The sun lit up the copper trimmings and the shiny varnish of the red hues caught fire. On the seat, Arthur, the driver, helmeted

158

in leather, was as rutilant as the vehicle. Hector, clad in an overcoat, his head masked by vast somber goggles that one might have mistaken for the carapace of a diving suit, tumbled out of the vehicle, which had come to a shuddering halt, and came toward the company.

"I'm going to make a little hundred-kilometer tour," he said, with the simple conceit of a great beater of records. He added: "If you don't see me appear at dinner, don't worry; perhaps I'll have picked up some invitation on the way."

"Take us!" cried Rolande, bounding to her feet, after having seized Clara's hand, whom she also forced to get to her feet. Then, in a tone that indicated peremptorily that she did not want to be accompanied on the tour by her husband, she added: "Take Clara and me. We'll be very good, the two of us. Julien is retained this afternoon and can't come."

"Oh!" said Hector, with a significant wink. "You can dispense with his company, then?"

Their eyes, the same keen and mobile eyes, animated by a similar fleeting uncertainty, battled for the space of a second after that intentionally-pronounced remark, but Rolande had such a desire to flee into the country that she did not react to the sarcasm. Gentler and more coaxing, she persisted,

"Take us, my dear Hector. It's so hot here! And there's nothing like an automobile for procuring a little fresh air..."

"No, my dear," the motorist cut her off definitively. "You can't go where I'm going. Besides which, I told you that I wouldn't be back for dinner, or perhaps to sleep. That depends a great deal on circumstances."

They responded to his conceited smile with a sulky about-turn. But without worrying about them, he said *au revoir*, shook hands and leapt into his automobile. He sounded the horn at length before departing, with a noisy persistence, without any other motive than to annoy Rolande. The young woman responded to him by thumbing her nose. Such exchanged amenity contented their fraternity.

Hector put the car in gear and went along the avenue of chestnut trees that led, via a gentle slope to the gate next to the

159

Grignons' lodge. There he had to stop and let his machine breathe for a moment. The gate was closed and in spite of repeated appeals, no one disturbed themselves to let him through. There was an unusual animation inside the house, a woman's screams of pain interrupted by silent pauses, which made the resumption of the plaints seem more terrible.

"Apologies," said Arthur. "It's mother, who's giving birth. The midwife has been here since yesterday, and she says that the child won't come because it's the wrong way round."

"Hasn't he doctor been informed?"

"I don't think so."

At that moment, Père Grignon appeared on the doorstep. Still a little drunk, he had a letter in his hand that he was waving joyfully. After him, Anatole, the soldier appeared, slovenly in his shirt-sleeves, his kepi over his ear and a cigarette in his mouth, bearing on his dirty face, which he had omitted to wash for several days, an expression of joy equal to his father's. Both of them, without paying any heed to the presence of the master, advanced toward Arthur to give him the good news.

"You seem very cheerful, Père Grignon," said Hector. "It's over, then?"

"Over? No it's not over; it'll go on for some time. The midwife has left until this evening."

"But what if your wife gives birth without her?"

"It won't be the first time, M'sieur Hector...the mother knows what to do."

"But if the child's the wrong way round..."

"Bah! It'll end up coming anyway!"

That was his entire morality as a creator, that indifference with regard to the being who was about to be born and that a fault in the natural mechanism might annihilate in the original womb, perhaps killing the mother. He had taken his pleasure brutally, in an alcoholic erethism, he had cast his semen without reflecting on the effect of his action, only calculating its sensuality.

While the rich had other pleasures, for him, poor and needy, was not that embrace, as often as possible, his only compensation for living and toiling? He said so, he admitted it frankly. By indulging his egotism, he had had eighteen children, and his wife had had stillbirths. A nineteenth was arriving, but he was no longer counting. At that figure, one more increasing the heap, or one fewer diminishing it, he scarcely cared. Mère Gigogne[7] had such a habit of emitting them that he had not even summoned the doctor to ward off the present difficulty.

And what was enthusing Père Grignon at present, what was impregnating his gaze with a brilliant gleam, was not the triumph of paternity, or the anguish of the complications that had arisen...no, it was something else. It was the letter that he was holding out to Arthur.

"News of Alphonsine," he said. "She's sent a hundred francs. She's not ingrate."

"She's a brave heart!" Arthur emphasized

Hector remembered Alphonsine, the eldest daughter, whose bold gaze and gangling figure he had once esteemed when passing before the lodge. Already promising vices, with the slim provocation of her hips, it did not seem impossible to him that he might distinguish her more efficaciously one day, but she had disappeared in order to go into service in Paris, and had rapidly fallen into gallantry. He even remembered having encountered her one evening in a public dance-hall, attractive, dressed in red and pompously dolled up. Only a cavalier who was holding her tightly had prevented the master from going to the former servant, transformed into a queen of the asphalt. She must be succeeding in the métier of her body, since she had sent a hundred francs and promised as much every month.

"But your wife...," said Hector, after that reflection.

---

[7] A joke, not a misprint; the reference is to a popular comic figure in fairground shows who had a great many children.

Père Grignon, brought back to the reality of events shook his head. Assuredly, it wasn't his fault, and it wasn't him who could help her. And while the woman in childbed continued screaming, he started to laugh, admitting that although he had been able to make the child, he was unable to unmake it.

"All right," said Hector, moved to pity even so by the cries emphasizing their distress. "I'll go as far as Doctor Bouret's house. I'll send him to you."

Once through the gate, the blond spaces of the roads were displayed, bordered by ditches delimiting woods of infinitely varied shades of green. Everything was sizzling in the sunlight. The air current provoked by speed combated the sweat-bath heat in vain.

Sensual reminiscences assailed Hector. They prevented him, when the road along the Seine straightened out and he no longer had the care of equilibrating his machine, from admiring the richness of the blond, crimson and green fields, and the fluttering of the river snaking with the belt of hills, powerfully decorated with foliage, spaced out by chalky cliff-faces. Even the water had overheated and languorous glints. Boats furrowed it, in which men covered in sweat raised and dispersed the methodical rhythm of streaming, shining oars.

A few bumps in the pavement that the pneumatic tires on the wheels scarcely transmitted to the carcass, a barrier to cross where the railway track emitted a vacillation of vaporous air, and then the quays of Rouen filed past, alive, swarming with activity and stuffed with heat. A rolling bridge suspended from an enormous metal armature enabled vehicles to cross the river.

Hector swerved, turned into the Rue Jeanne d'Arc and braked in front of a large stone dwelling signaled to the attention of passers-by by a brass plate engraved with a name; that was the physician's house. The joyful cries of a child playing with a ball emerged through the main door, which stood ajar beyond a flower garden with paths draped with spent bark.

He rang and went in. Ah, the good smile and the sincere welcome of the honest practitioner, aureoled by a white crown of hair and separated side-whiskers, which contrasted with the youth of the eyes arched by black eyebrows. Doctor Bouret extended his hand as soon as the visitor appeared, abandoning momentarily a monsieur and a lady whom he was escorting to the door.

"It's you, my dear monsieur…come in!"

And Hector felt himself caught by that sympathy, of which, deep down, he thought himself unworthy. The physician had a remarkable gift of inspiring it in his clients. Did he not have a certain coefficient of obscure faith in the importance that invalids accord to a healer? It was the only credulity of the sportsman. It had rendered him the service of allowing him to confide his venereal misadventure to Doctor Bouret, the damage that compromised his health gravely in that crepuscular era. In any other circumstance he would have limited himself to the resources of his innate science and his immense conceit.

Hector therefore accepted cordially the hand that was held out to him. Then, on approaching, he recognized the Fortin household in the monsieur and the lady who were getting ready to depart. The husband had taken his companion's arm; the latter was, however, less pale and less thin; her stance, straighter and firmer, no longer stigmatized the mysterious suffering in his abdomen. By virtue of a residue of habit, Monsieur Fortin was sustaining her, helping her to avoid bumping into things, looking at her fondly with fearful adoration. She defended herself now, drawing herself up to her full height without pain, with a little healthy color in her cheeks, protesting her valor.

"No, my friend let me go. At least let me show Doctor Bouret and Monsieur Hector how strong I am and what a transformation my surgeon has produced in less than three weeks."

And she accomplished a few steps, going back and forth, turning without her husband's aid, her face glad and her upper body proud. She added: "A little more and I'll dance a waltz."

"Come on, my dear! Doctor Caresco recommended not committing any imprudence before a month. It's already very good that he's allowed us to quit his house before the usual term. It would be insensate to compromise, out of vanity, the success of his operation."

"What!" said Hector, "You've come from Caresco's clinic?"

"You didn't know, then?" And, confronted by the ignorance of his interlocutor, Monsieur Fortin, with the approval of his wife, who underlined his words with little satisfied inflections of the head, explained what had happened, the recent intervention, accomplished by the master of the scalpel and destined to modify entirely the existence of his dear invalid.

Hector ought to remember; it was the day after the visit to Claude's laboratory, a visit made in the company of Professor Domesta, that Madame Fortin had suddenly made up her mind and had entered Caresco's clinic, in spite of the advice of certain friends, even in spite of the advice of Doctor Bouret, who, in the circumstance, had been ill-advised to preach abstention. And they had not had to regret their sudden impetuousness; far from it.

One could not imagine a house better kept and more seductive, of a luxury that was represented even in the operating room, so white, so neat and so aseptic in its shiny sterilizers and nickel-plated instruments, so ingenious disposed and bathed in light. And with that, a huge Christ protecting the great surgeon's gestures with his infinite commiseration—for Caresco was very pious, although a Semite by origin, subsequently converted, and he was surrounded by good sisters.

Oh, the good sisters, how active, vigilant and caring they were! They trotted like ants, modest ants in white cornets, silent and gentle. One of them, above all, was remarkable in devotion and cares, and very useful to the surgeon, whom she adored like a God. Her name was Sister Cunegonde, and she directed the house. She could do everything, knew everything and saw everything. It was her who had come to collect Madame Fortin from her bed on the morning of the operation in order to take her to the immolation. She found so many kind words that they dispelled, so to speak, the minute of fear in which you were laid on the bed covered with a sheet as white as a shroud and the chloroform compress with the reek of cider was applied to the face. That was a nasty moment, though, all the same!

"As for Caresco," Monsieur Fortin continued, "let no one speak evil to me about him. It's astonishing that evil rumors can be spread on the count of a man who, with a twist of the hand, can render you a health that has been tottering for such a long time. I admire that man. I want to make a friend of him, although he caused me to pass a nasty quarter of an hour when, from the room next door to the one in which he was operating, I heard him giving orders, when I saw his gestures, and the busy activity of his entourage designed on a screen on the door of polished glass—and above all when that door open to give passage to Sister Cunegonde carrying bloody linen in a bucket...."

And before that tremulous vision, and the memory of his idol delivered to the knife, Monsieur Fortin, with a movement that he must have repeated many times during the anxious wait, compressed his head with his hands, applied in anguish behind his temples grown old overnight. But was it beneficial still to think about that, since everything had succeeded? Was it not better to forget that drama and think about the present, and the future that was opening up in an illumination of fecund joys?

He raised his head, looked at his wife, and started to smile.

"What enthuses me the most, you see, Monsieur Fargeaud, is not knowing that my wife might be able henceforth, as she says, to dance a waltz and do the splits. No, we also envisage other results more immediate, and our happiness will be complete when the children arrive that we both desire madly.

On seeing her secret ambition thus revealed, Madame Fortin had started to blush. She did not like her previous amorous dismissal discussed before Hector; that hope of maternity allowed the tenderness of the alcove to be imagined, the creative act for which a modest education had inculcated her with a false shame. But her husband did not pay any heed to the embarrassment he was causing and continued.

"Would you believe, Monsieur Hector, that when Madame Fortin and I were married, we scarcely had affection for one another. The sole reason for our accord had been a common desire for a family. That desire was so profound, so absolute, that it took on from the outset of our marriage the importance of a veritable hypnosis. During our walks, we could not pass one of those blond and curly heads that run through the streets without falling into admiration. We continued on our way, squeezing one another's arms more forcefully, thinking that our amour was going to give birth to similar bright and candid eyes, similar adorable mouths and infantile tyranny.

"Oh, it was a rude disappointment when we perceived our incapacity! Which of us was responsible? We didn't know, but we suspected one another reciprocally. We read medical books, after which we blamed one another. Our confidence diminished, or characters became embittered, and I don't know where that might have led us if my wife hadn't begun to suffer. It required her malady to render us newly amorous. Isn't that curious? But bah! That's no longer anything but a bad memory. And now, my dear Monsieur Bouret, in spite of your advice, we're going to have children, since Caresco has affirmed it.

His delight cooled when he had observed that the physician remained skeptical. The creasing of the two bushy black eyebrows indicated incredulity. Monsieur Fortin attributed that reserve to a slight ruffling of self-respect, which was not impossible even in a great heart combined with a sound intelligence. In order not to manifest rancor, he shook the physician's hands warmly, thanking him again.

The latter, however, as he accompanied his client to the door while observing again the proud stance of the lady, shook

166

his head. He remained no less convinced that conception would be impossible henceforth. The examination carried out a little while before had clearly revealed to him the knavery of the clever Caresco, who, having promised an innocent operation, had, either by virtue of dilettantism or real surgical necessity, carried out a complete ablation of the maternal organs and ensured Madame Fortin's sterility.

A quarter of an hour later, Hector quit the doctor's study in his turn. The unexpected manifestation of a few stigmata of his secret disease had led to a new prescription, which he was holding in his hand. His face had darkened at the recommendations that the doctor had made. Chastity was a great deprivation of his appetite, ever awake with an unhealthy insatiability. And then, what would become of his collection, already rarefied by two years of relative continence?

The practitioner, who did not lack psychology, had few illusions about the observance of the abstinence he had just prescribed. However, he had been categorical in exposing the consequences of debauchery, not the least of which was the possibility of contagion. Almost immediately, it was given to him to pose another. Benjamin, his sixth child, arrived at a run in all the supple and agile force of his young limbs. He had a proud complexion and a boldness in his gaze. He approached without embarrassment, saluted the visitor, and then seized his father's hand seductively; a great tenderness emanated from their reciprocal adoration. With a gesture elevated to the level of the child's head, the physician estimated his statue, already considerable.

"Eleven years old! See, Monsieur, he's already something of a citizen. He goes to class, he's good. His hours of liberty he devotes to doing the gardening. And later, what will you do, child?"

"Later," relied the child, proudly, "I'll be a laborer. I'll have fields and plows, and I'll push the plowshare, cracking the whip, Hup, dia!"

And with a raised arm, the child brandished an imaginary whip. He seemed so determined, so serious, that Hector could not help laughing. But the doctor's grave lips murmured a sentence:

"There, my dear Monsieur, are joys that you will no longer be permitted."

"Which? Those of pushing a plow? Thank God!"

"No, not those. But of creating, of enabling little fellows like my Benjamin to grow, you must no longer think. At forty-five, your illness would render you a dangerous parent."

"Thank you for the advice, Doctor; but for the desire that I experience..."

"My duty was to warn you," the honest man concluded, showing the damaged individual out.

With his hand on the steering wheel, Hector released the brake and put the automobile into first gear. The motor shuddered, backfired noisily, exhaled, and then, with a more even rhythm, the vehicle drew away over the bumps in the pavement. The city filed past in rapid flight, the houses glided in a uniform flamboyance of sunlight. The monuments, so rich in legend, passed by; but this time, no more than any other, Hector did not spare them a glance.

Then there was the high road that extended, clumps of trees and small houses with incandescent tiles, so rapidly left behind, drowned in the wake of dust, that everything dissolved in a blinding and furious vision. Protected by his mask, the sportsman's mobile eyes no longer had any other anxiety than that of equilibrating his machine, directing his course surely and hastily. The physician's advice was scattered with the white dust lifted by the wheels, likewise sticking to the asperities of the road, remaining at the corners of houses. Soon, there was no more trace of it.

The forest of Roumare had been traversed almost in its entirety, and after a descent near a village named Saint-Martin, a château appeared behind a grove of poplars: the very modern château of Madame de Berge, the ardently covetous young widow, who had conserved from her wrestling match with Hector such a memory of a caressant embrace that she had already manifested he desire several times to welcome into intimacy the cavalier that she had felled.

"Madame is suffering…Madame cannot receive…Madame regrets…," said a footman summoned by two rings of the exterior bell announcing a visit.

Hector darted a rapid glance over the uniformed servant, whose face was amplified by broad red side-whiskers. The fellow was imposing; he had a far more ceremonious breadth than Louis, the Fargeauds' domestic. Behind his bulk, filling the doorway, the vestibule had a grandiosity, and banisters in sculpted wood extended toward the upper floor. Panoplies of precious arms accredited the nearby richness of drawing rooms. Hector uttered a sigh and was about to retire when the appearance of a pretty soubrette, coming down the stairs rapidly, gave him hope again that his presence had been signaled to the mistress of the house.

In fact, the pretty face approached smiled and then asked: "Is it really Monsieur Hector Fargeaud?"

"In person, my beauty."

"Would Monsieur care to follow me?"

She headed for the first floor. Hr slimness, the quivering grace of her hips and her ankles, from which the strong legs departed in black stockings, indicated the presence of treasures that the visitor would not have disdained. Although more harmonious, the girl was reminiscent of Rose, Clara Boswett's chambermaid. She explained in a respectful and low tone that Madame was not, in fact, receiving, having been suffering for a fortnight, but that, at the announcement of an automobile, she had thought that it might be Monsieur Fargeaud, and had given the order that, for him, the regulation could be infringed.

Hector listened to her, while gazing at her and smiling. Then there was the coquetry of a dressing room hung with mauve silk, which welcomed him before he penetrated into the bedroom, from which the young widow was already calling to him. Intimate utensils still filled with perfumed water were lying around, vases disposed for a secret hydrotherapy, and the

169

sight of them was not displeasing to him; his nostrils dilated as he inhaled.

"Excuse the disorder, my dear monsieur. My bedroom door is sealed and I had to oblige you to pass before those horrors..."

"Not at all...on the contrary..."

"But I'm receiving you as a comrade. Come in, then!"

Clad in an elegant vapor of sky blue muslin, she was lying on a chaise-longue net to the bed, of which a small baldaquin scarcely draped with two narrow silk curtains allowed all the richness and amplitude to be perceived. Before kissing the hand that she held out to him and taking his place on a mobile stool, Hector had time to accord the room a circular glance, to admire the harmony of the Empire style, the solid mahogany furniture ornamented by gilding, the marvelous clock-case with a visible pendulum, the cadence of which went between the colonettes of two heavy standard lamps. In a corner, a display case exhibited adorable trinkets of the epoch. A few paintings, a large Watteau panel and engravings on wood diversified the severity of the walls.

He sat down, extending his legs. "You've been suffering, then?"

"Yes a little annoyance quite common among women. But thanks to the good care of Madame Poupe, who comes to see me every day from Paris, I'm now almost better."

"Madame Poupe?"

"A doctress."

Madame Poupe? Hector reawakened in a corner of his memory that troubling vocable, belonging not to a doctress but to an equivocal midwife with the eyes of a bird of prey, a sorceress with hooked fingers whose specialty consisted of effacing the imprudence of lovers. Twice the matron's stylet, exercised on one of his mistresses, had aided him to escape the threat of paternity. Each time, simultaneously, the maker of angels had relieved his purse of twenty-five louis. The memory came back to him, all the crueler because it was accompanied by an affliction of his parsimony.

"You haven't had recourse to Doctor Bouret, then?" he persisted, to give more weight to his nascent conviction.

"No. Women have our complexion and understand better how to care for those miseries. I haven't asked for him."

In an indifferent manner, pierced nevertheless by the care of not allowing her questioner to engage in the path of indiscretion, she quickly changed the subject, recalling the amusement of the picnic that had been enlivened by their wrestling match.

"We fought rather well, eh? Were you thrown sufficiently? Didn't I make your shoulders touch rather shamefully? You have a revenge to take."

"I'll take it on another terrain," he said, conceitedly, "And you'll see whether I'm the weaker!"

The soubrette had slipped away some time before. He advanced his hand, as if unconsciously, toward her arm, which was dangling, stiff and sinewy, with rough dark skin. Then, having take possession of it, he squeezed it ardently without her resisting. He followed, through the veil of sky blue silk, the quiver of sensual augury that his contact caused to pass along the angular body. He saw his carnal invitation make the lungs pant and the breasts quiver, and climb with electric shocks all the way to the eyes, which became serious, ceased and revulsed, almost swooning.

Meanwhile, they chatted, they talked about other things, races, and theaters, exteriorizing a conversation motivated by a determined countenance, but which was belied by the more active pressure of he hands, the tickling of a fluid soon destined to exasperate their senses. However, the most elementary prudence counseled them on either part to momentary chastity. Fortunately, a heavy tread was heard in the next room, a rustle of skirts and heavy respiration.

"That's Madame Poupe; she never has herself announced," murmured the widow, modifying her attitude abruptly.

Hector turned his head and saw the woman appear. They were definitely the raptorial eyes that he knew. Their mercan-

171

tile intensity summarized the entire face; they shone as cruelly as two needle-sharp stylets. The outrageously black tress of a wig dominated them, shining the ears and going to join up behind the nape in a little curly twist. Beneath it the amplitude of an unhealthy, yellow-tinted fat unfurled, confounding the drooping nose, the mouth and the chin in the same sphericity, in which orifices and swollen appendices were drowned in the adipose bellows of the neck. The body, piled up on itself, clad in black silk with a floral pattern, was carved in a single block, so ample in the figure that one might have thought the corset lacking. The right hand was holding a large umbrella with a stork's-head handle, and from the left hand, gloved in white cotton, hung a reticule in which surgical instruments were clinking.

By virtue of what insouciance had Madame de Berge addressed herself to that matron, whose grotesquerie was only matched by her dubious cleanliness? Hector thought that the advertisement on page four of a newspaper of "discretion and propriety" had doubtless influenced the young widow's choice, as it had influenced his own.

In any case, the raptorial eyes did not seem to have recognized him. Madame Poupe leaned over her client heavily and kissed her forehead. "How pretty you are in that state of undress, my darling!"

The invalid endured the kiss; then, with a little scarcely dissimulated thrust of her lace handkerchief, she wiped away its damp trace. She was utterly contrite at having to support that scene of familiarity before Hector. What would the gentlemen augur from that conduct? Would he believe the explanation that made the repulsive matron a doctress? Would not so much effusion between the physician and her patient give rise to suspicions that would also be confirmed by her prolonged repose on the chaise-longue, the few imprudent words she had emitted at the outset regarding the nature of her suffering and the sight of the apparatus negligently exposed in the dressing-room?

The little ironic smile with which Hector gratified her tacit anxiety signified that she was right to doubt her visitor's credulity. She was very frightened, because she had read in the newspapers many times the story of judiciary entanglements following a simple denunciation. Trapped in her anxiety, adopting a new tactic, in order to deflect the presumption that she divined to be increasingly close to certainty, she confided aloud a symptom foreign to her illness.

"I feel a slight pain in the back, Madame Poupe. It's necessary for you to ausculate me."

"I have everything necessary here," replied the matron, who did not understand, indicating her reticule.

"Right! I'll leave you with your doctor," said Hector, emitting a little burst of complicit laughter.

Then, after having kissed the widow's hand, he retired, promising not to delay his return too long. As he passed through the dressing room he inhaled once again the aroma of the liquids contained in the bottles on the dressing table. Their odorous subtlety only served to mask antiseptics. Behind the charm of the perfume lurked the microbicide, the poison destructive of lives, embryonic lives destined one day, with the aid of fecundation, to become human lives.

He imagined the first movement of the amorous woman, when her senses were reanimated by the voluptuous *petit mort*. Without taking the trouble to dress, without even knotting her hair, fallen over the sinewy thinness of her still-quivering shoulders, in fear of the child, he saw her hastily having recourse to the destructive hydrotherapy. Her attitude, almost kneeling, would have been ridiculous if the anguish of the moment had not transformed her into a caryatid of fear. And yet, that frantic vigilance did not prevent the consequences reliably, since Madame Poupe had been obliged to intervene.

Nevertheless, Hector appreciated the care which rendered the meager esthetic of the widow more precious to him. He passed on, breathing deeply.

Thus nature, in spite of various hostilities, in spite of resistance inspired in men by solely egotistical lust, still launched semen, in its marvelous and absurd determination, and reached the creative goal. And its power was so great, its prodigality so stubborn, that in spite of precautions and obstacles created by social disfavor, and in spite of restrictions imposed by thought contrary to its brutal materialism it still arrived at its ends, still determined the obscure moment in which fecundation triumphed.

Then, in order to struggle against its obstinacy, the cruelest effort of intelligence was required: murder was necessary. Madame de Berge, so apt for creation, provided with such ardent instincts that solicited its accomplishment, and, on the other hand, so constrained by her egotism and the prejudices of opinion to prevent the eventuality, was one of those telling examples of the human paradox, the deplorable action of society conducting the individual to the supreme crime against life.

As soon as he had climbed into his automobile, Hector took out his watch, and observed that it was already five o'clock. That was the moment fixed for his rendezvous with Marthe Servant. The schoolteacher, after many hesitations, had ended up promising a meeting at the Epinettes tavern. She was to have gone in, under the pretext of refreshing herself after a walk, so that the encounter would seem entirely fortuitous, and would not lend itself to any malevolent interpretation. Nevertheless, in spite of the respect to which he was engaged, Hector hoped to draw the young woman into a private cabinet and retain her there to dinner. With the aid of a little champagne, he would finally reckon with a resistance by which his conceit was beginning to be astonished. He impelled his machine, and launched once again into the wooded countryside, which had become heavier and more depressing.

The tavern was situated on the water's edge. Beside the road, its roughcast white façade was distinguished by the deployment of a crudely illuminated sign representing rubicund and stout men at table before a bottle whose cork was springing forth in the midst of splashing foam. Behind, going down to the Seine, there was a meadow burned by the sun, equipped with rustic arbors garnished with tables and overheated benches, empty at present. Swings and games of boule remained inactive. A large Newfoundland dog, old and mangy, panting in the heat, its drooling tongue dangling, was collapsed in a shady corner. The vicinity of the water, the current of which rippled slowly, as if it too were fatigued by the torrid day, only left the illusion of freshness at that location.

Hector quit his vehicle outside, and while Arthur gave the engine the cares of the halt, he made a tour of the two common rooms in which peasants were drinking cider, prolonged his inspection as far as the arbors, and, not finding the person he was hoping to encounter, waited before a glass of absinthe.

He waited for two hours, still thinking that he might see her arrive, untiringly sustained in his expectation by his conceit. Never, during the numerous checks of his life replete with intrigues, during long moments spent looking out for the arrival of imaginary conquests, had he admitted that his ugliness and his miserliness might be the cause of the disappointments he experienced. In order to excuse them he had a marvelous imagination. He found original pretexts; he invented obstacles, unfortunate accidents, or the intervention of some lover or a jealous husband. He created those hindrances with such sincerity that he ended up believing in them.

When, importuned, sickened and, much of the time, fatigued by hoping for a remunerative generosity that was never manifest, a rebellious woman told him to go away, and threw him into the street, he still exculpated his disappointment by means of a corrective ingenuity. Doubtless the woman feared loving him too much and not being recompensed for the gift she made of her body by an equal amour; or she was rejecting him because of the foresight of her heart, in order not to have to suffer from his donjuanism. Thus, he had acquired he habit of long waits. He even found a certain spice in them. His mentality, always in erethism, prepared and caressed imminent debauches therein.

At seven o'clock, not having seen anyone arrive, but still hoping, he ordered dinner. The daylight was belatedly prolonged. The enchantment of sunset was pompously organized over the dentellate hills. Decorations of crimson, turquoise and mauve expanded in a prodigality of colored stripes. An apotheosis of gilded fringes departed from a red bulb and lost in infinity enchanted the location, making contours more precise before the star, as it sank, terminated the spectacle. But those splendors did not impress him. He ate without appetite, his gaze incessantly borne toward the bend in the road from which he still hoped to see the desired apparition emerge, in her robust blonde slimness.

A cup of bad coffee indisposed him against the meal, and at eight o'clock he got up and settled the bill. My God, what was he going do? Go home already, with the desired unsated that had caused him to travel the country, visit Madame de Berge, and spend three hours in a dirty tavern?

Then, the arrival of an unfamiliar mail-coach, filed with a joyous company coming to have supper at the Epinettes, caused him to remember Domesta. Had not the strange little man invited him, twice, to come and talk science with him. Did he not have at his property, scarcely two leagues away, an entire collection of pretty women who would open their arms to him? Another good fortune, with that; they were given hospitality by the professor; he might not even have to open his purse. That hope infused him with a new energy, and he was almost delighted when he rejoined his automobile, where Arthur was dining on the seat, on a crust of bread and a glass of alcohol.

The house of the master fecundator, situated in the environs of the village of Canteleu, near Rouen, was not, strictly speaking, a château, but a sort of characterless caravanserai erected in the middle of a vast and shady pleasure garden. Abundant woods and high walls isolated the habitation completely, protecting it from any importunate gaze, with the con-

176

sequence that, even from the road, one could not suspect the presence of a colony beyond the curtain of trees.

Hector spent a long moment searching for the bell dissimulated by the ivy of the wall. The darkness that had almost fallen, as much as the foliage, hid its presence, and he required the aid of one of his lanterns to discover it. After three appeals propagated by a rod of rusty iron, a valet in culottes appeared discreetly and demanded that he state his name.

The order to receive the visitor had probably been given in advance. The domestic opened the door, and with the same silent tread with which he had arrived, introduced him into the property.

To the right, in the opaque shadow, Hector vaguely distinguished the outbuildings. After a hundred paces, at a bed in the path, the house appeared, with the ground floor brilliantly illuminated, lights springing abundantly from wide open windows and distributing in the blackness of the garden great sheets of joyous clarity. At the same time a strange quavering soprano voice, hollowed out by gaps, escaped in sift and weary waves. Supported by the chords of a guitar, it was singing, with swooning modulations at the end of each line, "Santa Lucia," a barcarole popular in Italy, which players of nocturnal serenades trail along the watery routes of Venice bordered by princely facades, while the gondolier makes the surface radiant with stars quiver with the eddies of his graceful boat.

Hector paused for a moment, listening to the song which appeared to be coming from an old woman, doubtless the "Maman"; then, when the verse concluded, in the midst of enthusiastic applause, he turned to his guide with the intention of having himself announced; but the domestic had disappeared. Then, deliberately, he climbed the perron, traversed a vestibule, and pushed the door of the drawing room from which the noise and light were coming. The spectacle that he perceived filled him with surprise.

Occupying the center of a circular divan, Domesta resumed the second verse of the barcarole. Seated, with his legs crossed, simultaneously supporting the predominance of his

177

pear-shaped abdomen and the guitar that he was plucking with professional gestures, he was raising toward the heavens his little replete round head, which an abundant wig of long blond hair covered for the occasion. In addition, his face was made up, painted like a young woman's. The peeled eyebrows had been replaced by a circumflex accent traced in kohl; the lips, ordinarily absent and withdrawn into the mouth, were designed this time in carmine. A bright red velvet jacket, put on over a green silk chemise, culottes and black stockings, completed his costume and gave him an epic appearance of a Neapolitan singer.

Beside him, similarly made-up and dressed, was Cyrano, the pretty young man with the curly hair undulating in thick brown tresses. Around them, in various poses, covered in the multicolored frills of a hospitable house, holding one another by the waist and saddened by the melancholy of the song, were all the women of the seraglio: first the tall brunette Carmen, her temples bloodied by geraniums; then Mascotte, the blonde, anemically pale in spite of her make-up; and Sarah, the red-haired Jewess whose poor greasepaint was cracking; and Marquisette, gracious, frail and charming, with her Botticelli profile; and also Mignon, gilded with Venetian reflections. In a corner, Bamboula, the African woman, whom the music did not interest, was keeping the ever-dignified Madame company, who was knitting stockings.

Domesta was finishing his second verse when he perceived the visitor, but the moment was too solemn for him to suspend a trill, the execution of which made him stock out his neck like a bird, and the emission of which he accompanied with a lofty gesture of his stout and monastic hand. He even made Hector the tribute of his final notes, uttering them in his direction. Then having finished, disdainful of the applause, after having confided his guitar to Cyrano, he hurried forward.

"*Favoritas, Signor, favoritas!* It's kind of you to come!"

At the same time he extended his hands and drew Hector with an entirely southern effusion to a seat in which he obliged him to sit down. The women flocked around the gentleman.

Each one kissed him and interrogated him, taking pleasure in a temporary contact with exterior life, with the male, of which the claustral severity of the domain had deprived them for a month. Yes, truly, they confessed that there had been a lack, in spite of the broad wellbeing, the good food, the daily excursions in the mail-coach, and in spite of the presence of Cyrano. Delighted, Hector allowed himself to be surrounded and fêted, accepting as a tribute to his person that overflow of enthusiasm exclusively provoked by a unaccustomed deprivation. He distributed kisses and fluttering caresses right and left. His mobile eyes blinked.

"Yes, my princesses, yes! I love you all...all of you! Are you content?"

Domesta, however, protested anxiously. He moved them away, obliged them to return to more decent sentiments, to persevere in the chastity that they had suffered thus far without default, for the triumph of his scientific experiments. He had seized the arms of Carmen, the most ardent, who wanted sit on the gentleman's knees, and Bamboula, who, having taken off her bright yellow peignoir, was impudently displaying the fuliginous pride of her flesh with a customary audacity and wiggling her tongue. He pushed both of them away, deflecting them from masculine peril, fluting and lisping, hilarious in his gaudy ornamentation.

"Will you remain tranquil! A little patience, damn it! Another fortnight and I'll permit you...you'll have the right, yes, the right...even the duty!"

And turning to Hector, half-laughing and half-irritated, he reproached him for falling upon him like a cock in a henhouse.

"My experiments, Signor! You're going to compromise my experiments! Here, we're a family, they must remain your sisters as they are Cyrano's sisters, aren't they, my dear Cyrano?"

With the back of his plump hand he caressed the undulating brown hair of the handsome head. Finally, Madame— "Maman"—having resumed some authority over her boarders

179

having commanded them to dignity in a serious manner, they obeyed and returned to their places around the circular divan; and the soirée was prolonged for a further hour, Hector participating therein with the worldly reserve from which he would not have departed in the milieu of a salon.

Domesta had picked up his guitar again, and again he emitted in his guttural soprano voice, which failed at times, no longer pagan songs but liturgies, pious *Ave Marias* and *O salutaris hostias*, such as one hears in chapels. The ladies took them up in chorus, and in spite of the hoarseness and falsetto of their voices, one sensed a grave and contained emotion in them, impregnated with evocations of mystic piety, a return to childhood hours when hands were joined before symbolic altar ornamented with gold and plumed with incense; they melted into the unreal, the immense unknown of the troubling after-life.

When nine o'clock chimed, two valets brought iced drinks. Domesta got up, slid his guitar into a case, and then, taking a little bottle from his pocket, approached the table where he cups had been deposited. One by one the courtesans approached, took a glass and held it out, in order for him to mix ten drops from his bottle therein. Then they had to drink the liquid before his eyes.

Hector expressed his astonishment.

"It's a soporific, Signor, in order that they don't have bad thoughts. My experiment, you understand…?"

"Ah! It's very good, that," proclaimed the gentleman, whose hope that practice disappointed.

"*Fate bene, trovate bene; fate male, trovate male,*" Italianized the professor, measuring his diction without any evident reason.

The narcotic had an almost immediate effect. Eyes grew heavy, and Madame had to sustain Mignon, who was falling asleep as she walked. A retreat was effected to the vestibule, where candle-trays had been prepared. Carmen, less sensitive to opium, had a return of imploring tenderness toward Hector, and tried to whisper her plea in his ear, but Domesta, having perceived that she was indicating the third window on the right on the first floor, sent her to bed brutally. The procession of polychromatic peignoirs, dimly illuminated by the candles, went upstairs, with Madame at the head, and disappeared in a dismal retreat.

"Now, Signor, I render you your liberty," signified the poussah, escorting Hector toward the exterior.

They went out. Domesta had taken Cyrano's arm and was leaning on it languidly. They walked slowly along a part of the path that led to the gate. Hector saw the valets extinguishing the lights on the ground floor, while the rooms on the first floor were illuminated successively, and weary shadows passed back and forth behind the screen of the blinds. However, the third window to the right opened, and Carmen appeared in a nightgown, and blew him a kiss. The irruption of Madame, whose majestic presence was divined rather than seen, caused the ardent boarder to withdraw immediately.

"Don't look, Signor; it's futile," said Domesta, his strangely accentuated lips smiling, the redness of which had become black in the penumbra, under the cascade of hair, which gave him, in contrast with the iridescent powder that covered his cheeks, the mask of an old wanderer of the nocturnal boulevards.

"Later," he said, "you'll make up for your repressed desire. Desire, Signor, is the sole spice of sensuality. Return home. I permit you to recount what you have seen, if you desire to do so."

"What would I recount?" stammered the gentleman. "I don't understand any of it!"

"That's true, poor fellow—he doesn't understand...doubtless the thought that all those women...oh how mistaken he is! I ,Signor, am a great scientist, and the women...oh, the women, oh, my little Cyrano..."

He only finished his thought for his companion by expressing it as a more energetic squeeze of the arm. Then, Hector, increasingly stupefied as the eccentric individual spoke, heard him restate his method, recount his practices, and affirm the glorious goal of science and life that he was pursuing. Soon, a communication to the Biological Society, to the Academies and the Institut would reveal the surprising result of his irrefutable experiments: how, on terrain seemingly so hostile to fecundation, he had, after a month of rural chastity, sown by means of his method the good seed—Cyrano's—and succeeded in creating, thanks to his implements—"sterilized, Signor, sterilized!"—at the whim of his will, boys or girls, brown-haired or blond, in accordance with the epoch and the time, and above all in accordance with the incontestable influence of the moon.

Today, it had been Mignon's turn, and she had resisted, the child; but that would not prevent her, the moon being red, the weather dry and the date very near, from having a blond boy. In addition, the nature of alimentation was as important as the sight of ambient objects. That was why, for a fortnight, Mignon would be nourished on roast meats, potatoes, carrots and asparagus. Furthermore, her eyes, as they closed for slumber, would import into her dreams the spectacle of a phallus set above her bed, which also disposed to the creation of a male.

Sarah, for her part, desired a girl. She was presented at each meal with the pancreas of a calf or a lamb, green vegetables, oranges and aubergines. She would, on going to sleep, dream about the hips of the pretty woman depicted by the engraving decorating her alcove. At the same time, in order to correct by means of a sort of plastic suggestion what the Semitic face sometimes offered of the disgraceful, the young woman in question bore a spicy Parisienne head with a slightly turned-up nose.

That was how children would be made henceforth, if the world would consent to emerge from the rut of custom in order to rise into the more positive spheres of science.

These charlatanesque ramblings were proffered with such assurances that Hector, a paradoxical mind incessantly led only to conceive phenomena eccentrically and to accept it as the concrete verity, already added credence to them. Later, he would become a convinced partisan of those crude subterfuges, he would disperse the legend among the public of dupes or illuminates that the scientific masquerade convinces easily. He even accepted the deceit of the kind of chaste life that Domesta led in the midst of his seraglio, the eccentric asceticism whose deviation, summarized in the person of Cyrano, was easy to suspect.

He took the hand of the fecundator and, in a manner penetrated by the utmost sincerity, wished him bonsoir.

"Go, Signor, and I don't discourage you from recounting that I am a scientist, and not a schemer, as people say."

"I shall recount it, Doctor."

Arthur was asleep on the seat of the automobile. Hector took the wheel, which oscillated between his enervated fingers.

The afternoon's pursuit of an impossible satisfaction, first the enervating skirmish with Madame de Berge, then waiting for Marthe Servant, and then, to complete the exasperation, the caressant, perfumed, vicious and colorful brush with those women, all of whom, including the black woman, had taken their place in the panels of his collection—all of that had irritated his bulimia, pushed him to the final pitch of frenzy.

Hesitant, overheated, he gazed at the countryside. To the left, the red moon had just disappeared, and there was a black collapse, a sky crushed by large, opaque clouds, presages of an imminent storm, extending like a veil before his voluptuous impossibility. To the right, by contrast, there was a vague, distant illumination, suspected rather than actual, describing a pallor in the enigma of the horizon. Was that the incandescence of Paris awakening to its nocturnal pleasures? That pale stain, which was only a dot in the immensity, grew in Hector's eyes, took on the importance of a conflagration that a few hours of travel would bring nearer, which he could rapidly reach with his engine activated by twenty horsepower. He saw again the streets and boulevards, flamboyant at present, and the prostitution overflowing from houses and pouring variegated temptations on to the asphalt of the great arteries.

Yes, reaching Paris would compensate him for his successive disappointments, open the safety-valve on his intimate boiling, his compressed senses.

He turned to Arthur. He suspected him, so thin, so emaciated and perhaps so lit up, that he wondered how he was going to support the night of vigil and waiting that he was about to impose on him—because, for reasons of economy, the gentleman did not put his vehicle in a garage during his nights of adventure, and Arthur remained on the seat. But once again he stifled the rudiments of his pity.

"We're going to Paris, Arthur."

"Let's go!"

And on the road creaking with dust, after the luminous traversal of Rouen, there were two and a half hours of mad travel through the blackness—enervating, bruising, exhausting travel—toward the pallor of the horizon. The machine spat out its effort in panting breath. The storm seemed to be pursuing them; it gained ground, extended and rumbled, without attaining them. The headlights striped the shadow with a scattering of fluid, and nocturnal moths struck by the impact of the rapid vehicle broke their wings thereon. Toward what ill-fated flame was he racing, too, in order to annihilate himself therein?

He went like a whirlwind, balancing his engine with the precision of a tightrope-walker, unconscious of danger, the catastrophes that were lurking at the bends in the road, the insults with which the drivers of heavy market-gardeners' carts, brushed by the monster, saluted his furious passage. The more the slopes rose or descended, the more the houses loomed up in the black phantasmagoria, and the more the machine activated its thrust, belching its gasoline breath, the more the pale stain was magnified, which sometimes disappeared, only to reappear again closer, like the incandescence of a great sensual crater.

Pont-de-l'Arche, Gaillon and Vernon filed past thus, and villages of which he did not even know the names. People sitting on their doorsteps, respiring the cool nocturnal air, cried folly, mothers shuddered and clasped their children against them. Mantes was only a vision; Saint-Germain, Le Vesinet and Rueil passed in a vertigo. Then there was the descent from Suresnes, the brief stop and declaration at the customs barrier, next to a night café from which the shrill voice of a singer emerged, supported by a string orchestra. The foliage of the Bois de Boulogne was animated by a few streaks of light, encounters with rapid automobiles and slow fiacres in which enlaced couples were kissing.

Then Paris surged forth, the terraces of the Porte-Maillot swarming with customers, their forecourts cluttered with vehicles and bicycles; and the grave mass of the Arc de Triomphe at the summit drowned by storm; and the Avenue des Chanps-Élysées, at the end of which the Place de la Concorde spread out sumptuously illuminated. In the environs, open air concerts were underlined by a variegation of girandoles and posters, by bursts of orchestral music, by all the thunder of the fête, all the ardent racket of inferior recreations. Finally, the great boulevards: Hector stopped his machine in front of the Opéra. He was chewing dust; he was thirsty. He took off his mask and his overcoat and leapt on to the sidewalk.

"A beer, Arthur?"

"A grog, rather."

"Give my chauffeur a grog," he ordered a waiter who hastened forth.

Now, a first glass of beer hastily absorbed, seated before a second beer, embellished with a collar of white foam, his nostrils taut and his eyes avid, Hector took pleasure in reanimating his frisson at the spectacle of the movement of the world. In the foreground, on the sidewalk, in an uninterrupted flood, all the seekers of joy and all the miseries to which they delivered themselves went past. There were patrons of the Opéra or the theaters, still open, ladies in evening gowns going to supper on the arms of young or old cavaliers; foreigners unleashed by travel agencies, strolling in bewilderment; howling newsvendors; enlivened bourgeois couples; provocative prostitutes with dyed hair and projecting hips; pale, equivocal, asexual young men; an entire mélange, a confusion of suits, bright dresses and ragged garments, a display of provincial exoticism, a whirl of heads in top hats and straw hats—all of that coming and going, rubbing shoulders, squeezing and confounding wealth and poverty, vice and virtue, drawn away in the same luminous turbulence. And behind, on the causeway, the encumbrance was no less, with the snorting of horses drawing carriages, the trotting of fiacres, victorias and delivery carts, a plethoric and prosaic embarkation for Cythera taking couples toward amorous destinations.

Hector inhaled the flux and reflux of that human tide. Everything that passed, he appropriated to his sensual hypnosis. Female rumps, gazes with gleams illuminated bizarrely by electricity, the bright patches of skirts, smiles that burst forth in carmine mouths, and evocatively swaying hips all alimented his desire; he threw them into the seething cauldron of his exasperation. He transformed the most innocent visions in order to feed his frenzy. His innate hysteria was charged with fluid on contact with ambulant prostitution, with nearby lasciviousness suspected in the movements and gestures of that living cinematograph, which was about to be extinguished where the alcove opened.

He recognized several friends dissolved in the crowd, club companions; women were leaning on their arms, their eyes and necks inclined. He leaned back in order not to be recognized. Their presence would have harmed the prompt realization of his piercing desires. He paid for his drinks, swiftly resumed his place in his vehicle, and aimed the machine toward the Place Blanche.

There, in a café noisy with music, on the terrace and inside, artists, painters, students and imprecise individuals, the fake needy of art and science, were gossiping. Amid the clouds of tobacco smoke and the rage of violins, alcoholic voices rose up in hoarse exclamations, songs and laughter, only dominated by the noisy clinking of saucers propelled by the busy personnel. Young women scarcely coiffed in straw boaters, some harmonious and undulating, doubtless models, were coming and going, smiling provocatively in a rustle of fabrics. There were old women whose make-up redecorated them with an illusion of youth; there were young ones whose make-up gave them the pretention of aged vice. An entire meat-stall was extended there, in dirty red leather banquettes, a fairground of lust, a market of joy whose rarest pieces were not the newest.

How many miseries there were behind those garish costumes, how much distress behind the tempting smiles, how many tears on the edge of those eyelids darkened by kohl! They waited, in front of glasses of liquor, on the lookout for the louis that they would abandon tomorrow to the teeth of the money-lender, their hands only retaining the trace of it; the hard-won metal fled them, as if from a barrel of the Danaïdes. They were the worst of the oppressed, the slave laborers of the great convict prison of amour.

Hector spotted an aged procuress, a celebrated courtesan under the Empire, who now subsisted lamentably selling fans and earning a few coins from the sales of flesh that she facilitated. Her name was Mina. He knew her; she was his supplier. He called to her.

"Mina! Come and sit down for a moment."

"What are you paying for?" the wretch demanded, sitting down

"Whatever you want."

"An absinthe, then."

She opalized the liquor methodically. An ethyl breath passed through her broken and fuliginous teeth. As she leaned over, a thousand wrinkles were designed in the skin of her neck, tanned and stretched. Her arm, bent in order to pour the water betrayed the distress of her bodice, perforated by wear and tear.

"Have you anything new?" Hector asked,

"Yes, look over there. A pearl!"

She pointed at a blonde woman, neatly dressed, who got up at her summons and came toward them, taking care not to snag her dress on the customers' chairs. Then Hector laughed, for he had just recognized, as she arrived, the daughter of the Grignons. Arthur's sister Alphonsine.

"Alphonsine! No! She's very good!"

"You've already had her, then?" asked Mina. "They've all had her, this kid!"

Discreetly and politely, Alphonsine had taken her place. She declared that she was glad to see the master again, but she wanted to know his intentions right away, because she didn't have a minute to lose, being very busy and careful not to waste her time in futile chat. Then Mina declared her admirable in the order of economy. She confessed all her regret at not having conducted herself likewise. Surely, Alphonsine must be on the road to fortune, since she "lifted" a man every evening, and worked even in the daytime. She was making a métier, wasn't she? A métier like the others, like those who gave lessons, or practiced millinery or couture. Her body was her capital, and she cared for it, surrounding it with a thousand precautions and avoiding contagions. And she was quite right, for later, she would have an income.

"That's true," admitted the laborious prostitute. "I never offer myself any caprice. It's not the temptation that I lack, but it's necessary to think of the future. When one is old, men no longer think about you."

She took her handkerchief from a reticule, carefully, in order to wipe her lips. The bag, left ajar, allowed a battery of intimate toilet apparatus to be divined, and other utensils that were protective devices. All of that was meticulously arranged and packaged. Hector, remembering the same measures uselessly taken by Madame de Berge, started to smile.

"Arthur's here, waiting for me outside," he confided.

"That's nice," replied Alphonsine, serenely. "I'll go and say bonsoir to him."

She had a good heart; she did not neglect her family; she sent them money. But she forgot to enquire about her other relatives. She truly did not have time to waste. She concluded the price, after having haggled a little, and honestly handed Mina her commission. Then, followed by her cavalier, she took the velvet-carpeted stairway that led to the private cabinets. Before entering, fearing too arduous a task, she wanted to recruit a companion; there were a number present who could be obtained cheaply; but Hector refused.

Behind the suspect walls, in the cabinet hung with cretonne, with mirrors striped with entwined initials and the names of girls, on the divan with fatigued springs, they renewed the work of sterile lust accomplished everywhere around them, and in the big cities and the rural areas gained by civilization, and abroad, everywhere that wealth facilitated egotism and enjoyment.

Thus, in consequence of the imprudent generosity of nature, the beautiful seed was squandered and dispersed, deflected from its original goal. And there was, accomplished once more, the counterpart of its madly absurd abundance, the lure of pleasure that it had linked inseparably to its dissemination.

XI

Julia, the Servants' farm-girl, arrived at Monsieur Fortin's house, and remained hesitant momentarily, uncertain of the fashion in which she ought to announce her arrival. The habitation, very modern, two stories high, formed the corner of a street in Rouen, and two doors, one large and one small, gave access to a neat sidewalk paved with blue sandstone, which a fine drizzle poured out incessantly by a low and heavy sky varnished with a streaming glaze. At each of the doors Julia remarked a bell-cord. Which was it necessary to pull? The worthy young woman oscillated, perplexed, desolate at being unaware, at the first step, the proprieties of the city. She deposited on the ground a wretched wicker basket containing the luggage of linen and effects that she had been able to pack in order to quit the farm and come to commence her service in the bourgeois home. Then, after having taken the time to draw breath for a moment, she smoothed her heavy pleated skirt falling over coarse ankle-boots of an unusual employ, and adjusted her white bonnet, neatly camped on the shock of her red hair.

Finally, determined to brave fate, she rang at the little door. Emotion made her heart beat faster and colored her full cheeks red, dotted with freckles. From inside, a domestic ran to open the door. But after having gripped her basket, she was hesitating again when Madame Fortin called from the vestibule: "Is that you, Julia? Come in, don't be afraid; no one's going to eat you. You'll do very well here."

"Better than out there, for sure!" she replied, this time rediscovering her fine laughter, which the deployment of her throat augmented as much as the healthy freshness of her mouth.

Then she went into the dwelling, walking on tiptoe. She no longer recognized the mistress of the house, whom she had seen suffering scarcely three months before, and whom she had been obliged to help and transport, in a faint, to her bed.

"My God! You're so changed, Madame!"

"Indeed, Julia, it's a true miracle. You remember how ill I was, and how I admired your strength! You picked me up like a feather...I weighed less then. But now I've had an operation that has returned my health."

A shadow of melancholy tinted the gaze of the pretty woman. She still praised her operation, but she put less enthusiasm into proclaiming the good results. Although the mastery of Caresco had eliminated the cause of her languor, it did not seem that the surgeon's prognosis on the subject of progeniture, which obsessed the household, would be confirmed. Two menstrual periods had gone by without anything indicating the realization of their wishes. However, immediately chasing away that bitter observation, Madame Fortin took the new maidservant to her room and gave her the first instructions.

"Here it is, Julia: you'll replace the chambermaid. You don't know anything about service, but don't worry. It will come quickly. You seem to be intelligent, and above all, a worthy young woman."

"I'll do my best, Madame. For sure I don't like quitting my place. If my master hadn't beaten me..."

At the memory of the thrashing that Père Servant had administered because she had dropped a basket of eggs, she started to weep. With a few kind words, Madame Fortin calmed that naïve dolor, in which she divined the credulous good faith of a wounded heart prompt to attachment. She wanted to undress her personally in order to rid her of everything that recalled her former servitude. While helping her to pass her arms through a supple woolen jersey, she admired under the coarse chemise the firmness of the upper body and the whiteness of the skin, where the transparency of delicately traced veins snaked at the birth of the breasts.

A corset abandoned by the previous chambermaid, which she succeeded in lacing, immediately designed the most har-

191

monious waist. The arms were plump and solid, padded with good flesh. A perfume of human animality emanated from the armpits, an acidulous aroma that she promised herself to modify subsequently by counseling simple elements of cleanliness. In ten minutes, Julia was transformed, and, seeing herself so pompous in the mirror she blushed with pleasure, with a grateful desire to hug her new employer. A simple and impulsive soul, she gave in to it. Secretly, Madame Fortin appreciated the rustic homage.

Then she took her to the kitchen. On the mosaic tiles, arabesques were interlaced on which Julia hardly dared to tread. On a line of hooks, the copper of saucepans shone. A cuckoo clock was hanging on the wall, which started to sing when she appeared. That was an unexpected, unsuspected luxury, which charmed her and gave her the most convincing evidence of hr social progress. She smiled at the cook and the coachman, who were about to constitute, with her, the entire staff. She was happy; she found, in that environment, scope for her innate elegance, which indicated the slimness of her waist, the graceful slenderness of her wrists and ankles, fixed to hands and feet damaged by vulgar tasks.

But Madame Fortin quit her; she advanced toward Julien Duverdon, who, having been invited to dinner, appeared in the vestibule in the company of Monsieur Fortin. The gentleman shook her hand gently and timidly; he extended his fine neck of a colossus, and caressed, with a familiar gesture, his long graying beard, which contrasted with his delicate and mild blue eyes. He had his usual attitude of gravity, was enveloped by a melancholy.

"Madame Duverdon isn't accompanying you?"

"Excuse my wife," he replied, effortfully. "At the moment when we were about to set out she was suffering slightly."

He blushed, for the memory of a painful altercation, even more than the dissimulation of the truth, had repercussions in his face. That morning, Rolande, after having accepted the Fortins' invitation, had suddenly changed her mind. She was obeying Clara, who preferred the solitary charm of a hunting party on the plain, under the aegis of Hector, who had become decidedly gracious toward the little couple. This time, Julien, stimulating his marital authority, had protested. Their superficial relationship was extended to breaking point. After years of constraint and dolorous indecision, Monsieur Duverdon had finally wearied of the complaisant role that was demanded of his weakness; a few small sharp shocks had served as preliminaries to that morning's scene.

Pleading at first and demanding afterwards, he had ordered Rolande to accompany him to Rouen. Stupefied by that will so suddenly manifest, she had refused dryly, for the American witnessed their argument. Her little mocking laugh had emphasized rather outrageously the supremacy of her friend, for which Julien experienced the bite of chagrin added to that of an amour always mocked. The germ of a resolution that opportunity would not take long to content was finally planted in his heart.

But all his cares ought not to offend the opinion of others. Julien temporarily dammed the flood that was ready to burst forth and resumed his appearance of debonair and resigned good humor. He accepted Madame Fortin's arm and the three of them went into the dining room. Under the influence of dull and rainy weather, the meal might have lacked gaiety, in spite of the succulence of the dishes, if the confusion of Julia, who was helping the valet de chambre to serve, had not distracted the guests somewhat. She deployed in the accomplishment of her task an expansive pride that combated amusingly with her inexperience. However, in spite of her awkward step, rendered heavy by the habit of wearing clogs and the exclamations that her inapt gestures, risking breaking a glass and overturning a dish of stewed fruit, caused her to utter, she nevertheless had a proud slimness of the upper body and a tawny aureole of hair that lit up the room triumphantly.

"What a pretty girl!" Monsieur Duverdon could not help exclaiming, at a moment when she had retired to the kitchen to fetch a dish.

"Excuse her awkwardness," begged Madame Fortin. "This morning she was still in the midst of her turkeys. But I believe her to be sufficiently intelligent and devoted enough to become an excellent maidservant. Women of her age adapt quickly to civilized habits."

"Above all," Monsieur Fortin insisted, "those who, like that girl, have almost aristocratic origins. Julia's father was, I'm told, a sub-officer of dragoons, who loved her mother sincerely and was loved. The child has retained from her ascendancy a remarkable purity of lines. It's not astonishing that the atavism in question has not been entirely dissipated by the vulgar habits of her childhood, denuded of education and instruction. There are mysterious laws of heredity that betray the will of life in making the creature resemble the creator, in spite of the physical and moral modeling imprinted by destiny."

"Let us hope, in any case," said Madame Fortin, "that she doesn't obtain from her mother such a highly-developed productive instinct. It appears that the poor woman brought a whole gang of children into the world. She offered herself to all and sundry."

"Keep watch on your husband, Madame," said the guest, laughing.

"Oh, I have confidence in him. We love one another, and understand one another."

The accord of the two spouses was expressed by a tender gaze filtering through the floral centerpiece that decorated the table. In fact, their adoration was completed by a beautiful comprehension of their characters, and by a reciprocal faith that no weakness could have eroded. Commenced in indifference, and deprived of the charming flirtation of the soul that precedes some marriages, their union had undergone two capital transformations, The first had been manifest from the outset when, having offered themselves to the communion of the senses, equally ignorant of sensuality, they had experienced exceedingly acute emotions. The astonishment and dazzlement of their nerves was so violent that they believed themselves to be endowed with a hyperesthesia unknown to mortals and esteemed themselves favored by a superhuman amour. Their frequent embraces repeated the surprise without causing them to weary of it.

It was then that Madame Fortin, perhaps by reason of those excessive vibrations, fell ill, and their passion was modified again. No longer having in his arms anyone but a wounded woman for whom the embrace had become painful, the husband became chaste again and applied himself to caring for her. He put an admirable devotion and forbearance into it, all the more so as his cares, if they were successful, might result in the child, the fruit of which they dreamed incessantly, the hope of which had dominated their dream during the tender age, their hopes during the marriage, and still attenuated their suffering during the illness. He was seen to be attentive, compassionate and more proven than her.

Whether at their country house or their house in Rouen, she never took a step without him, without being sustained by his vigorous arm, anticipating the slightest shock in walking, without being accompanied by his devoted gaze. He spent slow days of immobility next to her chaise-longue; he distracted her by reading to her; he set the table and encouraged her to eat. In the evening he laid her down, by night he watched over her slumber; and he adored her in a silent continence. They ran around medical consulting rooms, attempted a thousand fruitless treatments, ending in Caresco's curative operation: a treasure bitterly acquired, a capital jealously guarded, of which the magnificent interest ought to be a child.

For her husband, Madame Fortin summarized all that. Through the flowers of the centerpiece, by means of the fluid of their gaze, their eyes told one anther tacitly, in a canticle of immense mutuality, that tender story of the past, that desire for the future, which the results of the recent operation had not yet confirmed.

And Julien Duverdon, who knew about the virtuous abnegation of the husband and the disillusioned tenderness of the wife, understood the mute expression intensely. Once again, the occasion had led him to compare his fate with that of others. Was he not, even more so than the Fortins, disinherited by marriage? Had not destiny wounded and tortured him, even in the most secret coverts of his heart? He did not even have, like that charming and plaintive couple, the supreme consolation of a shared faith to enlace his efforts, to spur his projects, to put his miseries to sleep in a décor of illusions, to replace the sadness of the moment with the mirage of the future. He could only see the shadow.

Even the dream of posterity that still persisted here, through the flowers on the table, in the adoration of the spouses, that splendid dream, could not inspire him. Rolande, in the grip of deviant vice, had a horror of children expressed many times. For everything that sprang from the male act, from the generous insemination through the glorious sight of an abdomen bearing the fruit of masculine amour, to the blond head accrediting future destinies, she had always manifested a supreme disgust. The child, so victorious in its smile, so appeasing in its grace, the child that softened the frictions and animosities born of the incessant contact of two dissimilar beings, she declared to be insupportable, dirty and repulsive. That, as much as aversion, was why she rejected her husband. A cure could not even be attempted, since she avoided any attempt at deliverance, since she denied the remedy...

"What are you thinking about, Monsieur Duverdon?" said the mistress of the house, surprised by the silence that, succeeding her declaration was maintaining her guest, without speaking, without eating, his eyes staring into space and his hands crossed, brushed by the abundance of his long graying beard.

"I'm thinking...," confessed the gentleman, striving to overcome his melancholy, "...that you're very fortunate, even so, the two of you."

She sensed a secret dolor in that remark, and already, good and compassionate, she was about to try to attenuate the affliction by requesting the confidence of it—for some confessions soothe—when Julia reappeared, bringing the coffee, which they took at the table. The animation that she deployed in serving well, the joy of seeing that her blunders had not been held against her, the already-overflowing gratitude—that mixture of unexpected sentiments blossoming in her, in her new costume, rendered her more beautiful, more resplendent in her young, strong flesh. Becoming conscious of her recent social ascension, she harmonized more audaciously with it in the baring of her head, the prominence of her bosom, the arch of her hips and the promise of her productive loins.

An eternal sun entered with her and came to radiate over the three dispossessed of sunlight, dissipating the nascent question and deflecting their thoughts toward the admiration of a beautiful work of art. Often, the arrival thus of a person foreign to the guests expands like a fluid, causes ideas to evolve and evokes new ones. As they sipped the coffee, sending spirals of blue tobacco smoke in the air, they started to talk about bad weather, about the beautiful days that would return in October with delightful tones of light, to such a point that, in order to see them, the Fortins would return to their country house, which they had abandoned early that year.

Then Monsieur Fortin got up and invited his guest to take a tour of his property, not sparing him any corner of his dwelling. What surprised Monsieur Duverdon the most was to penetrate on the first floor into a spacious room hung with draperies of blue silk. The middle of it was occupied by a pink cradle garnished with gracious ribbons of brand new satin, which one might have thought set up by a mother's hand. Around it, on tables, there were all the preparations for an infantile toilette, a little bath, bowls, sponges, linen, little white woolen socks, everything disposed for bathing an infant, and a balance for weighing it. In one corner, boxes of toys had been opened, and then closed incompletely.

"The baby's room," declared Madame Fortin, speaking as if in a sanctuary.

"What baby?" asked the visitor, nonplussed.

"The one that we haven't despaired of having some day. Doctor Caresco has promised us."

A moving credulity! Already, on the faith of the surgeon, they were preparing to welcome the being that no symptom yet permitted the suspicion. And yet, in the voice of the young woman, in the cloudy expression of her physiognomy creasing the charming arc of her eyebrows, there was an anxiety, a disillusioned prescience that the magic thrust of the scalpel, having furrowed her loins with a scar that had barely dried, if it had rendered her strength to her, if it had ornamented her cheeks with a spring-like freshness, would never have the sole consequence of maternity, even more precious for her than health. And in confirmation of the suspicions to which her uncertain speech gave birth, Monsieur Duverdon saw her lean her afflicted head over her husband's shoulder, designating with a gesture the accumulation of objects prepared for the little Messiah, the cradle, the bowls the sponges and the toys on the tables.

"What a misfortune, my dear, if he doesn't come...!"

Julien made his adieux, and resumed the route to the château on foot, passing through the woods, for he had plenty of time.

On emerging from the city he went into a little plain framed by the trees, cleared by the harvest, where the hunting season, open for a week, was revealed by long noisy echoes. He thought he distinguished Rolande and Clara behind an apple orchard; their distant silhouettes were advancing along the edge of a field of beets, and the porters and dogs deployed in a horizontal line were preparing the murderous office. A flock of grouse spread out; two gunshots saluted their flight. The thinness of the sound indicated the small caliber of the weapon; it really was his wife and the American. Masculine costumes and masculine pleasures; everything confirmed their inversion. He passed on, with a rip in his heart, without caring any longer about the result of their skill. He respired deeply the pure air of the dusk that was almost falling already.

His thoughts slowed his pace. Why so many celestial beauties, so much joy in the azure, falling in red fringes over the caprice of the mountains; why so many plains cheered up by verdure, so much vivifying oxygen, so many breaths and perfumes, if he had to profit from them alone, in that captivating dusk? Rolande! He would have abandoned his entire fortune, his luxury, even his voyages, to become his wife's lover, to follow with her, in the enchantment of the locale, poorly but amorously, the route that was being followed in the inverse direction of his march by a peasant couple, vulgar primitives who were coming toward him. It was doubtless a household of rude field-workers, and they were returning to the cottage, to black bread and cabbage soup. Their youth, fatigued by the harrow, had a comforting fashion of adherence, arm in arm; and the man was carrying, with infinite precaution, a child at whom the mother was smiling. At the moment when they were about to pass him, the poor couple stopped, because the child had started to cry. The father suddenly became anxious.

"The kid's wailing! Give him the teat."

And the woman, simple and naively, with the sovereignly grave gesture of dispensers of life, parted the worn fabric of her bodice, took out the human gourd, white and pink, swollen with sap, and held it out to the infant, who threw himself upon it gluttonously, like a little seigneur upon his domain, took hold of it with his plump fingers, and imbibed the milk, the holy liquid, with the noise of a rippling stream. And Julien gazed at them, loving one another in that nursing attitude, as simple and as sumptuous as nature; and he understood, in a flash, the tenacity of creation making all passions, all embraces and all hopes end in that despotic little voracious beast, admired by the father and generously contented by the mother.

The paupers had resumed their route, their footfalls stirring up the dust of the road, their silhouette blurring in the gray of the evening, and he watched them flee, so rich in their poverty, so triumphant in their misery, and he could still hear the rustic remark resonating, the magnificent peroration of their primitive amour, the cry of instinct by virtue of which all the injustices of the world were tolerated and softened:

"The kid's wailing! Give him the teat."

Yes, in order to chant that ritual refrain of paternity in the language of those peasants, in order to sing it as the Fortins would have sung it, as all those palpitating around the mouth of a thirsty child repeated it, yes, for those few words he would have given his riches, his châteaux and his voyages, he would have toiled, he would have broken the blue-tinted stones on which he was treading. And an audacious thought came to him from that lesson of hazard, a temptation to finish with his cowardly abolition of will, to take Rolande as soon as she returned from the hunt, to throw himself upon her as a dominator, as a master, and fecundate her, in order that the child, arriving subsequently, would become the glorious bond of amour, the little despot whose voracity would reunite the two spouses under its plump fingers, who, heads inclined, would watch it tenderly taking its nourishment from the human spring, as the peasants had just done.

When he arrived at the château, his fever had not yet calmed down, in spite of two hours of walking. He felt the need to cool down somewhat. The desire to bathe in the cool water that the natural caprice of the stream winding around the domain accumulated behind a clump of verdure caused him to turn aside before going back inside, and take a path that led to a concrete kiosk permitting him go undress and put on a bathing costume. Would he not rediscover a little of Rolande, rock himself in a fictitious caress, a distant echo of her, by steeping himself in the water into which she dived almost every day, in the company of Clara?

Thus, he sought evidence that evoked her, embraced her with memories.

When he had almost arrived at his goal, however, a sound of voices made him hesitate and suspend his march. A man and a woman were talking in the thicket, one with a sharp, contained and ironic anger, the other with supplications that distress dissolved into sobs. And he learned involuntarily of the recent pregnancy of the soubrette Rose; he overheard the abominable advice that Louis, the valet de chambre, was giving her to quit her place and go to Paris in order to request

200

from a matron the thrust of the stylet abolishing the menace, already confirmed, of a maternity of which he had been the artisan.

In vain, the woman invoked the sentiments of justice and right that demanded, if not reparation, at least the sharing of the damage consecutive to imprudent caresses. In vain, more tender and more suppliant, she recalled their amour, their intoxicated promises and their hours of quivering abandonment. In vain she offered the savings accumulated over three years of service to attract her seducer to marriage, in order that they could remain together, in order that she should not be dispossessed of pride and wellbeing.

Louis resisted angrily, arguing his incredulity. Did he even know whether he was the father of the child? Had she not frequented others before him? And coldly, like a businessman haggling over a bargain, finding it too unequal, seeing the fissure by which to wriggle out of it, the valet disputed dates, extracted his arguments from the unknown, supporting himself on laws that shore up masculine egotism.

Julien, holding his breath, shuddered in listening to that odious conflict. It was all of social tyranny that as being expressed in that bushy corner of the wood, in hasty and angry words on the part of the man, imploring and weary ones on the part of the woman. It was the illegitimate atrocity of conventions, prejudices and slaveries, rebounding on the fecundity that human accord ought to have rendered glorious, displayed in broad daylight and recognized with a superb gratitude, but which, on the contrary, it condemned to shame, burdensomeness, and the stifling of contracts. Thus, it forced the seed to restriction, to annihilation; thus, it led the creator to despair, perhaps to crime, and sometimes to suicide.

Coming after the example of a little while ago, of the harassed peasants who rediscovered their energy in the contemplation of a child avidly suspended from his mother's breast, that information was now singularly saddening, singularly unfavorable to social or religious submissions that stigmatized duty and honor with the signature of a Maire or the unctuous employment of a sacerdotal benediction. Thus, as long as the research of paternity was forbidden, as long as semen flowed without it being legal to define the consequences, as long as, for the sake of pleasure and insouciant lust, the creative element could distribute semen in fertile ground without any preoccupation with the harvest and the care of shouldering the burden it had engendered, there would always be these abominations, maternities paralyzed by the somber action of avid matrons, dangerous expulsions of wretched debris under bloody skirts and sheets that often became shrouds. How many of those victims of mutual pressure disappeared in frightful agony, taking with them the imprecise souls of beings sacrificed before their dawn?

But nature was paradoxical and incoherent in everything. In consequence, was not the first duty of intelligent beings to conspire against it, to extract themselves from its afflictions, to ward off its brutality, to utilize their intelligence to seek remedies for the evils that it spread incessantly with an indefatigable blindness? In any case, why did humans not organize their defense better, protecting the individual by means of the mildness of their laws? Why did they seem, on the contrary, to ally their cruelty with that of the great bad mother? Why, finally, did they impose constraints capable ending in crime, as in the particular case of Rose, common to so many other unfortunates?

All the incoherence of life, all social infamy flowed back thus in exaggerated rancor into Julien's mind. Without him being pessimistic by temperament, his own disappointments and the conduct of events led him easily to a conception of the deplorable arrangement of the universe He quickly omitted therefrom the real wellbeing of others more favored; he forgot, this time, the sovereignly consoling tableau of the peasant couple who, an hour before, when he passed them on the road, had stimulated so much reassuring energy and so much personal encouragement in his heart.

He took a few steps toward the invisible speakers, with the intention of removing the scales from their eyes, showing

202

them the gravity of their projects and perhaps reconciling them; but they had already drawn away and he could not find them again. Having reached the edge of the pool of water, he stopped, suddenly weary, no longer having any desire to bathe. However, the location was admirable and tempting. The sound of a little waterfall, issuing from the rocks, advertised the coolness of the element and invited him to relax there. Framed by a grove of tall trees, the surface was brightened in the middle by a reflection of the sky reddened by the sunset.

Buttercups, little golden flowers, ferns vivid in their chlorophyll, pink-striped geraniums, nenuphars whose long serpentine petals were visible through the transparency, balancing flowers similar to white lilies, water trefoils with fringed corollas, and hottonias displayed in a thousand cuttings: an entire green and shiny flower-garden, intensely slothful, was slumbering in the vicinity, savoring the clear, incessantly renewed, beverage. Mosquitoes were buzzing, fish were darting with a zigzag of their tails, soon vanishing. Julien gazed at them, interrogating the misdeeds of their lives, the battles they fought, the murders they committed...

Nothing tempted him any longer.

Then he went back to the château. In the vestibule, he found Louis and Rose, who were laying the table for dinner. They seemed to be entirely devoted to their work, and nothing, except for the young woman's red eyes, would have betrayed the secret of their fault.

In the drawing room, into which he passed thereafter, a calm accord seemed to reign. Claude and Raoul, leaning over the table in the middle, already illuminated by the light of a lamp filtered through a green silk shade, were reading newspapers. Antonin Fargeaud had closed his book, and near his hand was the magnifying glass with which he assisted the weakness of his eyes.

Henriette, isolated in a corner, lying on a sofa, was considering pensively the three individuals so differently dear to her heart. Toward the old man, the guardian who had collected her and brought her up, went her commiserative gratitude. Pity also softened the gaze that she posed on her fiancé, whose stooped stance betrayed his disillusioned suffering, the vanquished effort of an anemic tree struggling against the parasites eating it away. But when she looked at Raoul, she could not avoid a strange frisson. He was the triumphant oak, the magnificent colossus that extends its arms, beneath which the weak come to shelter, repose and inspire themselves with the idea of strength.

Under the shadow of long blond hair his eyes with dilated pupils scarcely reflected the tranquil light of the soul; under the beard divided into two quivering points, the charming contour of the cheeks and the finesse of the chin scarcely revealed the great simplicity and mildness of his character. From his Christ-like head, however, a grave and powerful authority emanated. His shoulders were dominant in their broadness; the design of his vigorous torso, uncoupled by sport, sank into a pelvis solidly supported by the robustness of the legs.

And in contemplating him, so powerful next to the other two wrecks, Henriette admired him confusedly, and was dazzled by him. She criticized herself for the frisson that his approach invincibly procured, for the languor that followed his handshake. She strove to forget the bitter moment of transport that an error of obscurity had caused her to experience on the evening when, on the terrace, believing herself to have taken Claude's hand, she had shivered at a contact delectable in its burn. She no longer wanted to think about it, but she thought about it incessantly, and in bringing back the memory of it, she felt warm flushes in her face and choking sensations in her throat, an entire flux of passion departing m the heart and radiating through her being, which even the holy idea of Providence and the hypnosis of prayer could not succeed in dissipating.

When Julien came in she was glad of his exorcising presence. She went toward him swiftly.

"There you are, Julien! Roland and Clara aren't with you?"

"No. They preferred not to accompany me to Rouen and went hunting together."

"They should have been back by now," observed the old man, bitterly.

But at the same moment, a hubbub rose from the vestibule, a disorder of emotional voices. Julien ran out, Rolande, very pale, sustained by Clara, had just collapsed on the floor, and he was immediately alarmed when he learned of the accident that had occurred.

Hector, who was bringing the huntresses back in the automobile, had wanted to throw a flower to Marthe Servant, the schoolmistress, who was walking along the road. He had swerved awkwardly in her direction, with the consequence that, steered into a ditch, the vehicle had tipped over, and Rolande, thrown out of the auto into a recently-plowed field, was complaining of severe internal pains.

In fact, folded in two in the chair in which she had just be placed, holding her right side with her two small hands, she seemed ready to faint again, her face pale, chilled by sweat, her lips discolored, only the whites of her eyes showing under the veil of her eyelids.

Monsieur Duverdon knelt down next to her and informed her softly of his anguish. "My Rolande, my poor Rolande, you're in pain! Oh, my God, she's in pain, she's in pain!"

And seizing the hem of her dress, kissing it, he expressed again, after so many disappointments and rejections, the intense amour that had never ceased to keep vigil in his heart, the forgiveness ready to spread. On the other side, Clara had taken a hand and was patting it coldly, with measured little blows Only the more emphatic wrinkles of her eyes indicated her emotion, contained and correct, the enemy of bluff. Doubtless she was also congratulating herself on having escaped the peril.

And it was a lamentable rivalry that was manifest at that moment around the young woman: on the one hand the constantly rejected, constantly wounded husband, allowing his male pride to burst in an explosion of real participation; on the other hand, the perverse friend conquering masculine privileges, conserving, even in confrontation with suffering, her egotism of character softened by sensuality, intimately satisfied that the accident had been more favorable to her than to her companion.

The antagonism was even more evident when it was necessary to take Rolande to her room. The American, wanting to accomplish that effort alone, had pushed Julien aside, whose protests did not move her, and strove to maintain the injured woman, to aid her to reach the stairway; but Rolande's cries had died away; almost unconscious, fainting, she was about to drag her supporter down, when Julien, revolted, shoved Clara out of the way, picked his wife up in his arms, and with a simple play of his Herculean muscles, carried her upstairs.

He heard plaintive thanks that troubled him more intensely than the adherence of the supple body that he adored. Encouraged by that first triumph, he turned abruptly to the foreigner who wanted to go in within him. His eyes blazed.

"Go away. Your place is not here."

"I shall care for my friend."

"You shall not care for her."

"I shall."

Then, exasperated, he deposited Rolande on the bed. Returning to the American, who was already installed, he took her by the arm and, without a word, threw her out. Having shot the bolt and returned to his wife, he was surprised to see that she was gazing at him without anger, and that there was even a sight glint of astonishment and admiration in her eyes.

XII

"I've finished, Mademoiselle," said the hairdresser, removing her last iron curler from Marthe Servant's head.

The young woman, sitting in front of the triple mirror, darted a glance at the nape of her neck. She smiled at the artiste who had been brought expressly from Paris to undulate the actresses. She had never seen herself so beautiful. She admired the expert waves imprinted on the blonde sheet of her tress, with ringlets dangling from the temples. A slight application of oil rendered the harmoniously staged folds more evident. The golden mass was distributed in curls hiding the slenderness of the neck, but in front, the throat and the shoulders, exposed by the slightly low cut of her dress, were full and gracious, as tempting as a ripe fruit, and a transparency of blue veins ran there that one might have thought sketched by the pencil of a skillful painter. By leaning over a little more, the corsage permitted a glimpse of the proud emergence of her breasts.

It was the first time that it had been given to her to show in public the secret splendors that women of the world exposed manifestly almost every evening. Her coquetry found itself satisfied in imitating them. She rejoiced again at the abrupt caprice of Rolande, who, having recovered from her accident, had wanted to enjoy a play before returning to Paris. Hector had immediately taken charge of facilitating that whim. Hoping to attract to the château the still defiant Marthe, still closed to his attempts, and to find in the rehearsals the opportunity for a more persuasive courtship, he had confided to the young woman the role of a soubrette in a play of his own composition—for he prided himself on his literary ability.

The pretext of Claude's recovery had sufficed to obtain from Antonin Fargeaud the authorization to turn the orangery upside-down, to erect a stage, and to construct dressing-rooms for the actors, draped with red percale and equipped with mirrors. That was why Marthe found herself that evening in such noble society, ready to act before the local château-dwellers, palpitating with the effect that she was about to produce on a choice public, and also frightened by the idea of losing her voice at the start of her role. She felt both a great delight and a great disturbance.

"Thank you, Monsieur," she said, politely, to the hair-dresser.

The latter, having already judged by the naiveties with which she punctuated the conversation the country-dweller with whom he was dealing, smiled, pursing his lips with a protective expression.

"I've never been so chic," she added, more loudly, in order to emphasize the remark.

And as the compliment seduced the fellow, he offered to make her up.

"Make me up? Why? I put powder on before coming. Isn't that sufficient? If it's the fashion, though…"

"You can't think, Mademoiselle, of going on stage without blackening the eyes, reddening the cheeks and whitening the throat and hands? You'd look frightful!"

"Please, then, Monsieur…!"

She abandoned herself again to the figaro with the blinking eyes. Before commencing his task, he planted his comb in the crown of curly hair bordering his bald spot, and, with a gesture that embraced the universe, he pulled back the white cotton of his sleeves, fixed by elastic. Then, his hands free, he spread a layer of vaseline over the young woman's face and shoulders. He amassed the pomade, prolonging it all the way to the breasts with an insistence whose significance she did not understand, because, at the same time as being interested by that work, she was dreaming of other things, in the fashion of the stars in great theaters preparing to endure the fire of opera-glasses.

With a cotton tampon, the hairdresser dabbed her with a white and agreeable scented powder. The red freckles that the sun had caused to appear on the young woman's forehead, which caused her despair every morning when she interrogated her beauty in front of a mirror, had already disappeared. The hare's foot caressed her as it colored her cheeks.

She knew, having read it in a novel, what happens in actresses' dressing rooms, and how those women experienced the delight of being made beautiful every evening. Was she not an actress too? Would she not collect, in the warm effluvia of the wings and the stage, the applause of admirers, the homages of amorous men, the flowers that are worn in padded coupés and at suppers in great restaurants? She would be virtuous, certainly, since triumphant actresses were cited who were adored for their talent alone, singers to whose feet princes came, solely by virtue of the contentment of art, to deposit fortunes, and sometimes a title.

Oh, to laugh, to shine, to parade, to perfume oneself like so many others less pretty than her, whose names were in the newspapers, whose glory was revered by writers, praised in print! Might there not be, in the rich assembly before whom she was about to appear, a seigneur generous enough to take her out of the rut in which she was stuck, the Lilloise family in which half a domestic, she advertised lessons in orthography, in order also to get away from odious vacations passed in the vicinity of the farmyard dung-heap, in paltry or vulgar company? Some man who might open the horizon of luxury and light to which she aspired, beneath her placid surface of a respectable young woman? Yes, what man…? Hector, perhaps…?

And just as the hairdresser finished penciling her eyes, enlarging the clefts and blue-tinting them, the gentleman in question came into the dressing-room, having opened the door without knocking. He was red-faced and congested. Surprised at first by the presence of a stranger, he quickly recovered his aplomb, went toward her, inspected her shoulders, iridescent with powder, and her face, where the make-up caused each feature to stand out more energetically.

"God! How pretty you are, my charming interpreter!" Then, turning to the man, in order to get rid of him, he added: "I believe the ladies are impatient to have you..."

In fact, from the next dressing-room, Rolande and Clara could be heard demanding their turn. The importunate picked up his implements and disappeared. Hector took the beauty's hand and drew it to his lips. She surrendered it to him with a surge of gratitude, which his conceit immediately attributed to another motive.

"Do you love me, Marthe?"

"Not yet. That depends on you."

"What is it necessary to do to render myself worthy?"

"Launch me...make me a actress. Your literary relations, about which you've told me so much, authorize that hope..."

"Yes...certainly!"

Ready to promise anything, in order not to delay anything, he had taken her waist and had penetrated audaciously into the gap in her corsage. She began to understand the immensity of certain sacrifices. He leaned over her and she had to move away his head before the mobile eyes, which were fluttering with the desire that set them ablaze with a covetousness like that of a hungry dog in a poultry-yard. She liked his astonishingly crimson face even less, and the curve of his nose, with an abrupt ridge, describing an angle above his moustache, evidently tinted with a chestnut too raw, sensing old age in their usurped youth. However, she did not resist too much, and did not inhibit the investigation of his hand. He resumed, foraging further.

"Yes I'd like to aid you with all my power. Fortune, influence, steps, I'll utilize everything for your success. You've become my protégé, the one whom I'd be proud to launch into the arena of glory. But it's also necessary that, on such capital thrown at your feet, you'll pay me interest, and that a little should be paid out on account..."

"What account are you talking about?"

She was playing the innocent, and he divined that she was wilier than she wanted to appear. For a moment, he hesitated, thinking about his money. A further glance at the attractive flesh immediately caused a turnaround.

"What account? You know very well."

"I don't know…I'm not a loose woman."

That confession signified precisely the opposite; did it not at least express a candor of ideas? Then, burning his ships, he explained himself. Marthe, after the performance, was to stay overnight at the château, for it would be too late for her to return to the farm. Only let her neglect to lock her bedroom door. Since she was sage she would remain sage; he was a gallant man. But at least she would permit him to come and talk to her about the future…

"Don't reproach me now, if that annoys you," he finished. "Such assents are always difficult to obtain from a young woman like you. Don't reply; just take this sprig of tea-roses that I'm wearing in my buttonhole. If you accept it; if, during the performance, I see you slide it into your hair, I'll understand that you consent, and your fortune will be made. If, on the contrary, you don't put it there, well, I'll strive to forget you, and I'll conclude that you prefer to remain a petty school-teacher eternally destined to frequent goose-girls during the vacations…"

He had taken the flowers from his jacket and had put them between her fingers, without her making any effort of revolt, subjugated by the mirage of future times. Again his head had inclined and he was able to feast on the spectacle of the shoulders framed by the curls of her hair. Over those treasures the candlelight slid gentle pastel shades.

They were both so absorbed by the skirmish in which they were engaged that they did not hear the door of the dressing room close discreetly. Claude had witnessed the entire duel and overheard every word.

Hector got up, compressing his congested forehead. "The audience must be arriving," he said. "I have a headache, doubtless owed to all this fuss. I'll leave you. Above all, don't forget your reply in the first scene: 'Personally, I'm an art nouveau servant.' There's a great deal of wit, by virtue of the contrast of epochs, in that sentence. Say it with a hint of malice."

"I'll try, Monsieur Hector."

When he had retired, she was extraordinarily troubled. What was she going do with those flowers she was holding in her hand?

Frankly, Hector displeased her. But was he not a master, who could raise his vassal up as far as him, like the ancient seigneurs? Although they were no longer in feudal times, that homage could not fail to be flattering. On the other hand, was she going to throw her bonnet over the windmill on the strength of a simple promise? Her bonnet was intact; it had value...

She made a little gesture of carelessness, and slipped the sprig of roses into her hair. There would still be time to bolt her bedroom door.

She went on to the stage contiguous with her dressing-room.

The curtain was lowered. It was a circumstantial curtain constructed from two drapes joined together. The acetylene footlights, scarcely lit, illuminated obscurely the backcloth of a crudely brushed landscape, opening to the right upon the forecourt of a Medieval hostelry and to the left upon a peasant hut. That decor was worthy of the play, as banal as possible, the mediocre intellectuality of which Hector had not been able to extend beyond a petty intrigue. The adaptation of a old operetta was also recognizable in the set-up of the three characters: a seigneur on his travels, the fiancé of a young chatelaine, whom he did not know, encountered the latter costumed as a shepherd, the whim having taken the young woman to employ that ruse in order to observe in advance the character of her future husband. Under those borrowed rags she extended multiple traps, which the seigneur avoided, to his honor. She went so far as to try to convince him of the amour of a maidservant, which he rejected in spite of the girl's coquetries. To conclude, the fake shepherd, wounded in an improbable duel with the seigneur, and cared for by him, finally revealed her identity.

Miss Boswett had not neglected the opportunity to affirm her tastes by taking possession of the only masculine role;

Rolande was playing the shepherd and Marthe the soubrette. For that minuscule effort of cerebration, five hundred local notables had been invited, the greenhouse turned upside-down, a stage constructed and a buffet prepared.

Marthe went to open the curtain and peer out into the hall. A surge of pride flowed beneath her make-up. All the local château-dwellers were there, all those whose wealth and luxury signaled them to her wonderment, in an unexpected tableau of diamond-embellished shoulders and black coats. There were even some red coats, the brightness of which out-shone the feminine costumes. Other individuals of lesser im-portance in her eyes, but for whose life she was nevertheless also ambitious: local bourgeois, fat crimson ladies exception-ally decked in silk; messieurs whose frock-coats were too tight and whose starched collars held their heads ceremoniously high; and college students strapped into the tunics, stretching their gloves long since buttoned—an entire improvised public invited to fill the emptiness of the hall and fortify the stifling success, was relegated to the back rows, stacked on simple benches, all the way to the trophies on the wall framed by foli-age, while the gilt of the chairs in the front rows and the claret velvet of the banquettes glistened under the incandescence of acetylene.

Marthe received, as a tribute addressed to her, the flutter-ing luminosity of jewelry, the musky perfume dispatched by the waving of fans, and the hubbub of conversations enlivened with laughter to which the wait gave birth. Nothing was worth as much to her as the imminent adulation and the clapping of hands that were about to salute the few sallies of her role. She arched her waist, and repeated a few items of dialogue insuffi-ciently possessed. Then, sure of herself, she returned her atten-tion to the audience.

She observed, not without satisfaction, that her parents, invited by ricochet, had abstained. She would not have wanted to be chagrined by Père Servant's antique frock-coat; she would not feel her mother's old fake calico shawl weighing upon her, embarrassing her stride, paralyzing her voice. On the contrary, this evening everyone would adore her, they would all exult at her talent, including the Fortins, whom she could see so tenderly coupled a few meters away; and Raoul, next to Henriette, separated by an empty chair—Claude's—both expansive in a charming intimacy; and Madame de Berge, who was flirting with a young man whose moustache put a superb flourish beneath his monocle; and Julien Duverdon, the timid Hercules, caressing his beard with a elegant gesture; and Doctor Bouret, whose serious white head was imposing, framed by his family—children, grandchildren, all in attendance—and a quantity of other fine seigneurs and ladies with casual, precious or languid gestures.

Yes, they were all there, all those she did not know but whose sonorous carriages she envied as they drew them along the chalky roads, and all those, humbler, that she knew and whose homage she wanted, including Louis and Rose, in charge of the cloakroom and coming on occasion to cast a glance into the hall, and even the Grignons' sons: Arthur, the mechanic, transformed into a footman, wedged in a coat with gilded buttons; and Anatole, the soldier, in his tunic, with slightly alcoholic cheeks, chatting to the gendarmes, recounting his campaigns, in a back corner of blue uniforms. They were all there to admire her.

She continued looking for a long time, but the presence of Claude arriving on stage deflected her attention. The young man arrived from the wings. A severity seemed to spring from the coat he was wearing, and from his pale face, gracious and fatigued. At least, that was the impression that he made on Marthe when he had approached her, when she had observed the disillusionment of his eyes, when she had heard the gravity of his voice, tinted with a hint of irony.

"You're about to affirm yourself an artiste, Mademoiselle. That Louis XIV costume suits you marvelously. But why are you wearing that sprig of roses in your hair?"

"I don't know, Monsieur Claude. The flowers were given to me and I put them there without any other intention..."

"Without intention?"

"What intention do you expect me to have?"

The lie weighed upon them, and their embarrassment was expressed in a constrained smile.

"Believe me, Mademoiselle, take them out of your coiffure. Those flowers are not in the taste of the epoch. I know your role, which is all simplicity. Believe me, remove them..."

He said no more than that, and withdrew, stepping over the stool that permitted access to the public.

What did he know? What double meaning was there in his remark; 'I know your role'? Had Hector told him something? She remained nonplussed, raised her hand to her head in order to remove the significant adornment, but she stopped on the way and transformed her action into another gesture of carelessness. Yes, there would still be time to lock her bedroom door.

She returned to the curtain, parted it again and plunged her gaze into the hall. Claude had returned to his seat. She divined intuitively the embarrassment to which his presence gave rise between Raoul and Henriette, although the latter seemed to welcome him with an amicable tenderness and recoiled slightly to make room for him, picking up her skirt. Hector had also returned to make contact with the public, to receive in advance a few whiffs of incense. He sat down near Madame de Berge and extracted her from her flirtation with the young man with the flourishing moustache. Their conversation reached Marthe's ears, and on hearing it she felt the bite of chagrin.

"Well, favorite of the Muses, you're about to triumph?"

"You'll aid me in that, my charmer."

"I've already chosen the place on the parquet where my stamping feet will make the most noise."

"Your pretty little feet?"

"Still unworthy of your jolly play. It's said that you've sown therein a great deal of wit and a great deal of amour. How have you done it?"

"For the amour, I thought of you; for the wit I drank champagne while writing the text."

"Why champagne?"

"Because my ideas and my style always reflect the condition of my stomach."

"God, how prosaic you are! So when you have to talk about a deceived husband…"

"I swallow sauerkraut."

"And when it's a widow?"

"When it's a widow who resembles you, its cantharides that I absorb."

Madame de Berge laughed behind the screen of her fan. She was delighted by the spicy tone of the dialogue, which continued in a low tone without Marthe being able to perceive the rest. But in the audience, the eddies of gestures and voices became feverish; people were waiting less patiently for the lifting of the curtain, which the good pleasure of Rolande and Clara kept lowered. The two friends had not finished donning their costumes. Marthe could hear their enervated appeals to the dresser and the hairdresser. One wit manifested his impatience to the rhythm of a drinking song, and the crowd imitated him with amused laughter. A few animal cries even went up, and the furious Hector had great difficulty preventing the joker from imitating the crow of a cockerel. He believed that he sensed a hostility in those innocent manifestations.

The racket was suddenly interrupted by a charming entrance. Antonin Fargeaud, who has sworn at first that he would not attend the soirée, had changed his mind, and he arrived holding the hand of an adorable child five years old, one of Doctor Bouret's grandsons. The infant allowed himself to be guided contritely through the packed rows of spectators. His exquisite Raphaelesque head, the oval purity of his delicate face, the delightful contrast between his rosy cheeks and his bright blue eyes, the vaporous blond expanse of his hair falling over a turned-down collar of white lace, the theatrical elegance of his black velvet costume, which a yellow leather belt secured at the waist, the grace of his little calves and feet shod in the varnished shoes of a doll, and, above all, his expression of embarrassed candor, resolved in a smile of adorable confusion, that apparition of a dainty jewel worthy of a showcase, delicately escorted by the old man with a hesitant step, ill-served by his defective sight, suddenly calmed the cries and caused the impatience to shut up. Afterwards, people took possession of him, fêted him, complimented the grandfather, Doctor Bouret, who was radiant, and added a new strophe to the celebrated poem by Victor Hugo, "When the Child Appeared."

The sterile Fortin household, above all, only had eyes for the child. Madame Fortin, having drawn him toward her, caressed his blond curls, and then drew them aside in order to admire the radiant clarity of his forehead and the frail charm of his oval face. And Monsieur Fortin watched her do it, comforting with that charming scene his indefatigable hope of a posterity that nature refused to accord him.

Then it was Henriette who drew the infant to her, took him on her knee and interested herself in his hesitant conversation.

And Marthe Servant, who, from her observation post had remarked the sudden appeasement of the noise on the appearance of the little being, and the sort of veneration and admiring tenderness that accompanied his presence, understood, in a flash of discernment, the child's power, all that his fragility summarized of participation, of cares, efforts, of amour, all that he awakened of perspectives, convictions, resources, and grandeurs. In him the past was made precise, by means of him the imperishable future opened. He was the treasure that the generations bequeathed, with the sacred preoccupation of conserving excellence superbly.

And it was doubtless because there was in him so much charm, so much savor, so much authority, that people invincibly felt protective toward him and adored him, from the moment when, having emerged from his mother's womb, he absorbed her nourishing sap, until, having become bigger and stronger, he would be able to advance alone into the world, to suffer its rude contacts, avoid its dangers and perversions, in order to distinguish himself by splendid deeds and make his creators proud.

Thinking about all of that, Marthe had a veritable moment of hesitation. The sterile life of enjoyment that she desired, in her inexperience, the perpetual celebration that she believed to be the attribute of the actress, the adoration of males and the stamping feet of the crowd, suddenly seemed to her to be very paltry ambitions compared to the one that consisted of creating and bringing up such beautiful little children, so elegant and so ornamented with beautiful frills. Her parents had made a bourgeoise of her; why should she not have children of whom she could make seigneurs?

Oh, the frightful flowers, stigmatizing her determination to fall, how they weighed upon her head now! She raised her hand to her coiffure in order to snatch them away and trample them underfoot. But again her gesture stopped half way. Rolande and Clara appeared on stage and her good resolutions evaporated. The two friends, both dressed as men, had their arms around one another's waists.

Rolande's grace adapted well enough to her equivocal costume of a young shepherd. An unkempt wig under which her hair was gathered, gave a certain piquancy to the yellow mobility of her eyes, and the delicacy of her carmined mouth, in which the whiteness of her young teeth was vibrant. It would have been impossible to specify her sex, so much did she have the appearance of a charming gamin.

By contrast, Clara Boswett, as a seigneur, was ridiculously disquieting. Her long wig, covered by a plumed hat, shaded the fatigue of her face and made the pastiness of the cheeks more precise. Her customary facial make-up, which still decorated her with a renewal of youth in the penumbra, betrayed this time in the footlights, now fully illuminated, the wrinkles issuing from the corners of the eye and deployed in goose-feet. In spite of the long basques of her costume, the amplitude of her hips, compressed by her corset, was divinable, and the long coat did not prevent the thinness of her legs being obvious. She was saddened thus, less by the treason of her forms than by her malaise, the inexpressible disappointment that one experiences in recognizing oneself so mature. However, convinced of her charm, she smiled victoriously at Rolande, The latter was chagrined to see her, tripped over her sword, and stumbled.

But Hector, radiant on seeing his flowers sported by Marthe, had just struck the three blows. An approving murmur ran through the audience. Chairs creaked and shifted. Some applause approved on the décor that the curtain, scarcely drawn, revealed. The interpreters only just had time to disappear into the wings before returning to commence their stilted dialogue.

XIII

The performance had just finished. A final hubbub of voices, the sound of horses' hooves on the gravel and the clicking of carriage doors accompanied the retreat of the guests, who climbed into carriages, tightening their mantles against the cold, because the atmosphere had become precociously fresh, presaging bad weather. On the perron, Antonin Fargeaud, Claude and Henriette addressed *bonsoirs* and shook the hands of those departing. Behind them, in the vestibule and in the vast dining room where a buffet had been set up, the guests of the château were commenting on the evening, the welcome, simply polite, given to the play.

Julian Duverdon, caressing his beard softly, was serving Rolande. He presented her with champagne and a glazed chicken wing. He also offered some to Clara, who was sitting nearby, although she was now less audacious in sharing their intimacy. After the scene that had taken place on the evening of the fall, the husband, incapable of conserving his anger any longer, had become once again he slave of his tolerant timidity, and he endured the presence of the foreigner as if nothing had happened; his rancor vanished before the slightest whim of his dominatrix. This time, very glad to have obtained an almost amicable smile, he tried to divine the reason for the change of attitude. Had he been a more skillful psychologist he would only have had to turn his head and look at Clara. He would then have attributed it to the buffoonery of her costume, which she had not taken off.

Marthe Servant, whose humble origin kept her somewhat apart, had been joined by Raoul, who complimented her on her unexpected talent. The schoolteacher had sensed the sly homage of a few men extending toward her, and that made her exultant with pleasure. She raised her head more proudly and braced her lower back, of which her little hand embraced the curve. She was still on parade.

Hector, finally, close to the door, inclined before every-one, inhaling the incense of conventional compliments. The mobility of his shifty eyes went from Marthe's low neckline to the spines of ladies fleeing in their wraps. His headache had persisted for several days and he thought that the preoccupation and movement of the evening had exasperated the claw-ing dolor, circumscribed beneath his skull to a precise point on the left side, but it did not prevent him counting in advance on the feast that the tea-roses pinned in the young woman's hair promised him. The society, the perfumes and the shoulders exasperated his nerves, tightening them to the point of suffer-ing, and at vey new ignition of his desire he was obliged to put his hand to his forehead, as if to compress it and reduce the dolorous pulsations. When Madame de Berge, the last to de-part, passed close to him, he seized her wrist with such vio-lence that she let out a stifled cry.

Eventually, Claude came back in. The cold air oppressed his bronchi and he was coughing. Henriette, who followed the modifications of his physiognomy with solicitude, was sur-prised to find him less resigned. She interrogated him, fearing that the torment had been increased. By virtue of a play of psychology making it manifest that Claude was no longer the only one to have taken a place in her heart, she turned her head toward Raoul, still occupied in chatting to Marthe Serv-ant. The company of that young woman, whose coquetry and artificiality she did not like, displeased her so much that she could not dissimulate the expression on her face, with the con-sequence that this time, it was her fiancé who interrogated her. He approached her, disguising his anguish under a feigned good humor that he could not sustain for long.

"A cloud over your beautiful eyes, Henriette! The soirée didn't amuse you, then?"

"I was about to ask you the same question, Claude."

"Permit me to specify it in a different sense. You don't like Raoul keeping company with the young schoolteacher."

"No, I confess."

"Why?"

Why? She had not even asked herself that. But on seeing its clarification requested by the fiancé, she finally understood, in a start of conscience, the antagonism implanted in her a long time ago, the rivalry now established between the two friends, unknown to them, unknown especially to Raoul. Confused and troubled, her torso was animated by a more precipitate breath, shivering at the frightful discovery, which she judged culpable, as a treason.

She dared not respond, and lowered her eyelids, behind which it appeared to her that Claude would be able to divine the terrible truth. A futile precaution, alas; he had divined it without searching her gaze, when he had seen Henriette's smiles, her mute interrogations, the caresses of her heart addressed to Raoul and not to him, when he had understood fully, after that silent play of their sympathies, than after any verbal declaration, how much the strength and beauty of his friend impressed the heart of his fiancé, involuntarily.

They remained thus for some time, without speaking, sensing their emotion palpitate. The irremediable had been declared. They had not said anything, but everything had been said, in a secret eruption that paralyzed them. So Henriette, having been surprised by her senses, was surprised to see Claude advance toward Marthe and go up to her harshly.

"Aren't you going home to your parents' house, Mademoiselle? A carriage could be harnessed to take you back."

"Gladly. I'd like nothing better, but I thought...," she replied, nonplussed, understanding this time the significance of the glance that he darted at the flowers pinned in her hair.

"Not at all!" protested Hector. "Mademoiselle Marthe has her room at the château. It wouldn't be pleasant if anyone took my charming interpreter away from me so soon."

"And what do you want to do to your interpreter?" Claude said to him, drawing him to one side.

"Eh! Damn it, can't you see that she needs to go to bed...," said Hector with a tone of implication.

The advent of Antonin Fargeaud suspended the conversation that Claude was about to cause to degenerate into a bitter diatribe. The old man, whose footsteps were more uncertain in the lamplight, requested, in order to go upstairs, the help of his preferred son. Hector saw with satisfaction the two censors, his eternal killjoys, draw away. He turned toward Marthe, now alone, extremely troubled.

"Soon," he breathed to her, rapidly.

"I don't know whether I should..."

"You must. Your future depends on it!" he affirmed, and disappeared.

In her turn, conducted by Rose, the chambermaid, she went to her room. Raoul and Henriette had retired. Only the Duverdon household and Clara remained downstairs, finishing supper.

Rolande was only nibbling. Her amity for the foreigner seemed less sincere. In addition, all her nervousness was irritated that evening by pains in her right side, doubtless a recollection of the fall due to the fatigue of the performance. She complained, and Julien pressed her to go to bed. The proposition received the support of Clara, who offered her cares. She was devoted enough to spend the night with her friend if necessary. That plan pleased Rolande, but Julien, with an unaccustomed vivacity, rejected it.

"No, thank you. I'm here and it's me who ought to watch." In spite of the accord of the two women he took Rolande's arm and went up to the first floor. Two rooms separated by a dressing room constituted their apartment. Every evening, after an adieu that was content with a touch of hands, the spouses separated and Madame bolted her door. This time she put less haste into dismissing her husband. She was really suffering from her side, and her physical cowardice beat a retreat before the strong man, whose disappointed amour she sensed to be ever ready, nevertheless, to protect her, to cherish her and to save her. She did not want to ring for the chambermaid who usually undressed her, and she confided the care of unlacing her corset to Julien. The troubled fingers of the colossus were embarrassed in the fastenings and tangled the strings. She took a proud pleasure in observing his confusion and started smiling.

"You'll never get there. Would you like me to ring...?"

"No, I beg you, Rolande. The favor of undressing you isn't accorded to me often..."

"It's the second time since our wedding night," she insisted, with a hint of cruelty. "It's necessary, in order for you to serve as my chambermaid, for me to be very naïve, or suffering a great deal!"

"In fact, it is the second time. Don't rob me of all the joy I experience in it."

She smiled differently, for her suffering had just dissipated. And he mistook the significance of her good humor. Activating his task, he imagined that she had been play-acting before Clara and that she was now about to return to him, that she was shortly about to attempt a new amorous experiment, to bite once again into the fruit whose initial taste had been followed by a recoil of surprise, dolor and revolt.

Finally, after many efforts, the upper body emerged from the corset, as resplendent as the blossoming of a flower, all the beloved flesh, before which Julien, for years, had been silently breathless: the delicate shoulders, satined by the reflection of candlelight, where, in the penumbra, the shoulder-blades designed their charming undulations under the play of movements; and the full and firm arms, entwining and odorous, the armpits of which were embalmed by the savant artifice of ambergris, sufficiently musky for the human aroma not to be entirely annihilate it; and the waist that the mauve corset still retained, but which would soon be disengaged from its grip would unveil beneath the diaphanous chemise the gracious harmony of the hips; everything, in sum, that his imagination, after the assault of a single evening, recalled in magnificent surprises, splendid astonishments and also thwarted lusts; all that flesh was there, within range of his violence, divinely offered in sacrifice to his passion, which had been seething for too long.

He shuddered. He drew her toward him. He burned his hands on contact with her skin. Tears filled his eyes, for his heart was also dying of desire.

"Rolande…! Rolande…! If you knew how I have wept…! If you knew how much I love you!"

A little mechanical, artificial, stinging laugh responded to his declaration and immediately chilled the overheating, casting him down, in a vertiginous fall from the paradise that he thought he had attained. She stiffened and pushed him away, her arms taut, turning away he lips that he wanted to take.

"Come on, my friend, you're mad!"

"Mad for wanting what belongs to me?"

"Mad for not admitting that your brutality has turned me away from you forever!"

"I'm your husband! I'm your master!" he howled, standing up menacingly.

But she retorted, reasoning coldly: "That's all right! Take me! I'm your thing; wound me again! Wound a woman already suffering…augment the aversion I already have for your caresses! I was beginning to forget the memory and to feel amity toward you. You want more? That's all right! Go on, do it. You'll lose me forever."

That disconcerting logic of forced immolation made him let go of the wrist he was gripping. She sat down on the edge of the bed, her legs dangling. For a moment he thought of laying her down there and slaking his rage, ready to sacrifice everything to that intoxication and kill himself afterwards. But her attitude of the proud victim, ready for the violation, to the dolorous tearing, made him hesitate, and that second delay was sufficient to steer him toward prudent ideas that suddenly calmed the excitement of his nerves. He took a few steps across the room, compressing his forehead with both hands, and then returned meekly toward her.

"You're right, Rolande, I'm a brute. You're suffering, and it's necessary to be anxious about these pains reawakened by every fatigue. Tomorrow, I'll ask Doctor Bouret.

"I've already seen him on that subject. He told me that there's nothing wrong with me."

"Then we'll go to consult a specialist, Rolande."

"You're good, and I love you like this," she said, holding out a hand that he took in order to kiss it devotedly.

She thought she had tamed him, and discouraged any new attempt forever, but she was mistaken, for Julien, after conserving the hand momentarily, sat down on the bed beside her and, spoke gravely, like a friend.

"My dear Rolande, you push me away, you don't like my caresses and you've seen how I've manifested my love for you with a continence of which another man might not be capable. Yes, in that there's a veritable heroism on my part. But it's not for my sake, this time, that I want to beg you to be less rebellious; it's for yours."

"For mine?" she said, surprised. "And how is that, if you please?"

"You're still in the full expansion of your youth and your beauty, Rolande, and you've doubtless never thought that their splendor would dissipate one day. However, old age will arrive, the dark and sad hour when the amorous distraction, dupery and sentiments that you seek outside marriage will no longer be possible..."

She listened to him with amazement, because it was the first time he had declared Clara's amity suspect. She blushed, frightened to hear expressed aloud a revelation that Julien had thus far hidden in his heart, and to which she had not thought him capable of ever making allusion. She gazed at him profoundly, and wanted to penetrate further into the science of life.

"So?"

"So, still young, you're pardoned; old, you'll be scorned. Will I have the courage to continue this existence, in which I'm playing the third, the collaborator, the stranger? I don't know. Perhaps, one day, my revolt and my lassitude will lead me to reject you in my turn, to separate myself from you. Then you'll be alone."

"Well?"

"Well, that doesn't frighten you, the prospect of no longer having anyone to cherish when you have white hair? The fear of solitude at the approach of the tomb, the fear common to all mortals, doesn't make you shiver? You've never said to yourself that when the limbs go cold, when the apprehensions of the imminent end paralyze the smiles and extinguish the illusions, that it's good and comforting to have beside you, to care for you, to put your sadness to sleep, to close your eyes, a child…children?"

"Children! Oh, the horror!"

She had stood up, indignantly, in a start of androgynous protestation, with the cry of a failed woman, for whom maternity is summarized by the miseries and sickenings of pregnancy, and the pain of childbirth. For if, once, a man's caresses had wounded her, if, from a single act, she had emerged wounded forever and aroused by rancor, the charges of maternity had made her incline even more toward gentler feminine effusions, a less soiling sensuality, erasing forever any creative aspiration.

"Children!" she repeated in a more acerbic tone. "Children! You dare to propose that to me, and mask with that pretext the offer of your egotistical satisfactions? Oh no! I divine you! Your disgusting motive is obvious behind your apparent solicitude. You're no different from the rest, my dear. You're as worthless as the common run of men, whom Clara has taught me to disdain. Children to deform my waist and round me out ridiculously! Children, to suffer during the birth, to wither my breasts, for you'll doubtless demand that I nourish them, your children! Oh, pooh! Children…"

She circled the room several times, like a beast in a cage, and then aggravated her sarcasm with a shrill laugh, more disconcerting than her great anger. Her comings and goings, distancing her from the lights, gave her face strange and lugubrious tones, sticking patches of shadow to her eyes, to the projection of her cheekbones, and blackening her mouth, designing a skeleton beneath the flesh—with the result that, so young

227

and so alive, her husband, in the optical effect of his prediction, dressed her in a lugubrious mantle of old age and death,
realizing at a distance of forty years the death-throes he had
just anticipated.

That vision troubled Julien even more than her revolt. He
quit her without a word, but with his brain upset by a project
brooded for a long time, but the audacity of which, at the moment when he made the irrevocable decision, made him quiver
with dread at first. He meditated for a long time.

Finally resolute, in an impulsion of irresistible courage,
such as the weak sometimes have, he sat down at his writing-
desk and drafted a long letter, the embarrassing tenor of which
necessitated so many erasures that he was obliged to copy it
out again. His hand moved over the paper in fits and starts,
reflecting the twitches of his Herculean shoulders, those of a
collapsing bull. Dawn was turning his window gray when,
after having extinguished his lamp, he lay down on his bed,
exhausted.

That was not the only drama that unfolded at the château
that night. Hector, having retired to his room, took off his coat
and donned an indoor jacket in Pyrenean wool, put on slip-
pers, and then sat down in an armchair in order to wait for the
moment when all sounds ceased and the retirement of the staff
would permit him to go to Marthe's room without being perceived.

He did not experience the ordinary enthusiasm of his
amorous prowess. His headache had got worse; the entire left
side of his head as now encircled by a paroxysm. One might
have thought that a leaden hand was weighing upon the cerebral hemisphere and compressing it. His distress, exasperated
by solitude, became so violent that he looked at his bed with
the desire to lunge into it. The sheets, parted in advance by the
valet de chambre, were white, embalmed with lavender, and
invited repose. Would his nape not be less painful, softly sustained by a feather pillow?

But he resisted his suffering, as certain fearful people resist cowardice. An encouragement and a pride came to him

from the walls garnished with photographs. So many smiles descended therefrom, so many voluptuous recollections; and those carnal poses, languid or superb, the vicious expression with which some had been able to impregnate their attitudes, launched such multiple effluvia that he placed a special point of honor in once again not failing, this time, to reawaken his virility stifled by illness. Marthe was about to be a royal feast; he already possessed her photograph, and in a few hours he would proudly pin it to the panel of virgins, next to the Madonna profile surrounded by a black frame.

An association of ideas revived in his mind the broad face and honest white side-whiskers of Doctor Bouret, and he shrugged his shoulders at the pessimism of the preacher of continence. And as the clock sounded two slow chimes, he got up, drank a glass of sherry brandy, and then went to open the door and listen to the silence of the château. No sound transpierced it; repose seemed to be imposed on everyone.

Then, at a pace that trailed more than usual but the heaviness of which he did not notice, under the whip of his desire, he went into the darkness of the corridor, reached the staircase leading to the second floor, where Marthe's room was, climbed it, following the banisters, reached the landing, counted three doors to the right and stopped, ready to reveal his presence by two knocks.

"Where are you going? What are you doing?"

The light of a previously-hidden lantern struck him full in the face, and behind its radiation he distinguished, vaguely, the halo of a masculine silhouette. But the voice that rose up in the silence betrayed Claude.

Without wanting to explain his importunate presence in that place at that hour he immediately attributed it to a rivalry that had led his half-brother to the same door at the same time.

"Where are you going?" repeated the voice that emotion had difficulty keeping calm.

"Well, what about you? Are we hunting on the same terrain? My word, that's amusing!"

"Imbecile!"

"By the same entitlement as you, I thank you. Come on, little brother, let me pass. I have the right of priority and age. Make way for the elder! I have the author's rights to collect as well. Later, it will be your turn…"

"Imbecile! Imbecile!"

Claude's abuse became almost painful, but the disdain that it revealed irritated Hector more sharply than any insult, for it attained his conceit. He moved aside the lantern that the young man was holding out toward him and, free from its dazzle, felt more disposed to riposte.

"Come on, have you gone mad? Cease this bad joke, I implore you!"

"I'm not mad and I'm not joking."

"Then go away; let me pass."

"You shall not pass."

"Why?"

"Because I won't allow you deliberately to commit a crime."

"A crime? Oh, this time it's really delirium! Go to bed; you need it."

He tried to shove him away; but Claude had planted himself in front of the door and was hanging on with all of his frail energy in order not to be displaced. At the same time, he continued his protestations in a low voice, in a hasty stammer that his shortness of breath rendered more halting. Hector had torn the lantern from his hands and now it was him who was illuminating the other, able to appreciate all the intensity of his emotion.

"Listen," said Claude. "I know everything. I overheard this evening in that coquette's dressing-room the rendezvous that you gave her. I heard you promise to ensure her future if she yielded to you tonight. I saw her consent, the dupe. You were lying, you were lying! Before how many unfortunate women have you extended the same lure? From how many have you stolen away thereafter, after having stolen your pleasure? But it's not as a defender of probity that I'm posing. That's a role that wouldn't suit me…and then, if the woman sells herself, she alone should suffer not being paid. No, I've come to fulfill a much graver duty, to prevent you, as I said, from committing a crime..."

He stopped momentarily, in order to combat a spasm that seized his throat, for he did not want to cough. An anguish gripped him, cold sweat bathed his brow. He continued, breathlessly: "There...there, in that room, have you reflected that that woman is healthy? Have you thought that your intercourse will vitiate her?"

"I'm cured."

"No, you're not cured. It's two years since you confided the secret of your disease to me, and a month since you confessed its new manifestations. One isn't cured in a month; you know that as well as I do. After two years one can still be contagious."

"One can also not be—and I'm not, any longer."

"And even when you aren't any longer! The danger doesn't just exist for the woman...it also exists for the child, the child you're about to commence! You haven't thought that far, have you? You haven't thought, in your boastfulness of a seducer, in your fury of lust, that a little being might emerge from your intercourse, and for that being, as soon as he is in the cradle, is reserved the disease carried in your blood, the odious disease that will eat away his bones, deform his features and suspend over his scarcely-hatched existence, meningitis, paralyses, perhaps madness, all mental and physical flaws, a lot of suffering and ugliness such as the worst torturers have never invented!

"No, you haven't thought of that. Do you understand now, what I'm saying? Can you envisage the responsibility that is incumbent on you, the abomination that you're about to commit, for a momentary enjoyment? Go away! Withdraw. Go back to your room; go to sleep. And tomorrow, you'll understand that you've avoided an evil action by letting that vain girl, that girl who's selling herself—for her amour is a bargain concluded on the faith of an illusory promise—by letting that girl wait for you all night. Go away, my brother. Go away, I beg you."

His final words broke his voice. He was no longer ordering now; he was imploring. And it was all the clamor of disinherited children that was passing through his voice, the plaint of being conceived in insouciance; it was the great sob of a creation sacrificed to pleasure, to lust, to egotism, to base instincts; it was the long calvary of a humankind spoiled in its essence, the issue of inconsiderately pullulating semen, overflowing in its infinity, springing forth blindly, immeasurably, without reflection, to the extent of crime. It was also the process of social villainy, lowering the sacred act of creation to a voluptuous spasm, attributing to woman the debased role of waste-remover and to the man that of brutal fecundator.

Incoherence! The great principle of the world!

More than anyone else, he foresaw the unpleasant aftertaste eloquently; more than anyone else, he expressed the bitterness dolorously, because he was a victim of it himself, because he measured the evil fate of his brothers in humanity by the extent of his own disillusionment, his heritage of tortures, by the defect that Antonin Fargeaud, his father, had unknowingly bequeathed to him. The insinuating vibrion, the obscure infiltrating protoplasm, the spermatozoon containing in its essence the entire destiny of the being, all the casuistry of conscience, all the problems of health or malady, dolor or joy, he perceived clearly the care of offering it intact and sowing it in good flesh; he foresaw lucidly the burden of atavism with which bestial coupling would charge it. And his voice, almost weeping, said all that.

But Hector did not understand. He started laughing, stupidly, finding in the end that the lesson had lasted too long and delaying excessively his entry into Marthe's room.

"Come on, don't play the schoolteacher. You're ridiculous, I swear. If one tried to reflect on the consequences of every instinct that one satisfied, life would no longer be possible. One wouldn't eat any longer, because eating gives typhoids transmissible to others! One wouldn't breathe any longer, because respiration introduces bacilli that one might infect one's neighbors later! One wouldn't walk any longer, in order not to displace the dust! How do I know what one wouldn't do any longer? Come on, let me pass! That's enough!"

"No logic has any purchase on you. That's all right: think what you like, but you shan't go in," said Claude, resolutely, barring the doorway again with his arms extended in a cross.

Then Hector got carried away. A flux of blood rose to his head, rendering more tenacious, bristling with a thousand points, the leaden hand compressing the left side of his brain. A fury of annihilation precipitated him upon his brother, made him raise his right first...

"Get out of the way, or..."

But the fratricidal arm that he raised suddenly slackened, started tingling and fell back along his body like the mast of a ship broke by a tempest. In vain he tried to lift it again; it remained inert, no longer obedient to his anger. At the same time, a dazzling light was displayed before his eyes, soon followed by an obscurity paralyzing his thought. He dropped the lantern that he was holding in the other hand, stammering his fear, which he still tried to mask with a smile.

"What's the matter with me...? What's wrong with me...?"

And after making an instinctive effort to cling on to his brother, he fell.

A few convulsions agitated him in the darkness, for the light had gone out. There was a second of immense distress, in which Claude, sensing death pass, palpated in the obscurity a recumbent body that, after having struggled, stiffened and already seemed to be losing its heat.

A sudden illumination rendered the scene its veritable cruelty. Marthe, attracted by the noise, emerged from her room and let out the first scream that had been emitted in that familial drama. And as Claude, having leaned over his brother again, reassured her, after having checked, that he was only unconscious, the right side of his body paralyzed, she shivered

233

on seeing an odious rictus twist the lips through which the respiration was passing explosively, and seeing the partly-open eyelids showing the whites of the eyes, from which the soul seemed absent. She turned away, horrified, her teeth chattering, livid with fear.

"I beg you," said Claude, finally, "not to make any fuss, not to wake anyone. Hector's fall on the threshold of your room will remain a secret between you and me. He's the victim of a fit of paralysis that was foreseeable. Help me to transport him back to his apartment."

A long and difficult effort! A macabre and improbable exodus! Marthe had taken the legs, Claude gripped the torso; as they descended the staircase, their hands trembled, exhausted by the suddenness of the event, making superhuman efforts to sustain the now-flaccid body, half of which fled with the jolts of the march. In order to avoid it bumping along the banisters, to keep their footfalls on the carpet and stifle the noise, in order to spare their retreat any scandal, they stretched their nerves expending fluid immeasurably. They could hear their exhausted respiration in the darkness.

Finally, out of energy, they reached the goal. When the human rag was reintegrated into his realm; when, an unnamable wreck, it was extended on the bed, Claude could not help being seized by the irony of things, remarking the carnal effluvia coming from the portraits, the still-vibrant evocation of actresses, courtesans, prostitutes an streetwalkers—all the decanters of sterile energy, all the destroyers of original vigor who, stuck to the wall, reviving in their fixed poses, appeared to be smiling, contemplating their work, applauding their task of annihilation. And in the panel of virgins, in her black frame, the little face of the Madonna with the chaste tresses, the one who had given him the disease, seemed more triumphant than the others, more resplendent with cruel joy in her adornment of mourning.

XIV

The month of September had been quite lovely, with a spring-like warmth, and sumptuous sunsets eclipsing in crimson apotheoses behind the dentellate hills. As soon as the star disappeared, the earth draped itself with mist, as if to protect the wealth of its soil, where germination reposed. It seemed that amour was brooding under that cloudy down, ready to emerge and manifest itself in all the tenderness of enlacements dispersing seeds. The beginning of October was no less radiant. The trees were stripped a little more; gold was falling everywhere, crackling in the woods, even extending to the roads and bordering the bed of the Seine, which was flowing gently. It was a spring that had changed color.

Now that Doctor Bouret was more reassuring with regard to Hector's fate, Monsieur and Madame Duverdon, invited by the beauty of the day, and also seduced by a diversion from the monotony of a fortnight's anxious suspension regarding the outcome of the malady, had decided on a journey to Paris. They kept its objective secret; Rolande did not like being represented as a woman having recourse to a specialist. Even Clara had believed in the necessity of a few purchases and had authorized an absence limited to ten hours of separation.

When Julien came down from his room, preceding Rolande, interminable in her preparations, he saw Louis, the valet de chambre, in the vestibule, pushing the wheelchair in which Hector was extended. It was the invalid's first venture outside, and in order to accompany him, to enable him to accept the pitiful excursion with less bitterness, Claude, Raoul and Henriette were forming an amiable cortege for him. Even Rose, the chambermaid, had been unable to resist the desire to see the gentleman wheeled away, and was gripped by his transformation, frightened by the illness that had abruptly fallen upon a man of such conquering appearance and, by paralyzing half his body, had twisted his mouth and hampered his speech.

In a corner, Antonin Fargeaud, still clasping under his arm his inseparable big book and holding in one hand the magnifying-glass that aided him to read it, employed the last lucidity of his eyes watching that disdained son, the first disillusionment of his life careful of paternity, pass by in a fog. Since the accident, of which the physician had been able to conceal the specification from him, he had not addressed a word to him, and had not gone to see him A embittered old man, he was no longer suffering; he was cursing. Beneath his long white hair, behind the walls of his thick cranium, in the mysterious laboratory of his thoughts, which were ossifying now, strange doctrines were being implanted, utopias of upheaval and annihilation, which the book he clasped tightly under his arm was helping to fortify. He had watched the invalid being brought downstairs on a stretcher and installed in the vehicle without manifesting a gesture of pity or quivering with mercy.

Julien approached. "Bonjour Hector. You're doing well, from what I can see. The treatment of injections is succeeding, the doctor tells me…I'm delighted."

"Yes…I'm…better," the invalid pronounced, with infinite difficulty, while his left hand, having made a gesture of thanks, seized the inert right hand and brought it closer to his chest.

"But…," he resumed, with a new difficulty, the words impeded in his deviated lips, "arms...legs…don't work!"

"That will come back, Hector. A little patience my friend."

However, his eyes had not lost their strange mobility, and Julien was alarmed to rediscover, in the anxiety of the gaze, its tormented and anxious agitation, the same expression of nervousness that he had observed many times in Rolande. Immediately, however, he was reassured in remembering the cause of the hemiplegia. He had caught sight of a medical prescription, and the nature of the treatment was significant, mer-

236

cury being special to Venus. So there was nothing hereditary in the sledgehammer that had felled the debauchee, nothing that could menace Rolande. Only the imprudence of the invalid had prepared his sojourn in the little vehicle. It was necessary to attribute to him the just consequences of his excesses and his irreflection.

And yet, ought one not to feel sorry for him too? Was not the hostile criticism that Antonin Fargeaud's attitude revealed, in no longer approaching his son, letting him pass like a guilty party being punished in his rolling jail, without giving him the alms of any pity, without extending a hand or addressing a smile to him, attributable to the old man himself, to the father who had blindly married a hysterical first wife, who had engendered two children charged, from their first breath, with a hereditary nervousness that the years had confirmed and that the blossoming of their instincts had consecrated?

What part was it necessary to reserve to free will, to conscience, to responsibility, to the influence of the self, when sensual fatalism weighed upon them, determining the frenzy of the elder toward numerous feminine adventures and the aspiration of the younger in turning her away from her husband's love? Were they not the slaves of destiny? Had their will not been subsidiary to their atavism? And who was culpable—yes, who was culpable, the one who was the cause or those who were subject to it, in the grip of the hereditary vice?

And thinking of that, Julien experienced more pity for Rolande. She arrived then; she came downstairs in a rustle of her tight-fitting dress, giving her hips all their harmonious value. The deportment of her head was gracious, not denuded of an aristocratic manner. Her white-gloved hands were holding a red umbrella. So elegant, so sumptuous, and also so distant from her husband's modest amour, turned away from him by aberration, he found her worthy of indulgence even so; he reanimated, under the splendor of her form, the hereditary misery, saw transparently the patrimonial claw behind her equivocal beauty. Poor enfevered creature! Was there not a beautiful and noble charity in caring for her, in transforming her, in rendering her mental health by any means?

Clara, by chance, was not following her. He approached her swiftly and drew her to one side.

"You're ready, Rolande! We're about to leave. Above all, keep our secret."

"Have no fear my friend. I don't want anyone to know..."

They said adieu, taking away with them Hector's envious disappointment.

In three-quarters of an hour the victoria took them to Rouen railway station. Another carriage arrived at the same time as theirs. The Fortins got down from it, and there were salutations and amities on both sides, and expressions of joy—deceptive, however—in traveling together.

Monsieur Fortin occupied himself with the luggage. Julia, who had come to accompany the household to the station, passed him the bags. She was treated almost as a lady companion now. She had accomplished the journey sitting opposite the couple, and she was proud of that consideration, which distinguished her from an ordinary domestic. Her figure seemed more harmonious in the black dress that she was wearing, her laughter more bursting with health under the veil that extended beneath her little boater. She was visibly refined.

Monsieur Duverdon noticed that. "But it's Julia! How changed she is!"

"Yes, it's her," confessed Monsieur Fortin. "Hasn't she been transformed? They say that the habit makes the monk, but I believe the robe is making the nun."

"Many great ladies would envy her that silhouette."

"And her hair! Look at her hair! I marvel at it every time I see it."

In fact, a cares of the sunlight set it ablaze, displaying its tawny richness sumptuously. Involuntarily, the admiration of the two men for that beautiful fruit evolved toward an unconscious desire.

"And with that," confessed her master, "she has a delicacy of sentiments improbable in a girl emerged from her cowshed. Every day we observe the astonishing reality of it. My wife almost has deference for her. She's been teaching her to read. Would you believe that she's succeeded in a month? If it continues, she'll soon be one of the family."

"Ha ha!" said Julien, supporting his exclamation with a nudge of the elbow.

"Oh! No…I love my wife too much…"

He confirmed the confession with a tender smile addressed to his idol. The latter welcomed the homage politely. Her valor was affirmed by an assured stride and the incarnadine of her cheeks. A ring still subsisted around her eyelids, but it indicated that conjugal joys were no longer refused to her, and that the household was being compensated for long years of abstinence.

Madame Fortin gave a few orders to Julia, speaking to her in a condescending tone. Then, the train being in the station, they hastened their embarkation. The conversation, jolted and muffled by the wheels of the carriage, was restricted to banalities. Everyone avoided confessing the real reason for their journey, and as soon as they arrived in Paris the households hastened to separate.

"The doctor has given us an appointment at three o'clock," Julien said to his wife, "after having consulted his watch. We have time to go on foot, it's not far, in the Boulevard Haussmann."

"Let's walk," Rolande consented.

They went along the Rue Saint-Lazare toward the church of Saint-Augustin. The crowd was dense, abrupt and busy, under the pale October sky that gives the Parisian atmosphere, always blurred by dust, a lukewarm and discreet light, as if filtered by the activity of particles in the air. Rolande marched at a deliberate pace. For ten days she had no longer been suffering from her fall, and it was a simple precaution, her husband affirmed, that necessitated the examination to which she was about to be subjected. Out of simple fear of illness she had seconded Julien's secret projects and surmounted her horror of the medical consultation from which, even more than modesty, her aversion to being touched by a masculine hand had deterred her.

They had not covered a hundred meters when she asked: "In fact, where are we going? You haven't told me the specialist's name."

Julien hesitated before replying. To yield the name of the practitioner was to enunciate the nature of his profession, rendered rather notorious by newspaper advertisements. It would, at the same time, suppress at a stroke the confidence that Rolande still accorded to him, adding mountains to what already separated them. But since the conflict that he had engaged against Clara, and against Rolande, in the latter's favor, his timorous character had suddenly evolved. Having understood the necessity of audacity, he had suddenly acquired, by reaction, a boldness bordering on temerity.

"We're going to see Doctor Domesta."

"Domesta...yes, that name is celebrated...he's a great specialist?"

"A great one... a professor!"

She searched for a moment, trying to reanimate a memory in her frivolous little head. She had heard mention of the man, but she had never seen him when he presented himself at the château. The name floated like something distant in the ocean of thought. Yes, Domesta...?

The slightest chore of memory was painful for her; she passed on, continuing to beat the asphalt lightly with her victorious foot and to make the silk of her skirt crease. In any case, she was being admired. As she passed by, men did not hide their persistence in looking at her. They turned round; they breathed in; and that homage, although it should only have awakened a slightly more manifest arrogance, nevertheless tickled her vanity. An exquisite fruit of amour, which an aberration rendered inappreciable!

Julien was subject more intensely than anyone else to the attraction of her savor, the seduction of her velvet. Those treasures, approached during the space of a single night, which his overly vivid amour had alienated, to what an odious subterfuge was he about to condemn them! That proud and hostile head, under what humiliation, under what dupery, which she would probably never forgive!

At that moment, he was on the point of saying: "No! Don't cross the threshold of that man, who will soil you with a seed that repels you; let's turn our errant life around, from which no hearth releases us...let's return to that Clara, whose subterfuge is sufficient for you and whose presence debases and tortures me...for I still prefer your scornful amity to your hatred!"

Yes, he had the temptation, in one last act of cowardice, to say that to her, to undermine the scaffold that he had had the courage to build by means of letters for a fortnight. But they had arrived at Domesta's door, and Rolande, deciding her fate herself, had just placed a gloved finger on the button of the electric bell fitted into the wall beside a large door of sculpted wood, which opened to her appeal.

They went in, and immediately, the luxury of the house was revealed. A vault extended for twenty meters, at the end of which a garden could be seen, withered by autumn, and then outbuildings, a garage, the door of which, left open intentionally, permitted the display of several vehicles: a victoria, a landau, a coupé and a cab, decorated in red, silver and gold.

To the left, under the vault, there was a perron, at the top of which two valets in culottes, marvelous in their amaranth livery with white trimmings, mounted guard. One of them, the more majestic, parted the two battens without saying a word, and immediately, a third valet appeared, a sort of majordomo more braided than the others, coming from the depths of a vestibule decorated with panels whose bad modern paintings exhibited crude depictions of bestial amour, nudes embracing one another against backgrounds of verdure and flowers. The panels were separated by columns of fake marble. The banisters of the monumental staircase originated there commenced with the enlacement of a faun and a nymph, in varnished plaster also pretending to be marble. An Oriental gallery in pale pink climbed the steps, fixed by triangular stems in gilded copper.

The majordomo advanced. Large separated side-whiskers fled toward the adornments of his circus costume, and he reeked of alcohol.

"Are Madame and Monsieur expected by the master?"

"I have an appointment, in fact," replied Julien, disquieted by the décor.

"In that case, I shall go and ask Monsieur Cyrano."

The handsome young man did not take long to appear. He was clad in a beige jacket and his brown hair, harmoniously divided by a median parting, with kiss-curls plastered over his forehead, covered with wrinkles of lassitude and ennui. When he was in the presence of the visitors, however, he did not take long to recover consciousness of his importance.

"Monsieur Duverdon, no doubt? The professor will receive you in a few moments. In the meantime, would you like to visit the house, the gallery of paintings, that of marbles, or the bedrooms, for we also have boarders, or the gallery of autographs? That's it! I divine your desire. We'll show you the gallery of autographs...."

Before Julien had manifested any desire whatsoever, he had opened a low door giving access to a room disposed in a rotunda and containing, pinned to the wall, thousands of letters framed in gold. Rolling ladders permitted access to the most elevated. There was no armchair nor divan, nothing on which to sit own. It was necessary, when one was there, to look at the certificates praising the apostle, making them party to the births that testified to his skill, in spite of the proper names having been effaced.

"Enter!" said Cyrano, in a monotonous tone that revealed a learned lesson. "You will see here letters signed by the greatest names of France, of foreign courts, of ambassadors, princes and kings. We even have one that Monsignor Siapina, the apostolic nuncio approved with his seal. Enter, then!"

But Julien retained his wife, who tried to obey the invitation. The tenor of the evidently false letters might have enlightened Rolande regarding the subterfuge of which she was about to be the victim.

"Thank you," he said, "we'll wait elsewhere. Above all, we don't want to be perceived by anyone."

"Have no fear, Monsieur. Here, everyone is received separately. The master understands fully everyone's suscepti-bilities"—the handsome Cyrano pronounced it *sustibilities*—"and we have private cabinets, and even champagne to help things along a little." As he concluded he smiled equivocally at Rolande, with the full range of his perfect teeth.

"A strange individual! Perhaps he's drunk?" the young woman murmured in her husband's ear.

"Undoubtedly," Monsieur Duverdon hastened to pro-nounce, pushing her toward an obscure drawing room without windows that Cyrano had just opened, and where he left them alone, closing the door on them.

They did not remain in the dark for long. Electricity switched on from outside set the room ablaze and showed fur-ther paintings of an offensive realism, of a brothel: enlaced nudities depicted in maladroit colors by an inferior artist.

"What are these horrors?" exclaimed the young woman, looking at her husband in amazement. "Are you quite sure, my friend, that we're in a doctor's house?"

She was suspicious now; she no longer understood any-thing, and Julien sensed that it would be difficult to go on to the end. He did not lose his composure, however. He did not seem to share his wife's astonishment, and, caressing his beard with his delicate and timid gesture, withdrawing his thick neck into his shoulders, he explained: "I'm absolutely sure of it. But why are you astonished, my friend? Modern painting, as you know very well, no longer knows any limits. In any case, the invalids who come to be treated here are, in general, not alarmed by any boldness."

They did not have to discuss the matter any longer, for Domesta suddenly appeared before them. He had arrived like a gnome, his strange bumpy cranium kneaded by the devil and his peeled face having appeared without it being possible to suspect their entry. He seemed to be fond of procuring his clientele one astonishment after another, and his entire house was adapted as if for conjuring tricks. His short person was still amassed in the long frock-coast diversified by the 1830 collar and the ruffle, but with his forearms imprisoned in white taffeta sleeves; this time he was more disquieting than grotesque. His thin lips, withdrawn into the mouth, sketched a smile. He inclined with an abrupt gesture; his two little arms, brought forward, designed a gesture of Oriental prostration: an ineradicable habit conserved through the usages of new courts like the indelible stigma of a former servitude. At the same time, his lisping, high-pitched voice declared, volubly:

"You're early...that's good...would you like to follow me, Signor and Signora..."

Julien had had the time to make him a sign of intelligence, to which he responded by an inclination of the occiput. Then there were somber corridors, a passage through rooms similar to the one they had just quit, all ornamented by erotic paintings. Rolande followed them with a surprise mingled with emotion, and in order to traverse that maze, alternately obscure and flamboyant with electric light, she had taken the hand of her husband, who sensed all his faith in masculine predominance avowed at that moment.

Finally, they reached a larger cabinet with two large arched windows, with pieces of stained glass recounting through the caprices of their arabesques, a mythological subject and a Christian mystery, but circumstantial: Leda and the Swan, and the Immaculate Conception. The light that fell from them illuminated, in soft polychromy, tables and glass trays laden with nickel-plated instruments of bizarre form, bathing in antiseptic liquids with emanations of phenol. A large item of swinging furniture, half-table and half armchair, with advancing leg-guards of a sort, occupied the middle of the room. Alongside it, a mobile electric lamp was still burning. All around there was still a orgy of paintings, decorations and tapestries, the display of a luxury devoid of eclecticism of art, fake and gaudy, thrown as if in profusion in order to dazzle and doubtless also to distract patients from their preoccupations.

The Italian turned to Monsieur Duverdon and showed him with a gesture of his plump hand the ensemble of his implements.

"Sterilized, you see, Signor, sterilized! You can have confidence..."

"I have confidence, Monsieur le Professeur."

"*Bene, bene!* Now, withdraw into the next room and leave me alone with Madame. It's the affair of a moment."

"What!" exclaimed Rolande. "My husband isn't going to stay with me?"

"No, Signora...it's the custom of the house."

"Oh! But I don't want that! I don't want that!"

She exclaimed furiously, her hackles raised, launching toward her husband, even more than the professor, the indignation fulminating in her eyes. And it was necessary to calm her down, to persuade her that it was for her own good, to convince her of the necessity of solitude and the benignity of the examination. It was necessary to spend a full quarter of a hour in dissertations that broke against her logic, refractory to the distancing of Monsieur Duverdon. Finally, Domesta, who was perorating with forceful gestures, found the supreme argument.

"What about professional secrecy, Signora? Am I not bound be professional secrecy?

She as nonplussed by that, bewildered, nor understanding, and at the limit of her resistance, she gave in abruptly and allowed the unctuous little man to guide her by the arm to the chair. Monsieur Duverdon had disappeared. Then there were minutes of enervating practices during which all her masculine aversion was exasperated. She remembered later that the sound of a gypsy orchestra playing the wedding march from *Lohengrin* had suddenly risen up, doubtless to cover up the cry that an intimate tear caused her to utter and the click of an instrument penetrating her. She also remembered a lisping voice piping: "There! Don't budge...it'll be over soon, Signo-

245

ra. I'll insensibilize you..." and the release of a trapdoor in the wall, through which a hand held out a little cup, while the professor, with a superabundance of words and questions, was manifestly striving to deflect her attention. Then she no longer felt anything. Domesta had just made a sign of the cross and the implements and the hands were working under complete anesthesia.

Finally back on her feet, enervated, confused and indignant, she nevertheless took pleasure in hearing the Italian give his opinion to Monsieur Duverdon, who had reappeared, very red, and affirm that no organ had been damaged by the fall from the automobile, and that she would conserve no trace of it in future.

"That's all that we wanted to know, Monsieur le Professeur. Now we're reassured. It only remains for me to thank you..."

And the heroic husband handed the little man the honorarium for the operation, an envelope containing four thousand francs, which was pocketed with an undisguised satisfaction, disappearing into the long frock-coat behind the pleats of the ruffle. The more emphatic inclination of the little rotund body affirmed the importance of the salary.

Rolande was in haste to get out. She stamped her feet as she passed once again through the sequence of cabinets and corridors drowned in the mystery of the seraglio. A final salutation from the professor confided her to the handsome Cyrano, who was lying in wait for their exit in the vestibule and who welcomed them with an equivocal smile. The braided majordomo and the lackeys in culottes, the sounds of the orchestra, the garish amplitude of the vestibule, the red, silver and gilded vehicles in the garage, all that racket of lurid luxury, cruel to the eyes, glided over Rolande's enervation; she hastened her pace, escaping aristocratically, like an honest lady traversing a bacchanal.

Before leaving, she poured further scorn upon her husband, murmuring: "You'll never get me back, you know. You don't have any respect for your wife, to subject her to such an examination!"

And she pulled the door violently, which the concierge came to open. But her surprise was complete on perceiving, arriving to ring the bell at the precise moment when she was leaving, Monsieur and Madame Fortin—who, for their part, experienced a great confusion at having been encountered. She went by, proudly, without saluting, while Julien sketched a smile, caressing his beard softly, his Herculean neck having emerged proudly from his massive shoulders.

XV

The middle of the month of October was soiled by a tempest. A fresh wind from the sea passed in a torment over the château, took possession of the slightest fissures under the roof, and lifted up a few tiles that it caused to fly a hundred meters away. The old tower, sunk in its thick masonry, remained insensible to its assaults, but the adjacent construction, although solid, trembled. Groans shook it carcass; the windows quivered; and by night, the squalls collided with the rigidity of the block, made the wood crack, were engulfed in the corners, with rumors of the afterlife. In the park, great trees were torn up, falling to the ground with a frightful din. Whirlwinds brought back the same cones and branches a hundred times, and then scattered them.

On the terrace, the centenarian oak opposed all the effort of its aged carcass to the fury. Its roots gripped. There was fear for its life, used up by longevity; but in its distress it still protected with its enormous span the exotic plants placed beneath it, shuddering with agitation.

In the distance, the plain and the checkerboard of cliffs seemed to have advanced toward the château. The chalky patches whose whiteness was displayed stood out more distinctly. The clouds above passed rapidly. Swept like consistent tissues, they rolled, mingled and dissipated, only to group again and dissociate again, in an endless course. Sometimes, however, it happened that the eclipsed sun triumphed over the chaos even so. There was a rent in the storm, two opaque shreds drew apart and revealed within their brilliant silver fringes the blue-green of the immensity

Antonin Fargeaud, without bothering to ensure his footfalls, which his eyes rendered uncertain, headed for the terrace. He sank into an elastic wet carpet made of dead leaves and saturated clay. Hesitating at the bifurcation of a path, the groping of his stick no longer being sufficient to indicate the right route to him, he called: "Claude! Are you there, Claude?"

"Yes, I'm here, nearby," relied the voice of his son, who soon arrived in the vicinity of the old man.

"What are you doing outside in this weather? I was anxious about you. You went out without an overcoat, little wretch! I'm obliged to watch over you like a three-year-old."

"I was getting a breath of fresh air, Father."

"The doctor recommended air, but not a tempest! You're trembling, you're icy. Here. Put on the mantle you didn't even take the trouble to bring with you."

His hands, agitated by senility, held out a cloak that Claude put on, as much to please his father as to expel the cold of the day, which was almost over. They returned to the château, arm in arm. A little warmth departing from the old body calmed the shivers of the young man. There was no one in the drawing room into which they penetrated. Antonin Fargeaud sat down.

"Why isn't Henriette with you?"

"She was there just now, Father, and we were watching the tempest together; but she must have quit me."

"For what reason?"

"To go and pray in the chapel."

"She's too pious, that child," observed the old man, with a hint of impatience. "She'd do better to occupy herself a little more with terrestrial things and preventing her fiancé's imprudences."

"Leave her be, Father. She's so happy to be able to pray."

There was so much bitterness in Claude's remark that his father was anxious. With the delicacy particular to the blind, who compensate for the abolition of sight by the hyperacuity of the other senses, he had been struck by that sadness; he had sensed his child's voice trembling more forcefully.

"You're not happy then, my son?"

For a moment, Claude had a desire to confide his distress and lay out all his heart, to talk about the slow fall of his hopes

249

and the increasingly formal certainty that no happiness was any longer possible for him, because the malady had paralyzed the flight of his amour, because, above all, Henriette, the fiancée, the adored fiancée, was abandoning the devotion that she had for him, obedient to a inconceivable detachment that nothing affirmed but everything betrayed—everything, from the indifference of her grip to the attenuation of her solicitude and her cares. But would it not be very cruel to confess that to his poor old father, already so disappointed and near to the grave? Would it not be to plunge pincers into a wound that oblivion would soon close?

However, a confidence at that moment would have soothed Claude; to weep would have been a release; his bitterness would have been mollified by the warmth of tears. And in his desperation, which the clamors of the tempest accompanied with a savage accord, he sought a fraternal heart from which to request moral assistance; he evoked the blond vigor of Raoul, the tranquil charm of his soul. But the memory of the head of a victorious Christ, the blue eyes with pupils so dilated that they seemed black, the memory of the meditative calm that he had once loved to remain when he had finished reading and put his book down in order to reflect, the memory of that happy and healthy placidity caused Claude pain, stabbing him profoundly.

Not that Raoul had lost any of his frank cordiality, nor that the suspicion of a weakness could darken his magnificence. But alas, there was a enigma, only too certain, between Henriette and him; nature had provided one too generously with grace and the other with strength, for them not to have taken pleasure in a reciprocal admiration that relegated the fiancé to the background, posing him as disinherited, as a victim of fatality, of the fate that evidently moved them but for which incessant pity would eventually end up seeming monotonous and burdensome.

And of that lassitude Claude recalled the increasingly evident symptoms, as he also observed the unconscious transformations by which Raoul responded to the admiration of the young woman. Both of them were engaged in a chain of events of which they could not see the danger. She followed too complaisantly the movements of the friend when he went to look for a book, when he walked across the lawn, exposing the slimness of his tall stature, the harmonious squareness of his shoulders, which he now took an innocent pleasure in showing off before her. Her eyes widened as she gazed at him and seemed to interrogate his stature. Immediately, it is true, she lowered them to her needlework. Immediately, she wanted to return to her fiancé, or to God. But the redness that invaded her cheeks, the transparent surges of emotion beneath her diaphanous skin, signified eloquently enough the interest that she never ceased to conserve for him.

And Claude saw all that, and suffered from it.

"You're not happy, then, my son?" Antonin Fargeaud asked, again, surprised by the silence that had followed his question.

"Yes, Father, I assure you."

"So much the better…so much the better," confided the old man. "For you see, when I think that a doubt or a disturbance might have been introduced into your heart, that upsets me, my son. You're the only one whose happiness I desire. Humankind no longer exists after you. You, my Claude, you, the son of the only woman I've ever loved, you who have warmed me with so much radiation, you whose first smile burst forth like the dawn…what would become of me if your health weren't restored, if you didn't give me grandchildren? I think about that sometimes, and then ideas of annihilation pass through my head; I see gulfs in which everything is extinct, into which everything sinks, into which I'd like to throw humanity entire. For what's the point of living, if evil reigns, if happiness down here is impossible, if eternity is unfathomable, and doesn't permit future compensation to be envisaged?"

His eyes, opalized by cataracts, started into the void, and it seemed that a little madness might be traversing the leucoma and swirling in the sclerotized cage of ideas. He got up, groped his way toward the table, searched with a tremulous

251

hand through the books that were deposited there, and recognized a large quarto volume, the mysterious vade-mecum of his recent meditations, printed in large characters, which he read with the aid of a magnifying glass.

"Everything that I tell you, a great philosopher, Malthus, has felt like me, and expressed in these pages."

"Yes, I've seen you reading that abominable book."

"It's full of good sense."

"No, Father, it's full of unreason. It's the doctrine of a disabused mind, and you leave it lying on the table, at the risk of a single page of it being read by Henriette?"

"There's more sage philosophy and less license in Malthus than in the Bible, with which she inspires herself every day."

"Oh, Father!" Claude criticized, wanting to stop the conversation at that single reproach, for he feared losing all respect.

But the old man had his idea, which he wanted to be shared. He drew Claude to the window that overlooked the plain. The day was now almost done, and the tempest continued to rage furiously.

"Listen with your good ears," he said. "Mine are hard and serve me poorly. Listen to that wind passing by, howling and destroying. You know that at the same time as it destroys, it transports seeds; it implants strange species in our soil, which live there wretchedly, if they don't die. Why that paradox? Why does that wind ravage and why does it aid creation? Don't you find there the proof of the absurdity of nature?

"Look now, look with your good eyes...mine can no longer see. There, to the right, beyond the river, if I have a good memory, you can admire the fecundity of fields of wheat in which each ear is born and grows harmoniously, endowed with its share of soil and sunlight; further away there's an alignment of vines, the clusters of which grow, are gilded and end up in the juice-press where the vintage is crushed under the joyful feet of young lads; opposite, in that orchard, there's the beautiful organization of plum-trees, apple-trees and pear-

trees, whose fruits ripen, enclosed by walls, sheltered from
the rage of tempests; there's all the succulence of flowers and
fruits amassed in a corner of fecundity...

"And before those spectacles, which satisfy your hunger
and rejoice your sight in advance, you proclaim the excellence
of the earth and the invariable bounty of creation! Think, however, think of everything that might have happened to that
field of wheat if the generous hand of the sower hadn't extended over the plain, in its methodical rhythm, in order to
spread the seed efficaciously; and to those blonde vines if viti-
culture hadn't diverted the water from the spring to bring re-
freshment to the ceps; and to that orchard where so many
fruits grow for your palate, and so many flowers are ornamented for your eyes, if the gardener hadn't guaranteed their
development, protecting their lives against adversities? Do
you see, those ears, those clusters and those corollas born on
the ardent plains, where the overheated and humid soil calls
for four harvests a year? What crushing then under the pullulating pressure of the sun, what chaos! If you saw them transplanted here, what would become of them, tell me? They
wouldn't live; their dawn would be their decline; they'd be
aborted, stifled, sacrificed by number..."

He stopped for a moment, turned his finger toward the
visible terrace, whose miscellaneous tangle was astonishing
above that landscape of vegetal order and harmony.

"Look to the left now, toward that space where I didn't
want to put my hand, by virtue of I know not what eccentricity. There, humans don't interfere, and only nature acts. You
can, by leaning over, remark plants born in hot countries, near
the equator. The wind brings their seeds. They're paltry here;
they're anemic under our sky, and the soil where fatality has
sown them is poor nourishment. The sun is too far away for
them, and they toil and they suffer, to end in their etiolation.
Only that oak, which is at home, in its climate, has grown,
crushing everything, absorbing everything. Its laborious roots
plunge profoundly, insinuating and extending, going in search
of the juice of the soil, which climbs again as generous sap

and chlorophyll, all the way to the crown, to the last twigs and leaves...

"Well, I don't know of any more telling example of the incoherence of creation. Why did those plants come here to anemiate in a terrain that isn't their own? How many seeds must have been annihilated during their peregrination before a single one was implanted? How many vital hopes were thus destroyed? Tell me, is that logic? Yes, it's necessary to admire the creative will of nature, its dogged generosity in creating, always creating, in spite of all the brutalities and disorders of the elements. But what it's necessary to admire even more is the human thought that disciplines that nature, which moderates its impetuosity in order to aid the excellence of products, which restricts abundance in order to let the individual develop better.

Well, the moderation that agriculture posits in principle before plowing the earth, that sage restriction of seed, Malthus, the great philosopher, demands for human culture; in order not to have to clear the field of humans, in order that superabundance doesn't lead to some crushing others, he teaches the limitation of creation. That's the doctrine of Malthus. Isn't it utterly logical?"

The old man's speech had given birth in Claude's mind to a host of observations that he was on the point of confessing. Was the greater part of social misery not due to the accumulation of fatherlands and the usurpation of capital? Were there not beyond the seas numerous riches that attachment to the native soil left unexploited? An entire world was there, waiting for someone to profit from its treasures. The plethoric people restricted by its frontiers had only to overflow from the cities where it was stifling, and the rural areas where it snatched every parcel of property, in order to flow toward that world and subsist there broadly, on the fecundities quivering in its womb. But above all, Claude would have been able to extract another consequence from Malthusian theories terrible for the old man: that was the fault imputable to those who launched the bad seed, or those who, like Antonin Fargeaud, confided their good seed to bad ground.

The arrival of Henriette cut the conversation short. The young woman kissed her guardian with a greater air of reserve than usual. She seemed to be carrying within her a little of the devotion that she had just employed in praying. However, a certain animation, the nervousness of a soul divided between meditation and the exterior layer of piety, was manifest in her.

She confessed: "I've just done the illumination of the chapel. If you knew how beautiful it is when everything shines and gleams! The altar cloth that I embroidered and he paintings I made have a magnificent effect. You'll come and see it after dinner, won't you, Claude?

"Claude would do well not to go out this evening," rectified the old man.

"Oh, that's true...I forgot."

She did not insist, and headed for the dining room, where the table bought together all the château's guests. Only Hector was missing; he had not been seen that day, the bad weather having prevented his excursion in a wheelchair. Dinner was rather morose. Rolande did not eat. She had been subject for a month to extraordinary distastes, of bouts of ill-humor, which this time fell upon Louis, the valet de chambre.

"Louis! That's three times I've asked you for bread! You're serving in spite of common sense. In any case, this meal is detestable."

In fact, Louis was subject to an evident preoccupation. He dropped a plate when he heard Clara announce the imminent visit of the doctor. She had sent for him to examine Rose, the soubrette. The latter, on returning from Paris, where she had spent the day. had been obliged to go to bed, afflicted by frightful blood loss. The ancillary Don Juan knew the origin of that hemorrhage, inexplicable to the American, for Rose had just come back from surrendering herself to a somber matron.

His advice to get rid of an inconvenient maternity had been followed by the frightened girl. He had even given her the address; and Madame Poupe, the midwife, had drawn a

255

new benefit from her publicity in the newspapers: propriety and discretion. But who could divine what the doctor would say? Certainly, he knew that he was bound by professional secrecy. And whether or not the physician observed it, what was he going he do with the human egg that he was carrying in the basque of his livery, with a dishrag as a shroud? In what place of shame was he going to hide it? To what parcel of ground was he going to confide that embryo of death, which he could feel bumping his thigh while he offered the dishes to the guests?

The idea of his responsibility had suddenly come to him, credited by the memory of judiciary reading, by the verdicts striking simultaneously the practitioner, the victim and the accomplice. And the suspicion of that still-warm cadaver weighed frightfully upon his leg. You wouldn't catch him loving good girls again!

After dinner the honest white head of Doctor Bouret appeared. He had been snatched from a dinner of family gaiety, all of his dispersed children having returned to the original hearth in order to celebrate the victory of one of them, the new achievement of the second son, who had just passed his thesis in medicine and installed himself in Rouen with his father. Oh, the painful demands of that perpetual labor, that professional annexation making him the true victim of human miseries, the forced laborer of the social prison that the slightest appeal displaces immediately, abstracting him from the calm joys and the repose well due to his white hair! The long immolation of those obscure servants of wellbeing will never be recognized sufficiently.

However, the worthy man did not seem too annoyed. He was dominated by habit. He abandoned the reins to the domestic, gravely climbed the steps of the perron, obtained information from Louis who ran to met him, leaned his head to listen to his embarrassed explanation, and, already suspicious of the truth, went up to the second floor, where the soubrette's room was. Rose was lying there, very pale, emptied by her loss.

"What's wrong, my girl? Where are you in pain?"

Alas, always to suffer the same dirtiness, always to suffer the same silences, to hear the same lies; always to run into the same marks of fear, of gehenna, of cowardice. He palpated, he interrogated the mysterious organs,

"No, my dear, you're not telling me the truth. You've had a miscarriage..."

"Oh, Monsieur le docteur! How can one say that?"

"Yes, one can say that. What did you do this afternoon?"

"Nothing. I went to Paris."

"That's what it is."

The abominable calvary, the bloody calvary! He divined the phases, and as much as his examination, Rose's response affirmed the provocation of the accident. And once again indignation gripped him, not against the unfortunate young woman, a victim of male egotism, a victim also of detestable social organization, going because of the dread of shame, because of the dread of misery, to confide her womb to the needle of a mercenary, and coming back panting, dying, charged with a crime, but against that hypocritical and tyrannical society, debasing the most beautiful human manifestation, reducing the creative act, the sumptuous act, to the price of mockery or opprobrium.

A disastrous consequence of prejudices, orthodox and civil stiflings, narrownesses whose collectivity grips and strangles the individual, he detested it more bitterly than ever, because the girl was pretty, young and velvety with life; because, in sum, she had not committed any sin but loving and allowing herself to be loved; because, in offering herself in her ignorance and her naivety, she had been more generous that others already wilier, alert and experienced in fraud.

And the sovereignly pleasant scene of the family that he had just quit, of children and grandchildren united around a familial table in a common felicity, passed before his eyes again, measuring even more eloquently the glaring injustice of social divisions, the great immanent iniquity making the same work of amour end in such diametrically opposite conclusions:

bounty, joy and honor for Madame Bouret; rancor, sadness and infamy for Rose.

The young woman was sobbing now. She had taken the doctor's hand and was squeezing it in a reckless supplication through which all her distress passed.

"Cure me, Doctor. And don't tell my masters. I have so much need of my place! They'll dismiss me! I have my mother to nourish, Doctor...my mother, who is old and has no one but me; my mother, who loves me so much and who calls me her little one. Oh, if you knew her, if she knew...I beg you, Doctor!" And she had undoubtedly weighed upon the point of the soul where the old man's sensitivity was most vibrant. Under the austere surface, behind the upright and decisive simplicity of the scientist palpated the heart of a child, a naïve tenderness that the least complicated procedures caused to succumb.

"No, I won't say anything...I don't have the right. And I'll cure you, my little one, but on one condition, which is that you marry your seducer."

"I've asked him. He didn't want to."

"In that case, I demand your formal promise not to do it again."

"On my mother's head, Doctor!" she said, extending her hand and spitting on the ground to confirm her oath with a quasi-religious ritual.

The doctor smiled, and then wrote a prescription. Having returned downstairs he responded evasively to Clara's questions. The American's artificially tinted hair displeased him. He counseled repose for a fortnight, to the great disappointment of her mistress, who, always on Rolande's heels, was leaving the country in two days; time in order to install themselves in Paris. In the end, he was about to depart when he noted Claude's dejection. He took him aside.

"A little fiber, damn it! And gaiety! You're on the way to being cured. Three months in the Midi, and you'll be as solid as the old tower of your château!"

"You think so, Doctor? You say so, and I consent to it...but, solid as I am...excuse this question, which has been burning me since the first day of my illness: will I be in a condition to marry?"

"Ah! That, we'll talk about later..."

And in order to elude further explanations, which Claude's anguish was about to provoke, he took an escape route, turning to Monsieur Duverdon and asking him for a cigarette, which he lit.

"With this damned weather—excuse me, ladies—it will be impossible for me to light one outside. Let's go! Au revoir!"

They had to close the door on him, which the tempest was pushing. They saw him make sure of his hat, climb into his cabriolet and take the reins. The wheels were manifestly jolting his aged person. He disappeared quickly into the fallen darkness. Then, as the tinkle of a silvery bell that the wind was blowing from a distance reached them indistinctly, Henriette ran to the wardrobe and took possession of a long cloak, which she wrapped around herself. She was very animated, fearing to arrive late at the mass that the local curé was to celebrate at her request.

"You're going out, Henriette?" asked Claude.

"Yes, I'm going to pray for you and for Hector."

"It's a long way to the chapel. I can't accompany you."

"Raoul will come...won't you, Raoul?"

They drew away, struggling cheerfully against the anger of the weather. And not being able to go with them, being nailed down there to wait for them, Claude was invaded by a great sadness, at the same time as a suspicion clawed him, a frightful amorous suspicion, the first that he had experienced seriously. The abominable fatality that always kept him apart from them! In that trio of intimacy, it was always from him, then, who had the most rights, that circumstances stole sweet familiarity. And how lightly, almost with contentment, Henriette dispensed with his company in order to accept Raoul's!

The bite of suspicion became crueler, suddenly pushing him to abandon the prudent care that he was obliged to observe. He darted a glance around the vestibule and found himself alone and unobserved, all the others having retired. Then, without even taking the trouble to cover himself, he ran after them. The cold made him shiver.

As soon as she had entered the chapel, Henriette forgot the exterior world. Her attitude was modified, humiliated, impregnated with the sanctity of the place. She made herself very small, very contrite, before the flamboyant symbol of so many great things, so many problems of the afterlife that her intelligence accepted with the inspiration of Faith without wanting to calculate their depth. Often, in the convent, her candid mysticism of an orphan, whom no maternal smile had ever soothed, had gone to request protection and courage from the great guardians of the dream: Christ, whose head was so sadly ennobled by suffering, and above all from the Virgin, the blue virgin whose arms, bearers of the infant Jesus, materialized maternity, the sinless conception of the sacred fruit, whom she would have liked to be, whom she sometimes believed that she was.

Then, at the fall of the day, when the ritual was deployed, when a thousand tremulous golden flames lit up before the tabernacle, when the organ poured out soft or loud waves accompanying puerile plainsongs, when the incense rose in blue swirls toward the age-old vault, she experienced a sort of intoxication, at the same time as a desire to melt into all that radiance, to become an intangible element, like the dove, like the saints, like the angels adorned with white wings, the beating of which took them into the sky. And if the completion of the ceremony brought her back to reality, if the proximity of her little companions and the return to the dormitory made her conceive the impossibility of so much peace and isolation on earth, then she thought of preparing it in the future by renouncing the superficial joys of the world, immolating herself, and becoming a saint already, in the habit of a nun, one praying incessantly for the unfortunates whose unsuspected sins rendered them inaccessible to celestial beauty and bliss.

She rediscovered this evening, more concrete, more consistent and closer to possibility, her visions of old. The little girls of the area had come in a host to admire the pomp of the altar. Kneeling, with hands joined, they were praying and they were singing before the golden vacillations, before the colored images and the embroideries that were her work. In contrast to the exterior cold of the tempest, the noises of which, dominated by the voices and the harmonium, were not even perceptible, a mild warmth reigned in the sanctuary, a calmness, an appeasement of incomparable suggestion.

She wanted to become once again the child of old, to relive her ecstasies, to isolate herself in the magnificent apparatus of piety, to sense once again the brush of angelic wings passing over her curbed head, to hear once again lyrical invitations to an effacement of supreme purity, and to obey it. And, no longer finding the elements of it in her heart, already modified by the troubling contacts of worldly existence, she sought inspiration in the image of the divine Savior, the one who, his arms in a cross, his torso bleeding, and his head so dolorously tilted over his shoulder, was weeping and dying for humankind, for the petty souls who were launching their naïve incantations toward his distress at that moment.

How many resources there were in him; how much energy in his legend! What power there was in his thinness, what strength in his stretched muscles, emptied by torture, in his thorax, where the skin was plastered, designing the curve of the ribs, where the wound, the abominable murderous wound, was still bleeding! So paltry, so reduced, so pitiable, he dominated everything, he inspired all sacred valor; and his extended arms, in accepting the prayers of the humble, still protected the Universe! Yes, it was to him that it was necessary to have recourse when the soul vacillated; it was from his lips that it was necessary to collect the great cordial; it was from his calvary that it was necessary to take inspiration in order to remain pure, holy and immaculate.

And for a long time, a very long time, in a sort of hypnosis, she considered the Christ. His livid seemed to be at the end of so much suffering and so much dying. She aureoled herself with the waves of his hair, falling with a melancholy grace over the lassitude of his shoulders. What a poem there was in the agony of his half-closed eyes, ringed by martyrdom, the hollowness of his cheeks, manifest under the long beard, and the plaintive smile of his pale lips, in their expression of distress and pardon!

Oh, why did he not return down here, he who had overturned the world, in order that she could give her pure flesh and her compassionate soul to the divine man from whom so much dolorous radiance emerged? Why could she not see him detach himself, escape from the cross that had retained him for centuries, raise his head again, respire and walk, resuscitated as she had been resuscitated once before? Then, she would travel the earth with him, she would enter with him into the cottages of the poor and the drawing rooms of the rich, in order to hear him, vibrant with pity, preach once again goodness, virtue and mercy. Yes, to follow him, as Mary Magdalen had followed him...

Fascinated, she stared at him, so handsome, so vanquished, so powerful. And it suddenly seemed to her that the insensate dream was realized, that the eye of the divine man began to shine again, dissipating his veil of agony, that his cheeks were colored, that the mutism of his lips, more widely parted, was about to be converted into speech. Dazzled, she saw a precursory frisson of movement run through the body, the chest rise and respire. The arms extended, the nostrils palpitated. A crease formed that opened the mouth and made it smile more manifestly. At the same time, his hair and his beard changed hue, becoming brighter, blond and silky, animated by health and life. He was no longer the crucified; he was no longer the inaccessible toward whom the world's dolors and prayers rose up. He was human.

He was Raoul.

And Raoul-Christ spoke. Raoul-Christ spoke words of an ineffable tenderness, an entire divine murmur of passion, which only lovers are able to whisper. She listened to him, in a rapture, proclaim the irresistible sovereignty of intoxicating communions, the charm of caresses in which bodies touched, in which arms were knotted and breaths fused. Their kisses sealed two lives together, became the fecund source of other lives similar to theirs, by means of which they persisted, by means of which they engendered a perpetuity of vigor, potency and amour. And the appeal of the lips was so magnificent, their canticle vibrated in such a sweet harmony, the evocation that they elevated stirred so many profound an unknown fibers, cast such a quivering disturbance into her heart that she believed that she could no longer wait to go toward the Resuscitated, in order to take the blond hair in her hands and cares it, to be able to place her lips on that smiling mouth and breathe into it all her servitude, all her adoration. And in not being able to budge, in being held there, in a distant worship, by an unconscious reserve, she felt her breast heave and lack air, as if a hand were clutching her throat.

"O Lord! Christ! Come to me…come!"

Her amorous incantation had been heard. The divine man descended, approached her, and took her in his arms. A long spasm caused her to totter.

"What's the matter, Henriette? Are you in pain?"

Raoul had run forward. A moment ago, not taking his eyes off her, he had seen her svelte body shiver. Her breast was projected forward, her throat offered, and in the sanctity of the place, a sacrilegious fluid was emanated from her person, which attained him and troubled him delectably; he drew her toward him at the moment when she fainted. Oh, the intense acuity, the voluptuous emotion of that contact of scarcely a minute!

She came round. The sanctuary had already been empty for an instant. The Christ who had come toward her and who was leaning his blond head, imprinted with surprise and anguish, was not the true Christ, for that one was still on the cross, livid in his torture, in his eternal death. But it was only Raoul who had spoken in her heart, who had vibrated in her senses, and who was now interrogating her affectionately and sustaining her so that she would not fall. And then, understanding the drama that had agitated within her, the profanation with which she had soiled the great dolorous figure, she felt a shiver run through her, horrified by an abominable sin.

She stammered a few inconsequential words, unable to resist her sadness, which was confined again to sensuality, and, leaning on the shoulder of the troubled young man, she started weeping copiously.

A stifled sigh, something like the fracture of a soul, responded to her tears from a corner of the church, without her or Raoul hearing it. It was her fiancé, who, from the dark corner where he had placed himself, had witnessed the entire scene and had understood its irremediable significance. Desperate, maddened, he took flight without entering the stage, and plunged back into the tempest outside with the sensation that he was finding his true element there, the veritable accord of his irreparable wound.

Having returned to his apartment, Claude was unable to go to bed. Far more than the rumbling voice of the tempest at its paroxysm, the frightful discovery that he had just made kept him agitated in his room for an hour, pacing back and forth nervously. He would have liked at that moment no longer to be alive; he would have liked the dwelling, toppled by the tempest, to crush him. Why had his breath not been extinguished when the hemorrhage springing from his breast seemed to affirm that the last drop of life was about to escape with the last drop of blood?

He went back and forth, extraordinarily stirred, drying up involuntarily, with the back of his sleeve, the cold sweat that was flowing abundantly from his forehead. And in stirring thus, in being so distressed, in feeling his heart palpitate so much, he understood that his health was oscillating once again, and that he was about to reenter the cortege of miseries already experienced and then escaped by five months of solicitude and cares.

He was not mistaken. A little cough absent for a long time, sounded like the definitive knell of his mirages. A warm and irksome hand, seemingly coming from the depths of his being, rose to his throat and tried momentarily to choke him. He put his handkerchief to his lips and stained it with blood. Blood, more blood! He gazed, without alarm now, at the foam staining the whiteness of the linen, spreading out there in a crimson splash strewn with little bubbles of air. Was it finally death, this time? Would his despair follow the current of his vital fluid, would he go with it toward the shores of oblivion?

And as the blood seemed to dry up he opened wide the window battered by the squall. A torrent of cold water inundated him. All the disorder of nature was expressed in the roaring breaths that penetrated the room, swirling here, extinguishing the lamp. What struggles, what ferocities and what mournings there were in that monstrous orgy of the elements! For a full hour he was subjected to the attack, exacting the mortal thrust therefrom, the blow that would fell hm.

Finally, the arm hand came back to grip his throat, and in the darkness, he spat out a flood of life for a long time, mingling it with the icy water that was streaming over his clothing.

XVI

The following morning, there was an upheaval in the château when it was learned that Claude had vomited blood again. In spite of the precautions that the young man took to dissimulate his hemoptysis, Louis, the domestic, had discovered a handkerchief under his pillow freshly sprinkled with revelatory stains. He immediately took charge of spreading the news.

It was the father to whom he addressed himself first. Antonin Fargeaud received it as a sledgehammer blow. He vacillated under the impact, the tremor of his hands increased. He was obliged to vanquish the stubbornness of the invalid to make him accept a new auscultation by Doctor Bouret. The latter, disorientated by the new hitch, advised a few days of repose and then a rapid departure for the Midi.

Cannes was chosen, where the air would be more favorable to the acuity of the disease and where life was less ardent than in Nice. Claude greeted the physician's prescription with a disabused smile, judging the cure futile and the season of improbable efficacy. He was the only one to know that, before caring for the pitiable body, it would have been necessary to bandage the soul. The conflagration departed from the heart, and of that burn, only one person could heal the wound; it was Henriette who had produced it, and who suspected as much.

The recurrence of the illness brought back around his bed the same vigilant urgency of three individuals anxious to cure him. He welcomed their cares with less cordial gratitude. He did not put any bitterness into receiving them, he even recompensed them occasionally with thanks; but most of the time, he could not help allowing his lassitude to be perceived, accepting their cares with a disappointed mutism, as eloquent as the revolt of words.

He was never left alone. Antonin Fargeaud, rendered incapable of useful movement by his cataracts, came to stand guard at the same time as the valet de chambre. As before, he sat in the large armchair beside the fireplace, and he spent hours there listening. When he sensed that his son was awake, he sometimes broke the silence with a benevolent word, a word of encouragement long meditated, in order not to say anything to frighten him. His opalized gaze, wandering over the imperceptibility of things, had a mild expression, distant and plaintive, but behind the unpolished window of ideas, there was a shifting gulf, all his tenderness drowned in an abyss of despair and rage against fatality. When Claude coughed, he shivered; the cough perforated his heart, and then, the silverless mirror of his eyes was covered by a mist.

Raoul succeeded him next to the invalid. He still retained his apparent good humor, his superb confidence that nothing seemed to alter, but if he forced himself to joyful speech, if he made the future shine, he also thought about Henriette, whose attitude had been suddenly modified. Having observed the glacial, almost hostile change that had succeeded her act of abandonment, he explained those complex manifestations by a nervousness common in young men of twenty, and did not want to seek any further Nevertheless, without trying to define a psychology that his moral simplicity was incapable of allowing him to fathom, he could not help noticing the strange nervous disturbance to which he was subject himself.

Twice, hazard had rendered him the active witness of a faint on the part of the young woman, and each time that faint had been translated by a caress by which he was bowled over. One evening, before the magical night, their hands had met and united; another evening, he had received her in his arms, amorously tremulous and bewildered; and those two contacts, the first so slight, the second so violent, had awakened his senses, numbed until then in a fine equality of temperament, as if enclosed in a tabernacle of chastity that no divine hand had yet opened. Afterwards, he had dreamed about it by night; he had returned breathless in burning sheets; he had seen voluptuous forms passing in his dreams, which all took on the form of Henriette. By day, violent exercise and the tension of

267

work calmed him somewhat by imposing reality upon him. He told himself then that the young woman was still destined for Claude; they would marry later, after the cure. There was nothing else to imagine, and nothing else was possible.

Claude, therefore, sensed that he was as loyal, as sincere and as unconscious as before. He had not addressed any reproach to him; he had not allowed him to suspect that he saw him approach as the cup-bearer of amour, the man who had first poured intoxication into his fiancée's heart; but he could no longer smile at him.

Henriette employed a prodigality of excessive cares, as if she needed to be forgiven. She wanted to stun herself, to distract herself from an intimate fever, the symptom of which was emphasized in her face by a worry line creasing the eyebrows, and immobilizing he charming hollows of the dimples in her chin and cheeks. When the blond head of Christ appeared to her, when she heard again the murmurs pronounced by his transformed lips, and most of all when the inconceivable desire of their approach was reborn, her religiosity was alarmed; she was frightened to see how easily one can end in culpable profanation, how easily the evil genius had captured her heart.

She shivered under the stab of an intimate spur; her upper body quivered on the seat she occupied, she had a desire to rack herself, to wring her hands, to lacerate them with her fingernails, to subdue the demon of ideas by means of some physical torture. She stood up; she looked at the clock; she counted the minutes until the time prescribed for the potion. If Claude was drowsy, she picked up a rosary and told the ivory beads, she stared dolorously at the cross, the symbol of great martyrdom. But it was Christ, again, who reappeared on that cross, and then she rejected it. Or, if the invalid was awake, she revived every moment of their childhood. Neither of them took pleasure in those memories, brought back for the sole purpose of a deliberate diversion, so the conversation became anemic, and then died away. Claude closed his eyes, turned over on his bed, and his silence brought them back to face the troubling haunting.

On the evening of the third day, however, as she held out a bowl of tisane to him, he took possession of her hand and conserved it for a moment in his own, trembling with emotion. What he had to say was grave.

"Henriette," he commenced. "We're soon going to return to Paris, and then I'll depart again immediately for Cannes, probably alone."

"Alone? You don't want me to accompany you, Claude? You no longer have need of my cares and my presence, then?"

"The air will suffice to cure me. I'd reproach myself for imposing a longer sacrifice on you."

She started before the harshness of the term he had just employed. It was the first time that a direct allusion had been made to her detachment, and the phrase revealed the extent to which Claude had had the complete divination of it. It therefore offered her the opportunity, perhaps exceptional, to liberate herself, to break an engagement that her natural aspirations rendered so heavy at that moment. She understood all the gravity of the words that were about to follow. Her heart oscillated, believed itself to be close to a confession. The blondness of Christ returned again to radiate over future enchantments; the tender appeal of his lips murmured again a supplication inflated by caresses. She was on the point of confessing her weariness of immolation, of asking Claude for a forgiveness that he would have granted before separating their destinies.

But he had resumed coughing and the heart-rending sonority of his voice suddenly brought her back into confrontation with her duty and her pity.

"My sacrifice?" she said, softly. "It isn't a sacrifice to give all one's liberty to the man who is one's fiancé...to the man one loves."

"No, Henriette. You no longer love me...you've never loved me. You've mistaken for love the condescension of not contradicting my father, who wanted to unite us. Don't protest, my poor Henriette...you're not culpable, and I'd lose the little voice I still possess in demonstrating your innocence, for it fatigues me dolorously to speak at present...my breath is running out. Let me tell you, therefore; for a long time I've understood—the heart has clairvoyances of which reason is ignorant—I understood, before you were able to suspect its existence, the transformation that you've undergone...for you didn't analyze yourself; you blossomed unconsciously in a gracious and primitive purity, as a chrysalid is modified, as it one day acquires wings and flies away. Alas, I'd be a very sad pollen for you, and it would be the crime of my life to want to imprison you, to reduce to a ant-like servitude the golden dragonfly that you are."

She could have enunciated in advance the lament that she was hearing, and yet its suddenness left her confused and disarmed, lowering her eyes. Only the motion of her breast, the more pronounced activity of her respiration, the fever with which she twisted the crest of her armchair, revealed her distress; and her silence became a further argument for Claude.

"You're not responding...what response could you make, in any case? You're now as convinced as I am of a verity that still escaped you yesterday. It's therefore up to me to resolve the situation, to determine the fate of our two existences before the bond is broken..."

This time the measure was surpassed, and with a generous surge she extracted herself from her mutism.

"What are you saying, Claude? Separate us!"

"It's necessary. If we don't concede the point deliberately, destiny will take charge of it, for I'm fatally touched, you see. I sense it; I'm carrying death within me...or if, by chance, I don't die, what a wreck I am! Can I take you in tow with my miserable body, which would drag you, resigned, to spas, searching for the climate most favorable to my bronchi? Can I ask you to be the incessant spectator of my decline, of everything that can repel a delicate sensibility like yours? Envisage all that! Envisage also that a family would be impossible for us, that after having created children I would always have the terrible suspicion of wondering what victims I had made and what tears were reserved for them. That frightful burden doesn't frighten you, as it does me? Can you, who hang on children's smiles, who desire to cradle their little bodies, imagine the perpetual anguish of thinking that they mighty bear within them their father's malady, and that agony might be suspended above their cradles?"

That was the invincible argument, the only one capable, by its dramatic evocation, of touching her. She was extraordinarily moved by it, and she had to stiffen herself in order to retain her appearance of serenity. She got up, approached the bed, and passed a handkerchief over the forehead of the invalid, which was dotted with sweat.

"You still have a fever, Claude; you'll tire yourself out searching all these foolish ideas and expressing them to me when my route is traced, when my resolution can't change. We'll marry as soon as you're cured."

"What if I'm not cured? What if I disappear? Anything is possible."

"If you disappear, Claude—hear me well, I'm not able to lie—I shall enter a convent and I'll pray for your eternal repose."

The statement had been pronounced so slowly that he sensed it to be vibrant with verity and resolution. Then, losing all reserve this time, he got carried away. A nun! Become a nun! Oh, could she say that seriously? Could she even think it? She did not have the right to immure herself in a cloister, to annihilate, for the sake of mystical egotism, the living forces with which nature had endowed her, to cheat, by a willful sterility, the creation that had provided her with fecund faculties. There were other fashions, far more noble and more magnificent, of serving God, in whom she believed. There was founding a family, and consecrating to its glorious progression all the reserves of mental foresight, devotion and virtue that were her prerogative.

Oh, people admired the devotion of sterile women who withdrew from the world, avoiding the charges of life in order to subsist in the paltry commerce of their dream, in anticipation of future compensations! They were said to be making sacrifices? No, they were simply self-interested. How much greater, how much more respectable, was the heroism of the mother who obeyed the sacred laws of hereditary duty, of the perpetuation of the race, and who gave all her efforts, all her abnegation, all her servitude and all her blood to the child emerged from her womb. For him, she labored and suffered, for him she submitted to anguish such as celestial dreads never brought. And that was the true devotion, the only one for which the great God, in his justice, ought to conserve gratitude, the only one that he ought to recompense later.

Henriette listened, surprised, to that language, so new, opening the broad perspective of eternity, establishing, in its just division, what one owes to reality, and what one accords too generously to the symbol. Then, in a reversion, more to calm her invalid than out of conviction, she approved it. She took his hands with words of tenderness, infantile appellations that did not conclude anything, which did not indicate any new orientation, but which soothed Claude and calmed him—when, exhausted, he let his head fall back on the pillow.

PART TWO

XVII

'

The last Sunday in December was particularly beautiful in Cannes that year. While the newspapers signaled meteorological upheavals in the rest of France, with snow and ice everywhere, the Mediterranean calmly bathed its coast in an azure warmth plumed with fringes of foam, under a spring-like sun. The white down of waves extended to infinity, broadening out, separating and joining up again in a thousand small weary embraces that died tenderly on the shore. The vegetation traversed its annual crisis, and yet, it seemed scarcely to want to slow down, hurrying to strip away the old adornment of the year in order to put on the new briskly, remaining smart, shiny with chlorophyll, varnished with the mild limpidity sent by the blue waves, which attenuated the flight of the surrounding rocky masses, the Esterel and Cap Roux, and the emergence of the islands of Saint-Marguerite and Saint-Honorat. A fresh rain, abundant during the last fortnight of November, had washed the soil, condensed the dust, cleared what the summer had accumulated of crumbs and worm-casts, and the entire country, swept, laundered and redecorated, passed for new, awaiting the advent of its guests, the pleasure-ground of the rich or the gehenna of the sick.

Arm in arm, Claude and Raoul were stationed before the little square of the church near the pathways of the flower-market, which they visited every morning. This time their pilgrimage had stopped at the porch, and their idleness took pleasure in watching the faithful emerge from mass and descend the parvis, invaded by a host of beggars whom it was necessary to avoid.

The sanctuary poured out households, families and children who, having conserved in their faces for one moment

273

longer the reflection of the holy place, suddenly blossomed as soon as the last step was crossed, rediscovering the joy of the sunlit Eden, the intimate satisfaction of communing with the charm of nature, of respiring, all the way to the most secret fibers of their lungs, the scents of the air perfumed by eucalyptus and the marine breeze. Even the invalids—and they were very evident: poor, sickly, jaundiced creatures wrapped up warmly, with limbs like sticks poorly adapted loose garments; and the cacochymic, whose tremulous footsteps and shortness of breath revealed all their interior lamentation—rediscovered a fictitious energy, swelling their frail torsos, extending their muscles more vigorously, still strutting, while their eyes gave infinite thanks to that generous nature and the sky that soothed their miseries so splendidly.

The pious individuals were still descending, so numerous that every exotic element seemed to be brought together there, forming a living spring tide, animated by a variegation in which bright colors dominated, filling the parvis, flowing toward the nearby issues: toward the Rue d'Antibes, bordered with houses several stories high and furrowed by sprightly little trams; toward the Allées de la Liberté in which the polychromy of the flower-market extended, sheltered by booths; and above all toward the Croisette, the delightful dike on the edge of the sea, battered by the monotonous rhythm of curt waves, devoid of a beach or tidal zone, always within range of bathers.

The spectacle was so colorful, so swarming, so jovial with the special good humor of that region of election, that the two friends could not take their eyes off it, and they delayed for a moment their customary stroll on the jetty, the moment of untiring seduction that came from the great luminous gorge opening on the Esterel on one side and the islands of Lérins on the other.

Suddenly, Raoul squeezed Claude's arm, and indicated several people walking toward them

"If I'm not mistaken…that's Madame de Berge, and the Fortins with her!"

"Who's Madame de Berge?" asked Claude, who had forgotten the widow once glimpsed at a picnic.

But Raoul did not have time to respond, for the petite lady, moving ahead of her companions, was already abreast of them and manifesting her joy at the unexpected encounter noisily. She still had her provocative manner, thin and muscular, the same aspect of a dry Spaniard with eyes sharpened by an intimate consumption of the senses, her hair and complexion reminiscent of a layer of amber. One particularity deformed her, however: in her white piqué dress, her thick waist, which seemed tortured by her corset.

Immediately, she explained her presence with a loose volubility that Claude's manifest astonishment did not succeed in moderating.

"What a coincidence! Have you been on the Côte d'Azur long? I've just arrived...yes, you've been ill...me too, it's to patch me up that I'm here. I must have committed an imprudence, you see, when I wrestled with your brother Hector...is he well, your brother? Oh, that picnic on the bank of the Seine...do you remember? We amused ourselves! But I think I came out of it broken down. I put too much conviction into my wrestling. I'd be quite incapable of recommencing now!"

The arrival of the Fortins stopped her momentarily. There were further astonishments and handshakes. The loud voice and intemperate laughter of Madame de Berge made heads turn, but the curiosity she awoke did not moderate her enthusiasm, and after scarcely leaving time for the first compliments she resumed, sweeping the air with a circular movement of her red umbrella.

"No, I couldn't recommence. I've scarcely emerged from a grave operation, which kept me in my bedroom for another month, after two months of immobility. Yes, an operation. Can you imagine that my belly has been burgled?"

She burst out laughing, finding the expression funny, expressing her infirmity with an unconsciousness that Claude found suddenly embarrassing, for people passing by had heard and two messieurs following her closely had just stopped, smiling.

"I had inconvenient things there," she continued, "riches of pathology, Caresco affirmed, who made the cut. Now I'm fashionable, I no longer have my ovaries. It's a genre; it's very chic. Do you know Caresco? No? Oh, what a conjurer!"

"What, Madame! It's Doctor Caresco who operated on you?" asked Madame Fortin, suddenly interested.

Then Madame de Berge explained her operation, insisting on the result, that she could no longer have children because the organs of conception had been suppressed. She had drawn nearer to Raoul, whose musculature seduced her, and seemed to be addressing him more particularly. In the recklessness of her confidence, she had even seized one of the buttons of the young man's jacket, tugging it and twisting it, accentuating the torsion at the moments when she was speaking about her impotence.

Madame Fortin, who had adopted an expression of sympathetic gravity in order to listen, could not get over her amazement when the speech, peppered with technical terms, enabled her to suspect the satisfaction that Madame de Berge experienced in being henceforth infertile. She found that sentiment so dissimilar to her own, so contrary to the logic of natural aspirations, that she wanted to clarify the matter.

"Truly, Madame, it doesn't cause you despair to know that you can no longer be a mother?"

"No, my dear Madame, on the contrary. In any case, I don't like children, and what had put me off marriage was precisely the faculty of having them."

"That's not like us," confessed Madame Fortin, darting a sad glance at her husband. The he added: "Monsieur Fortin and I only dreamed of a family. When we got married we scarcely loved one another, but that soon changed. From that moment on, our sole penchant for one another gave rise to an equal desire for posterity. That desire has only increased since. Alas, Heaven hasn't favored us. The treatments of specialists—and God knows that we've consulted them, including your Caresco—haven't had any result. We were desperate when Monsieur Fortin proposed to me to cheat destiny by bringing up an abandoned child for some time. So we went to the Public Assistance, and chose from among the disinherited in its charge a little boy, three years old. His name in Emile; he has no other. We'll keep him for a few years and then we'll put him in boarding school. Look, here he is! He's playing with Julia, who's looking after him..."

Everyone turned round, following her gesture, and did indeed see Julia, the domestic, holding the hand of a blond little boy in a short white dress ornamented by a belt of knotted roses, with a broad creased hat sheltering a eccentric and willful face. Julia was preventing him from playing with the soil and making his little white-gloved hands dirty, with the consequence that the child, who was irascible, suddenly flew into a terrible temper, and started to howl, kicking and punching his nurse. The spectacle attracted attention and Madame Fortin, confused, had to go and calm the child down—who did not yield to the tenderness of her voice, and continued to cry more loudly, stamping his feet with rage.

"I must admit," confided Monsieur Fortin, while his wife was employed in futile coaxing, "that our attempt has so far been very poorly recompensed. The child will be difficult to bring up. But we'll do our best to keep him until the day when more clement nature will finally permit us to have another, of our own."

"Do you know the origins of that child?" Claude asked.

"In truth, no. I didn't think to worry about it…"

"It is, however, a capital precaution!"

Claude did not insist. The imprudence of the couple, avid for posterity, going blindly to collect from so many abandoned children the fruit that they imposed it upon themselves to ripen, without worrying about the original branch, without knowing whether he carried innate ancestral defects or criminal dispositions, the entire menace of hereditary decadence that the amours of the gutter prepared and suspended over young heads, seemed formidable to him, only having its excuse in the creative hypnosis of the unhappy household.

And Claude, obedient to his obsession, to the mania that he now had for the incessant contemplation of life and nature, reflected once again, as always, on the illogical division of the creative instinct, of which he had before his eyes at that moment two subjects so differently endowed.

On the one hand, there was Madame Fortin, so blonde, so charming, so anxious about fecundity, with a soul so near to the fundamental instincts of the simple nature that she had, like animals, the need of reproduction, and her entrails were tormented by remaining neuter, strangers to the great mechanism of life, of creation. She had striven for that in the early days of her marriage, and then had been reduced, after years of distress, days and nights of wounding disappointment, to offer herself to the surgeon's scalpel. A new scorn succeeded the dangerous gesture of Caresco; she had fallen even lower into dupery, having recourse too belatedly to the charlatanism of Domesta.

Finally, deceived by everyone and still possessed by the child, in order to possess at least the illusion, to obtain the lure, she had addressed herself to the Public Assistance, choosing there a plaything for her disappointed maternity, wanting to lavish on that lottery prize all the imperious solicitudes that were seething within her, having been fermenting there since the age of her first affections. And that was yet another disappointment. Emile did not know her, did not react to her tenderness; Emile was unquiet and vicious; he obeyed atavistic impulses that frightened his mother on occasion and ended up throwing her into disarray, demonstrating to her lucidly that families cannot be improvised, that their fruits cannot be picked at random, that they ought to derive from at least one of the two members of the community. Virtuous, however, loving her husband, she had not thought of deceiving him or going to demand a more generous semen elsewhere. She knew, in any case, that the creative fault was in her, and not in him. And she lamented that impossibility, like a laborer sitting down in a field that remains sterile in spite of his efforts.

The other specimen, the directly contrary subject of observation, was Madame de Berge. That one was as far away from nature as Madame Fortin was proximal to it. A prototype of degenerate civilizations, in which bastardized fluids, exhausted by neurosis, vacillated before extinguishing, she only wanted to adopt instinctive phenomena in order to accomplish enjoyments. After having expressed the essence of pleasures, she rejected afar the generative night-light that threatened to be a burden too heavy for her narrow shoulders. It was sufficient to look at her to be convinced of it. Everything in her revealed the unique will of ferocious egotism, the disdain and fear of maternal elaborations. Her atrophied reproductive organs scarcely existed, concentrated in a nucleus where sensuality was obtained.

Her instinct only ignited in order to possess, and then immediately decamped; and if, perchance, an ungallant lover surpassed the measure, and all precautions remained ineffective, if lassitude or forgetfulness permitted nature to utilize its blind force and implant the seed, immediately, at the first symptoms, she ran to the criminal hand and demanded the abortive gesture. A despicable positivist, a fraudster of life, always on the lookout for an apparition, the transports of which were incessantly spoiled by the anxiety of procreation, how numerous women like her were in the civilized world!

Destroyers of future energies, debasing amour by shameful perplexities, running to the basin when the intoxication was consummated, they were legion: socialites, bourgeoises, even daughters of the people, now as informed as one another, they were the multitude, for whom a equal concern for infertility caused to terminate the divine rapprochement with the interrogation of sheets, the canticle of adoration with the movement of a vase or the ridiculous plaint of a bellows.

And that alarm, excusable in the poor woman who, in creating, prepared miserable destinies, the refusal that social plethora might excuse if immense fallow lands did not still

279

exist, entire corners of the world, vast colonies susceptible of giving nourishment and wellbeing to new beings, that avoidance became, in Madame de Berge and her peers in wealth, a abominable act, the simple expression of a cowardice, a flight from the first duty of being, the sacred obligation to perpetuate the race, to reproduce in one's image, to utilize the generative force up to the measure of possible resources. And the poltroonery of that woman was so great that it had almost given her courage in pushing her all the way to the surgeon's operating table. She had emerged from it castrated, and she could now offer herself to any debauchery without incurring the consequences that she feared so much.

All of that, the movement of a small nervous hand on Raoul's jacket expressed shamelessly, without the latter seeming to understand, or to obey the appeal of her dark eyes, burning with evil desires.

"Shall we go?" asked Claude, coldly, taking his friend's arm, without any further explanation of his retreat.

They made their adieux to the Fortins, whose child had now calmed down. They promised to dine together one evening. Madame de Berge, who hoped that the invitation might attain her by ricochet was very chagrined not to be touched by it. Nevertheless, she allowed him to depart without adding a word. She knew that her ordinary promenade along the Croisette would put her in their presence again, and counted on having more effect on another day on Raoul's refractory virility.

The two friends quit the parvis of the church, now deserted, and went into the pathways where the attraction of the flower-market drew a swarming crowd, a compact throng of strollers in their Sunday clothes before the pretty displays, perfumed with the scents of roses and carnation. They were closely surrounded by baritone southern voices, stressing the penultimate syllable, the shrill cries of the merchants, the acidic voices of Englishwomen and a whole confusion of exotic consonants; an ensemble of Babel animated that eccentric corner of the town.

Claude was not speaking. That coming and going, that noise, that dazzle, instead of enchanting him, resounded in his soul in a dolorous reflex. He had taken Raoul's arm again and allowed himself to be conducted. The memory of his fiancée had expelled from his thought the bitterness inspired by the conversation of Madame de Berge. Henriette was far away, but their separation had not banished her from his heart. He took pleasure in imagining her in the company of Antonin Fargeaud, watching over him, surrounding his infirmity with a filial solicitude. She ought to be appeased, not having the same reasons for suffering as him; she ought to have rediscovered, in her monotonous existence, a claustral calm, the neutralization that she had desired from an early age in the convent.

Winter was holding her by the fireside, doubtless embroidering, or absorbed in some pious reading, her head leaning over the symbolic illuminations of a missal. He loved to envisage her thus, relieved of the conflict hat had risen up within her and tortured her conscience when Raoul was there. He could not believe that she was other than he dreamed her. In order to bring her that peace he had preferred to come to Cannes without her, in spite of her insistence, in spite of the pain that it caused him, and to be accompanied by Raoul, with whom he wanted to finish his book. Thus, he believed that he had put her to sleep in a kind of truce, and he lamented not being similarly put to sleep, although everything invited it: the perfume of flowers, the warmth of the sun, and the splendor of the scenery.

But Raoul! What must Raoul be thinking? Clearly as he had previously been able to read the heart of his friend, such a loyal heart, so wide open to each of his investigations, he recognized now the wall that he had formed, which, on one question, at least, the one from which he was suffering, he rendered insurmountable. But by reason of that very impenetrability, that determination, observed many times, to avoid any idea relative to the young woman, he understood that Raoul had not passed alongside that revolution without feeling its

281

repercussion, that he had not remained, like a beautiful marble, indifferent to the admiration that he had provoked, or like a Stradivarius, insensible to the sounds that it is made to render. He had surprised, in his gestures, his gazes and his hours of silence, the same concern that the young woman experienced, not to allow the storms that was agitating within them to appear.

Before their departure from the station in Paris, to which they had been escorted by the whole family, he had observed both of them, and, already certain of the sentiments of his fiancée, he had also understood the distress of his friend when the latter, his throat constricted, had thrown himself on to the banquette in the sleeping car, turning his head in order to dissimulate the contraction of his features.

Since then, during the first two weeks of their sojourn in Cannes, the cares of the installation in a small furnished villa, the choice of a domestic and the concerns of the physician had occupied all their leisure hours, not leaving them sufficient respite to chat, to return to the perceptions of general philosophy that their serious minds loved to deduce from the observation of particular facts. At the same time, the memory of his fiancée had been too vivid for Claude until then for him to attempt to subject it to the rigors of a new destiny.

Now, however, the obscure dissentiment was blurred; his love for Henriette was filtered through the perfumes of flowers, emerging therefrom as if embalmed, lukewarm, and converted, thanks to the mildness of his transformed life, into a sort of melancholy amity, an infinitely grave worship of a past that was still life, but also contained death. And that past, so brutally broken by a fissure, Claude wanted to reanimate, no longer for his profit, but for the benefit of Raoul, under the aegis of a great solution of humanity—with the consequence that, under the fête of the sky, everything seemed to have been smoothed out.

There really was a truce that had been tacitly declared, and they both enjoyed that armistice imposed on their antagonism by the clemency of nature. There resulted from it, for the invalid, less bitterness in having his vigorous friend by his side, less of the inevitable rancor for his triumphant rival; there also resulted an infinite gratitude to the man who had consented to abandon his studies, ready to conclude with his doctorate in sciences, in order to accompany him and care for him, fraternally, and in order to perfect the work commenced the book on *The Amours of Plants*, the completion of which was so dear to Claude's heart. They were about to be able to return to their cherished visions, the exchanges of their perceptions of life.

Madame de Berge furnished them with the first opportunity. After having traversed the whole flower market, and after having given a silver coin for the pretty smile full of southern devilry and the coquettish gesture of the young merchant who had supplied their buttonholes with pink carnations, they had returned toward the sea and were strolling slowly along the promenade of the Croisette, bordered to the left by dry palm trees, sumptuous hotels, gardens and villas, with a distant backcloth of verdant hills, and caressed to the right by the dying warm waves of the sea. The sunlight was striking the curt and shiny waves directly, and their variegation came, went, ran, dazzled and dissolved, vanishing in a sprinkling of light foam. They could not support the glare, and turned their heads in the direction of the road running alongside the Croisette, where vehicles were passing. It was then that they perceived Madame de Berge.

Her wry silhouette, with her white piqué dress, her hat garnished with white lilacs and protected by a red umbrella, was leaning over the edge of the sidewalk, interrogating the file of vehicles, more compact at that moment. She seemed to be searching for a gap by means of which to reenter the town; and after having risked herself several times, she had returned to her place, feigning a excessive fear, of which two correct messieurs, the same ones who had been following her before, were offering to calm her. One of them having offered her his arm, she leaned on it excessively in order to reach the other sidewalk

"Well, my poor old friend," said Claude, smiling sadly, "you've already been replaced in the young widow's heart."

"You noticed, then…?" asked Raoul.

"That she was inviting you to the bagatelle? Of course—it was quite obvious. If you wished, that woman would only ask to faint in your arms. Yes, in your arms, right away. And it's admirable, that genital thirst persisting as keenly in a creature still throbbing from Caresco's knife. Don't you think, like me, that it's a fortunate augury for society, on the day on which it will be renewed?

"You don't understand? I'll explain. In time, Humanity will be modified. It will make laws of wisdom and hygiene. Thus the Jews acted when they had great pastors. In those times, perhaps imminent, Humanity, finally alerted to the criminal imprudences committed by individuals who create inconsiderately, will organize generation, and equilibrate prolificity in accordance with the resources available for well-being, as it calculates taxes and revenues. The state of courtesan, becoming a public function, similar to that of postmistress or schoolteacher, will necessitate a preliminary castration. There will be patented castrators, Carescos invested with honorable employment, in order to tell you that it will not be displeasing to masculine conceit to be persuaded that it can still dispense a little intoxication, to give a tip of pleasure to the Madame de Berges of the future, or, rather to the functionaries of sensuality, for Madame de Berge herself will only be one benevolent individual…"

Raoul found that utopia amusing and he started to laugh. However, Claude reflected for a moment and a bitter crease furrowed his forehead. Everything brought him back to his obsession, to the point of enabling him find verity even in the most eccentric propositions. He continued:

"You think I'm joking? Does one ever know whether one is joking? May not some theory that seems paradoxical today become the expression of the truth tomorrow? When Harvey announced the circulation of the blood, when Galileo declared that the world rotated, people laughed uproariously. To regulate creation, to submit it to restrictive laws; to prevent the bad male from sowing his bad seed, or to order the good male only to restrict his seed to terrains of election, in order to produce perfect fruit, seems a chimera now, an odious constraint, over-turning our ideas of paltry modesty and familial convention. Think of it! To bring men back to the role of stallion, to organize humankind like a stud farm, what a cataclysm for our prejudices! And yet...how many charges and dolors Society would avoid by turning vitiated semen away from heredity and only authorizing the birth of beings excellent in their physique and, in consequence, in their mental beauty. In sum, isn't that Society's right?"

"It isn't its right, because it would sacrifice individual liberty in consequence."

"Indeed; it would sacrifice particular interests to the general interest."

"The individual ought not to suffer from the conditions in which destiny causes him to be born."

"Don't say destiny; say irreflection and incoherence. And ought not the individual liberty for which you're invoking respect exist first to enable the healthy man to work and to act—in sum, to live—without being exposed to toil in order to nourish the sick and the mad, to respire the dangerous miasmas of the former and be subject to the inconsiderate actions of the latter? That man has more right to liberty than the sick person whose destiny is to harm him. He has that right because he is a force in the community, while the other is a burden..."

"You'll end up with an inquest on marriage, then?"

Ah! The great problem of humanitarian future that Raoul was raising there! The conversation, commenced by a joke as inoffensive as the caress of the limited waves they could see, had suddenly become as bitter and vague as the immensity. It rebounded from the shiny calm of the water to the tormented rock of the Esterel, which, sumptuously distant, was profiled by the glory of the sun

Then Claude spoke like an illuminate, without taking his eyes off the summit of the mountain, at the level of which his ideas were soaring.

"Why not an inquest on marriage? Think about it, as I have done, and you'll conceive that it's abominable to allow couples unite, of which one of the subjects, even if he does not contaminate the other, is destined to procreate a lineage doomed to morbid heredity. Why should health in marriage not be a obligation, like customs duties, like military service, the duty of every citizen to the generality, submission to the demands the ensure the strength and security of the country in which we live, from which we draw the profits as we are subject to the rigors, for the sake of general harmony?

"What is the point of science having labored as much, of having clarified so many problems, of having accomplished so many magnificent discoveries, if it is not to arrive at perfecting human destinies? The old religion, the one that is based on precepts once capable of directing blind flocks, is disappearing, tending to be replaced by another deriving from practical genius. It will come; that is logic; that is enlightenment. And science by its progressive efforts, will dissipate the ancient errors, and reorganize the world, with the aid of a morality that will be simultaneously an esthetic, edifying a new humankind, superior to modern humankind, just as modern humankind is superior to primitive humankind.

"Then, science will throw out all religion, as well as all morality, in a time of mental trouble; it will establish conflicts between the old brutal instincts and its new laws, between the reasons of interest and egotism and the superior obligations it creates; it will be oppressive, like everything that reforms, but nobly oppressive, by reason of its justice and its sovereign goal. But in the end, everything will be leveled, smoothed out; and I glimpse, in an apotheosis, the race, finally reformed, able to be considered as a beautiful work of art submissive to principles of reflection, order and beauty entirely contrary to the incoherence, hazard and ugliness that reign on earth today,"

"A dreamer's utopia," murmured Raoul.

"Is it really a dream? Isn't it rather an illumination of an invalid, a man scythed down before the hour, who can imagine the amelioration of others by virtue of what he has suffered himself, who envisages the new era in which the first concern will be to supervise heredity, the integrity of the species and the health of the human seed? 'Love, have children as numerous as the stars in the firmament,' preached the ancient dogmas, careless of a fate, often unfortunate, reserved for posterity by the fault of nature. 'Love, have children,' the new religion will respond, 'but before creating brutally, reflect on the act you are about to commit, inspire yourself with reasons that will ensure the physical and mental excellence—the happiness, in a word—of the individual that you are about to launch into the world.'

"And the hour will sound when marriage, a sacrament of science, protected, enlightened and ordered thereby, will henceforth be accomplished in accordance with conditions of the most absolute security. It will become customary, logical and inevitable to be presented to the physician priest, to be offered to his examination in order to obtain a bill of health, just as those summoned to military service are submitted to the draft board. With the result that, by virtue of those salutary dispositions the calamities due to unconsciousness or ignorance will be avoided; crimes—homicides by imprudence or veritable legal murders inspired by cupidity—will be avoided. Everything will be improved there, society by ameliorating the species and eliminating degeneracy, parents in being spared the remorse of having engendered beings doomed to misery, and the children—the children above all—in avoiding being born only to suffer."

His voice had altered in his final words, and Raoul, surprised by that unexpected logic, finally understood the intimate despair that had given birth to that language. Claude was suffering, Claude was atrociously unhappy, and a struggle between his conscience and his amour had been engaged a long time ago, since the day when he had spat out the first mouthful of blood, looming up like a crimson disk before his most legitimate aspirations. And he was not alone, alas, in his desperation; others, curbed like him, suffocated and breathless like him, were passing with them along the gilded promenade of the Croisette. Their hacking coughs could be heard mingling with the cadence of the waves. They had clamored the same lamentation; their enfeebled footsteps, their limbs temporarily revived by the mild warmth, in vain, expressed eloquent distress.

And yet, how much light there was in the sky, how many perfumes in the air, how much joyful incandescence on the sea, what magnificent flights of mountains and landscapes! All of nature, that careless and madly prodigal nature, was singing divinely at that moment. One might have thought that it wanted to be pardoned, by virtue of its beauty, for what the invalid had just said, like a pretty woman excusing her treason with a smile. The Esterel, to the right, climbed superbly in the azure in golden splendor, and to the left, the Île Sainte-Marguerite extended like a bouquet of verdure bathing in the blue waves. And behind them, there was an entire cascade of green lands, radiations of universal joy in expanses of adorable spring.

Noon had already chimed, the bells of the hotels had summoned guests to the midday meal, the roads had emptied, the Croisette was almost deserted, but they were still there, stunned by the flamboyance, untiringly seduced by the coquetry of the vegetation and the iridescent water, where, to the right, toward the port dominated by the old town, the white, green and yellow hulls of little yachts agitated the arrogance of their flags in the pure breeze and remained motionless before the neighboring gravity of the aqueous immensity, limited on the horizon, at the end of the luminous gorge, by a line of darker blue.

They experienced devotedly the eternal canticle of things, invariable admiration for a splendor that the brutality of the elements might convert tomorrow into a cataclysm, with the mute consternation of being alone in sensing it, of not having beside them, comprehending and vibrating with them, the person whom Claude's language had just invoked: Henriette. And suddenly, their joy was transformed into sadness, form, tacitly, they had understood. Raoul had to make an effort to speak.

"You've just spoken for yourself," he said. "Are you going to criticize nature at the moment when you're being cured?"

Claude looked at him almost with fear. He sensed that their rivalry was about to be reborn in their language, because their arms were disunited. Nevertheless, he engaged in his response stubbornly.

"Cure? What deviation of consciousness are you obeying? You know very well that my disease is too profound. And if I were cured, I'd still be a man dangerous to his posterity. There's too much reflection, too much striking observation in what I've just expressed for me to want to contravene it later, to commit an ulterior cowardice toward my conviction today."

"But Henriette is waiting for you, Henriette loves you!"

"Is it me she's waiting for? Dare to affirm it to me! Is it me that she loves? Dare to tell me so! Raoul, she has never loved me. She has mistaken the intentions of her heart; she has obeyed a foreign suggestion, the pressure that my father has exerted on her will since an early age. And since...oh yes, since..."

"You're not, however, going to annihilate behind the four walls of a convent that creative force, that divine incarnation of the family!" Raoul hastened to add. "She's religious, you know that, and she has told us both of her intention to disappear piously if you don't marry her!"

The formidable question suddenly burst forth, so feared and so desired by both of them, which had been palpitating with the anguish of their breasts. Then the invalid stiffened himself, for the moment had come to respond, to define the role of obscurity and sacrifice that he intended to play henceforth, to the profit of his friend, the magnificent man who was almost his brother.

"No," he said, with difficulty, "I don't want her to disappear into a cloister, in default of the creation for which life has endowed her. There are riches that should not be buried, treasures that ought to prosper. I am renouncing her because I am unworthy of her, because fatality has broken me...but I want to be generous enough to give her to another, who merits her, another, whom she loves...yes, whom she loves, I'm certain of it..."

"Who is that other?" stammered Raoul, tremulously. "Oh, tell me...who? Who?"

But the effort had been too heroic for the invalid, and had vanquished his will. Suffocating, he was obliged to stop, leaning against a tree, seized by vertigo.

"Let's go back," he said, "I beg you! How cruel you are! You can see, I can't do any more..."

An empty fiacre was passing by. Raoul hailed it and installed his fainting friend therein. The wheels stirred up a little dust. The variegation of the water, the pretty islands, the sunlit Esterel, the yellow palm trees, and the white and green villas, all disappeared in a flight. The carriage had to stop at a level crossing of the railway, which a strident locomotive furrowed. A glance at the platform allowed them to distinguish Madame de Berge in the company of her two followers. She was embarking for Monaco.

XVIII

Slowly, Monsieur and Madame Fortin climbed the winding road that led to their villa, on the road to Valergues. It was a delightful walk when the weather was fine. Orange trees covered with golden balls, flowering mimosas, palm-trees enlaced with ivy, odorous eucalypti and magnolias ornamented the route, and when the caprice of the terrain brought them level with fields, entre areas could be se to the right and left bright with roses, geraniums and carnations. Streams descending from the mountains flowed along the rocky border with sonorous haste. On dark nights one could guide oneself entirely by means of its urgent voice, extinguished in places by a subterranean section; but it soon reappeared, a little noisier and a little more rapid, and its shrill cascade mingled with gusts of orange-blossom coming with it from the heights.

The household had chosen that quarter because of its isolation, and also because of the splendid view that one had from the first floor. All of Cannes extended beneath their feet, with the slope of the Esterel as a background to the scene, and the blue tints of the gulf of Naples perceptible through the branches of gigantic palm trees.

That day, however, the weather was disorderly. Large gray clouds were jostling one another, fighting, crushing the sky and then bursting, pouring down masses of cold water—with the consequence that on the sullen and dirty road of yellow earth, soaked by the rain, the feet of the walkers skidded incessantly and sank into the mud. Nothing was as awkward as that ascent, so briskly accomplished when the ground was dry. Madame Fortin, exhausted by effort, all her courage abolished, stopped in front of a bench and abandoned her husband's arm.

"I can't do any more. Let's rest, please."

"I told you, my darling, that the route would be difficult. Why are you obstinate in refusing a carriage?"

"My poor friend, it isn't the road that's breaking my legs...it's the doctor's consultation."

"It's necessary not to think about it any longer, my darling."

She shook her head sadly, as a sign of impossibility. The last stroke of the scythe had just been given to her hopes and cast them definitively to the ground. A little while ago, the examination of a physician celebrated in the region, an examination for which suspicions consecutive to Madame de Berge's loquacity had inspired the desire, had finally revealed brutally the nature of the operation carried out by Doctor Caresco, certainly curing the malady but rendering maternity impossible henceforth, since the organs of fecundation had been suppressed by the hand of the skillful surgeon.

At the same time, Domesta's fraud had also been revealed, and that mingled anger with their sadness, the shame of being fooled by the glabrous poussah, of having lent themselves ridiculously to an unrealizable insemination, having been subjected to debasing practices. Oh, it was complete now, and nothing had been spared them: cruelty on the one hand and grotesquerie on the other! And their disappointment brought back more intensely the memory of what they had endured, revived the metallic gaze of the operator, the alarming display of his instruments, the white table, the cold walls coated with varnish, the chloroform, the bloody linen and the agony of breath that seemed to want to be extinguished.

Terrorized and happy, they had believed then; they had adored the sacrificer. Then, later, when their faith had already been shaken, there had been a further illumination of the mirage, a new dream that they had nourished in their hearts, pushing them almost to repeat the first operation, but a buffoonish repetition, charged with drama, the husband and the wife separated again, her extended again on the fecundator's table, him in the next room seeing a woman with made-up features suddenly appear in a mystical half-light, only clad in a long pink peignoir...

"Oh, the wretches! Have they lied to us both enough?" stammered Madame Fortin in a rage, the first that her good and simple nature had ever experienced. "Caresco especially! That Caresco, whom I considered almost as a god…! Can I pardon him for having cured me, now that he's reduced me to the condition of Madame de Berge, that's he's doomed me to sterility?"

"What do you want, my darling? It's done. Let's not think about it anymore. We'll arrange our life differently; we'll love one another more."

"We won't be able to love one another in our child, alas… And the room we prepared…and the cradle, the baby-clothes, the toys that were waiting for him…"

At that memory, her sadness exploded in a flood of tears, warm tears that she dabbed away with little thrusts of a lace handkerchief. She had leaned her head on Monsieur Fortin's shoulder, and it was a relief to let her dolor out thus, to recount her annihilation to the person who knew it as well as she did and was no less afflicted by it.

Sitting on the bench with their backs to the rock, they seemed, in their attitude, paled by the approaching night, to be a dolorous frieze, two individuals shoring themselves up in order to support the weight of a enormous distress. Passers-by, couples who advanced arm in arm, united against the bad weather, continued their route without daring to turn their heads, carrying away in their enlacements a little of their dejection.

A frisson of wind threaded over them droplets of cold rain that were dripping from the leaves of trees overhanging the rock, but they did not perceive the glacial impression. He tried to calm her down, however, to persuade her of his amour, before which the other objects of the world would henceforth be effaced, since it was a fusion of their two hearts, a paradise of tenderness in which they would both be exalted until their last breath. But she shook her head, no longer even finding the strength to smile at the coaxing expressions, the abbreviations of adorable intimacy that he employed in smoothing her hair with the back of his hand, as he did every time he had to console her for some petty chagrin.

"No, no! Your benevolence is trying to distract me, bandage the frightful wound, but you know very well that it's irremediable, since nothing can now fill the empty hearth, since the little heads that I hoped to see agitating around us, those other yous and other mes, will never smile at us. I've thought about it all my life, the child, since the age when I was hugging my dolls. It was to obtain it that I married you, first, and then loved you. My marriage, my affection for you, had no other goal...and now all that has been sacrificed by that wretch Caresco...!"

She did not continue, for a new order of ideas was agitating her mind, a sudden hope on to which she clung. And the more she thought about it, the more a desire took form to scrutinize the youth of Monsieur Fortin, to learn that he had succumbed like others to the pressures of nature, that he had loved before her, that he had had mistresses.

Oh, if a child had ever born of an old liaison and if he still existed, with what enthusiasm she would have opened her arms to welcome that unknown, and how gladly she would give the disinherited individual the place he merited occupying in their hearth! For if that child had not emerged from her flesh, at least he would have come from her husband, and that was enough for her to forgive him the other half of his extraction, for her to excuse the fault that had been his origin, for her to adore him.

A sublime fiction, an implausible suggestion! She was almost hoping for it now, building an entire anterior romance of which the gracious and unfortunate baby as he hero. From there to envisaging a combination of circumstances, a voyage, a temporary separation impelling Monsieur Fortin to deliver himself to another woman, to choose temporarily another, more fecund, terrain to inseminate, and to bring back therefrom the fruit that she was impotent to give him, there was only a single step to take, only one further concession to admit. Certainly, that anti-natural amorous scheme, the sacrifice that it would have made of marital fidelity, resulted from a certain logic in her hypnosis. Certainly, too, that monstrous renunciation for others only existed within her in a confused state. But she was in a moment of inexpressible distress, in which the heart accepts all solutions. And by dint of thinking about it, by dint of wanting the eventuality, she arrived at wanting to sow the first ferments. In any case, she desired to know, to be informed.

"If only," she continued, in a lower voice, "you had been married before, and, your first wife having disappeared, I had her cherub to care for and caress, at least I would still have a consoling goal in my misery, How many households are there in which the child of another bed is bought up preciously by an adoptive mother? We know enough of them, don't we? And I wouldn't even care, I tell you, my darling, if Monsieur le Curé hadn't been involved. You're young, you've doubtless loved…don't all children come from the good God?"

He looked at her with eyes widened by surprise, and in his astonishment he had abandoned his familiar gesture of caressing the back of her neck and smoothing her wet hair.

"Is it you, my wife, who is saying that? You, who were once so absolute on the unity of the family?"

"Well, yes, it's me. Once, I was only an egotist; now my impotence recalls me to generosity. I understand that love is beyond prejudices, and that there are no longer any vanities or social categorizations to respect when one has a void in the heart to fill. So, I repeat to you, all children come from the good God; and if I learned of the life of one of them, engendered by you before our marriage, I would ask you to bring him to me, to offer him to me, to keep him and love him as if he were my own."

He did not even respond with the arguments easy to oppose to such a prayer. The child, if he existed, would not be his, and a mother would never be dispossessed of him. But that would have been reasoning, and it was not an occasion for reasoning. He contented himself with raising his hand in a sign of negation, excusing that simple and great delirium, not finding it ridiculous, as he would have excused the caprice of an invalid.

Then, Madame Fortin's last hope having evaporated, having dissolved in the fine drizzle that had recommenced falling in the severity of the approaching dusk, she stood up, very wearily, and they both resumed the route to the villa. Vehicles whose brakes were screeching were descending the slippery hill, bringing back chilly excursionists wrapped up in their damp cloaks. Behind them, Cannes lit up, and an opacity of water and nocturnal mist veiled its satellite, the Esterel, and the sea that bathed it. For the first time, the solitude weighed upon them heavily.

That impression of emptiness only dissipated at the moment when they perceived, at a bend in the road, the white façade of the house. It was visible through the branches of tall palm trees, its windows illuminated, under the projection of a large perforated stone balcony framing the only story, and the contiguous hallway was flamboyant behind a thin and translucent texture of wooden blinds. In that hallway, Julia must be waiting for them, watching Emile, the baby extracted from the Public Assistance, who had seemed calmer for a few days.

But that was another false hope, for as soon as they entered the garden by a door hidden in the ivy, to which Monsieur Fortin had the key, they heard the child wailing.

"Oh, that child is insupportable," said Madame Fortin, enervated.

"We can't keep him," said the husband, supportively.

They were beginning to admit their imprudence. They regretted having yielded to a caprice too hastily contented, the child having been chosen on the basis of his original appearance, without them worrying greatly about his character or the moral aptitudes already sketched at that age. After having admired him, and ornamented him with ribbons like a pretty doll, after having smiled at his first fits of anger, now they found his unhealthy tantrums, impulsive crises of a sort that twisted his mouth and made him roll on the ground, disquieting.

And then, their hearts were not in it; they were no longer able to forgive. The plaything wearied them; it was continually breaking down. He remained impassive to all the tender solicitations of his temporary mother, all the hearty laughter of Julia, whom he scratched on the sly, like certain cats that one pays with caresses and which return the change in treacherous thrusts of the paw. He liked to break and destroy things. Although voracious, he refused obstinately to eat when begged to do so. The muffled elaboration of base instincts could already be sensed in him, the precursory rumbles of crime, al the torment of morbid heredity revealed by a cranium receding under the coquetry of blond hair.

On opening the door they found the infant swollen with rage, almost blue, trying in vain to struggle in the solid grip of Julia, who, having sat him on her knees, was paralyzing his arms and hands. The little boy was writhing convulsively under torn and dirty garments, and simultaneously uttering a shrill and uninterrupted howl.

"Well, what is it now?" Monsieur Fortin asked.

Julia raised her tawny head, leaning over the child, and very angrily she explained the new avatar. The kid was surely vicious, and they would never get to the end of it. Had the little wretch not plunged his hand a moment ago into the goldfish bowl to seize one of them? Then, having taken possession of it, had he not crushed it under his foot? That cruelty had been punished by a good slap, and that was why he was now crying and struggling. Yes, surely he was vicious, and Madame had been very good to want to raise such a brat, descended from who knew where.

Madame Fortin approached and attempted a futile appeasement. Her maternal virtue was not put off so easily, and found once again, in the presence of difficulties, an astonishing patience.

"Come on, Baby, please be nicer to your maid! Be good, Baby, and you can have cake. Come on, my baby…"

She extended her hand to caress him, but her gesture had no other effect that to augment the infant's fury; he began to

297

squirm like an eel on Julia's knees. A gleam of manifest hatred appeared in his gaze. And as his immobilized hands and legs did not permit him to assuage his paroxysm, he suddenly advanced his mouth toward Julia's breast, projecting beneath the supple woolen bodice, and bit it. The pretty girl uttered a scream, and let go of the child, who tumbled to the ground, suddenly calmed by the success of his vengeance.

"He bit me, the brute! He bit me, and I'm bleeding!"

The couple immediately hastened around the wounded girl, pale with dolor. The bodice being buttoned at the back, it was necessary to remove it completely in order to uncover the wound. As it was taken away, the white cleavage of the firm breasts appeared, damascened by light veins, the nacreous plenitude of the shoulders and the harmonious lines of the arms, still strong, but refined in their contours since they had been liberated from rough labor. But what caused them to marvel most of all, emerging from a chemise of coarse fabric like two beautiful jewels deposited in a case unworthy of their splendor, were the firm, arrogant, glorious breasts, with a clarity of polished marble, terminated by a halo of exquisite rosiness. Forceful and gracious at the same time, one would have thought them ready to swell with a generous sap or to quiver under creative kisses. And their appearance, presaging so many other dissimulated beauties, as so unexpected and so dazzling that they forgot the drama, the red droplet oozing from one of the teats, and the stain spreading over the chemise, and Julia's pain, in order to pause in their care and admire.

"It's true that the bite has drawn blood," said Madame Fortin. But she was speaking to give herself countenance, and, not daring to touch the wound, she stood aside and left it to her husband. The latter strove to tend to the wound. With a piece of cotton steeped in antiseptic liquid he compressed the gap and collected the crimson fluid that was already flowing less abundantly. His hand was trembling and tried to hasten the task; he could not have said whether it was only precipitation and alarm that moved him to that degree, for at the same time as he was trying to stem the blood, he had her two vigorous nipples of the beautiful young woman directly before his eyes, which pain rendered more erect. On seeing them pointing their plasticity, so radiant, so promising, he experienced an infinite disturbance.

In order to finish the dressing, to make the strip of fabric that he wound around the chest hold its place, he had to take the entire globe of flesh in his hand, and palpate the grain, as soft as satin. A burning fluid emitted by the superb form contracted his fingers over the marmoreal beauty, and then flowed all the way to his brain in a quivering tide. And to complete the temptation, the movement forcing Julia to raise her arms, he perceived the gilded tufts under the armpits, and respired the feminine odor, the aroma of human animality emanated therefrom, so gripping, so sovereignly evocative that he received a shock of delectable desire that stunned him and made him close his eyes.

Finally, after a pause, he opened them again, and avoided thereafter looking at the cleavage, and the emergence of the other breast, which the bandage left free.

In any case, Madame Fortin had drawn nearer. After a twitch produced by the surprise of a voluptuous rivalry, the importance of which she sensed, she showed herself very cheerful now; she was smiling, and she joked: "Come on! That's nothing. Baby will have done it for his greed. The morsel was worth the trouble, anyway. Isn't it true, my friend, that one would gladly bite there?"

She took Monsieur Fortin's arm in order to go to table. Throughout the meal she was very attentive to him, not allowing him to carve in accordance with his habit, but demanding, on the contrary, that he accept the finest morsels. She was talkative, and the sadness of the previous moment had evaporated. Several times she stopped talking; her mouth creased for a mute confession; her mime designated the attentive and superb allure of Julia, who was assisting with the service, and the supple movement of her undulating hips when she walked.

299

Later, however, when they had retired to their room Monsieur Fortin found her manner strange. She got undressed briskly, deploying a nervous haste in unlacing her corset and unbuckling the elastic girdle of which the consequences of her operation still demanded the employment. Finally, when she was no longer wearing anything but her chemise, she sat down on the edge of the bed and drew her husband against her, seductively, with an expression of proud tenderness and inexpressible devotion. There was also a solemnity in the fashion in which she started the conversation, in which she asked: "You're mine?"

"Eternally."

"Yes, I know; I have an absolute conviction of it. Our amour will defy even death. Nothing is above and nothing equals it. You love me, and you've never ceased to love me, even when you were touching Julia's breasts."

"What are you saying?"

"Oh, don't defend yourself, my darling, since we adore one another...but I saw! I saw your emotion; I saw your hand tremble; I glimpsed the flame that lit up in your eyes..."

Stupefied, he was opening his mouth to protest when she put her arms around him, gently. She was ready to weep, and yet she held back her tears. After a sigh, inflated by her sacrifice, she went on:

"Don't excuse yourself, my darling; it's so natural to desire what is beautiful, and she's so beautiful, that Julia! You're still a man, and I no longer have the right to call myself a woman. Yes, she is beautiful compared to me, fatigued and worn away by malady. Look at my breasts, compare them with hers!"

With a gesture of supreme abnegation, she parted her chemise and exposed the lassitude of her breasts, still meager in spite of several months of recovery, and the projection of the clavicles under which two profound hollows were designed, shadowed by the oblique illumination of the lamp.

"Yes compare this flesh, which has suffered, with the other, which is new; compare the sterile with the fecund! It would therefore be necessary for me to be blind to hold it against you because you desired her! Your instinct spoke, your senses were stirred involuntarily; and that isn't your fault, and I forgive you, because, as for me, it's your entire soul that I possess, my darling."

Again he tried to stop her in order to calm her folly, which he sensed becoming painful; but she closed his mouth with a violent kiss. No dike, now that she had launched forth, would have been able to oppose her confession, and she threw her heart, breathlessly, into a suffocated speech, punctuated by hoarse sounds.

"Look! You can see that I adore you, since I'm kissing you at this moment; but let me say everything...I need to say it! Perhaps tomorrow there'll no longer be time, for I won't have the courage any longer...listen! That woman, so beautiful, that marvelous instrument of flesh, I want...I want, you hear!...I want you to take her; I want you to draw away from me, I want you to use yourself as a machine for creation, in order to bring back to me...in order to bring back to me that which I can't give you...!"

She did not finish, for she had finally understood, and now it was him who had wrapped his arms around her and was soothing her delirium with caresses that led them to the utmost limits of sensuality: infecund caresses of which, when the communion had been celebrated, he ruminated the strange debut, while, with her eyes closed, she reposed in the large bed, after having placed her weary pretty head on his shoulder. Her parted chemise displayed the meager sinews of the neck, the jutting of the clavicles, and the lassitude of the two poor breasts, annihilated by suffering, so contrary, in their poverty, to the sumptuous erection of the former farm-girl.

XIX

As Julien Duverdon went past the hotel office, the porter, a self-important, clean-shaven fellow braided in every seam, approached him, cap in hand. His obsequious smile revealed the crenellations of three absent teeth, and he jabbered in an exotic accent formed of polyglot sounds:

"Monsieur, Madame he is suffering. Just now, when he came back with Miss Bowett, he suddenly fell in faint."

"Where is she?"

"In his room."

Without waiting for more ample explanations, the gentleman plunged into the stairwell. An Oriental gallery favored the length of his stride. He went past the elevator contiguous with the banisters, filled with Englishmen, who, thinking that it was a race, laughed noisily, shaking drooping moustaches yellowed by pipe smoke. Having arrived at the second floor he turned left, stopped in front of a somber door characterized by a serial number, and was about to enter without knocking when he remembered that Rolande detested his unexpected irruptions. Then his broad shoulders suddenly became hesitant, he breathed and listened, caressing his large graying beard.

Two familiar feminine voices, one adored and the other hated, filtered through the interstices of the door. Their babble reassured him and he started to smile. Now he suspected the cause of her faint. Domesta had warned him. Then he decided to knock, and to turn the key in the lock after Rolande had given him authorization from inside.

On seeing her husband appear, Madame Duverdon suddenly resumed a certain languor that her friend's conversation had made her forget to observe. She extended her upper body, scarcely protected by an unfastened blouse—for it had required the fresh air from the open window to reanimate her—

on her chaise-longue. Then she accepted Julien's hand graciously.

"Oh, my poor friend, you were lacking just now..."

"No, I was there...," Clara interrupted, nervously.

"You, Miss Clara, are only a woman, and you lost your head. That's why I say that my husband was lacking, truly. Can you imagine, Julien, that something amazing happened to me? I suddenly lost consciousness and fell into the porter's arms. You can imagine the turmoil that my fall caused in the hotel. The entire staff, management and flunkeys, and all of Albion, around my inanimate body!"

"Yes, I know."

"Personally, I didn't perceive anything. It's very mild, that fashion of going away. When I woke up, I was on this chaise-longue. I had Miss Clara on one side and on the other, taking my pulse, a bearded physician in a white cravat, summoned in haste."

She burst out laughing, delighted to be alive again, joyful at the memory that crossed her mind.

"Do you know what he asked me, that bearded fellow? He asked me if I might be pregnant. No! Can you image that? By what operation of the Holy Spirit?"

She was laughing now, although a little while before, certain questions ventured by the doctor regarding her monthly periods had surprised her by their precision. Monsieur Duverdon, anxious at first about the intervention of the practitioner, also started to laugh when he understood that the request had not had any effect. The Holy Spirit, operating with sterilized instruments, appeared to him in the form of the adipose little charlatan, glabrous and lisping, solemnly ensconced in his 1830 high collar. Nevertheless, he thought it wise to reassure her more completely and to erase completely the impression caused by that inexplicable faint.

"Come on! It'll be nothing, my dear Rolande. You must expect a few snags consecutive to your automobile accident, but the doctor has taken care to inform us of their innocence...you remember!"

"That's true. Would you believe, though that such a slight bump could have such distant consequences? Hector paralyzed...me subject to bizarre troubles..."

"Accidents consequent to trauma. They disappear in time..."

"It's only Miss Clara who's remained valiant," Rolande concluded, smiling at her friend.

The American did not reply. Beneath her make-up, her green eyes were glinting strangely. She moved all of a piece, her neck tight in her masculine collar. Her mahogany hair, in short curls, radiated false tints. She went to button her friend's blouse in order that Julien would not have the spectacle, and that modest gesture revealed a supreme immodesty.

The husband, in any case, shrugging his shoulders, had posted himself at the window that overlooked the street and was amusing himself watching the movement of Nice, which, between eleven o'clock and midday, through the broad streets furrowed by packed trams, was announcing the battle of confetti.

That February day was superb, and the fête was already quivering, with multicolored carts heading separately for the rendezvous in the Place Masséna, with the sound of trumpets, the roll of drums, and appeals and cries proclaiming in advance the brutal gaiety of the afternoon.

"Will you have the strength to accompany our friends from Cannes to the battle?" asked Monsieur Duverdon, turning to his wife.

"Certainly, my dear; I want to amuse myself."

Here malaise had passed. She got up, went to her swiveling mirror and began to repair the disorder of her hair.

"I'm a little tight in my corset," she admitted to Clara. "I think I'm definitely putting on weight."

"I haven't noticed. In any case, it's necessary not to allow yourself to get a paunch, my dear friend. We'll go cycling."

Julien protested. That sport was forbidden by the doctor, as well as all other violence. Complications might ensue that could put Rolande's life in danger, and he believed that he ought to use his friendly authority to recommend Clara not to draw the invalid into shaking up organs already weakened. When the American replied, citing the example of the girls of her country, always in motion, always careful to develop their corporeal strength, and were all the better for it, Monsieur Duverdon finally became irritated and cut the discussion short with a brief word.

"My wife isn't a girl."

"Oh, she's hardly your wife!" replied the American, with a nasty smile of triumph."

"What do you know about it?"

The expression in their eyes aggravated the skirmish. For a long time they had been making war thus, with thrusts of implication, the husband having decided, in his prudent timidity, no longer to have recourse to acts of violence susceptible of compromising the success of his subterfuge. He let things go, pulling his neck back into his square shoulders; he even submitted to the scratches of his rival without bringing down the crushing club. And this time, like the others, he was the first to lower the flag, for he was sure henceforth of a vengeance indicated by a few symptoms unsuspected by the two friends, including Rolande's recent faint. He even started smiling ironically, and the foreigner remained anxious at that mockery, the presage of an upset.

Fortunately, Rose, Clara's chambermaid, appeared. She was thinner, rendered pale by the journey from Paris, accomplished the previous day. Her eyes, drawn by fatigue, and her delicate nose, sensual and palpitating, narrowed at the root, confirmed eloquently the rings around the eyelids. It is true that the journey had been made second class in an almost empty carriage occupied with her by Louis, Antonin Fargeaud's valet de chambre, who was going to join his master's son in Cannes. The jolts of the route had exhausted her, and she was almost fainting with lassitude. She announced the presence in the hotel lounge of Monsieur and Madame Fortin, Raoul,

Claude and Madame de Berge, all invited to lunch by the Duverdons.

"That's all right, my child; we'll come down," said Rolande, who had completed her toilette.

Rose turned to Clara and, lowering her eyes, asked for permission to rest during the afternoon. She declared that she was exhausted by the journey. But when the authorization had been granted to her she found a new vigor in order to reach her room on the fifth floor, where Louis, similarly provided with a leave, was waiting for her. She opened her arms, still a slave to that man, who dominated her egotistically with a brutal irreflection. She adored his caresses sufficiently to have forgotten the dangerous consequences, once set aside already by the midwife. He took her again, not without hr murmuring between two caresses her supplication to be prudent, which he omitted to do.

The masters' lunch was imprinted with a mild cordiality. They all had the pleasure of finding themselves almost a family in the private dining-room with gilded paneling. The menu, exempt from the sauces and ingredients of cheap restaurants, was washed down with vintage wines. Bowls crammed with exquisite fruits—blond bananas, velvety peaches and large blue grapes—garnished the tablecloth, strewn with rose-petals. Wellbeing warmed their cheeks and refined their sentiments, temporarily putting Madame de Berge's ardors to sleep; she forgot to gaze at Raoul with all the eloquence of her indefatigable desire, but she compensated herself over coffee by lighting a cigarette. The young man had to withdraw his foot, too violently touched, and that audacity made him think of the sage Henriette.

Since Claude's confession, in any case, since the moment when the disillusioned invalid had declared his renunciation, Raoul had been living in an inexpressible turmoil. His character of frankness and broad cordiality had been entirely disorientated by that event. Although his friend's unexpected confession had been interrupted by emotion, he knew that he had been designated by it, and he knew that he was the man chosen to replace him in Henriette's affection. Such a sublime sacrifice confounded him with admiration and devotion, and he strove every day to manifest it in effusion, astonished that Claude, who was subject to a very human reaction, responded to his expansive tenderness with an almost hostile concentration, which was even echoed in the cordiality of their common endeavor, in the moments of clear labor that they spent edifying their work.

In consequence, Raoul had crazy alternatives of hope and doubt, imagining one day that he might attain the purity of the young woman, and believing the next day that he would be insensate even to brush her with desire, according to whether his companion's face, on which he kept watch, brightened a little or darkened in the silence. Nevertheless the ferment cast into his heart developed there with a seething activity, dilating its every fiber with an incredible force, to the point of making it burst. Thus amour acts on new souls, thus its flame suddenly grows. His nights were troubled by acute dreams from which he extracted himself with a sentiment of melancholy surprise.

The rest of his wakefulness he spent drawing analogies, researching small events, recalling memories, building marvelous castles in the air, the materials for which he had acquired long ago. He stirred all his adoration and was astonished to find it older than he thought. The rare manifestations of his penchant, blurred until that moment by the surprises of the journey, the unexpectedness of the panoramas, took on an active life, a luminous evidence. He recalled the involuntary pleasure that they had both experienced in finding themselves incessantly united, savoring the same admirations and sharing the same cares around the bedridden Claude. Henriette's smiles were repainted with their charm of unconscious confession, and he knew that he had responded in the same fashion.

And yet other evidence: the delectable shiver that he had shared with her on the evening when, by mistake, in the darkness on the terrace, under the palpitating sky, she had seized his hand, thinking that she was possessing Claude's; and those unexpected tears, the strange kind of swoon in the chapel, after the adoration of Christ, after which she had almost fainted in his arms. All of that now constituted a formidable sheaf of plausibilities, an accumulation that intoxication crushed and that anxiety also overturned, for he saw looming up against the realization of Claude's wish the great religiosity of the young woman.

Sometimes, in their walks along the roads bordered with flowers, along the Croisette caressed by the sea, new questions burned his lips, and he wanted to talk, to interrogate his friend; but he dared not awaken so much dolor, and he contented himself then with ruminating his obsession silently, as he had just done throughout the meal, shivering at the slightest word.

But Rolande had just stood up.

"It's time to get ready," she said. "Let's go put on our masks and dominos. We've ordered two landaus and a hundred kilos of plaster. They ought to be waiting for us outside the hotel.

Suddenly, her expression became anxious. She counted the guests. One of them was missing. "Where's Monsieur Fortin?"

"My husband has had to retire already," Madame Fortin confessed, timidly. "He regrets not being able to be with us his afternoon. Occupations retain him."

"Occupations on a day of Mardi Gras!"

"Yes, serious occupations," she affirmed, pursing her lips, with a deep sigh of intimate restriction.

Rolande did not insist. They took the elevator again in order to go and put on costumes adapted for the occasion, enveloping themselves in coarse cloth that protects garments, and masks with iron lattices that protect the face against the brutality of plaster pellets.

Claude had not followed the surge of the others. He had stopped in the vestibule of the hotel and collapsed on a sofa, as if exhausted. All that heavy joy was unsuited to his sadness, and he felt too isolated to share it. Raoul, astonished that he had not followed him in order to dress up, came back down to search for him. His apparition, draped in a long brown domino tightened at the waist by a rope, had something heroic about it, and his mask, which he was holding in his hand, not dissimulating the power of his energetic head, gave him a vague allure of the warrior monks of legend. Not being ridiculous in his costume, he became handsome. Claude observed him bitterly.

"Well? What are you waiting for to dress?"

"I won't go to respire the plaster dust. It would suffocate me."

"Come on! You need distraction."

"No, I'll go for a walk somewhere else."

"In that case, I'll go with you."

"Leave me alone, I beg you. I need to be alone. Go away! Go!"

"My poor Claude," Raoul murmured, who understood that intimate dilapidation, and who withdrew, his pleasure in the day spoiled.

Madame Fortin, for her part, on entering the room that had been reserved for him, found her husband melancholy, slumped in an armchair. She advanced toward him, smiling, and remarked that he scarcely dared look at her.

"What! You're still here? You haven't left yet?"

"It isn't time," he said, taking out his watch, which he then replaced in his fob pocket, with the piteous expression of a beaten dog. "To what folly are you pushing me?" he continued, gravely. "Now, you see, I'm hesitating to accomplish what you're asking of me. Since the day when you launched me on this track, when your persuasion penetrated me with a little of your extravagance, I believe that I've no longer been living on the intelligent earth, I've been respiring in a domain of formidable fantasy, guided by a angel, who is you...I've become blind, with returns to the light that frighten me. At this moment I'm in one of those instants of vision, and I'm hesitating. I'm hesitating, because you might reproach me later for what you're making me do..."

She listened to him, confusedly shaken, abstracted by his speech from the obsession that had been pursuing her for two months, sensing that if he continued to argue, all the courage of her sacrifice would capsize, and she would return to their simple, dolorous and infecund amour.

"Shut up, shut up!" she said. "Your logic would quickly reckon with my dream. It's necessary to be able to be mad for a minute, for so much consequent happiness; it's necessary to be able to agitate in the shadow for the sake of so much subsequent illumination. I'll never reproach you for the sin to which I've deliberately engaged you. And then, don't reflect any longer...don't think any longer! Do as I've told you to do, my darling, whom I love infinitely!"

Her voice had softened with al he tenderness of her heart. He wanted to draw her to his lips, but she understood that if she delivered herself to them, he would remain deliberately attached to them, and that her wish would collapse under that weakness. Then, rapidly, she undressed, took hold of her mask and her domino, and disappeared, blowing him a kiss.

"Go! I love you!"

Monsieur Fortin took his head between his hands. He felt himself gripped again by the contagious folly of the adored woman who had just fled. It bewitched him; it drove him to obey mechanically. He looked at his watch and observed that he still had ten minutes before the train.

Leaning out of the window he saw the two landaus draw away. His wife's yellow domino could be distinguished in the first. The color did not even make him smile, and the last adieu that she sent him with the end of her mask, which she was holding in her white-gloved hand, moved him. Yes, she was mad; her maternal hypnosis had unhinged him; perhaps the recent operation, in removing her essential organs, had simultaneously taken away part of her reason. Oh, the wretched Caresco! Everything he touched went to ruin and destruction!

He circled the room momentarily, and finally took hold of his cane and his hat. He obeyed.

A few minutes of jostling in the crowded street, the blasts of trumpets, rapid visions of grotesque street-performers, false noses, carnivalesque polychromy, soldiers bawling and nursemaids dragging costumed children; then cafés and more cafés swarming, infecting the empyrean by cooking with garlic, and after a bleaker detour going along the railway, he was outside the station.

A crowd from a train was coming out. He stood on tiptoe, searched, interrogated the groups that were breaking up at the exit, and saw nothing. Oh, what if she didn't come! What if a respite were about to be granted to him, which would permit him to collect himself, to bring his wife back to sane reason! What if she didn't come!

But no; suddenly, he perceived her, so dazzlingly robust and healthy in her simple black outfit that men moved by a similar frisson of desire turned round brazenly to look at her.

He called to her: "Julia! This way, Julia!"

She smiled on seeing him. Her teeth shone in the sunlight. With an undulating gait still heavy with agrarian atavism, she veered in his direction, cleaving through the flood of people. A little boater was perched awkwardly on her thick hair; a veil with wide mesh hindered the freshness of her cheeks; a texture of white floss silk gloved her fingers crudely; but she was carrying her umbrella elegantly. On considering nothing but her hat, her veil and her gloves, one might have taken her for a country schoolteacher; but her waist, her bosom imprisoned in a corset that espoused its contours, the arch of her lower back, and he harmonious curve of her rump and legs, manifest under her tight dress, indicated a queen of the flesh, the eternal idol of healthy sensuality. That was the only impression that Monsieur Fortin retained when she had joined him, when he spoke to her,

"Well, Julia, have you had a good journey? You're very pretty today! Everyone's looking at you!"

"Oh, idlers…I don't pay any attention."

However, she blushed with pleasure at the compliment. She found a very particular air about Monsieur Fortin, the same air of violence and dread, of dominance and submission, that she had once had before Douvard, the schoolteacher, which she had already noticed in her master several times, notably on the evening when the baby had bitten her. That flattered her, and moved her slightly without her being able to explain the nature of her emotion. In order to change the subject, as a respectful servant, having already adopted polite formulae some time ago, with the subtle transformation common to women, she asked:

"Is Madame not with Monsieur?"

"No, Julia. Madame has gone to the fête, and has confided to me the care of occupying myself with you."

"Are we going to the professor's house, then?"

"Yes, we're going there. It's this way. Take my arm, Julia."

"Oh! I wouldn't dare!"

"But yes! Let's go! We're in carnival."

A paltry subterfuge that she accepted naively! In order to attract her to Nice they had used the pretext of an instruction henceforth indispensable to her new employment as a lady companion. It had required a long time to convince her that the education in Cannes was poor. Her enthusiasm to become a demoiselle admitted without reserve the idea of traveling several times a week to Nice and receiving there the elements of pedagogy necessitated by her new position, learning to read, to write and to speak faultlessly. She had even been enabled to hope that she would one day place her fingers on a piano keyboard, and that pride, more than any other, delighted her. She allowed herself to be conducted, charmed by becoming a friend for her employers, one of whom, at least, was paying a very particular attention to her that day, since he had taken her arm in order to take her to the professor's abode.

Monsieur Fortin was only thinking any longer about his wife with a distant tenderness, which dissipated as they advanced. The prayer that he had received from her, the order that he was obeying, facilitated singularly his audacity of a man refractory to adventures of his sort. He foresaw trouble; he was engaged in a lacuna that he would fill in later by forgetfulness, in order to return to adorable conjugal slavery.

The only casuistry that still agitated him, which the carnal suggestion of Julia would soon vanquish, was the scruple of drawing into sin a virgin whom no preliminary invitation permitted him to deflower. His maidservant had not offered herself; he was taking her, in a machination. It would have required, in order to accomplish that act of monstrous possession deliberately, the unconscious knavery of a Don Juan, and he was only the mandatory of a strangely inspired wife.

Numerous attenuations, it is true, lessened his culpability. What fate, in fact, would have been reserved for that girl if she had continued to milk cows and agitate the butter churn out there on Père Servant's farm? Some Douvard, one warm evening, would have pushed her over in the straw, and she would finally have ceded to the unavoidable demands of victorious instincts A little more violence, subsequently, and she would have succumbed, subject to the atavistic influence, the empire of natural legacy, the sensual heredity of her mother, the prowler of the high roads who passed bestially from ne man to another on the edge of ditches and in odorous fields of hay. Yes, that was doubtless the future that lay in wait for her, a future of brutal subjection, of splashing mud. Since then, in extracting her from the dung-heap in transforming her, in civilizing her, had he not offered her the finest fate that she could desire, had he not accomplished a role of magnificent protection?

Certainly, those advantages she would pay for with a collaboration of flesh, with the abandonment of a child, a broken heart, perhaps, if maternal love bloomed within her as other vibrations had developed there of a soul awakening beneath a rough-hewn envelope. But later, extracted from poverty and indolent vice, refined, endowed and married to Douvard, would she not still be in his debt, having got the better part of the bargain, she giving her body and the fruit of her body temporarily, and he offering social promotion, intellectual renovation, liberty and wellbeing? He tightened his grip on her arm.

Although astonished by the insistence of that pressure, she did not revolt, by virtue of the habitude of passive obedience, respect for the master, and also by a sudden awakening of instinctive sensuality, all of her being submitting hereditarily to masculine provocation, and shuddering intimately. She looked away; she gazed, in a absent-minded, confused vision, at masks passing by and the fine dust raised by the wheels of the noisy carriages.

Monsieur Fortin was talking to her, inclining his head over her slightly-uncovered cleavage, and his voice seemed to be a caress that ran all along her neck, a fluid that was disseminated over the entire surface of her skin, tickling her agreeably, bringing her, successively, warmth and frissons. But she scarcely understood all the pretty things that he was recounting, the terms of admiration that he was employing, by which she was nevertheless moved. At a bend in the road, in front of a low door surmounted by a notice indicating furnished lets, he stopped, and then pushed her into the darkness of a corridor.

"It's here?"

"Go on, then; it's here."

Her eyes, dazzled by light and surprise, barely distinguished a steep staircase leading to a narrow landing painted green, In order to climb it she aided herself with the banister-rail, but the arm of her cavalier guided her insistently by the waist. A door was open and the arm plunged her into a room with lowered curtains, which seemed cheerful and reminded her of her room in Cannes.

In any case, she did not have the possibility of estimating its comfort for longer. She felt two warm hands weighing upon her and fumbling at the fastenings of her bodice. The friction of a soft beard enervated her with a thousand prickles and compressed her throat. Two kisses made her sovereignly languid. She abandoned herself, swooning, to the devotion of her master, who was no longer talking, and was savoring, in the accomplishment of his mandate, an exalting intoxication. A poor amorous beast, she succumbed, without a struggle, in a lamentation dolorous at first, passionately voluptuous thereafter.

XX

Sitting next to her lamp, her elbow leaning on the table and her hand sustaining her attentive forehead, Henriette was reading. Her profile, softly engraved by the yellow glow of a silk lampshade, clearly delimited the two sides of her face, one illuminated in demi-tints, with the tonality of living ivory, warmer at the eyes and lips; the other lost in shadow, but recovering violently at moments the reflection of large logs burning in the hearth. Above was the glaze of smooth hair, the mirror of which shone or tarnished, according to whether the hearth was activated or reentered into calm.

Her serious silhouette, thus exposed to constant placid light on one side and passing on the other through successions of darkness and illumination, symbolized the two aspects of her heart, the two states of her complex soul. The languid light, with its blurs and its unhealthy pallors, it was Claude who sent it to her and impregnated her with it; the reflections of the fire, the reddenings of brutal conflagration that faded almost immediately unto blackness, came from Raoul.

For three months her mental life had been alimented by those contrasts, those oppositions of effluvia, those uninterrupted struggles between the continuity of mystic radiations, attributable to her fiancé, and sudden and imperious flares followed by an abysmal obscurity, inspired by Raoul.

She put down *The Imitation of Christ*, which she was reading, and extended her hand over the colored engraving that filled an entire insert of the book, in order not to see it any longer. Why, infallibly, among the works that the young woman's bookshelf contained, did she choose the one in which the beautiful imploring head of the divine man was found on almost every page? Why, wanting to flee an obsession whose haunting tortured her, did she return incessantly, with a delectable regret, to that leaf of the work in which the great Sacrificed was agonizing amid the adoration of women

315

prostrate at his feet? What evil genus hypnotized her, directed her fingers toward that same figure, constraining her to weigh upon it when she strove to turn away from it, and to bring back the memory, always identical, of a maddening and ineffable minute?

Her desire to banish the evocation persisted; her resolution to obey her duty was as convinced; her fear of the demon—a strange demon, which took the form of Christ!—did not abandon her; and she fought with obstinacy. Alas, she remained the weaker.

Moreover, everything was in league against the energy of her heart. If she cast her eyes on the photographs scattered on the walls or the furniture, she saw Claude, but Claude made her think of Raoul. If she heard mention of the absentees, people spoke to her about the health of her fiancé, but they did not neglect to recount the devotion of his friend. If she received a letter from the Midi, whether that letter came from the Duverdons or the invalid himself, there was almost always question of nothing but the faithful companion, his strength, his goodness and his abnegation. She lived with him, while wanting to expel him from her heart; she respired his memory, while striving to find bad air therein. She succumbed mentally to those alternatives of wishes and rejections, those fits of attraction and recoil, as pulmonary sufferers do from successions of heat and cold. However, she did not lose either her beautiful coloration or her youthful charm. Disengaged from her envelope of mysticism, she had become more woman. Amour, in metamorphosing her, had enabled her to bloom.

The roll of a sonorous vehicle under the arch beneath the room where she was—the large elegant drawing room of a luxurious Parisian town house, in the heart of the Monceau quarter, with three ogival windows overlooking the Rue de Courcelles—and then the dull grating of the coaching entrance being closed brought her back to reality. Hector was back. In a moment, she would see him appear, dragging his ameliorated hemiplegia, his right arm contracted in a simian fashion. She would hear his still-hesitant speech, emitted by contorted lips;

she would sense the disquieting flutter of his eyes weighing upon her; she saw herself constrained to accept the pressure, always too long, of his right hand—the only valid one, for the other still dangled, only effecting movements with difficulty, under the exertion of the will.

Nevertheless, she had prayed for the invalid's recovery, and Providence still listened to the implorations of the profane, since Hector was better, since he had abandoned his wheelchair to live like others, to sit down at table, where his food was cut up for him, and to make a few excursions in a coupé.

She turned her head, for she heard a noise and thought he was already present; but it was another hesitant step that came through the door, another invalid who advanced into the room. Antonin Fargeaud orientated himself among the chairs and tables, groping for their placement with the tip of his cane. Immediately, Henriette got up, ran to her godfather and offer him her helpful arm.

"Bonsoir, father!"

"My daughter! My Antigone! Unique help of my uncertain stride, sole ray of light in my obscurity!"

Gravely she received the kiss that he deposited on her forehead. She sensed that he was less acrimonious, less disabused, and wanted to know the reason.

"You seem content this evening, Father."

"I've just received a letter from Cannes."

"Ah!"

The young woman's exclamation was emitted without enthusiasm. Every return to reality, every flow of events, extracted her from the neutral state of uncertainty in which she had been floating for two months; every manifestation of the absentees announced the approach of their return, causing her an impression of dread, the terror of an imminent denouement in which her heart could no longer oscillate, when a determination had to be made.

After having searched in his pocket the old man handed her the letter.

"Take it, my child…so that I can hear your dear voice read the dearest of writings."

"It is, in fact, from Claude."

She cut the envelope sealed with wax, and took out the wad of bristol paper, which was lumpy, because two carnations, one red and the other white, were contained therein, and stained the paper with their colored juice. She put them to one side and then started reading the epistle, which was addressed to both the old man and to her. And an astonishment seized her this time, again, for after a few phrases relating to his state of health, increasingly satisfactory, Claude no longer talked about himself, but consecrated the rest of the four pages to eulogizing Raoul. He praised the surety of his amity, the continuity of his devotion. He insisted on his physical beauty, on his moral magnificence, on the fortunate fate of the woman who would eventually become his wife. And the postscript terminating the dithyramb had a supreme ambiguity that astonished the two readers variously.

It said: *Raoul has slipped into the letter a white carnation and I have inserted a red carnation. You will attribute to each of you one of these emissaries of your affection. The white will be for charm, grace and innocence; the red will be welcomed by the heart that, all its life, burned for the convalescent…*

The letter fell from her hands. Did that not express significantly enough that, via the intermediary of the invalid, Raoul destined a flower personally for her? What enigma, what intention was there in that fashion of bringing together two beings whom everything separated? She shivered. But Antonin Fargeaud raised his voice.

"That's several times, my child, that your fiancé's letters have surprised and disconcerted me. Perhaps my suspicion is due to an excess of reflection, and perhaps I'm going astray in reading to read too much into simple coincidences of a grateful amity, but it seems to me that Claude doesn't put enough insistence into talking about you at the same time as himself, in recalling the situation of definitive attachment in which you find yourselves in regard to one another. Isn't that your opinion?"

She did not reply, utterly nonplussed by that question, fundamentally of a passionate interest. He sensed that she was troubled and took her in his arms.

"My child, I can only see any longer with my heart, but the heart is often more perspicacious than the eyes. Reply to me frankly, affirm to me that before Claude's departure, nothing was modified in your relationship..."

"I affirm it to you, Father!"

"And that you are still destined for one another?"

"I affirm that to you also."

"Forgive those questions...that worry oppressed me...for ten years I have only had one thought, that of seeing you united. Only your possible accord consoles me for still being alive. By virtue of it, I'm patient in waiting to die. By virtue of it, I tolerate the villainy of the world; by virtue of it, I've set aside a hundred times the inspiration of troubling books that counsel me to annihilation. Oh, I'm not the first to have detested life, to have claimed the right to destruction. Yes, you alone make my philosophy oscillate; you alone direct it toward better conceptions...or worse! And to foresee your separation, the collapse of all my desires, would be the end of everything for me, would plunge me into I know not what abyss. But you've reassured me, and there are still smiles amid my disappointments."

Henriette did not reply. She abandoned her insensible and cold hand to the old man, who squeezed it, and was astonished not to be paid in return. The young woman's mind was captivated by another concern than that of dissipating the illuminate's preoccupations. Suddenly, in a flash of discernment, the struggle had just appeared before her, and she saw the opposed elements of it camped facing one another.

On one side, there was her love for Raoul, slowly hatched, the impulsion of nature directing her toward the powerful man of election, glorious and handsome, capable of assuring the magnificence of future destinies. That amour was favored by the very man who would perish of its realization, by Claude. On the other side, there was her respect for the promise sworn; her obedience to the old man who had taken her in and raised her; her conviction also that by accepting her fiancé's renunciation she would be dealing a mortal blow to both of them.

Did Raoul, who found himself in the middle of the conflict, suspect his triumph? Was he astonished to move so many sentiments? Oh, the somber struggle, when there was so much light elsewhere! For in which direction would she go? What solution would finally dissipate these cruel alternatives?

Was it not preferable to detach herself from the world, to look higher, to raise her eyes toward celestial purity, no longer to turn away from it, since one saw there, in streams of gold, rippling with a thousand harmonious canticles, God and the angels and the saints, the entire cortege of immaterial substances with which it was gently reposing to mingle, in a sort of infinite adoration, so far from humanity and the appetites that agitated there? No more torments then, no more of these procrastinations of conscience, no more of these desperate leaps in which she passed importunately from duty to revolt, from what was good to what she believed to be evil. And above all, no more of these stabbing pains that exasperated her soul, that mingled the down-to-earth with mysticism, base instinct with the ideal, transforming ecstasy into shameful realizations, and making her glimpse in the head of Christ agonized eyes that awoke in order to admire her, and in his gesture of sublime protection, arms that forsook heir nails in order to embrace her passionately and cherish her with transports of culpable intoxication.

A domestic came in to announce that dinner was served. They waited for Hector, who did not appear. And as Antonin Fargeaud became anxious about that, the domestic announced that the invalid had been taken to a boulevard café where he was awaited by ladies, and then had sent the carriage back, saying that he would be returning later that evening. Antonin

Fargeaud did not protest. His son, scarcely better, was resuming debauchery.

The dinner was melancholy.

XXI

They had quit Nice at two o'clock in the afternoon. After the end of a tiring day, the train was racing at top speed through the enigma of the night, intercut by the sudden illumination of stations hastily surpassed. The isochronic hammering of the wheels on the rails, the trepidation of the springs, more accentuated at bifurcations in the track and the stridency of the locomotive saluting the signals—the whole disciplined jolting tumult of the great express—became insupportable to Julien Duverdon; as he could not sleep, he decided to go and smoke a cigarette in the corridor of the sleeping car. He threw back his blanket, and got down with as little noise as possible from his upper couchette; then, before opening the door, he cast a glance over the compartment hired for their return to Paris, in which only three of the four places were occupied, one entire side having been reserved for the suffering Rolande, while Clara and he had taken possession of the two superimposed bunks opposite.

His glance reassured him. Rolande's crisis had finally calmed down, and she was lying fully extended, torpid, protected by thick furs. In the semi-darkness of the carriage she had closed her eyes and seemed to be asleep. She was exquisitely pretty in that blur of things. Her unfastened bodice, covered by a white chenille shawl, allowed the more accentuated development of her breasts to be divined.

By contrast, the silhouette of Clara, folded and gathered in a large overcoat with a turned-up collar resembled in the shadow the body of a fat adolescent. All that could be seen emerging of the woman was the artificially dyed hair, cut and curled. The face, the make-up of which had greenish fluorescences, was very small, lost between two fleeces, that of the fur and that of the hair. A smile of contented irony creased Monsieur Duverdon's lips, and, as the foreigner appeared to have succumbed to slumber, he turned the catch gently and slipped out, drawing his neck back into this massive shoulders.

But Clara was not asleep. A thousand ideas were agitating her intensely, a thousand suppositions that she wanted to be only hypotheses, but which the repetition of phenomena were forcing her to envisage as probabilities, For two months her liaison with Rolande had been subjected to assaults that she had observed with an increasing surprise. The creature that she had subjugated with a slow infiltration of vices was less docile in the acceptance of her morbid slavery. She had inexplicable revolts, variations of character that, without detaching her from her, indicated a certain evolution.

At any moment, without apparent reason, she passed through exaggerations of tears or laughter that the pettiest contretemps or the slightest satisfactions provoked. Further fainting fits had felled her, laying her down very pale, as if dead. Then disgusts had arrived for certain aliments, sudden caprices of the stomach, nausea consecutive to innocent absorptions; at other times, ravenous hungers caused her to precipitate toward the first patisserie encountered and throw herself on the *petit fours* or puddings in order to stuff herself. It was, in brief, a complete upheaval of health, which could only be attributed to intimate troubles, a nervous breakdown that astonished the American and caused her to reflect, to interrogate the red dates of which the epoch was becoming remote, lost in the forgetfulness of months.

The husband, prudently consulted, had only responded with a strange smile, and his insouciance signified more knowledge that he wanted to be supposed; and the suspicion increased of an anguishing rivalry, of a Rolande weary of incomplete sensations, having allowed herself to be taken again by a man—by the husband, since he was the only one who could have approached her. Their common life and the surveillance she exercised denied the possibility of any other weakness. In addition, the question of the doctor in Nice, asking Rolande whether she might be pregnant, had confirmed the American's belief.

And merely thinking about it, imagining the act that could have rendered her a mother, gave her a cold anger, concentrated rages during which she overturned their three existences, planning tortures and plotting murders with a savage determination, but which she veiled with a smile and an artificial tenderness as soon as Rolande showed herself more docile to the tyranny of her sensuality. She was on the lookout for an opportunity to investigate, which the preparations for the departure had not permitted.

That evening, after the crisis that had forced her friend to undress in front of her, the light of the sleeping-car, falling from above, had so manifestly illuminated the unusual amplitude of her breasts and the abnormal development of the hips, two symptoms of pregnancy already suspected in Nice, that they could not now be attributed to any other cause. In a few days nature had taken an enormous step, and Rolande's advanced maternity had become evident. In any case, if nature had not taken charge of declaring the event, the radiant attitude of the husband when, as he went out while caressing his beard, he had considered the midriff of his recumbent wife, and the victorious irony of the smile allowed to fall afterwards upon the foreigner, would have informed Clara completely.

Those observations were not the result of an imagination overheated by distress; Julien really had expressed the joy of a rapist in looking at the wife that a subterfuge was bringing back to him; he really had thereafter, in a moment of pride, crushed with his scorn the loser in that amorous battle.

The American waited, therefore, until Monsieur Duverdon had disappeared and had closed the door. A gap in the curtain showed her the husband innocently occupied in lighting his cigarette. Then she got up with a bound and woke her friend, seizing her by the arm.

"Are you asleep, darling?" she said, in her accent tinted with exoticism, the expression of which she tried not to render too tragic. And almost before Rolande had opened her eyes, she added: "Your tyrant has just gone out, we can talk. Do you know that I'm very anxious about your health...very? Your continual suffering desolates me, and desolates me all the more because I've divined the reason for it. Something mysterious is happening within you...yes something exceedingly mysterious."

Her eyes pierced the darkness. She would have liked to observe that her insinuation produced an alarm in the young woman, but she only troubled the apathy of a gross lassitude that her sudden intervention could not succeed in extracting room the toils of slumber. She went on in a bittersweet voice:

"Are you less attentive than me to your person, darling, or is my tenderness giving me the illusion of a peril that does not exist in reality? I don't know, but I'm frightened by the changes I observe in you. Come on, Rolande! Seek, reassure me or confess! I have a heart loving enough to forgive you if you confess to me."

"Confess what?" Rolande asked, finally; she did not understand and was astonished to see the ardent hair and the made-up face move, come closer, come very close to her and exhale their distress, cheek to cheek.

"You don't want to tell me, my darling, but you know very well, and it would be necessary to be ignorant to an extent that it isn't possible that you are, to attribute the illness that's ravaging you to any other cause than a pregnancy."

"A pregnancy!" exclaimed Rolande, nonplussed.

"Yes! Everything affirms that interior upheaval, everything, from your hollow features to your developing bosom, to your amplified loins."

"My poor Clara, I swear to you..."

"Don't try to deceive me, darling. Look! Look!"

With a nervous hand she parted, almost tore, the bodice and the chenille shawl that covered the invalid, to lay bare the increased vigor of the breasts that emerged, swollen, shadowed at their summit by a brown tint more distinct under the half-light of the electric lamp, incompletely filtered by the blue cotton curtain. Her anger was exasperated by the memory of joys that she had experienced in admiring the flavorsome roundness and the virginal rosiness of the areola.

325

"Oh, if I were sure…!" she said, in a crazed tone, "I'd destroy, I'd crush all these beauties, if I were sure that a man, even your husband, had been their possessor!"

"You're making me ill, and you're going mad!" exclaimed Rolande, finally, pained by the abruptness of the attack, pushing her away.

But the foreigner wanted to know, and was obstinate in thinking that her friend was feigning innocence. Then she evoked the memory of the end of the evening after the play at the château, when Rolande, fatigued and wounded, had rejected her offer to take her back to her room. She had accepted Monsieur Duverdon's arm; she had locked herself in with him. To what shameful domination had she yielded? For since that incident, there had been a relaxation in their amity, a kind of interposition that had separated them, which had spoiled their tenderness. The rare reprises had not been engaged with the mad enthusiasm of the first moments; and for a month, since their sojourn in Nice, the sentimental rupture had been accentuated by an indifference to all the sharing of pleasure that she had offered her. Why was that? Why did Rolande not lend herself as before to their effusions, if not because her new condition edified between them insurmountable horrors, because her friend had returned to the disgusting submissions of nature?

The invalid was stupefied. She finally protested.

"No, no! You're mistaken, you're rambling. Julien is no more my husband than before, and it's not to him that it's necessary to attribute these modifications in my character and my health. Only my fall from the automobile is responsible. You're ambling, I assure you, and if I'm filling out, it's because I'm at an age where one fills out."

In order to calm her down she took her hand and squeezed it tenderly; and Clara, ever a slave to her aberration, careless of the possible reentry of the husband, was about to convert that mark of amity into a subtler audacity when a few words added by Rolande, words destined to reassure her, suddenly put her back in confrontation with her maddening enigma.

"Besides which, these troubles, the specialist warned me about them."

"What specialist?"

Rolande bit her lip. She had said too much. In order not to worry her friend, in order that she could not oppose an examination that Julien's authority and the fear of her suffering had made her accept, she had hidden her visit to Domesta from her. And now, in this moment of extreme lassitude, when every effort became difficult, she was going to have to confess a weakness, to submit to reproaches, to soothe a new crisis of indignation! She was distressed by her imprudence.

"What specialist?" the American repeated.

"That's true, forgive me, I didn't tell you about it in order not to torment you, my dear Clara. But I had so much dread of no longer being able to remain your pretty Rolande, and of suffering like many of us who look after themselves too late. Know, then, that Julien and I went to consult Professor Domesta,"

"Domesta!"

Her cry was a laugh of ironic distress, and her fingernails dug into Rolande's skin.

Domesta! It was him that they had gone to see in secret! It was Domesta, the sinister ape, the Sixtine cantor of Rome, the guardian of a seraglio in Constantinople, the clownish fecundator of Paris. In those three stages she had encountered him, she who traveled incessantly, whose deviation pushed her to hazard all acquaintanceships, all extraordinary researches of stupor, who sniffed all the exhalations of pestilence and tasted all the abnormal spices of the generative instinct. And every time the obese asexual, the deprived soprano, a shady mercenary of her curiosities, a hybrid procurer of her morbid exaltation, every time, Domesta had put a black stain on her life, like the mere gaze of an evil sorcerer intervening in a destiny, like a screech-owl uttering a hoarse cry and deciding an evil fate.

In Rome, an intermediary between her and a Megaera who sold her daughter, he had cheated her and flown, not furnishing her with the pleasure for which she had paid in advance. In Constantinople, accepting his services again in a kind of unconsciousness, introduced into the seraglio that the eunuch was guarding, in order to follow the two beautiful black eyes of an alma shining in the whiteness of her veil, she had been beaten and then imprisoned for a month. And now in Paris, the city of all liberties and all extravagances, she found him looming up in her path again, a grotesque evil dwarf, profaning and destroying what she loved most in the world, her friend's beauty!

Her physiognomy, at that moment, reflected the maddening certainty that she was not mistaken, that Rolande was a victim whose misfortune was rebounding on her. And, still holding her tightly in her grip, she was about to proclaim her woe, to open her mind to the conception of an ignominious subterfuge, when the door of the compartment opened and the debonair face of the husband reappeared. Then she let go of the wrist she was gripping, did not say another word, went back to bed, lowered her eyelids over the fire of her rage, and allowed herself to be lulled by the metallic voice of the train that was racing in the rumblings of formidable murder.

Everyone was silent, but no one slept in the wearying warmth of the sleeping car, the windows of which the belated March frost was decorating with a fantasy of cracked arabesques, imperceptibly born, growing and displaying themselves magnificently, with the determination, the constancy and the discipline of the slightest phenomena of nature, of its indefatigable creative activity.

They disembarked early in the morning. Shivering, their eyes heavy, their hair unkempt and their clothing crumpled, they mingled with the crowd of travelers, carrying their overcoats and their traveling bags. Clara's make-up emerged from her long fur coat with the dirty hues of poorly washed porcelain. She had not taken care to repair the nocturnal damage, so great was the anxiety that clawed her. Once again, Julien Duverdon was astonished by his wife's choice.

At the exit, an ugliness was detached from the compact mass of people waiting, hoisting himself up like a leaping grimace. That was Hector, who had come to collect them. Laughing with his twisted lips, striving to demonstrate his reconquered valor, he declared that he had only gone to bed that night for the moments necessary to overturn an alcove that was not his own. The rest of the time he had trailed around the taverns of Les Halles, and he had two photographs in his pocket that he counted on adding to his collection. His mouth was drooling, he reeked of alcohol and tobacco. Such unconsciousness disarmed Julien Duverdon, converting his repugnance into pity. Hector took his place with the travelers in the vast hired omnibus that was waiting at the exit; he was delighted to save the forty sous of a cab fare.

And as Louis, the valet de chambre, helped to load the trunks at the front of the vehicle, Clara suddenly perceived the absence of Rose. Having sent her on a few days in advance, she had ordered her to be present at the arrival.

"What about Rose? Where's Rose?" she demanded.

Louis responded, and his distraught expression was noticeable. Rose, suffering and unable to continue her work, had been obliged to retire to the home of one of her cousins. She begged Mademoiselle to excuse her. When she was cured, probably in a fortnight, she would resume her service, if Mademoiselle had not replaced her.

"What a nuisance!" affirmed the American. "She's so nice, that child, so attentive. Is she gravely ill? I'll go to see her. Give me her address."

The man hesitated. An anxious crease was sketched in his brow. Mademoiselle had no need to disturb herself; it wasn't serious, doubtless a little fatigue, which rest would repair. In any case, Rose's mother, a peasant from Berri, summoned in haste, was at her bedside. But as the mistress insisted, in order that suspicions would not weigh upon him later and render him an accomplice of what might happen, he hastily uttered the number of a sleazy hotel in the Montmartre quarter. He could not suppress a grimace on seeing Clara make a note of the address; then he took his place on the seat, next to the coachman.

The clanking omnibus reached the quays, which the misty cold of the morning kept deserted, abandoned to the effort of the road-sweepers. They could be seen under their hoods and raged accoutrements turning their faces violet and extending their arms, pushing the scoria of the pavement into the Seine. For the pleasure of the city, in order that the carriages of the rich should not be splashed, they toiled miserably, sustaining their activity with murderous flames of alcohol. That simple slavery was so customary that the travelers did not even notice it. Clara was more preoccupied by a nausea of Rolande's, which forced her to open a window.

The Rue de Rivoli was reached; they entered the heart of Paris. Snow, suddenly falling, put the panorama in tune with their melancholy. On the sidewalks of the Avenue de l'Opéra, umbrellas opened; functionaries, bureaucrats and employees were walking rapidly. The monument could no longer be seen, although it was very close. A white swell framed it, scarcely allowing the sight of the hasty pedestrians.

After many skids, the horses stopped in front of one of the principal houses in the Rue Scribe. It was there that the American had a costly apartment, kept all the year round. She descended without saluting Julien or Hector. Her fur coat snaked between the snowflakes; her shrill voice gave orders to the porter; she distinguished her luggage from those of others. Finally, returning to the open window, she took Rolande's hand.

"Go to bed, my friend, rest. Then, at three o'clock, come to collect me here. We have a very important visit to make."

When Monsieur Duverdon, astonished, asked for an explanation of the nature of that visit, she made no response and turned on her heel.

"She's scarcely gracious for the messieurs today," Hector criticized, with a simian smile charged with an evident intention.

The omnibus resumed its route more painfully, and finally reached Antonin Fargeaud's house. Only Henriette was waiting for them there; the old man did not appear even at lunch, which was silent.

Rolande did not sleep, got dressed, and went out at three o'clock.

Julien waited for her all afternoon. He strove to calm the fever of his nerves by reading, but the ideas that his book suggested did not succeed in dissipating the anguish of his presentiments. The letters danced before his eyes; between them and his vision, phantasmagorias neighboring hallucination were imposed, a diabolical flesh-eating Clara, grimacing faces with bloody lips and fingers gripping a prey, which was Rolande, livid in her arms, her loins lacerated.

He rationalized his delirium, trying to attribute it to the fatigue of the journey, to an overactive imagination that his ordinary pessimism engendered. But when common sense got the upper hand again, he was convinced that his fears derived from the real state of things, from the perspicacious rivalry of the foreigner, who must have discovered his secret; and then his fear was redoubled. To what consequences, to what flight, to what crime would the odious pervert push Rolande? She possessed her to such an extent, had impregnated her so much with her vice, and dominated her with such corruption!

At eight o'clock, Rolande had not returned. It happened so frequently that she prolonged her absences extremely, only coming to sit down at table at the end of dinner, scarcely taking care to excuse her lateness by the duration of visits or excursions, that Julien remained patient and nibbled his food. But when nine o'clock chimed, he was alarmed, put on his overcoat, went out into the street, hailed a fiacre and gave the address of the house in the Rue Scribe.

The snow had ceased; melted by the salt, it transformed the causeway into a lake of black mud where the trenchant reflections of gaslight floated. Almost empty trams bathed in the submerged rails; the appeals of their horns seemed like sinister lamentations. Oh, running after the fugitive like this, in the gray dirtiness of deserted streets! Where would he find her? What would he say to her when he saw her? What audacity would he inspire by interrogating her about the employment of her time? And then, what new lie would be suspect behind the calm transparency of the adored eyes, to what new shame, perhaps a rebuff, would he be subjected?

At the house he was told that Miss Clara, having gone out in the afternoon in the company of a lady, had not returned. And that news augmented his perplexity. He paid the coachman, and for two hours, without losing sight of the flamboyant door, he paced back and forth in the Rue Scribe, posting himself in doorways, behaving like an evicted and anxious lover. There was a performance at the Opéra. Shivering, he watched the warmth of the fête evident in the flamboyant windows, and the carriages occupied by couples in evening dress engulfed by the portico reserves for vehicles.

He looked at the poster. Celebrated singers were interpreting *Lohengrin...Lohengrin!* The knight, the swan, the wedding march, and the full hall, glittering with diamonds and gilt, low necklines, smiles and lies, so many ironic visions, so many sharp points in his gaping wound. *Lohengrin*, every phrase of which he knew by heart, every breath of lyricism of which he could murmur, having heard it frequently in the company of Rolande and her friend, when, relegated to a corner of the box, he had witnessed the happy egotism of the two women, had seen their bare shoulders lean over to collect the homage of opera-glasses, shoulders nacreous in the radiation of the great chandelier!

The glaucous reality of the street gripped him again. He shivered with cold. And when the two braided grooms of the house finally noticed him and pointed at him, he became shamed and leapt into another cab, calling out the number in the Rue de Courcelles. Having reached the intersection of that street and the Rue de Lisbonne, almost at the end of his journey, his breast suddenly began to beat the charge, for he perceived Rolande going home on foot, alone in the wet street.

She was walking like a drunken woman, her dress trailing in the puddles; her otter-fur muff and her jacket were hanging down, abandoned by her ungloved hands, indifferent to the cold. He saw her stop outside the door and press the button automatically. Then he ran forward.

"Rolande! My Rolande!"

She did not reply. She was very pale, her eyes widened, impregnated with a mysterious gleam of fear or rage; he could not define their expression. She passed, or rather slid, into the concierge's lodge, went upstairs, went into her lightless apartment like a hallucinate going blindly to her destination, unaware of the surroundings. He heard her collapse in an armchair with a great sigh. Then he switched on the electric light and saw her prostrate in her seat, weeping.

"Rolande! My Rolande!" he stammered, kneeling before her in an attitude of infinite desolation, for he knew, at that moment that he was the instigator of that dolor, and he cursed the audacity that had been the cause of it.

But she shoved him away with a protestation of disgust, shame and anger. Imprecations emerged from her taut lips, a lava of excessive words that astounded him.

"Miserable coward! Ignoble individual! Soiler of women! You've soiled me! You've degraded me! Go away! Go away! I'll kill you!"

He dared not budge, gripped again by his timidity, by his anguish. He feared, by risking a gesture, driving her to the ultimate consequences, to the murderous eruption of the revolted volcano that was seething within her. She seemed to be searching the vicinity of her hand for an object that she could hurl at his head in order to crush it, in order to annihilate him; and not finding one, she resumed her diatribe, hurling a further volley of imprecations at him.

"Swine! You've made a fool of me by abusing my naivety and taking me unknowingly to the house of that Domesta, a eunuch! Yes, you didn't know that he's a eunuch! What shameful buffoonery! Me, lying there, soiled by that charlatan; you, hiding, doing even worse. Oh, the grotesque filthiness! How the poussah must have laughed! And I didn't suspect, no, I didn't suspect! I delivered myself innocently! Even though you're only a neuter and spineless, I trusted you, I thought that you loved me to much not to respect me. Good God, was I an imbecile! To believe in the good faith of a man! Was I stupid! Then, all this illness, all these symptoms...you considered them with a joyful expression! And I still didn't know! But now I know everything. Clara has just taken me to a physician, and his diagnosis didn't take long. I'm carrying the fruit of your filthiness inside me, I'm pregnant! Pregnant!"

Exasperated, she stood up, and she began to undress herself in an increasing folly, tugging and tearing hr garments, her skirt, soiled with mud, which fell to the floor, breaking the fastenings of her excessively tight corset, which burst under her nervous fingers. Finally, almost naked, she lifted up her chemise and displayed her abnormally developed abdomen.

"Look! It's there, your child; it's filling me; it's stifling me. Tomorrow it will deform my flesh, of which I was proud, and which isn't yours. Tomorrow it will double my waist and render me ridiculous. Tomorrow it will wrench cries of pain from me! And you think that I'm going to wait patiently for the hour of its emergence, and offer you the gift of my belly, you, the liar, you, the thief of my beauty? You think that? Brute, to think that. Here, look! I'm breaking it, your child, I'm killing it, I'm annihilating it!"

Having arrived at the paroxysm of her wrath, she started beating the importunate guest of her flesh with her fist. Anesthetized by fury, she did not feel the pain that the repeated blows provoked, and she augmented their destructive force, hammering her hated sphericity, which rendered a dull sound. Then Julien hastened to prevent that abominable murder, to snatch from annihilation the treasure of life that his subterfuge had accumulated: a contest of fear on one side and folly on the other!

He had seized her wrists and he tried to paralyze them in a cold embrace in which their hostile breaths were confounded, in which their bodies, for the second time in their marriage, were enlaced. She struggled, shoved him away, dug her fingernails into his face, tried to attain the eyes in order to abolish their flame. And as he recoiled, blinded and bowled over, vanquished by the pain, Rolande, disengaged momentarily, perceived the bed, one of the uprights of which formed a peak at the height of her waist. Rolande, whose age caused her to forget momentarily her customary fear of pain, launched herself forward and leapt up in order to fall on the child she bore, to crush it in embryo. Before she could accomplish her design, however, a spasm gripped her throat; a vertigo, entangling her feet in the carpet, caused her to fall flat, her head bumping into the mirror-fronted cupboard.

Darkness falling within her had subdued her, burying her in the mute rigidity of a faint.

When she woke up, she was warmly wrapped up in the whiteness of sheets. The room seemed to be empty, things were languishing in the penumbra of a single candle, filtered by a globe of pink silk. However, a powerful hand, from which she could not disengage her own, was caressing her gently.

And even gentler than the hand, an imploring voice, a grave and penetrating voice, filled with tones of broad humanity, was talking about the child, about the splendor of the maternal role, the promise of ulterior joys, sovereign consolations that could only be bought by the little being that nature would soon case to be born. And she listened, still half-absent; she listened, as if to a strange, unknown thing, to that captivating and magnificent song of the love of the race, by means of which all destinies are perpetuated, by means of which the decline of life finds a new dawn, beneficent and fecund, perfumed by a breath of tenderness and purity. But on turning her head, on looking at the preacher, she shivered and withdrew her hand abruptly, because the person who was speaking was her husband.

XXII

A hired coupé carried Miss Boswett and Rolande through the Temple quarter. The two friends were talking without the spectacle, unusual for them, of streets swarming with a society overflowing from the narrow sidewalks into the causeway, being able to distract them from their conversation. A young and rapid chestnut was pulling them; the impatient thrusts of its rump, often moderated by the encumbrance of carriages caused a cinema reel of shops, stalls and display-windows, already gas-lit in the declining daylight of six o'clock. The quarter filed past, brutal in its materiality, reddening alembics and shiny zincs, crimson meat trimmed with white by the butchers, edifices of tins and jars in grocer's shops, displays of metal, multiple varieties of clinking utensils, and in pharmacies, polychromatic bottles, red, blue and yellow, radiating nascent shadows of sheets of cheerful color. Coming and going, hastening, elbowing and shoving, an entire dull population was moving, busy with work that would soon finish, a universal fever made of a little of the misery and cares and of the profits and joys, of everyone.

But neither Rolande nor Clara savored the picturesque quality of that spectacle. Having met up ten minutes before, because it had been necessary to deceive for an entire day the comedy of Monsieur Duverdon's surveillance, they were entirely given to their confidences, their impressions, and their desire for a prompt vengeance. After a moment of silence, the American turned her equivocal head toward her friend, and asked: "What did he say, then, darling, when he knew that you didn't want to remain in that condition?"

"He didn't say anything. I was suffering, crazy. I must have been delirious throughout the night he spent watching over me, sitting at my bedside. Then, this morning, when I felt better, he let me get up and no longer talked about anything. To see us, one would have thought that I was just as ignorant as the day before and that he was as insouciant about his crime. I had lunch at the common table. I ate a little, and people commented on the latest news from Cannes. Hector was suffering more and wasn't at the meal. He has bizarre ideas, he seems to be going mad, and everyone is anxious about him. But between my husband and me there was no allusion to our common emotion, no reminder of yesterday's scene, except for the state of his face, which I had lacerated—I don't know how he explained the damage—and his sad and soft expression, without manifest rancor, although he was on the lookout for my impressions and my intentions..."

"So?"

"So, at five o'clock, when Julien, overwhelmed by fatigue, went to sleep on the divan in the small drawing room. I decked myself out damnably quickly and I came running. Where are we going, Clara?"

"You'll find out in a minute, darling," replied Clara, seizing her friend's hand authoritatively. Then, more quietly: "Do you still trust me, darling?"

"Yes, Clara."

"And are you still determined to get rid of that?"

"Yes, yes!"

They brought their faces closer together, effusively. And yet, it appeared to both of them that that testimony lacked real abandon, that it was more the result of circumstances, the confirmation of a common determination than the intention to reanimate the embraces of the past. Now, dissociating and effacing their tenderness there was a monstrous act, a kind of degrading stain that had to be erased before their nervous amity could resume its flight. Rolande, even more than the foreigner, resented that temporary incohesion. Although she was not culpable, she was at least a victim, and she experienced by virtue of that a sensation of inferiority that rendered her more fearful, and also more reflective, and imposed on her, once again, the astonishment of the degrading yoke to which she had been subjected by the revolt of masculine brutality, by the idleness of amour, and by passionate atavism. She even went

337

as far as recognizing—but only in a flash of discernment—the scant seduction of her friend, the lie of her made-up face, treated in contrasting tones, the fake mahogany of her androgynous hair and the pallor of the withered complexion, pasty and creased under the enamel.

The carriage had reached the intersection of one of the streets perpendicular to the Rue Charlot. Clara pressed the rubber bulb that rendered a whistle-blast signaling a halt.

"We've arrived," she said, getting out first; then, to the coachman: "Wait for us."

Before moving away she consulted by the light of the lantern a little notebook in which an address was written. She raised her eyes toward the plaque indicating the name of the street, looked at the numbers of the houses, and then started walking along the sidewalk at a deliberate pace They covered two hundred meters thus. The street they took narrowed, becoming black, choking and oppressive; it was almost deserted. The street-lamps seemed to have difficulty illuminating the poverty, their luminosity hesitating before the mud of the pavement, before the detritus accumulated at the borders, and the troubled oozing of the walls. Passers-by in caps turned round to look at their elegance; prostitutes already on the prowl laughed. Finally, a less disreputable house loomed up palely. A balcony gilded by the sign of a midwife distinguished the windows of the first floor.

"It's here," indicated Clara, plunging into a corridor impregnated with an odor of burnt fat that was emerging, with smoke, from the concierge's narrow lodge.

A few paces took them alongside an indecisive mural decoration of floral-patterned wallpaper, old and dirty; then a rather steep staircase where a rope carpet maintained by tarnished tringles trailed lamentably; then a landing with two doors, one characterized by a copper plate bearing a name: *Madame Poupe*; they had reached the goal of their excursion.

The casual attitude of the American, her coolness in tugging the bell-rope, did not calm Rolande, whose heart was palpitating with emotion. A young maid wearing a Breton

338

bonnet introduced them, without saying a word, into a banal drawing room hung with rep burned by age, with an ebony table, stripped of its polish by the stagnation of sticky liquids, disparate seats upholstered in worn and dusty red velvet, and beneath their feet a carpet in fake tapestry, bright in its newness, the motif of which was a green dog holding a basket full of fruits in its mouth. By contrast, hanging from the wall, there was an old engraving on wood, showing in a frame of flowers, Psyche at grips with Eros. Nothing could define the malaise due to that miserable and pretentious furniture, where, above everything, floated a sickened odor of old and neglected things, mingled with the reek of antiseptics and cooking.

"I'm afraid!" said Rolande, collapsing on a rickety chair, which groaned as if it were suffering from her weight.

Clara did not have time to stimulate her, for Madame Poupe came in, She was clad in a coarse woolen peignoir, gray with horizontal mauve stripes; her outrageously black wig, disciplined into two wavy bangs twisted at the back and covering her ears, did not mask the sharp avidity of her eyes; her nose, like an eagle's beak, curved over a wide, energetic, violent mouth of ferocious designation, in the midst of the nasty fat. Immediately, she apologized.

"I didn't want to make these ladies wait, and the ladies will excuse me for presenting myself in a peignoir...ordinarily, I dress in silk...black silk, because that's more serious."

She indicated chairs and all three sat down. Madame Poupe look at them complaisantly, wondering which of the two would be her prey, for she divined what brought them. But it was first necessary that she encourage their confidences, and that, by implication, she signified in advance the confession of her complicity. Laying a scarcely engaging stout hand with dirty fingernails on the table, she said:

"In what way can I be useful to these ladies? These ladies can confide in me. Discretion and propriety, that's my motto. In our profession, we so often have to calm anxieties,

339

and to console dolors, that we're a little like the Sisters of Charity, aren't we…?"

She smiled, showing the disposition of excessively pretty false teeth, manifestly incompatible with the usury of her features. And as her verbiage chilled the two friends, and no proposition emerged from their cold lips, she became impatient, and took on the authoritarian tone of a woman in a hurry who has sacrificed enough time to preliminaries.

"Is it for Madame? Or is it for Madame?"

"It's for me," said Rolande.

"I see…we're pregnant…"

"Then it was Clara who gave an explanation surging from her inventive brain. The pretext had been found in advance: her friend, a married woman, had had the imprudence, while her husband was away traveling, to commit a sin for which she found herself, alas, well punished, for the husband was about to return, and one did not know to what consequences his outraged honor might impel him. It was a question of humanity, of pity, of making disappear, with the shortest delay, that cause of rupture, perhaps of murder, in a united household.

But the practitioner had started and her stout destructive hand with tarnished nails protested at the same time as her words.

"But it's very serious, what you're asking of me! I don't do such things."

"Get away!" said Miss Boswett. "It's Madame de Berge who indicated you to us."

"Oh, if you've come on the part of Madame de Berge…! It was necessary to say that when you came in."

It was nothing of the sort. Madame de Berge had never confided to Clara the participation of the matron in her amorous repairs. It was a simple suspicion that made her employ the support of that name, and fortunately, she had guessed correctly. The woman's eyes began to shine intensely, lit up by the covetousness of a lucrative clientele. Madame de Berge not been one of her banal patients. She remembered her emotion and her nervous resistance at the first visits, and her indolence thereafter when habitude had come to offer its expert hand. Practitioner and patient had become friends, one accomplishing her little task easily, like an insignificant act of her métier, the other delivering herself without mortification, chatting while she worked, recounting her adventures, and only lamenting the egotism of men and their lack of foresight, and yet, regretting nothing, for pleasure had to be paid for. And Madame Poupe confided her gratitude, accompanying it with a lament.

"Yes, Madame de Berge as one of my good clients, and genteel with it, not proud for a liard. Unfortunately, Caresco has usurped me. Under the pretext that she was suffering in consequence of one of her…accidents, he's operated and rid her of everything, Oh, these surgeons! They don't respect anything!"

The reproach acquired, in the circumstance, the appearance of an accusation. The matron emphasized that character by giving her advice in a tone of mealy-mouthed protection, which already permitted their solidarity in the sin.

"Believe me, dear Madame, don't ever go to see Caresco; never have yourself opened up. First of all, the woman thus dispossessed is no longer a woman. She grows fat, she often loses all pleasure; she becomes apathetic and slack, she fades like a flower out of water. And then you know, it's dangerous, that game! How many times I've seen my poor patients butchered like that! While me, never any risk…a fortnight's rest and Cupid recovers his rights."

Clara became impatient with that loquacity. She divined Rolande's intimate torture; her bosom was heaving with apprehension. She cut her off.

"Then you accept to render that service to Madame?"

"That depends on the conditions. I have my risks, you understand. The police aren't tender with us. In addition I ought to declare that a married woman is dearer. Sometimes husbands have an interest in causing a scandal. I don't know how Madame stands with her Monsieur, but it depends...yes, it depends..."

"Anything you wish," the American concluded

Madame Poupe, her eyebrows furrowed, reflected for a moment—not because she was hesitating but because she was making a calculation. The risk was in fact, great, and she had recently acquired the persuasion of it because a chambermaid on whom she had operated two days before for fifty francs had been suddenly gripped by an infectious fever and had caused her great annoyance. She no longer wanted to work in such wretched conditions, now that her clientele had almost enriched her, now that she possessed a nice yellow-painted villa in Joinville-le-Pont, on the edge of the water, with a summer-house from which one could see the silvery river rippling and hear joyful boating songs. She assessed the luxury of the visitors, the sable jacket of one and the pearl necklace of the other. It was real; she knew that, having been something of a clothes merchant before making angels. Her dark eyes were ardently mercantile when she raised them again to her interlocutors, risking a large figure, with the conviction that she would be beaten down by half.

"Two thousand, paid in advance," she launched through the joints of her false teeth.

"Agreed. Where and when?"

Then she felt remorse; she regretted not having been more demanding. She had a desire to renegotiate the price, to ask for double. But she was too businesslike to play thus with a lady who would doubtless become her client. It was necessary not to discourage her by skinning her. And then, she only had a promise.

"Where and when?" Clara repeated.

"Whenever you like, but not here. I never operate at home. I'll come to your house tomorrow, if you wish. It will be more comfortable for Madame, who won't have to be displaced."

"It's impossible at her house."

"Hire a room in a hotel, then. Give me the number in advance, in order that I don't have to be noticed at the office, and everything will go smoothly. That's how I generally do it."

There was no need to prolong the conversation. Clara and Rolande got up and hastened to flee the abortionist's obsequious smile, her shady ambience, the green dog on the carpet, the burned rep on the wall, the threadbare velvet of the seats and the odor of burnt fat coming from the kitchen, mingled with the unspeakable reek of antiseptics. In the antechamber on the way out they passed a fat man with a shiny cranium with an outrageously cosmetic beard and a large golden chain ornamenting his abdomen, with the air of an old captain emerged from the ranks, having become, by virtue of a new situation, a well-to-do bourgeois. That was Monsieur Poupe, a tranquil soul beneath his martial face, having never done anything other than serve to bring respectability to his wife. In addition, he kept the accounts, bought merchandise and fished with a road and line. He had a top hat and an odor of absinthe, although the string bag containing comestibles suspended from his right arm indicated that before the aperitif he had been to buy provisions. He bowed deeply to the two visitors, who did not respond.

Once outside, Rolande and Clara felt the need to respire before climbing back into the carriage. They walked a short way, followed by the vehicle. It was nearly seven o'clock, and in the Rue de Saintonge, then further on in the Boulevard des Filles-du-Calvaire, a new movement was produced, a fluctuation of people hastening toward the hearth. Seamstresses of wigs went past them; the workshops in the vicinity poured them out in hundreds, with thin torsos and chlorotic faces, the anemic fruit of generations nearing extinction. The fatigue of their atavism, the flight of their vital force due to years of attrition, was betrayed in the plaintive gleam of their eyes. Blood never regenerated, lungs stifled by noxious air, the colors of life dissolved by precocious labor, they went, squeezing under the shoulders of poor cloaks that a fantasy, a certain chic in the fashion of wearing them, rendered them less pitiful. Some were laughing as they listened to the words of gallantry that pursued them.

How many of them, under harsh social oppression, because love impoverishes, because love kills, had gone to Madame Poupe or her peers; how many would go to her in future to request the gesture destructive of degrading maternity? How many would subordinate their creative need to the monthly apparition? How many, after getting drunk, after the voluptuous spasm that held them exhausted in a lover's arms, suddenly sobering up, would bound out of the embrace and have no other haste that to clear away the conception like a shameful and dangerous virus? Rolande thought about that on seeing them pass by and hearing their laughter. But Clara had just stopped, having seized her by the arm.

"I think, darling, that I ought to go and see Rose, my chambermaid, who is suffering, as you know. Do you want to accompany me?"

And as Rolande hesitated, because of the lateness of the hour, and also because she had had enough of suspecting and seeing so much misery, the American insisted: "Come on, darling, you have plenty of time. And then, we have to arrange our day tomorrow. Come on, then!"

Then she followed her, taking her place in the vehicle again in her company. In the room in the sleazy hotel to which the carriage took them, in the environment of strange desolation that is a redoubt opening to the exterior by an obscure skylight, pitifully furnished with vague rejects from public sales, large dirty cretonne curtains fell pretentiously over a mahogany bed with sheets dirtied by temporary contacts and a worn mattress, a table and chairs of rickety wicker, and, in a corner, the vestige of a broken marble wash-basin and a greasy bowl, in that stifling and vitiated mansard, Rose, Clara's genteel and sprightly soubrette, was agonizing.

Two days ago, on returning from Nice, without even bothering to have her luggage taken to the Rue Scribe, in her haste to finish promptly with her two-month pregnancy, she had rented that hotel room for a fortnight, telegraphed her mother to request her care, and then, methodically, with the tranquil air of an orderly young woman foreseeing everything, given confidence by the benign consequences of a first operation, she had gone to bed and asked for Madame Poupe. And death had entered the room at the same time as the midwife had left it. It had only required a dirty stylet introducing infectious germs into the human egg for the malady to flare up. The next day, after a calm night, an intense frisson had woken her up. Her teeth were chattering, and an abundant sweat chilled her. Then, without transition, fever had plunged her abruptly into boiling fever.

When her mother, an old peasant-woman from Berri with a suntanned face tormented by multiple wrinkles, had arrived, she scarcely recognized her. It was a catastrophic septicemia, the kind that kills in forty-eight hours. A local physician, summoned by the landlady, in his ignorance of the cause, had diagnosed typhoid fever and advised transferring her to a hospital, but the old woman had opposed that separation with the stubbornness of a country-dweller frightened by the word *hospital*.

And the following night had passed in futile cares, listening to the gasping breath and the rattle of the chest lifting up the sheets, pressing the hand dried by the fire in the veins, watching Rose's face, first livid, transform, blue-tinted and then ablaze, before the final extinction, while fetid excretions that she tried to collect and clean up with the only napkin in the room impregnated the atmosphere with poison. A night of calamity, an abysmal night, in which her old hardened heart broke a hundred times, after having hoped a hundred times: an indescribable torture suffered in the macabre gloom, the lamp having gone out for want of fuel; a despair that the dull dawn filtered through the skylight could not dissipate, although a remission had been produced at that moment in the condition of the dying woman, although her eyes had opened again to salute it and she had surprised the tender gratitude of her gaze there.

345

But almost immediately, Rose had fallen back into her furnace and now she was mildly delirious. In that supreme hour, ingenuous terms, appellations of childhood, all the sweet evocation of moments when as a child, she had felt herself soothed by maternal love, passed softly through her lips, emerging at the same time as plaintive hiccups from her dry mouth, exhaling with the nauseating ejection of stomach liquids. A heartrending contrast: extreme childhood, extreme life dissolving in the same stammering! The purity of the one and the corruption of the other accompanied by the same appeals for maternal protection!

She was dying, a new victim of the society that made so many others, a martyr to the community whose tyranny is formidable, whose oppression is stupidly illogical, since it stifles under shame and frames in misery those who commit no other sin than yielding to natural instincts and obeying the creative necessities that life imposes on them. Such holocausts are necessary, then, to that society and that nature! Injustice, cruelty and incoherence: the protestations were audible in the halting breath of the dying woman, in her stammers of agony.

Heard passing, at the same time as hers, were the lamentations of an entire category of humble young women surprised in their innocence, delivered to the savage impulsion of the male, driven to the utmost limits of despair, finding in their distress, the misery and infamy that accompany it, no other resources than prostitution or the crime of abortion. For alas, the liberation and redemption so much vaunted were illusory; rare were those who, dissimulating their fault, resumed a life of rough labor, calculations and incessant privations, in order to nourish and raise the child immediately snatched from heir breast, the child that they did not know, whom a distant mercenary adopted in some unknown hole in the country and swaddled in her stead, and laid down in a cradle that was often converted into a tomb.

When, then, will the pastors of peoples, those who organize so rigorously the laws of the family, the monopolists of terrestrial enjoyments to whom, by dint of legality or money, all the joys of amour are permitted, sense a little humanity radiating within them, and comprehend the beauty, the grandeur and the holy excuse of maternity, the right of every being to love and to create in full light, without affront even being able to brush the woman whose dolorous loins have just opened to give birth?

When, then, will society finally honor the primal act of life, not by brandishing and adoring sex organs, as in the epochs of ancient decadence, but by glorifying those whom men inseminate and inspiring in adolescents respect for the seed, instead of allowing it to be mocked, and then by collecting the fruit that is neglected or abandoned, in order to enable it to ripen sumptuously, in the radiance of the sun?

Rose's rattle said all of that, but the old woman did not understand its frightful eloquence. And yet, her dolor was another form of protestation. Intoxicated by despair, the creases of her face exaggerated by the heartbreak that accentuated every wrinkle of her tan-colored skin, her lips parted over the absence of teeth, respiring the odor of imminent death, she remained immobile, petrified before the agonizing woman. At the same time, a dull and fearful anger seized her against the big city whose streets she had seen full of an alarming movement when she had disembarked the day before: a monstrous and voracious city that attracted children from the country, killed them and ate them like a kind of carnivorous giant. Her fear and her rage were, in sum, a primitive fashion of protesting against the cruel and all-consuming society, against the despotic and exploitative community.

And she stayed there, sitting at her daughter's bedside, sunk in her impotence, all her activity reduced to watching for the approaching death, listening to the increasing hindrance of the respiration and gazing, by the favor of an obscure daylight coming from the skylight at the transformation of Rose's face as it was kneaded by agony, and her eyes were hollowed out by darkness and veiled, lost in mysterious abysms. She did not budge when the physician returned and announced the imminent end; she did not hear the bustle of movement in the hotel, the doors banging and the footsteps that made the uncarpeted staircase cry out.

At about three o'clock in the afternoon there was a racket in the next room. A couple of lovers had been introduced to it, who started laughing and singing. The thinness of the wall allowed every outburst of voices to pass through. The singing was soon succeeded by a plaint, that of a woman entering into amour. Her breath was panting, like Rose's; the creative rhythm was strangely confounded with that of the agonizing woman. A layer of plaster scarcely separated that work of life from that work of annihilation, and they were expressed by the same gasping. The old woman did not understand; she thought that a similar fatality was unfolding and concluding behind the wall.

At that moment, a ray of sunlight, which the caprice of the neighboring roofs allowed to reach as far as the skylight, appeared momentarily, revealing more repulsively the squalor of the redoubt; but at the same time it evoked the joys of the fields, the open air, the gaiety of young women dancing in arbors, the heath of young men harrowing the ground. And that ray illuminated the old woman's true dolor, caused a profound sob to explode in her entrails and denounced the taut strings of her old heart. She wept for a long time, and that was almost a relief.

Then she took Rose's hand again, which was going cold and turning blue, and she covered it with her tears, stammering and appealing to her "little one," begging her not to go away, to come back to her, to her love, to the large spaces around the thatch where the air was pure and where lungs dilated easily. But the ray was extinguished almost immediately, as an ironic smile vanishes, and left her plunged in her bleak contemplation, in her abyssal interment.

And she had been there for hours that distilled an eternity when there was a knock. Almost at the same time, Clara and Rolande opened the door. Immediately, however, they recoiled, frightened by the odor of the redoubt and the spectacle of the bed.

Eventually, they came in. Their attire was radiant in the sadness of the mansard. Already they had taken out their bottles of perfumed salts and were reanimating their sense of smell, ready to make them faint. The mother had not budged, but Clara approached and touched her on the shoulder.

"So, Rose isn't well? You're looking after her? You're a relative?"

The old woman finally raised her head. She opened her mouth, revealing her lack of teeth. Grimacing, she moaned: "She's my little one. She's dying."

"What's the matter, then, poor girl? You don't know? Has anyone sent for a doctor? She seems very poorly... Reply, then!"

She was interrogating nervously, impatiently, and the other, as at the irruption of the sunlight a little while before, had now recovered from the tears that had paralyzed her voice; she still did not respond to the foreigner's questions, however. She consented herself with calling to her "little one" in the tone of a wounded animal, at which Rolande, pale with emotion, started to tremble, and withdrew to the farthest corner of the room, near the door. Then the American approached the bed, became the mistress again, and wanted determinedly to penetrate the mystery of the malady that had felled her chambermaid so abruptly. She had suspected her relationship with Louis.

"Well, Rose? Are you asleep? Wake up, my child. Do you recognize me?"

She had seized her arm, impregnated with a burning moisture, and imprinted shocks to it that were transmitted all the way to the unfortunate woman's head, extracting her from her oblivion, parting momentarily the veil of agony extended before her eyes. Rose lifted her heavy eyelids, looked, and recognized the new arrival.

"It's Madame!" she breathed.

"Yes, it's me. I've come to obtain news of you. You have a fever, my child? What can you have done to fall ill?

Come on, tell me, so that I can care for you! Tell me, I demand it!"

Oh, the atrocious annoyance of being disturbed in annihilation, of having to think, and still to obey! Rose struggled to reanimate her memories. The last heartbeats of her life were concentrated in a colossal research of lucidity, in order to subdue the voluntary fluid, the imperious suggestion of the mistress she feared. She turned her head, wanting to see whether there was anyone there who might hear her confidence; but her extinct eyesight could see no further than the face of Clara leaning over her, unable to distinguish either Rolande or her mother, equally suspended on her lips. She unstuck her dry tongue from her palate, and finally let through curt and expiring words, which signified phrases. And the formidable confession escaped, nailing all three of them with stupor.

"Forgive me, Madame…I sinned…Louis…I had him in the blood! Oh, those kisses...his voice…so cajoling..! Then, a first time…then a second…couldn't! Miserable the child, and me too…the shame…my place.... Then…then…"

"Then?" insisted Clara, shaking her again and forgetting, in her furious curiosity, the presence of Rolande, whom that confession might frighten."

Rose clenched herself in order not to fall back into her void. The authoritarian fluid of her mistress enveloped her, impregnated her totally, and, her semi-rational delirium still leaving her the memory of her servitude, she obeyed, as she would have obeyed the image of the Crucifix extended by a confessor, for the remission of her sin.

"Then," she replied, hiccupping, "I went…Madame Poupe…to get rid of the child!"

Another rattle escaped her; her effort had completed killing her. She gasped. Her lips, employed in struggling for the last breath, closed over her confidence. But she had said enough, and Clara, having understood, pushed her back on her bed.

Beside herself, corrupting that agony with a foam of violent imprecations, all her morbid rage against men suddenly brought back by that supreme confession, she cried: "Whore! Little whore! That's how you've betrayed me! You've delivered yourself to a man, like a bitch! Yes a bitch, a bitch of the streets, soiled by that pig! Oh, you're punished now! You're doubtless going to die! Well, that's good!"

In her androphobic fury she went astray abominably, to the point of madness. She wanted to strike, to break, to destroy. She raised her hand to slap the victim, but the old woman intervened. She bounded, leapt upon the arm that was about to come down, and there was a brief struggle, an all-out battle of two bodies and two adverse wills, in which words of natural love collided with ignoble terms before the indifferent Rose, who fell back with a frightful gasp that departed from the utmost depths of her breast.

From her corner, Rolande, her heart progressively constricted, watched the scene. At first, an astonishment had seized her on seeing her friend pursue her investigation so bitterly and not even to disarm before menacing death. A rudiment of conscience made her find Clara's tyranny exorbitant, in wanting to bend everything to the whim of her vices, not admitting that others might have different tastes, and choosing that moment of solemn expiation to reproach them as a crime. There was a despotism in it that wounded her, which made the domination to which she had submitted for years more debasing, and she was ashamed of it.

But she did not have the leisure to reflect on it at length, for Rose's confession rendered her a sentiment of curiosity, and when the madwoman's hand was raised over the dying woman she finally revolted; she applauded the impulse of the old woman, and her struggle, which paralyzed the foreigner. She was about to mingle in it, to launch herself against the violator of that agony when a strange intimate stir, a new manifestation of her pregnancy, nailed her in place. It was a shock that had just struck the partitions of her abdomen, and then several, the first appeals of the being she was carrying. And as that unexpected awakening, those stirrings of the dawn, denouncing the new life that was palpitating within her, was not

351

painful, she experienced a confused astonishment, a tender disturbance.

Ah! What a sudden enlightenment, what an advertisement of nature, proclaimed, in that minute of drama, that it was necessary not to contravene its laws, that no human power had the right to oppose a hatching in its first phase. The child was alive, then; the child was blooming within her; she felt it become animate, like a treasure of flesh that she ought to respect, that she ought to welcome with gratitude. And suddenly, the future seemed to her to be resplendent.

The child had kicked, the child had revealed itself, and the maternal instinct, deviated until then by vice, stifled by an odious amity, finally quivered, and its splendor threw far away, into the shadow, the enervating lie of her dead passions. An abominable liaison, which she detested now!

And as the little being became impatient and kicked again, Rolande, with a great gesture of renunciation for that death and that ignominy, ran away.

She marched hastily. She headed for the boulevards in order to respire better, in order to disengage herself from all that horror. She went past people who were going home for dinner, who were running to the hearth, and she received, from their urgency, a thousand gripping suggestions, a thousand evolutionary contrasts. They were numerous, then, those who loved and were loved in accordance with nature? There was, then, in that other intimacy, a charm she did not know, since all those men, a whole host, were hastening so urgently toward woman, since women, like Rose, sacrificed to men all their pains and joys, their entre bring, to the extent of dying!

And suddenly, she recalled the agony of the unfortunate young woman, her face already rendered livid by imminent death; then, the visit to Madame Poupe, the destroyer of that creature in full flower. She shivered; all her egotism trembled at it. What! It was to that end that Clara had tried to take her, to that death-rattle, that lividity! Oh, the abominable odious, perverted friend!

And there passed before her eyes, at the same time as the horrible spectacle of a little while before, the symbolic aspect of her previous degradation and the incomparable justice of tomorrow. She saw once again those two women who wanted to afflict the race, both collapsing: one vanquished, flagellated by the old woman, choking with rage, her red hair disorganized by the struggle, her dissolved make-up allowing the withering of age to become manifest; the other suffocating, dying amid pestilence. And that was the normal conclusion of things, simple love, creative love, felling vice, crushing its ugliness. She alone had the good fortune of having sensed the future result, of having heard, before the irreparable fall, the warning of nature's alarm.

And it was her child that had given it to her. It was kicking more forcefully now, as if to tell her to hasten her return. It also awoke unsuspected ideas and ravishing transports. It indicated, in striking its blows, the sumptuous perpetuity, the new egotism made of altruism, that would henceforth occupy all its mother's cares, which was about to hold her prostrate awaiting future evolutions Those who did not listen to such appeals were sacrilegious, as were those who prevented that flight, who did not favor those triumphant appearances. By virtue of those little beings, one was never extinguished; by virtue of them, life was prolonged; they were the sacred deposit of the past, the triumphant promise of the future.

And in confirmation of that magnificent vision, she recalled the mild visage, the blue, sad and loving eyes of her husband, and his neat beard, his gracious gestures, his shoulders of a timid Hercules. He had acted for her benefit, for her redemption. He was in the hearth that she was approaching; he was waiting in the warm room whose calm had been blessed. His conduct had had no determining reason but their common happiness, and the happiness of the child that was about to arrive. Oh, poor good Julien, the poor perplexed colossus she had so atrociously misunderstood!

She had already placed her finger on the doorbell of the house. The light of their window made her hope that he was in

353

her apartment. She ran, quivering with the need to love him. She opened the door. He was there.

"Oh, Julien...my great Julien!" she said, falling into his arms with huge sobs that shook her whole body.

XXIII

After having climbed the sill of the window, a ray of sunlight penetrated into the room. It slanted all the way to the silvering of a mirror, which reflected it toward the sleeper and woke him up. Every morning, the same salute of the light drew Raoul from his great repose and renewed his surprise in finding himself in the little bed in a furnished villa, which a white tulle mosquito-net protected from the inopportune activity of those flies and their cousins, pullulating in the warm season of April. The young man struggled for a moment before ridding himself of the last grip of slumber, but the concern of the cares to be devoted to his friend completed the stimulating work of the star.

He yawned, rubbed his eyes, propelled his limbs, relaxed by the long night, and leapt on to the uncarpeted tiles, red and shiny, where radiance trembled under his footfalls. He slipped into loose flannel pajamas, under which the grace and vigor of his esthetic was divinable. Finally, quietly, he opened the door of the next room, in which the invalid reposed. He saw him behind the transparency of the mosquito-net, his eyes still closed, his chest calm, rising rhythmically, inhaling the air of which an open casement allowed him all the purity.

The same caress of light, visiting every window in the dwelling, would soon wake Claude in his turn, but at the moment, it had only covered half its route; Raoul therefore had time. He closed the door again soundlessly and went down to the ground floor.

Thus they both lived in that villa enchanted by the sun and the flowers, which overlooked a bright and silent little street of La Californie. The deployment of tall palm trees with trunks enlaced by rose-bushes, flower-beds of veronicas, geraniums and carnations in bloom, rendered the access delightful. Climbing plants, wisteria and clematis, snaked along the white façade, diversified by shutters planted pale green, and enabled it with a charming polychromy. Honeysuckle was organized along a wooden structure to form an arbor that the afternoon heat respected. In addition, the garden was sheltered from indiscretions by a curtain of odorous eucalyptus linked by a chain of bamboos. There were also clumps of fleshy aloes reminiscent of opal, mimosas ornamented in yellow, magnolias and pepper plants weeping their melancholy mauve drooping clusters, and, near the entrance, voluminous cacti surging from red porphyry vases—in sum, an entire splendor, an entire warm vegetation, embedded in fine gravel, contrasting with the leprosy of the grass, burned by the sun.

Once the threshold was crossed, one penetrated on the same level into a drawing room that the two friends had transformed into a work-room. They had disposed therein an entire scientific baggage of microscopes and precision instruments utilizable for botany. To tell the truth, they did not spend much time in there, only a few hours a day, the rest of the time being employed in walks, excursions by carriage, long siestas and copious meals, for sleeping, eating and breathing the pure air was the whole secret of the treatment. The dining room, garnished with old furniture in sculpted oak, was contiguous with the drawing room, and the kitchen formed the background, with the stairway going up two floors, each composed of two rooms. The first was occupied by Claude and Raoul, the second abandoned to Pauline, the maid-of-all-work, a plump young woman from Arles whose voice betrayed an excessive tone of wine. She occupied that floor alone, since Louis, Antonin Fargeaud's valet de chambre, useless and idle, had been sent back to Paris without having been able to seduce her.

Raoul went into the kitchen, and the domestic's broad smile welcomed him. She was occupied in distilling the morning coffee in a corner of the stove, and the aroma embalmed the room every time she uncovered the filter to pour the boiling water into it. Her breasts filled the blouse disturbed by the lifting; her short hands, now habituated to cleanliness since she had be nerving her new masters, were laden with fake gold rings. She was immediately expansive.

"Bonjour, Monsieur Raoul. Has the night been at least good?"

"Perfect, Pauline."

"And has Monsieur Claude slept well too?"

"He's still asleep."

"Tribunal de Carcassonne!"

Pauline's language, independently of the local accent, was distinguished above all by the latter exclamation, which she threw into the conversation for no reason, and by which she expressed, depending on the tone of the expression, indifference, surprise, joy, anger, dolor or amour. The ritual refrain amused the two friends. They had taken possession of it, and employed it in their rare moments of gaiety. Between themselves, they no longer designated the soubrette other than by that phrase, emitted with the naïve and sparkling mimicry of an agreeable physiognomy.

Thus, "Tribunal de Carcassonne" was satisfied that the two messieurs had spent a good night. She served them with contentment, nevertheless reserving her preferences for Raoul, whose musculature impressed her, in spite of the respect to which she felt that her temperament of a bold young woman was obliged. She experienced for him a sympathy so exclusive that, in spite of her welcoming complaisance, she had rejected the attempts of Louis. On seeing him smile at her exclamation, she interrupted watering the coffee and placed both hands on her hips, ready to chatter.

"I've had a funny dream, Monsieur Raoul."

"You can tell me tomorrow, my dear," said the young man, serenely, to cut short any expansion, for he now wearied quickly of her loquacity, to which he had listened cheerfully in the beginning. Then he added: "Pass me the fresh eggs instead, and pay attention to the milk, which is about to boil over."

He deployed a wifely precision in the execution of those housekeeping cares, and supervised the alimentation of his friend like an autocrat's chef. Claude owed his amelioration, so manifest in three months, to that incessant stuffing, the dozen eggs that he swallowed raw, with meat extract and alimentary powders that were added to his nourishment. Raoul prepared them with his own hands, and insisted that the invalid absorb them, even when he later declared himself sickened, and pretexted the lassitude of his stomach. At each of his weekly visits, the doctor affirmed the value of that curative procedure, and the guardian carried out his instructions with a tenacity that had already been recompensed. He took the four eggs that the soubrette handed to him, therefore, and broke the shells over a bowl, without losing a drop. He even found the dose insufficient.

"They're very small today, Pauline, your eggs. Pass me another one."

"Tribunal de Carcassonne! Five eggs in one go, no less!"

She was amazed that anyone could ingurgitate so much substance without bursting. But Raoul broke the new egg immediately, and it did, in fact, make a respectable mass in the bottom of the bowl, which the young man started to beat energetically with a fork. He sprinkled it with salt and a few grains of pepper, agitated the yellow liquid again, in which bubbles of air were imprinted, and when the preparation was complete, holding the bowl of eggs in one hand and a cup of fuming milky coffee in the other, he went up to the bedroom again. He had quit him ten minutes ago; now, doubtless, the sun would have traveled far enough to have brought the awakening ray to Claude.

He was not mistaken, for on opening the door carefully, he remarked immediately the invalid's blue eyes fixed upon him, eyes with azure reflections, softening the expression of the face, hostile to the approaching overalimentation. Then he went into the room, whistling a military march.

"Tyrant!" cried Claude, sitting up in bed, half-laughing and half-annoyed.

"Ingurgitate first and insult me later."

Claude grimaced, and had to resume three times in order to swallow the detested mixture, a few gulps of milky coffee having difficulty dissipating the abominated taste.

"What's the point of these repeated tortures?" he said, putting the cup down on a nearby table.

"You're in a bad mood very early…didn't you sleep well? Come on, don't be a baby. The cure is at the end of this stuffing."

"Cure? What's the point of the cure?"

Raoul shrugged his shoulders, but a fit of coughing that had just taken possession of Claude stopped him at the moment when he was about to express his discontentment with that puerile resistance in another fashion. He watched him fold himself in two and flex his shoulders in order to rid himself of an inconvenient expectoration.

Every morning, Claude was subject to the same anguishing cough. However, he was benefiting visibly from his sojourn in Cannes; the projections of his cheekbones had lost the excessively vivid redness that contrasted with the mat pallor of his complexion; his eyes no longer had the unhealthy gleam that seemed to reflect an interior fever, and behind the brown beard, which he was now allowing to grow, one could judge the thickening that weight-gain rapidly gives the cheeks of tuberculosis sufferers.. His aspect was reassuring, therefore, and it required that stubborn cough at every awakening and the preoccupation of the physician, who still observed signs at the right summit, for one to watch out for the slightest imprudence and to suspect the ever-menacing consumption in the chest. He retained the dolorous persuasion himself, in spite of the sincere encouragements of his friend, who was involuntarily troubled by such a resurrection.

In fact, the success of the treatment determined a strange intimate debate in Raoul. The most valorous consciences are submissive to such failings in times of upheaval. Although he wanted Claude to recover his health and applauded the symptoms of amelioration observed by the physician, he felt at the same time, almost infallibly, a bitterness when the sweet vision of Henriette reappeared as a corollary to the transformation of her fiancé, with the memory of the rights that the latter still conserved over her. He wondered then whether

Claude would persist in the same intentions of abandonment, whether his reconquered health might make him forget the valiant words of renunciation he had pronounced one morning along the promenade of the Croisette, without getting to the end of his confession but significantly enough for Raoul to have understood that he was the replacement of election designated to the young woman's heart.

Since then, a tension in the relationship of the two friends had resulted therefrom. Both strove to hide the evidence of it by means of a more manifest cordiality, and there was a constant play of their behavior and their words, an increasing determination of their testimonies of sympathy, a deceptive exaggeration of their fraternity, succeeding long periods of sterile silence. But that did not prevent Claude, in the back of his mind, seeing in Raoul the fortunate beneficiary of a happiness that had been reserved for him, and Raoul wondering whether Claude had not been a poor estimator of the strength of his heart in causing to shine, before the eyes of the successor he had designated, a prey of foolish hope that he still had the liberty to keep for himself. That dispossession on the one part and that uncertainty on the other thus acted dully on the accord of the young men, but without elevating in either of them the slightest sentiment of animosity or manifest rancor, since the sacrifice of the one was voluntary and the hope of the other justified.

So, when Raoul brought Claude the morning bowl of aliments, and later took is friend by the arm in order to take him to respire sunlight and air before the iridescent sea; when, after the midday meal and the evening meal, he exerted all his tender solicitude again to force him to eat—in brief, every time he contributed by his attentions and his suggestive will to that amelioration, both desired and feared—the same obscure debate was reanimated in them. Every time, their hearts had a muted struggle to endure, before their sentiments of honesty and natural mercy got the upper hand. But every time, too, their conscience ended up reckoning with personal interest, and abolished evil desire in order to give way to innate generosity in such conformity with Raoul's exterior beauty and so analogous to the delicacy of Claude's malady.

With his more refined psychology, Claude had divined those alternatives in his companion, and he thanked him tacitly for allowing them to triumph to his advantage. He compared them to his own and found them similar. It was then that he saw clearly the only way out of the continuing moral impasse, which was to favor his friend's amour by means of a mortal sacrifice, and not to make the healthy young woman submit to the terrible consequences of such a gross egotism.

It was then that he addressed letters of Paris filed with eulogies to his rival; and when, vibrant with those new resolutions, he received Raul's cares, when the latter appeared, as he did this morning, with a bowl of aliments in his hand, he admired the abnegation of the young man more profoundly, because he divined that it was similar to his own. He experienced a sentiment of the most sincere gratitude, for he read in his friend, in order to give, efforts identical to those he was obliged to make himself, in order to accept.

For two months they had been living in those alternatives, more troubling than any declared situation. They hid the great embarrassment that resulted from it behind a false gaiety of which "Tribunal de Carcassonne" often paid the expense. But sometimes, in the midst of their laughter, they stopped suddenly, and confessions burned their lips. The same evocation paralyzed their enthusiasm. In reality, very little was required for that: a word evoking their former threefold intimacy, a silhouette of a woman recalling the proud grace of Henriette; a reflection of pure water fixing their common obsession. At the moment when they were about to speak, to confide their chagrin to one another and dissipate their doubt, their throats constricted and they were afraid of what they were about to say.

Finally, one evening, Claude, on emerging from the house of his physician, whom he had gone to consult, unknown to Raoul, had shut himself in his room and had written a long missive addressed to Henriette and which he had marked with the word "personal." The effort had been rude to deliver his entire heart thus, for in emerging from writing the letter in order to post it himself, he was trembling like an old man. It was three days since that act of heroism, and the response had not yet reached him.

The coughing fit that shook the invalid having finally calmed down, Claude got up and began to get dressed. He rejected with a gesture of thanks, the help of Raoul, who wanted to aid him. He went to his dressing-table, situated in front of one of the windows, and took off his night-shirt in order to devote himself to his ablutions. The mirror reflected the muscular sinews of his neck, the notch of the clavicles and the curve of the ribs, the bony framework that, in spite of his amelioration, thinness still caused to stick out. He had never observed the evidence so crudely. Perhaps he judged it more poignantly because he had slept badly.

He murmured: "See how I've melted away!"

But Raoul, sensing a black moment against which it was necessary to react, started joking: "Evidently, cannibals would disdain putting you on the skewer, but remember, my friend, that you've just put on more than a kilo in a fortnight, and that's a jolly good result..."

"What's the point?" he said, again, in his tone of ritual desolation. "Will I ever be a desirable husband? For that's my unique goal of living."

"Why not? When you're cured..."

They looked at one another, both sensing that a decisive moment was about to pass. The conversation this engaged could have no other conclusion than finally to establish, in a positive manner, their reciprocal situation with regard to Henriette. Claude, who was about to put on his cravat, placed his trembling hand on Raoul's shoulder. His face was suddenly excavated by great fissures of anguish, as if a skillful sculptor had just modeled a mask of despair. Then he spoke in a voice so low and hoarse that Raoul initially had difficulty grasping the meaning of the words.

"Let's see, my friend, my brother...I believed that you had understood and that I had no need to bring up the subject that is oppressing me again...for sixty days of the most intimate existence, in fact, an equivocation has existed between us; we dared not envisage a solution that is nevertheless very simple...and that is because I have not explained myself fully, to affirm what you needed to hear in order to be convinced...

"Listen: a man like me has only one word, because, when he pronounces it, that word results from a profoundly ripened conviction. Listen: no, I shall not be cured, or, if I am cured, it will be later, when there is no longer time to aspire to marriage. Don't protest: I know. Three days ago, I went without your knowing it to see the doctor. I explained our situation to him; he didn't smile. I asked him for the absolute truth, and he gave it to me; I asked him about the future, and he told me. He's a man of honor. Well, the tuberculosis is too deeply rooted in me. My mother, alas. sowed it there even before I was born. Can I marry in those conditions? Would I ever dare to create? I cannot plead the ignorance that excuses my father's creative act, of which I am the lamentable product, since I'm informed, since I know in advance the frightful consequences for any woman who married me, for the children I would have. Would you want me to reserve for the person I venerate, the torture of seeing her children condemned to my illness? Would you want me to be criminal; for my marriage would be a crime, death emerging from our kisses?"

"You know very well that you love her!" protested Raoul, raising his head, which he had kept lowered in order to listen to that lament.

"Yes, I love her, and it's because I love her that I'm thinking in this fashion. It's also because I want to behave as an honest man."

"One doesn't murder one's heart like that!" observed Raoul again.

"Can one compare the murder of a heart to the disaster of an entire lineage?" replied Claude. "And then, those wounds close. Time will end up scarring them over."

"Time is so horribly long in this case!"

"Do I not have other concerns that deflect my thoughts?"

His gesture, designating his chest, narrated his physiological misery, and the both thought of what would still be necessary in terms of intensive alimentation, auscultations and bacillary research before the return of health. How many years would be employed in those cares, during which the body would eke out its youth and its resistance; and what would finally remain to offer his fiancée at the end of that struggle except a premature old age, a ravaged beauty and the imperishable memory of rancors that make kisses hesitate? But thinking about those things was, at that moment, like a repose for them, a truce in the conversation that threatened to impel them finally to resolve their situation, which both of them feared. And they were glad of the silence.

Claude was the first to break it. His fit of dark humor pushed him to energetic resolutions; he was in haste to rid himself of the weight of sacrifice that was oppressing him. He continued: "In any case, there's another reason why my heart will be contented. I would already have told you, but a purely physical reason prevented me. Do you remember...?"

He was obliged to make a effort, quickly dissipated, and he continued almost coldly: "Henriette doesn't love me. Nature has conducted her toward another. I ought not even need to pronounce the name of that most fortunate of men. Your own emotion, at this moment, denounces it, and your eyes have already denounced to me that you knew that it was you."

Raoul stood up, in a fearful release of his entire person, and his two hands were propelled in a sign of imploring protestation.

"No! You know that's impossible! I can't! I can't!"

"You can and you must."

Claude had departed from his coldness and had adopted a attitude of grave benevolence to utter those last words. The effort that he had to make to express them was no longer transparent, and could only have been detected in the trembling of his fingers. The sublime faith of apostles illuminated his face, attenuated by the pitiful submission of his body, broken in two, subject to the fatality of events. The great speech had been made; but he had to soften the impact that struck his friend more than himself.

"Come on, Raoul, calm down. Sit down and listen to me with as much calm as I have. I've reflected hard, damn it, and the truth of those last words have matured me by ten years. Misfortune makes one wiser and leads the soul all the way to the roots of verity. One sees the world so differently then! One strips it of so many prejudices and false sentiments. Yes I've understood what part of pride is invested in the love of others, and weighs most frequently upon their conduct. I've also understood how sweet it is to be able to sacrifice oneself for two people one cherishes.

"Henriette and you are the only two elite beings that I have encountered on earth. Our childhood games were common, our minds awoke to the same conceptions, seduced or afflicted. Later, when our ages separated us from Henriette, when the atmosphere of the convent enveloped her in a mysticism that I deplore, but that all her nature fortunately denies, we continued to love one another in our collaboration, in our work, in our visions, equally honest and disdainful of the baseness of others.

"Our studies brought us precisely to the study of families and races. We were astonished by the brutal power of creation; we were saddened by the passions that humans added to it, for the misfortune of humankind. That concern and that information rendered us superior to others, better destined than them to perfect our hearth and embellish our posterity. Well, is it now that, when, imbued with those reasons, mastering prejudices and pride, you know as well as I do the inadmissibility of my marriage, you contradict them all by striving to lure me with unreasonable hopes, by making a false future shine before my eyes?

"There should not be between us, the pious lies dictated by an ill-advised amity. We are both too instructed in positive science to allow ourselves to be taken in by them. The facts ought to dominate our sensibility, and you ought to be able to recognize as sanely as I do my obligation to distance myself from Henriette. My amours would be limited to postponements, to putting off that projected union to a distant time, and even if, one day, when cured, I succumbed, I would have the frightful suspicion of having given mortal caresses, if not to my wife, at least to my children.

"Well, what one ought to respect, first of all, is the work of the race. I am too convinced of its burden of obligations to want to shoulder them. Now, I've discovered your undeniable amour. You are not responsible, for one is not responsible for the tractions of nature; and on the other hand, you have both put too much determination into not succumbing to them, in order that I could not criticize you. Love one another, then, you two, the only elect of my soul. Accomplish the work of perpetuity that would be dangerous if I took part in it. My unity will stand aside before your plurality; my weakness will be annihilated before your strength.

"Marry. My supreme consolation in still living will be to be the distant spectator of your happiness, of your success in posterity. I cherish you both enough to stifle the evil flame of jealousy that would illuminate in others, since the spectacle of life and the profundity of misery have inspired disdain for it in me. You will be beautiful, happy, strong and glorious for me. Your children will be mine; I shall cradle them like another father. I shall applaud the triumph of your couple, with the persuasion that my renunciation has contributed to a beautiful work of humanity. In brief, I shall have the supreme joy of having made your joy."

Raoul did not reply to the silence that followed the eruption of that tirade. He had listened to it with both sadness and happiness, passing through alternations of shadow and light, frightened by the enormous mass that was crushing a soul in order to enable two others to live. Such devotion, in spite of Claude having defined the motive for it with so much sincere simplicity, also seemed to him to be superhuman, dazzling his comprehension of a normal human being, disposed by good health to solutions of common egotism, surprised and a little frightened by an apostolate.

Yes, he was astonished. In truth, he had suspected that when his friend talked about a race, when, in their long conversations provoked by their studies in botany, he deduced propositions of beauty and goodness applicable to a species, by virtue of the fire of his language, that at those moments Claude was not a simple dilettante, one of those laboratory philosophers who comment on social problems, and envisage their solutions, but who, when a case arises that brings them into confrontation with reality, would not sacrifice an atom of their tranquility in order to put their admirable theories into action. But to go so superbly to the realization, to make the beat of his wings accord so cruelly with the principles of his reason, to immolate himself on the altar of Humanity! What an illuminated heart he had, then! And what grandeur there was in his simple speech, how many mirages of thought disappointed!

To judge by looking at him at that moment, one would surely be reassured regarding his cure, one would have affirmed the health that he denied, and the ruination of which dictated his conduct. The heroism of his conflict had brought the incarnadine back to his cheeks; he had straightened his ordinarily drooping shoulders; he was taking deep breaths amplified by emotion. His brown beard had warm glints and his sea-blue eyes, ablaze with exaltation, had lost the expression of sadness that was reflected in the lassitude of the features. And seeing him so vibrant, so transformed. Raoul had the conviction, momentarily, that he was advancing the hour of his condemnation and that his sacrifice was not legitimated by the future reality. And that thought dictated his response.

"No, Claude," he said, forcefully, "I can't admit that you make such a decision, so disastrous for your happiness. You're mistaken about your condition, you're deciding your future too rapidly; you'll regret it later when your health is completely recovered. And I can't profit from your discouragement; it would be a usurpation; it would be unworthy of my fraternity.

367

Yes, I love Henriette, but as an idol, as an inaccessible beauty, so far from me, so sacred by virtue of her engagement. She's a mystical child who will respond to you when you want her. She has never betrayed you voluntarily and a few pretty words of love will bring her back to you. So, I beg you, withdraw these follies, which your discouragement has counseled to you. I ought not to listen to them, I ought not to believe you. I don't want to accept them."

Claude, in his turn, esteemed his friend's fine moral organization and was distracted by that from the goal of the conversation, from numerous arguments that he could still have given, arguments drawn from his very suffering. The memory of the scene in the chapel in which Henriette had fallen into Raoul's arms under the effect of a veritable crisis of amour, was making his arteries beat in his temples at that moment. He could have recounted it; he preferred to admire his friend, as valiant as him in this battle of altruism. On that morning of clarity, however, their conversation took on a solemn amplitude, a decisive force that impelled Claude to go on to the end, to confess everything in a few words.

"There's no longer time," he replied. "What I've just said, I've already written to Henriette."

"You've done that!"

"Two words of reflection resolved me to do it. I've told her that I'm no longer her fiancé, I've told her that you love her."

"And what did she reply?" demanded Raoul, suffocating.

Footsteps climbed the stairs. Before anyone had knocked, Claude went to open the door and seized from the hands of the domestic the post that she was bringing. He leafed feverishly through the letters and newspapers, and finally discovered a missive sealed with white wax, the envelope of which bore an adored handwriting. He held it out to Raoul.

"Here's her response. Read it!"

Raoul had to make a violent effort to master his anguish, moderate the tremor that had taken possession of his hand, and insert a finger into the fissure of the envelope. His misted eyes had difficulty following the vacillating lines. When he had finished reading it he dropped the letter and sat down, very pale, his legs no longer having the strength to sustain him, suddenly crushed by an immense despair.

Then it was Claude who took possession of the response. He smiled; by virtue of a reversal, it was him who became the stronger now and who dominated the situation with an authority independent of the drama by which his heart was lightened. The letter was, in any case, rather brief and quickly scanned.

Henriette carefully neglected therein everything related to her love for Raoul and the young man's passion for her. She simply declared that Claude's conduct dictated hers and revived the intentions of her early youth. She would separate from the world, no longer having any reason to remain in it. She would return to God, whose servant she had always dreamed of being. In a fortnight, before the invalid's return to Paris, she would have entered the convent of Dominican nuns, and she bid her fiancé an eternal adieu.

"We'll leave this evening," cried Claude, as soon as he had read the final word, inscribed in the beautiful English handwriting that hides the soul of women beneath its uniformity, but which the emotion of the correspondent had rendered more nervous in its perfection this time.

And as Raoul, still downcast, did not reply to his decision with a cry of surprise, and remained sunk in his dolor, he went on with a false gaiety that hid tears: "Let's go, Christ! Get up! Your great ancestor emerged from his tomb the save his faithful. Won't you resuscitate to save Henriette?"

That evening they were at the railway station well before the time of the train. All day had been employed in hasty journeys, packing trunks, in a circumstantial displacement. Pauline the cook, suffocated by that abrupt departure, had lost her head. She confounded everything, and in order to rid themselves of her encumbering services, they had been obliged to send her to book places in the sleeping car and settle up with the suppliers. She was tearful, and pacing up and down on the platform.

"Oh, Tribunal de Carcassonne! Tribunal of the good God!"

At that moment, the young men perceived Madame Fortin. She was still nicely blonde, a little stouter, more expansive than ever, prettier than in the freshness of her renewal. They went up to her.

"You, Madame, and without Monsieur Fortin! What event can have separated you from him? Is he ill?"

No, Monsieur Fortin was marvelously well, as well as she was, and that was saying a lot. But he had had to absent himself for very serious affairs, to spend his afternoon in Nice, and she was expecting him by the same train that the young men were about to take in order to quit the land of the sun. She was shuffling her feet and talking avidly, as if to avoid other questions, but without being able to hide her nervousness.

Finally, she sighed noisily. The two large eyes of the puffing locomotive appeared around a bend in the track. She forgot to make her adieux; she ran toward a carriage door where a handkerchief was waving. That was Monsieur Fortin, who leapt out of the carriage before it had stopped and fell into his wife's arms. He had not recognized the travelers, and the latter heard him pronounce a sentence that they did not understand, but which had the gift of making Madame Fortin burst into tears in a surge of grateful tenderness.

That sentence was: "It's done, my poor dear; she's pregnant; you're going to be a mother!"

XXIV

When Julien Duverdon penetrated into the drawing room of Antonin Fargeaud's town house, where he and his wife were still resident, he found Rolande sitting in a low armchair, her eyes detached from the book that she was holding open on her knees. He understood immediately, from her expression, that she had a great subject of concern, and was anxious in consequence. Then he approached her on tiptoe.

"Bonjour, little wife!" he said, kissing her forehead.

The young woman was touched by that testimony, and welcomed it gracefully. She seized his large hand eagerly and pressed it with a charming manifestation of intimacy. The physiognomy of both had been transformed by recent events. Rolande had lost the air of anxious and sly nervousness that had previously given her angular profile, the vibrations of her ever-alert nostrils and the fluttering of her mobile eyes a kind of unhealthy harshness. Her face, slightly filled out, seemed to have blossomed, reposed and calm in her five-month maternity. As for Julien, his belated amorous triumph had clad him in a general contentment that was transparent in the fashion in which he now held his broad shoulders, and caressed with less timidity the long graying beard, elegantly disciplined by the hairdresser's tongs.

"Come and sit down here, next to me," she said, addressing him very softly as *tu*, revelatory of their complete liaison.

Then she added: "Have you retained the apartment in Passy?"

"I've given God's denier to the concierge."

"We'll do marvelously there."

"I'll always be content wherever you are, my darling."

They were installed. There was no more question of traveling now, nor of the encampments for a day that, immediately modified by Rolande's caprice, had incessantly disrupted their existence, making the husband a sort of quartermaster, always worried about their next move. They were about to have their own home, and await the arrival of their child there. And that was an indication of the complete revolution that had rendered Julien so perfectly happy, and enveloped Rolande in an amenity whose delights she felt more profoundly every day.

"Yes," Julien continued, "the house is very well inhabited. I've rented a stable at a good price and I've been to Tattersall's to look at horses."

"How good you are, my Julien!"

"No, I simply love you. I want you to be happy. Are you happy?"

As a cloud passed over her face he became alarmed again. He took hold again of the delicate hand that he had abandoned in order to play with her golden wedding ring.

"Is something still causing you chagrin?"

"Yes," confessed Rolande, in a low voice. "I didn't want to tell you. I feared that you'd suspect me of having returned again..."

She lowered her eyes, moved, not daring to explain further. But he had understood and protested immediately: "No, I trust you."

And as he insisted, putting into his pressure a little of his newly conquered authority, she said:

"Well, here it is; she's been writing to me. For a long time, she's been begging me to receive her. I didn't tell you about her letters for fear of tormenting you. I contented myself with burning them and leaving them unanswered. But this time, she's been more audacious, and she's fixed a rendezvous for today at four o'clock. She ought to be here already. I'm afraid of her visit. Not that I fear for my will—oh no! I scorn my past so much, I'm so impregnated by you, I have such concern for the little being that is stirring within me, that a return to my folly is no longer possible. No, all that's completely finished. But I know that she's violent, and I've sometimes glimpsed such strange gleam in her eyes that I wonder

372

whether a further conversation might lead her to some act of dementia..."

Since the first words of the confession Julien had not been obliged to ask about the identity of the unfortunate woman whom Rolande did not name; it could not be anyone but Clara; and that evocation, which he had thought banished forever, plunged him back into his former anxieties. He became thoughtful, and raised his fingers to the hairs scattered on his head. Rolande noticed that gesture, which was familiar to his torments. She leaned her delicate head toward him, which she imprinted with a design of a greater loyalty and a greater obedience.

"What is it necessary to do?" she asked

"It's necessary to receive her, of course. It's necessary to settle her account once and for all. And I'll take charge of it."

"No, not you!" she said, fearfully. "Let me do it. I'll send her away gently."

She got up with a start, for the valet de chambre announced Miss Clara Boswett. She had time, before the entrance of her audacious friend, to push her husband into a neighboring room, which had served Antonin Fargeaud as a work-room, and was now unused.

She had closed the door, with the consequence that Julien found himself in near-obscurity, the shutters of the room having been closed for a long time, scarcely permitting the passage of a thin beam of light, in which molecules of dust floated. He tried for a long time to perceive the sounds coming from the drawing room, but the movement in the street outside, the rumble of vehicles on the pavement and the customary racket of the great arteries, of a thousand discordant sounds, to which a Parisian's ear is accustomed, and the magnitude of which he only suspects when he needs to hear something else, all those various rumors kept him apart from the scene that was unfolding alongside, uncertain as to whether he ought to intervene or maintain his neutrality.

He thought at one moment, that he distinguished sobs followed by bursts of tragic voices, and the drawl of the accent particular to the foreigner. He had already found that the conversation was prolonged when a scream uttered by Rolande suddenly made up his mind. Rolande was in danger! Rolande was menaced!

He bounded toward the door and opened it. Immediately, he perceived his wife, maintaining with difficulty the wrists of Clara, who, mad with rage, with foam on her lips and intoxication in her eyes, had just leapt upon her in order to beat her or hurt her. Then, also seeing red, he threw himself upon the group. A surge of blood swelled the veins of his neck.

"Oh, the slut!"

He encircled her with his massive arms, squeezing like a vice, paralyzed her and possessed her mortally.

"Oh, the slut, the slut!"

For a long, frightful minute, he maintained her thus, enjoying sensing her bones creak. Not one word was pronounced, not one cry uttered. He crushed her in a horrible mutism. Nothing was heard but their panting breath, for Clara, already turning blue, scarcely felt the pain.

And in an abysmal silence, the Hercules was about to annihilate that enemy flesh definitively, to stifle in the mechanism of his arms the foreigner who had disorganized his household for so long, stolen his Rolande, corrupted his hearth with the infiltration of her vice, when the clock in the drawing room suddenly raised its crystalline voice, striking five blows, five clear warnings that recalled him to prudence to the notion of a futile murder.

At the same time, exterior life flooded in with all its normal intensity. It was like a current of cold reflection that suddenly chilled his hatred, made the danger of scandal shine, bought back the memory of Claude's return, of which the train, at that precise moment, ought to be pulling into the station. Thus the smallest causes avoid the greatest effects; thus events mingle with the actions of the soul and influence destiny.

Julien relaxed his vice, and perceived a gasp of deliverance; then, with a traction that was still powerful, he made the corseted corpulence of the androgyne pivot, spun her around and went to shove her against a table. Then he sought Rolande's gaze.

He discovered it confounded with admiration and grateful tenderness. It was not the first time that Julien had manifested his violent strength before her, nor that she had seen her usurper succumb with a ridiculous weakness at the moment when she wanted to play the male. Already, some time before, Rose's mother, the old countrywoman shaken by age, had reckoned with her with a disconcerting facility. False virility, false vigor, hair and complexion false, sensuality false: everything as therefore a lie in that unhinged individual! Nothing true, nothing positive, had ever vibrated within her. And Rolande wondered how she had ever been able to allow herself to be duped by such a mediocre deception. She had, therefore, never seen clearly, or the vice had troubled her with a very peculiar optical illusion.

In order to avoid so much torture for Julien, so much shame for herself, why had she not seen her in the beginning as she saw her now, pitiful and derisory, her mahogany curls disorganized, her make-up dissolved, her eyelids smeared by the displacement of the kohl, her cheeks and chin swollen with rage, dispossessed even of the animation of the complexion that revolt and rage give the ugliest?

She looked at her, and was filled with a definitive disgust, by contrast with the prestige with which she now aureoled the stature of the man who had become her master, and, by contrast, especially with the being who filled her loins, and whose birth was about to be a dawn of candor The daughter of the first wife of Antonin Fargeaud, she was necessarily subject even so to her atavism of nervous weakness; it was necessary that she felt dominated. Fortune had determined that it would not be by nature.

The three actors in the scene therefore remained immobile in the expectation of a word that, coming from another, would decide their attitude.

Clara Boswett was the first to depart from that fixed interrogation, as impressive as the outburst of a little while before. After having got up, she pivoted on her heels and headed with a stiff gait toward the exit without looking back, without even taking the trouble to readjust hr garments crumpled by the struggle. She seemed hallucinated, by virtue of the automatic fashion in which she moved her legs. With a mechanical gesture she opened the drawing room door, forgetting her handbag, placed on a chair, and her umbrella, leaning on another. The same unreal ambulation enabled her to traverse the vestibule, descend he steps of the perron and head for the coaching entrance, before which her carriage was stationed.

Having reached the street she walked, neglecting to respond to the interrogation of the footman who seeing her flee, advanced to take her orders and believed he understood that it was necessary to wait. She marched straight ahead, at hazard. The fibers of her thought were broken. The only thing that hindered her was a stifling sensation in the throat, which she wanted instinctively to vanquish with an abundance of air. Her brain was englobed by a heavy and obsessive helmet that she tried in vain to throw backwards by shaking her head in a tic.

She wandered at random There was a delightful spring warmth. A dust of sunlight powdered the summits of the roofs, and collided in gilded reflections with the widows of the upper stories. That afternoon fête had attracted an entire society outdoors, and idlers were treading the ground slowly while others beat it hastily in the last fever of affairs.

She went along a boulevard where the trees were already in bud, sowing white and green dots over the framework of denuded branches. She melted into the crowds disgorged from the Metro, where she was noticed. Soon she reached a large open space swarming with carriages and trams, bordered by pavements swarming with pedestrians. That was the Place Clichy, which she did not suspect. She turned right into the Rue de Douai and again marched straight ahead. The movement slowed down there, but audacious couples passed by, tall women who looked at her made-up orbits filled with nothing and turned away, instinctively frightened by observing the jerkiness of her gait and sensing her nascent madness approaching them. However, she distinguished a few young women who were staring at her more brazenly. They reminded her of the distant image of Rolande; they even provoked an exquisite memory, a savor of burning kisses tempered by the moist freshness of her pretty teeth. And that evocation, reanimating the evil frisson, was all that persisted of her wandering promenade, all that determined its continuation.

She walked on, following streets and crossing roads, risking being run over twenty times; she traversed a bridge under which the waters of the river, in undulating breakers, allowed themselves to be caressed at length by the crimson sun, as many kisses of the elements that made her shiver again, She kept walking; she walked in order to recover, among the passing women, he fresh evocation of Rolande's mouth, the smile of her jewel-case striped with nacre. Her morbid imagination descended lower, cased her reminiscence to gravitate around the naked breasts, around erect nipples with pink areolas.

And now, all those who came to encounter her were Rolande. The seamstresses emerging from work that she went past were Rolande, and the honest bourgeoises returning to the hearth, and the courtesans hurrying to their rendezvous, and the pauperesses begging. Her androgynous folly undressed them; she addressed smiles to them and murmured incomprehensible words of lust, chewing the kiss. The kiss, the sterile kiss; she ran to it, she evoked it; she implored it; she swooned from it; she brushed it in the dresses of the passers-by, advancing her hips; she fell upon skirts, which parted, seized by terror.

Behind her she amassed a mocking crowd, ever increasing, which she did not see, and whose gibes she did not hear. Someone shouted that she was drunk, for she was, in fact, tottering, and the ferocious joy of the people expanded in lewd jokes.

377

Suddenly, after covering a long distance, a vision dilated her eyes and she extended her arms forwards. She had arrived at a crossroads, and on a marble plinth, Etienne Dolet stood.[8] Toward his torture, a seated semi-naked woman of bronze was raising her consoling arms. It was Rolande! With a howl, she bounded on to the pedestal, bestrode the body, enlaced it, quivering, palpated the rigid breasts, and stuck her ardent mouth to the icy mouth; her eyes revulsed in a spasm. The people laughed.

And that was precisely the moment when, thanks to a delay to the train, the vehicle carrying Claude and Raoul from the station emerged into the Place Maubert. A barrage along the quays had necessitated that detour via the Boulevard Saint-Germain. The encumbrance made the carriage stop, and Claude, leaning his head out of the window, had the unexpected spectacle of the madwoman around whom the mass of louts was laughing and vociferating. Seized by pity, he was about to get down in order to seek information, and bring help if it were required, when he suddenly recognized the crazed faced of the American, whom two guardians had just seized, and who was struggling, uttering imprecations.

"Look! Miss Boswett!, Miss Clara Boswett!" he said to Raoul, who was also striving to see.

The madwoman's movements had drawn the policeman toward the carriage, and one of them, having heard the traveler's remark, approached, his hand on his kepi, with courtesy imposed on him by the luxury of the carriage, the shiny harness, and the coachman sitting stiffly in his seat.

---

[8] Etienne Dolet (1509-1546) was a French reformist scholar who attracted the ire of the Inquisition and the Faculty of the Sorbonne, whose combined efforts contrived his execution for heresy in the Place Maubert and the burning of his books. A bronze statue of him was erected in the Place Maubert in 1889, with the subsidiary statue of a woman to which the text refers, but it was melted down during the German occupation during the Second World War.

"Monsieur knows this woman?"

Claude was about to agree that he did, in fact, know her, and that she was a friend of the family; but the very confession he was about to make evoked the image of Rolande, of whose conversion Julien had informed him. He saw her again, as in the bad days of her liaison, her face agitated, nervous, bruised by the devouring intimacy of the foreigner. He heard her authoritarian and cutting voice again, giving orders to her Cassandra, disposing of him like a lackey, reducing that benevolent husband to a fearful and painful servitude, whose Herculean shoulders buckled under the insult and whose taurean neck folded back in his timidity, not daring to revolt and darken. It was that haggard possessed woman now maintained by the grip of the policemen who, on the terrain of the young woman's nervous atavism, had sown her element of stigma and stupor, disorganizing the household. He clothed her with all her sins, forgetting the initial vivacity of the husband that Julien had confessed to him, and which might equally have incriminated him.

In addition, the old leaven of intuitive virtue and honesty that had been slumbering within him since childhood and which the spectacle of recent events, in bringing him face to face with shameful reality, had reawakened; that instinctive moral propriety, hostile to sensual aberrations that utilized creative pleasure in order to appropriate it to a voluptuous egotism and stole away before the heavy and sumptuous obligations of life—a morbidity disastrous for the race, debasing it and extinguishing it—all boiled up in him at that moment, setting aside the magnificent pity of which he had given proof on more than one circumstance. And then, what would be the utility of his confession that he knew Clara? If she was mad, she would be interned without him getting involved, and if she was drunk she could sober up at the police station without his intervention. He looked at the policeman, who was waiting for his response.

"No," he said, "I don't know that woman." Then, addressing the coachman: "Go! Quickly, to the house!"

And as, now that he was ensconced again in the cushions of the coupé, Raoul, whose healthy candor had always wanted to ignore the role of the foreigner in the Duverdon household, was astonished by that lack of commiseration, he said, impatiently: "What do you want me to do? She's the concern of physicians. She isn't interesting. She'll be locked up tomorrow. We have better things to do than take her to the padded cell."

Then he fell silent. In the depths of his mind, however, the great problem of creation was reawakened again, at that moment when each rotation of the wheels of the carriage was like the circuit of the clock bringing him to the solution that would be definitive for his amour. Clara's mental ruination, her collapse into the straitjacket, was one of those catastrophes common to individuals who violate the holy laws of nature. The foreigner was concluding with one of the consequences in which physical or moral dramas always end, In this instance the nervous system, exhausted by false solicitations, had ended up lacking fluid, and leading from deviation to a cell Elsewhere, there would be another termination, no less deadly, of tears, dolor or death.

And more than ever, the recent lesson of events fortified Claude in his dolorous intention to unite the only two beings truly dear to him, those whom nature had favored with its elite gifts, and to enable them to perpetuate themselves in a radiant tribe. But would he have the courage to go on to the end, to massacre his ideal, to despoil himself of his dream, the divine hope of which had enthused him, in order to offer her to another? How difficult the terminus seemed to be to confront, how ready his will was to buckle!

At that moment, when he was drawing nearer to Henriette, when the flight of the carriage past the shops made him remember having gone into them with her in order to inspire her in the choice of purchases, his heart capsized. Was not the meeting with the young woman about to convert the weight rising in his throat to a sob? Out there in Cannes, distance had rendered his altruism less painful, less immediate.

He had written almost easily. But to speak, to restate his generous folly to his adored, to hear her responses, to find his arguments, to dominate his disturbance and convince her...! He would have liked to be able to order the vehicle to turn round, to go back to the station that it had just quit, and he started to tremble as he addressed Raoul, whose arm he had just touched.

"Raoul," he said, "We're getting close. It's time for me to give you the final instructions. You're going to quit me here. It's necessary that I act alone and that Henriette is unaware of your presence in Paris. I'm asking you to obey me blindly. Go home, and wait for a word from me in order to run to my father's house. If misfortune dictates that Henriette persists in her intention to disappear from the world, you'll never see her again; I'll come and find you, and we'll leave together. Far away, we'll mourn the dead woman. If, on the contrary, she listens to me, and understands..."

But it was impossible for him to continue. The hoarseness of his voice in the last phase finally betrayed his determination to be courageous and not to allow his disturbance to be perceptible. He opened the door to let his friend out, who was gripped by a emotion no less intense.

"Go! Go away, my dear Raoul."

He passed him his overcoat and some small items of luggage, then threw him an "*Au revoir* my dear friend, *à bientôt!*" accompanied by a cordial gesture.

As soon as Raoul had disappeared from his sight, Claude felt himself seized once again by his doubt. A tumult of ideas assailed him, and through their grip he tried to work out the psychological situation, to analyze Henriette's heart. He wondered whether the young woman's decision to take the veil resulted from a profound conviction, one of those convictions of faith that nothing can resist, or whether that decision, on the contrary, had been commanded by her fiancé's last letter, pushing her to respond to an act of renunciation by an act of abdication no less chivalrous.

Everything cried out that the latter supposition was the only plausible one. The kind of mystical enthusiasm to which the charming girl had been subject at the convent, the necessity of the heart, in a child deprived of her parents, to report the abundance of her affective sentiments to another object, and the seduction of the practices of religious ceremonial, had acted on her mind at a early age, and had developed later into the reckless love of the divine man.

Was she not, in her purity, also a kind of psychic deviant, as Rolande had been another, for her senses? Could she too not be cured, like her cousin, by means of a simple contact with nature? Yes, probably, since a simple rapprochement with the world, a first frisson of adolescence, had already been sufficient to disrupt her devotion, for her to confound Christ with the person who, in reality, resembled him so much. Evil—or rather, what she believed, in her innocence, to be evil—had then appeared under the form of Raoul, and life had resumed its rights sufficiently for her to let herself slide insensibly toward him, for her to identify in the same adoration the two images, the divine and the terrestrial, for her finally to feel the necessity to efface herself in the shadow of a cloister. From all those symptoms of a muted evolution, Claude had suffered too much not to have conceived them clearly.

At the same time as those difficulties and uncertainties of the present moment, Claude saw others as disquieting surging forth. Alongside the sweet face of Henriette, that of her guardian, Antonin Fargeaud appeared. With what dolorous astonishment would these complications and their result, whatever it might be, darken his declining old age? He was still deluded; he had moderated his fanatical hatred of human beings momentarily in the last hope of seeing Claude united with his ward, of seeing his son create a family to replace the one that had failed. At that new hearth, emerged nevertheless from his essence, due to his source via the intermediary of his dearest child, he would have been able to warm his weary limbs, he could have drunk the cordial that consoles for extinction, which puts death to sleep in the hope of future lineages.

Claude was, therefore, about to deal a death-blow to that poor credulity, to that illusion, which still made an old heart palpitate. To the scorn of all the sap there was in that old trunk, he was about to cut into the base, to bring about the collapse.

Simple gratitude counseled him against that fatal stroke. But immediately, logic—a logic that had a form other than pity—ordered him not to succumb to the weakness of sentimentality. Although Antonin Fargeaud had a right to filial respect, he must nevertheless support the consequences of his original irreflection, of the ruins that he had accumulated in creating inconsiderately, in destining a being to necessities like those that Claude was analyzing. But above all, Antonin Fargeaud, an old man near the tomb, did not have the right to oppose himself to a future of life that Raoul and Henriette might realize, even if he had to suffer from it.

In any case, the die was already cast, there was no longer time to turn back; the letter from Cannes now opposed that the young woman could become the fiancée of the invalid again, in the anticipation of a distant cure. The last act of the tragedy was about to be played. Provided that Claude arrived in time, provided that the young woman had not yet confided anything to the old man!

As soon as he arrived he had the positive sensation that nothing was lost. The carriage had scarcely gone under the porch when he perceived Antonin Fargeaud holding out his arms to him. His long white beard, his eyes almost extinct to light, his tremulous gestures—everything in his person, in sum—seemed radiant. Henriette was standing next to him, exceedingly pale, her legs buckling. Behind them, Monsieur and Madame Duverdon had wanted to welcome him with a gripping evidence of affection; they appeared arm-in-arm, united and smiling. The simian face of Hector, who had had to be put back into his wheelchair following recent accidents, formed the sole shadow on that picture of familial beauty.

"My son! My Claude!"

The poor father stammered his joy. He had grabbed the new arrival by the shudders, and caressed his face with his long fleshless fingers, in order to follow the contours that his sight no longer permitted him to distinguish.

"You've let your beard grow! You've done well; it's more virile. Oh, my son; you've come back, and cured—aren't you?—entirely cured; I sense it; I divine it! What good you're doing me, my Claude!"

The child responded to that effusion, but all of his acute attention was concentrated on Henriette. He had taken her hand, but he dared not squeeze it, because he sensed it distant from his own, even though he was holding it. He saw her lower her eyes with a sad confusion, unable to support the tender interrogation he addressed to her. Alas, how he had to admire her still, how he felt reborn, in that simple first rediscovery, the indelible surge of his amour!

Although she had not grown thinner, the new state of her heart having enabled her flesh to blossom in a matter of months, her red eyelids confessed her tears and her humble attitude already revealed, like a sacerdocy, the veil under which she wanted to take refuge, and it was another woman, entirely, that he had before him. And yet, he did not find her any less troubling in her mournful grace. She still had the piquant charm of the dimples in her cheeks and chin. Her dark velvet eyes, one so tremulous with sparkling joy when she sensed life, now had something grave and plaintive about them, like a dolorous mirage of her contrite soul.

Yes, perhaps he loved her more in her metamorphosis, in her harmonious fashion of incarnating sadness and solitude.

But she had just taken her hand away, gently, as if it would have been a sin to abandon it any longer. She sat down at table with the others, and in the middle of the conversation that animated the meal—for everyone was asking Claude questions to which he strove to respond in a detached manner—she conserved her distant, remote, veiled attitude, closed to all terrestrial pleasure, even to the contentment of welcoming the invalid. She ate very little.

However, at one moment she returned to earth. Antonin Fargeaud had just raised his voice and addressed his son.

"But what about Raoul? Is your savior not with you?"

"Raoul quit me at the station. He had to go home because he's suffering," Claude replied, taking note of Henriette's shudder and the glimmer of anxiety that her gaze had been unable to dominate.

XXV

Claude had had no repose all night. His amour, having become more imperious since he had seen Henriette again, had held him in a fever of reflections, tossed between two contrary solutions. When his mind, vanquished by the fatigue of the voyage and mental shocks, allowed itself to be entangled in a semblance of sleep, a dream immediately took possession of him. The same obsession gripped him again at each lapse of somnolence, and that obsession symbolized the present state of events.

He found himself, clad in a long black cloak trimmed with silver, in the choir of a church flamboyant with light. His marriage was being celebrated. Incense was rising toward the vault, and delightful hymns coming from invisible spaces resonated all the way to the slightest fibers of his soul. Before him, a priest was officiating with gestures of hieratic beauty. He could only see his back, his stole radiant with gold, possessing in the center a living dove, the gracious movements of whose neck and whose circular gaze he perceived distinctly. Behind him, there were guests, friends and relatives, all dressed in an ancient style, rutilant with crimson. And beside the pulpit toward which he inclined his head, a tall young brunette woman clad, beneath the vapor of the nuptial veil, in a long white dress with a train and a crown of orange-blossom, was praying and sighing.

He knew that the young woman was Henriette, but he could only divine her behind the opacity of thicker tulle at the level of the face.

He passed long moments of immaterial rapture thus, seeing the rite unfold, listening to the angelic songs, respiring the exquisite aroma of the incense, hoping for the nuptial benediction. The moment finally arrived. The officiant turned toward them. He had the head of Christ, the head of Raoul. He extended his arms, he summoned them, he pronounced incomprehensible words, but of which Claude grasped the meaning nevertheless, which were the sacramental terms of the union. Henriette advanced toward the priest, her long form undulating under the veil. He got ready to follow her, but the black cloak trimmed with silver that he was wearing over his shoulders, too heavy to be displaced, immobilized him, riveting him to his seat.

In that moment of fear, he sensed that he was about to lose his fiancée; he implored her, he begged her with a desperate eloquence, while she marched, splendidly resigned, toward the Christ-priest. What he suffered then surpassed the most frightful tortures, for as soon as Henriette had crossed the three steps that separated her from the altar, the altar was suddenly converted into a dark door, banded with iron: the door to a cloister, which she entered, resplendent in her white purity.

Claude could even see, through that open door, stone arches of a ogival architecture, designed under a radiant sky, and a procession of white nuns singing a canticle of actions of grace. Then the thick partition closed upon the recluse again heavily, with the sound of a coffin falling into a grave. Then, of the church, the priest, the audience, the flames and the canticles, nothing any longer remained, except for the dove of the stole, the living dove with the circular gaze, whose flight soared for moment longer over an abysmal immensity that Claude's dolor did not take long to fill, on its own.

That nightmare was reproduced, with the same faithful rigor, every time lassitude defeated him. The frightful denouement woke him up with a start, with the intensity of dolor that painful dreams leave behind. As soon as he was awake, a no less anguishing struggle recommenced in his consciousness, and although reflective, the sentiments of it were no less sharp.

He relived the phases of his amour for Henriette. He commenced with the first astonishments of his soul before the child's pure eyes, those eyes with dilated pupils, full of tender interrogation. Already, a pleasant sympathy caused them to collaborate in their games. He took her in his cart, pulled by a

387

little pony with a shiny coat; he took her out, alone with her, like a man going out with his wife. He protected her, he would have liked to defend her, sovereignly happy to sense that charming weakness entrusted to his strength. He was gallant too; he heaped her with treats and flowers, content to be paid by a smile that hollowed out the three adorable dimples.

Later, the infantile idyll was transformed into a real amour, which the young woman's mysticism did not reject. They were engaged, and he envisaged the tranquil splendor of the hearth and the family. Then...then, one day, everything had crumbled. Fatality had one of those abominable reversals. Nature duped him simultaneously in his body and his heart. For the unconscious evolution of Raoul and Henriette arrived, the magnetic attraction to which they were both subject, unknowingly at first, and then striving to repel it when they had understood its gravity. Finally, there were the words of renunciation that he had spoken to Raoul, and the letter that he had written to his fiancée, his entire heart thrown into a few words and a few lines.

And in the obscurity of the room in which he was lying, he heard sobs, which were his own; he saw the suppleness of a wedding-dress undulating, which was the one he had just seen passing through his slumber. Was he asleep or was he awake? The two states, reality and dream, were confounded. He had to hide his head under the pillow in order not to perceive anything any longer.

Later, toward dawn, his ideas were refreshed. As early morning winds blow over the tumult of the waters and sweep away the mists from the horizon, he estimated more positively and more bitterly the determinations of his heart. He imagined himself having resumed his rights over the young woman, having reconquered her, as the same time as a marvelous serum rendered him health. Could he, with deliberate words, based on a simple pessimistic conception of life, on the affirmation of a Cannes physician whose opinion was perhaps subject to caution, abandon to another such a prey of happiness? Were there not numerous examples of cured victims of tuberculosis engendering progeniture whom wellbeing and hygiene saved from morbid heredity? The world was pullulating with them, as well as young women married in spite of their sentiments who subsequently became the most loving and most faithful of wives.

No, nothing was absolute. His rights over Henriette had not been abolished by a simple letter of explanation, by the resolution that letter had made the young woman take to deny the world. If he simply withdrew that letter, explaining it as a caprice of his melancholy, their reciprocal relationship would resume as it had been before the voyage to Cannes, and Henriette would renounce her intentions of celibacy. Then there would be a radiation of incomparable felicity.

Immediately, however, his conscience rose up against the cowardice of those ambitions. It restated to him the poignant certainty of the poor state of his health. The diagnosis had been confirmed by two scientists worthy of faith: Doctor Bouret and the physician in Cannes. The evidence was further affirmed by the hereditary transmission, by the evil fire that, having condemned the mother, was consuming the son at a distance of a quarter of a century. The efficacy of a serum had already been proclaimed so many times, and belied so many times by the reality, that it still remained an improbability. And then, in curing him, would that serum have cured his heredity? What frightful question mark would be posed over his kisses, still staining them with a suspicion of murder? Refrain from the creative communion, then, soil that innocence with a debasing fraud? No, his amour was too pure, its object too candid, for him even to dare to think about it.

And then, there was Raoul: Raoul, about whom he thought now; Raoul, whose virtuous simplicity believed in his honesty; Raoul, to whom he had permitted a sentiment in embryo, and who ought to harvest the crop, under pain of another disaster comparable to his own.

Thus, everything overwhelmed him; everything impelled him toward the denouement that he had prepared, toward the supreme holocaust. And the resolution definitively acquired, after so many oscillations, he sensed as a warmth of the soul. He experienced a consolation in thinking that the arbitrariness of destiny had marked him for sacrifice, and that he would carry away, in his torture or in his tomb, the beneficent thought of having been the faithful servant of his philosophical convictions, of having realized, by means of a sublime personal effacement, a work of life that he could not accomplish himself.

So, this very day, he would talk to Henriette, he would demonstrate to her, with the persuasive tone of a self-sacrificing friend, what a sacrilege toward creation she was about to commit by abolishing herself in sterility, what a sin toward beauty and toward her own happiness she was preparing to accomplish in rejecting Raoul's amour. That very day he would take those two hands so desirous of being united and seal them definitively, utilizing as cement his broken heart, kneaded in tears.

When he got up after his abysmal night he was no longer recognizable. The benefit of five months of treatment had been resorbed in the twelve hours of the return to the parental hearth. The blue eyes that Antonin Fargeaud compared so willingly to the azure of Mediterranean waves had resumed their disquieting gleam of fever. His cheeks, filled out by a rapid increase in weight, rendered olive-tinted by a tan due to the dryness of the southern air, were swollen by insomnia behind the abundance of the brown beard, shiny and neglected. He was cold, shivering as much from the new climate as the difficulty he was about to have in following his destiny. He forgot the customary care of his coquetry, which he had never neglected before, even in the worst moments of his malady.

Then, clad in a discreet costume, in accord with his moral disturbance, he quit his room and went to a small drawing room on the ground floor, from which he could keep watch on the staircase. He had decided to wait there for Henriette and to obtain an explanation from her.

He did not have to wait for long. She soon appeared, followed by a chambermaid. She must be going to mass, for she was carrying a large prayer book. The gilt of the book, which she was holding under her arm, was the only gleam in her outfit, very simple, a costume tailored in dark blue with black trimmings. Her gloves were also black, and she was not wearing any jewelry. Beneath her modest accoutrement, however, beneath her vestment of shady mysticism, how much grace and radiance there still was! The skirt, tight around her hips in accordance with the caprice of current fashion, the bolero, which designed the increased firmness of her bosom, the gracious neck that extended, disengaged from the raised hair, toward the elegant plumes of her hat, and especially, the admirable seduction of her mat complexion, her brown eyes filled with velvet gleam, all declared that her former beauty was ready to triumph again soon under the spur of a little happiness. On seeing Claude stand up, who had taken a few steps toward her passage, she could not retain an undulation of surprise and recoil.

"I have something to say to you, Henriette..."

With a sign she ordered her chambermaid to wait for her, and she followed her fiancé into the drawing room, the door of which he closed. There she sat down, holding her book against her breast with a gesture that might have seemed of supreme reserve, with an intention of defending from the sight of her interlocutor the charms of which the clinging fabric permitted the divination, but which was in reality purely emotive, destined to constrain the violent beating of her heart. In any case, Claude was too much the slave of his own preoccupations to perceive the movement and to seek its significance. He commenced, in a voice broken by emotion with a statement that he had ruminated as an entry into the matter:

"Henriette, you're the only one to have been mute when everyone was congratulating me on my return; you're the only one to have understood its precipitation...is that true?"

"Yes, it's true," she replied, without raising her eyes.

"You reprove, then, the step that determined me to return sooner than I thought?"

"I can't approve, Claude. My letter replied to you suffi-ciently. There's no point in repeating that explanation..."

"What are you thinking, in replying to me thus? Is it to you or to me? Which of us will suffer most from what we're about to decide?

"We have nothing more to decide, Claude—no, nothing. And we're both suffering as much."

Each of her phrases was emitted with a view to extin-guishing the conversation, while Claude strove in vain to bring it back to the terrain he desired. Before that ill will, clearly designed at the outset, the young man understood that the skirmish might last longer still if he did not arrive immediately at the great effect, of throwing in the name of Raoul, which had not yet been pronounced.

"And Raoul," he said, "do you believe that he will be joyful?"

He saw her start. She must have expected that there would be question of him, and yet the redness of her cheeks, soon excessively paled by a contrary reflex, revealed the tur-moil that the evocation produced in her. And the fiancé under-stood more intensely, at that moment, how much empire the image of the absentee still had over the twenty-year-old heart that a deceptive faith was trying in vain to distract.

"Don't talk to me about Raoul," she said, finally domi-nating her disturbance. "I don't know what you've imag-ined..."

"I haven't imagined anything, my poor child! I've seen and I've understood. My solicitude for you rendered me per-spicacious, and perhaps I would have been blinder if I had been more smitten."

Thus, at the outset, benevolently, he denied his passion with an apparent ease by which any other woman would prob-ably have been offended but which did not succeed in striking with its evidence a mind momentarily troubled and captivated by the gravity of the discussion. And in order to render his artifice even more convincing, he went on:

"Come on, Henriette, remember and persuade yourself. I cannot reproach you for anything, for a soul as candid as yours allows itself to be transformed involuntarily Do you remember to whom your gaze went when the three of us were together? Toward him, always toward him. Was he not the worthier to fix it, in any case? Do you remember how frequently you loved to take him for a confidant? Do you remember your joy in finding yourself next to him during our excursions to the country, in noticing his laborious and grave head poring over a book when both of you were watching over me during my illness? It was me for whom you were caring, and with what tenderness—I shall never be sufficiently grateful—but it was at him that you smiled when I got better. Do you remember the sort of ecstasy that I surprised, one evening, in the chapel...yes, I was there; you didn't suspect it! You implored Christ, and it was Raoul who responded in your thought...and it was him who received you in his arms when you fell, overwhelmed by amour and dolor! Thus, you see, of all these arguments of your poor little soul, I have followed the phases. Are they not invincible proofs? Tell me that I'm mistaken, you who do not know how to lie, you whose soul is as honest as the sky is pure!"

"That's the past...the past is dead."

She had lowered her head again in confessing, for her statement was a confession without restriction. In the momentum of his pleading, Claude no longer felt the bite of it. He spoke on behalf of the other with the fire of certain advocates who seem to be sustaining their own cause.

"No," he said, "it isn't the past, since the flame that is burning within you, and of which you were doubtless unaware, until my letter of a few days ago caused it to burst forth anew, to the point of dictating that response in conformity with your desire not to betray the promise you had made to me. No, that past isn't dead, since my presence is reanimating it! Come on, Henriette, think, reflect on the enormity of the decision that is about to break two people, Raoul and you! No, haven't I told you that I couldn't remain your fiancé, and be-

393

come your husband, because the phthisis is still undermining me? Haven't I said that the substitution of Raoul for me would be accomplished as a normal act, since, dispossessed of the gifts of health and life that every man owes his wife, I perceived clearly the first error of my imagination, and that I no longer loved you, in sum, other than as a brother loves his sister..."

That last argument, as false as the others, but as apparently plausible in its generous impetus, left her enervated, compressing the arms of her armchair. In any case, her ideas were seething with her, and she had difficulty following her interlocutor's thesis; she listened to his speech as one hears a deafening torrent pass. Then, in her disarray, she too had recourse to her supreme resource: to the faith whose unquiet leaps in her soul she had so often attempted to appease. She saw again, with a clarity of impression that struck her optic sense more than her reason, the kaleidoscope of religious rites, so dear to the aspirations of her early childhood, and the lighted candles, the altar ornamented with gold, and the undulating silky costumes of saints of both sexes, and the blue robe of the Virgin, holding a pink infant Jesus in her arms.

Before that spectacle, kneeling in adoration, there were a thousand white and black nuns, a thousand praying women abstracted from the world, imploring the Lord for the remission of the sins of others. She found herself among them, mingled with their ecstasy, guaranteed by the same fluid of purity, bathed in the same bliss of isolation. And that evocation, magnificent in its serenity, deflected her ideas, provoked the argument that, she believed, would put an end to their conversation.

"I've promised God to go toward him if I didn't go toward you, Claude. You've just repeated to me that you can't marry me, that you don't love me anymore. If you hadn't confided the depths of your thought to me, if I sensed that you still wanted me as a wife, I'd follow you, I'd take your arms again. But we've pronounced one of those oaths that death alone can break. I can't marry Raoul...and in consequence, I'm obeying my vocation."

"Your vocation!" he said, raising his voice. "You're pretexting your vocation? Henriette! Does it exist, your vocation? Do you even know what it is? You're luring yourself with a word! Isn't your vocation to love, to have children, to found a family? Even your God, whom you're invoking..."

He had a second of hesitation before continuing. He regretted the pronoun with which he had preceded the word God. Saying "your God" was to express that he did not believe it, was to leave faith to Henriette alone and to deny it. And he feared that his incredulity might accentuate their difference at the critical moment when he ought to show himself most worthy of the young woman's confidence.

In truth, whenever he had thought about the Supreme Being, it was as a great myth, as a troubling mystery of which he did not feel any desire to fathom the nature or the existence, for fear of finding contradictions there. The positivism of his studies invariably brought him back to the materiality of things, and the new conquests of science, the progressive tread of human genius over the terrain of unknown forces, conceiving, explaining and reproducing experimentally phenomena once accepted as manifestations of divine will, plunged him into a great uncertainty when he reflected on the origins of the world.

In addition, he rejected necessarily on to the creator the incoherences of creation, and he could not admit a God who engendered anything but perfection, who allowed evil and dolor to increase, even to test the conscience of his creatures and recompense or punish them in an eternal survival. Goodness was so comfortable for some, sin so imposed on others!

Thus, his religious philosophy was limited to an immense question mark. He guided himself honestly by virtue of a latent generous atavism, by virtue of a fortunate disposition of his cerebral substance, a need for pity that was an even purer result of his studies, all of observation. He had never ventured on to that dubious terrain with Henriette. He respected

395

her principles, he had even favored her practices, but he had never been able to share them. This time, however, in his desire to succeed in his negotiation, he regretted having delimited the young woman's belief and his own by an improvident word. He therefore went on:

"Yes, God, whom you have just invoked, if you consult him..."

"I have consulted him, Claude. One interrogates the good God by means of prayer; he responds by means of grace."

"No! The faith that impels you toward reclusion results from a suggestion engendered by events. Have you not confessed to me, a moment ago, that if I still loved you, you would renounce the convent? Veritably summoned by God, you would not have been able to respond thus. You would have sacrificed everything to an illumination, even the anterior promise that linked you to me."

That reasoning confounded her. She could not find another to refute it; she sensed herself losing ground before such a concise argument. However, further words spoken by her fiancé rendered her the hope of not being definitively beaten in the struggle in which their former custom of sincerity caused her to estimate that, logically, she ought to reply by means of logic.

"Believe me, Henriette," Claude went on, "one serves God as magnificently in having children, in devoting oneself to their flight, as in taking refuge in the neutrality of a contemplative celibacy. I often ask myself on which side there is more real devotion. God made life in order that his creatures might live! He gave them pleasure in order that instincts could function; he gave them instinct in order that his creatures might create."

"God also made life in order that certain of them, the most favored, might have the abnegation of refusing terrestrial joys!"

He admired the triumphant way in which she had launched her response. Her upper body straightened, her bosom was thrust forward; her complexion became once again, under the ardor of the conversation, the manifestation of a brilliant nature; all of that cried out that she was not one of those whose soul ought to flee the body. He sensed how much her new appearance separated her from him now, she whom he had once judged closer in her poverty, floating, like him, in unreal regions. And that observation dictated Claude's eloquence.

"Refusing terrestrial joys, my dear Henriette, could you ever do it? Nature has provided you with senses, organs and instincts like everyone else, and their functioning, in spite of you and always, is accompanied by joys to which it will be impossible for you not to submit. You eat in recreating yourself because you are hungry; you respire gladly, because your lungs summon air; you marvel at the verdure of the trees because your eyes are obliged to see. You thus obtain a thousand pleasures from your senses that are nothing but terrestrial joys. Oh, I've penetrated your soul too deeply not to have appreciated it! I've understood the scant complication of your nature too well not to divine its positive satisfactions! Even when you wanted to take refuge in abstract ideas, even when you were praying, your head hypnotized by the altar, I divined that it was your flesh that was seduced and not your thought! Interrogate yourself, and you'll see that I'm expressing the truth.

"Know, then, that your senses will always revolt against the idea that is striving to murder them, and one day, you'll regret the decision you want to make, because it will not have had the result of the immolation you desire. And when, as well as all these realities of corporeal life that you're destined to savor in spite of yourself, I've shown you another more imperious still, because it summarizes our reason for being down here; when I say to you: we're put in the world in order to bring into the world in our turn; we exist in order to give existence, and that is an obligation so superior that, in order not to allow us to fail in it, God created amour and fecundity, and those who want to avoid them are cowards or insensate...when I display for you that superb law of eternity, Henriette, does your need for truth not shudder, and do you

397

not reject far away the paltry mirages by which you want to deceive your heart?"

In the young woman's wide-open eyes, with pupils dilated, there was such an anxious interrogation that he feared having exceeded the measure and wounded her sovereignly new candor with the friction of materiality. However, he rediscovered in her the air of grave attention that she had always manifested when, from the youngest age, she listened while he protected her, while he fashioned his first ideas, as one does with a creature of election and charm who is going to share one's intellectual life later. Yes, he rediscovered the same clarity of ingenuity, the same confessions of mute seduction for which he had loved her right away, which had impelled the first palpitations of his heart, because of her and for her. And that was an evocation of freshness and tenderness such that he sensed again how much he adored her, how much the sacrifice of his happiness for another surpassed the limits of terrestrial devotion.

He drew nearer to her, desperate but nevertheless decided; he took her by the hand, he allowed other words to flee, and in a voice quivering with the agony of his heart, speaking in favor of Raoul, it was still his own passion that he expressed.

"Henriette, my Henriette, understand me: the participation in amour that I can no longer offer you, another can offer you; the work of life of which I am incapable, another can perfect. That man is the man who animates your divine beauty and the splendor of your thought. On the day when he divined what light might come from a woman, on the day when he suspected the idol he bore in his heart and when he materialized it, it was you that he saw, you that he implored. Then, when the radiance emerging from you, as if escaping from star, to go toward him, became more intense, it warmed his more tremulous hope, from it he drew the illumination of his future. In dreams, you brushed his nights as a pale form; in reality, you bathed his days with a more triumphant energy. He wept, Henriette! I have seen him weep! And it's for him—

yes, for him—that I invoke your pity; it's for him that I have come to say: take that blood, take that life of a slave. He will keep you, he will save you, he will bless you, for he adores you, Henriette...my beloved Henriette!"

He had fallen to his knees, and he was weeping for them to be happy, in order for the life of which he was the apostle, and which he could only serve by immolating himself, to be triumphant in their union.

Then she understood, in a flash of discernment, the pious lie of his letter; she understood that he had never ceased to love her, that he was immolating himself before their altar. She leapt to her feet, seized the young man's head in her fearful hands and pulled it toward her.

"It's you! It's still you, that other! I sense that it's you!"

"Me!" exclaimed Claude, rising to his feet and pulling away, suddenly sobered up. He started to laugh, with a gurgle that made him feel ill, obstinate in the evident falsity of his protestation. "Me! It's insensate to say that it's me! Me, the son of a consumptive, and consumptive myself, dare to create! I know that the earth will reclaim me tomorrow, and that your God will punish me if I give mortal kisses and engender children for whom I would be reserving the tortures reserved for me. Me! Oh, me..."

He was still laughing, madly; but it was wasted effort. Henriette came to him, and looked at him again with all the sincerity of her honest soul,

"No, Claude, you're trying to deceive me. I've sensed your heart vibrating too powerfully. I can no longer turn away from the face of things. Because of you, because of the oath I made to you, which only death can break, I ought not to marry Raoul. It's necessary that I go into the convent. I've decided that definitively."

She went out. She had already resumed her appearance of melancholy, claustral humility. Claude stayed there for a long time, reflecting, his head in his hands, his eyes dried by a resolution of fear and the night.

XXVI

"Because of an oath that death alone can break...," she had said, twice.

Claude was still there, next to the chair that Henriette had abandoned, for a time which he could not delimit, which might have been minutes, or hours. His head plunged in his hands, occupying the same position of dolorous dejection, he reflected. Each of his own terms and each of the young woman's responses was reproduced in his memory with the fidelity of a manuscript one rereads; and now that he strove to appreciate their conversation more coldly, he read therein more evidently the transformation of his fiancée, the scant sincerity of her convictions, and how he had almost convinced her to renounce them in order to yielded to Raoul's amour. But the result had been suddenly set aside by his imprudent ardor in defending a cause that was too much his own, in letting his own passion show through the eloquence that he believed destined to enable his rival to triumph. And the same phrase, innocently pronounced was revived intensely, as the veritable motive for the chivalric refusal to which he had been subject.

The young woman had certainly not understood the gravity of her words. Pushed to the limit, she had simply emitted them as the reason for her decision. But Claude could not help feeling their voluntary cruelty; he could not help estimating that, in truth, that speech suggested the only means by which the situation could be resolved in accordance with his heroic effacement: if he disappeared. Henriette could marry Raoul.

Oh, the bitterness of those reflections, the frightful upheaval of that poor heart, which, after seeing itself dispossessed by destiny, after having been murdered by him and torn into shreds like a prey, now had to reunite its twitching fragments, its supreme energies, in order to rebound in one last leap, all the way to the altar of immolation. Oh, the miserable incoherence of the universal system, reflected in things and beings, springing back as far as humankind and crushing one of them, the most tender and sympathetic, and also the most enlightened, the most disposed to render generously to life what it had given to him, to establish his hearth, to radiate in the present and reverberate in the future!

Claude sensed that injustice violently, and he could not, alas, believe in the equilibrium of ulterior compensations, in survival in a world of appeasement. What compensation could there be, in any case, to balance the immense dolor that he felt at this moment? He could not even hope in some metempsychosis, harvesting the debris of his soul, in order to reunite it in a more favored entity and communicate a new fortune to it in a reparative evolution. No, in that he could not believe. He had observed too clearly that the soul is consequent on the thousand particles of cerebral matter—did it not stop, in fact, in a living body, when the brain stopped functioning under an organic influence, an unhealthy flaw?—and he suspected that it dispersed in the final hour, at the same time as the matter disaggregated.

Such was the disappointing result of his positive studies, but at that moment he would gladly have denied it in order to return to superstition, to find therein a palliative for his misery. He would have like to believe in a last refuge of ideas, in which everything is appeased in a calm firmament, or blurred in celestial neutrality, in which thought subsists, soaring, asleep in an infinitely pure psychic bliss. He would then have accepted more serenely the final proof; he would have inclined more piously before a incomprehensible edict of the great hand; he would not have felt that mute rancor against events, against the bad mother, creation, and also against the imprudence of the man who had prepared this web for him woven of fire and death, Antonin Fargeaud, whom he heard arriving at that precise moment, groping the floor with small taps of his cane, stopping at the door of the drawing room and asking, his voice rendered more high-pitched by the usury of the years:

"Are there, Claude? Are you there, my son?"

At that appeal, he awoke from his distress. He got up, exhausted, his legs weary, ad went to meet him. He took his arm and guided him with great precaution to a seat. A veneration further increased by the old man's infirmity protested within him nevertheless. He did not recognize in that enfeebled man any other fault than being ignorant. And then, had he not repaired his fault with a lifetime's affection?

"Sit down, Father. You have to talk to me?"

"Yes, my child," replied Antonin Fargeaud, vaguely surprised by the lassitude that was evident in Claude's question.

With the hyperacuity particular to those dispossessed of one sense, who compensate for that sense with another, the father's ear divined the dejection of the son. At first, however, he abstained from searching for its motive, and said: "Yesterday I had all the joy of welcoming you, and I wouldn't have had a mind tranquil enough to interrogate you; but the night has permitted me to reflect. I also thought that I'm very old, that death might take me at any moment...frequent leaps of my heart, palpitations and stiflings indicate certain disorders to me here in my chest. I haven't consulted the physicians, what can they do? But I want to know that you're happy before I go away, and I believe that it's time for you to make dispositions if you want me to obtain any profit from them..."

At another time, Claude might have escaped with a pious lie before his father's confession. He knew perfectly well what epilogue the old man was caressing for his romance of youth; he knew that he could not respond in accordance with the poor old man's views, and that would perhaps have given the fatal shake to the poorly-beating heart, haunted by the obsession of his union with Henriette. He would have temporized; he would have demanded to wait for a more certain cure; he would have eked out in several successive confessions the dolor to which his confession was about to give birth at a stroke. But in the state of demoralization he was in, and also under the flux of the involuntary rancor that he was experiencing against the imprudent instigator of his fall, he no longer felt the energy for mercy, for a further sacrifice added to the others.

"What dispositions are you talking about, Father?" he asked.

"Come on, child, don't avoid a question that interests you more than me..."

"You're talking about my marriage?"

"Certainly."

"That marriage is impossible, Father."

Antonin Fargeaud put his hand to his chest in order to contain its sudden beating. At the same time, Claude saw him go extremely pale, as if the death to which the old man has just alluded was about to take him away. His beauty of sculptural lividity, famed by the fleece of the great beard and the abundant hair falling to his shoulders, had a character of grandeur at that moment, truly so poignant, that the son could not help admiring him while being saddened. But the bitterness that replaced the seizure of the face relaxed the features almost immediately, engraving them with a expression of annoyance less calculated to inspire pity. The anger of his voice rose.

"Ah! I divined truly then, when, reading your letters, I discovered the detachment from the woman I reserved for you! So, you and Henriette are in league, plotting against my authority! I'll be reduced, then, to denying you as I've denied my other children! To think that I raised both of them in that unique hope! So you've understood nothing of the tenderness of my heart? I palpitate around you two. For the sake of that lost crop I have covered you with adoration! I haven't listened to my disgust for life, nor my attraction toward annihilation, in order to see you two extend your united hands over my old head! Oh, why didn't Malthus advise me sooner?"

All his ideas of sterile anarchy returned to him at that moment, agitating his sclerotic brain, stirring the mud troubled by his past revolts: ideas, in sum, similar to those of his son, similarly engendered by the disappointing spectacle of creation, but differing in their conclusions, which were in him a destructive revolution, while in Claude they were a great re-

403

parative pity, the powerful movement of a consoling, and above all far-sighted, humanity. He only envisaged the immediate result, banal in its brutality, the word ending at the same time as his aspirations crumbled. On the contrary, Claude glimpsed future destinies, the progression of civilizations toward happiness, by means of the prudent seeding of the race, and the more reflective organization of families.

A cataclysm annihilating the earth and drawing him into its disaster would have fulfilled the dearest wishes of the father at that moment; a stone falling into one of the hearths for which he wished, and wounding one of its members, would have upset the charity of the son.

The latter observed, impatiently: "Don't invoke Malthus, Father, don't think about annihilation. If you had let me speak, you would have understood why I can't marry Henriette, why I liberated her from her promise a little while ago. I'm not cured and perhaps never will be. See nothing there but an unfortunate episode of life, which might be beautiful elsewhere, where those who engender are careful of the beings to whom they gave birth!"

"The ingrates!" murmured the old man, who was having difficulty following his son's thought.

"For what ingratitude are you reproaching us?" Claude demanded.

"That of not obeying me!"

"Obeying you! Come on, Father, don't force me to pronounce words that are too harsh, of lacking the respect that I'm conscious of owing you, in spite of everything that has happened, alas."

"In spite of everything? So I'm the culpable here?"

"If you're not culpable, Father, you're responsible..." And as the old man made a movement of surprise: "Oh, how painful it is for me to talk to you like this...but it's necessary that I confess the truth to you in order for you not to blame Henriette or me.

"Listen, then: two responsibilities exist, of which the majority of men are unaware, and of which you have been ignorant, like the others. When a man creates, he ought to avoid for his descendancy the burden of hereditary transmissions, and you have not been able to spare me that. A man can dispose of himself, but he doesn't have the right to dispose of his children, to condemn innocents in advance to the tortures of a pathological heredity. That's why you can't reproach me for not marrying.

"Down here, our individuality doesn't exist; we are merely intermediaries, links in an immense chain that is the race, creditors of life, receiving from the past a legacy of immortality in order to confide it to our descendants. A man is not born and does not die; he radiates beyond himself through time and space; he continues the flesh and soul of those who created him; he persists in the flesh and soul of those who come from him.

"Well, tell me, Father, have you looked behind you? Have you seen the magnificent flow of ancestral virtues that the chain has alienated from stock to stock in order to bring it to you? What accumulated energies, what active splendors, to resolve in your person! Have you looked ahead of you, thereafter? Have you seen the atavistic route so golden with hopes, so wide open and so luminous, where, like your predecessors you might have launched your lineage sumptuously, your lineage furnished with all the resources of sap, potency, health and beauty? What a treasure you have received, Father! What a treasure you ought to have transmitted! But you have not looked!"

Scarcely had Claude finished than he regretted having been so cruel. The astonishment of such a speech had been succeeded by despair. The old man let a large tear fall, and nothing was as moving as the ooze of sadness emerging from those opal eyes devoid of light, hardened by the gel of years. All the result of the generative act, he involuntary case of such a disaster, rose up now in a whirlwind behind that sclerous cranium, which was like the monad of philosophy, with no window to the outside. Oh, the unfortunate father, the unfortunate creator!

Claude was convinced, at that moment more than ever, that he had been marked by the evil finger of destiny, that he was himself like those fatal birds whose wing-beats cast an evil spell on whomsoever is touched by them, whose lugubrious cry condemns. A little while ago, it was Henriette and Raoul whom his intervention had cast into the abyss; now it was Antonin Fargeaud, whose dream of twenty years he had severed at a stroke, whose weary shoulders he had laden with an unconscious and unknown crime.

Why had he spoken to his father? Why had he not left him in his tender ignorance, or even in his anger? Should he not have credited with a little more obedience, a little more of the blind adoration that one owes to one's parents, the man who, for years, had armed him with such a radiance of tenderness? Oh, the atrocious consequence of his science, of his philosophy, of his need for truth, of his frankness...and also his rancor!

"I've hurt you, Father," he said, softly, taking the two fleshless hands, where the cords of the tendons were spaced out.

"Yes, too much...don't remain near me any longer. Go away! You're making me suffer...go away!"

The old man pushed him way, and his entire body trembled. Then Claude feared provoking, by his presence, a further paroxysm of that dolor, and he withdrew.

He went to his room, encumbered by his trunks, impregnated with the atmosphere of changing residence, the mere observation of which fills the soul with disarray. The fire had not been lit; the fresh morning air passed into his bronchi like a burn. He started to cough.

He shivered, and all the life in his body flowed to his brain. He knocked over the boxes that obstructed his passage. He went to his writing-desk, opened it with an abrupt gesture, seized a pen, set out a sheet of paper, and got ready to write; but his fingers moved away from the sheet and he reflected.

Because of the oath that death alone can break... With what resolute calm she had pronounced the phrase that condemned him! And it was quite logical, in fact, that he could not continue to remain while everything turned against him, while his presence was an obstacle to the happiness of others. The poor child had not known, in innocently giving an argument favorable to her retreat, that she was pronouncing a death sentence. Suicide, a cowardice of men capable of still being useful to generation, to the flight of the hereditary proliferation of which Claude had just evoked the role before his father, became a heroic term for the man whose survival prevents the expansion of one of its roots.

His botanist's soul lingered voluntarily over that symbol. When a plant parasite prevents the growth of neighboring plants, one uproots it. The intelligence of the most modest gardener would have quickly adopted that measure favorable to new evolutions. Was not life a plain already sown with brambles? Ought he, Claude, not show himself, in the circumstances, to be a sublime gardener, and uproot himself from the atavistic soil whose sap he was draining, the terrain of which he was cluttering?

And the more he thought about the beings he had known, of those who had lived in his intimacy, and whose acts and motives he had discovered, the more he recognized the deadly role of creators, their blameworthy immixture in society. Yes, he was seeing clearly in this hour, so close to his last. Several, certainly, had been able to set an example of admirable prudence, and Doctor Bouret had created his eight children with a respectful concern for his seed. But the others, the generality, what a mass of slaves of their ferocious enjoyments, what a population subjugated by interest, by egotism or by incoherent passions!

Whichever way he turned, there was the same scorn for the human seed, the same incomprehension of the disasters that bad dispersal engenders, the same transgression of the patrimony of races; there was pathological heredity, the heavy charge of defects supported by the descendants; the frightful trio of alcoholism, syphilis and tuberculosis transmitted by the unconscious, ravaging everything, extinguishing everything.

How many masks grimacing agony there were in the world! How many others howling the crime of ancestors! Claude saw them all again at that moment, he heard the cries of suffering and death. Little degenerates, from the outset, convulsions and meningitis were lying in wait for them. In vain the helpful physician would lean over their cradles, in vain frightened mothers, in order to extract them from their delirium, in order to be recognized by them, would strive to lift their eyelids! The light of their innocent souls vacillated momentarily, but their breath was extinguished and they died. They died because the bestiality of their parents had engendered them.

And if, by chance a few, spared by the sledgehammer blows of early age, survived, then there were other tortures, other terrors. Vice, monstrous passions and madness were ready to seize them; some rediscovered at twenty the fury of ethyl alcohol, others consumptive decadence. What joy would they experience, those pariahs, dangerous to society, a burden for all, a burden to themselves, incapable of a smile? Claude knew that very well, he who was about to die of the initial fault of his father!

And all of that misery had been engendered in sexual intercourse.

Thus, the most beautiful part of creation suffered or crumbled. The somber authors of those dramas, the specimens that Claude knew, passed before his eyes again, as representatives of joyful humanity riveted to its base instincts, to its unconsciousness, to its calculations.

In his family, first, there was his father. Antonin Fargeaud had married twice, and both times, by virtue of ignorance, he had spoiled his descendancy. The fruits of the first marriage, Hector and Rolande, were designated already as two complete specimens of atavistic consumption.

Hector, hereditarily nervous, bearing his mother's hysterical flame in his marrow, had quickly fallen into debauchery, squandering his seed, abandoning it to all the winds of stupor, further aggravating his libertinage with monstrous boasting.

Extraordinary luck had spared him at first from the inevitable consequence of his numerous imprudences, but one day, syphilis had struck him, all the more brutally because it was belated, and now the grimaces of hemiplegia were succeeded by the progressive general paralysis of which he would die imminently, in a repulsive abjection.

Then there was Rolande, as nervous as her brother of the same bed, impelled like him toward sensual morbidity. The vivacity of the first man, Julien Duverdon, had sounded and sickened her, and cast her into a deceptive vice, appeasing her genesic avidity but hostile to creation. A subterfuge had cured her in spite of herself; she would now evolve normally around the child whose first palpitations had proclaimed her deliverance. By that means, she would reconquer the health of her instincts, the normal play of the organ around which female sensibility is concentrated, which is a second brain.

Those first disappointments had not opened Antonin Fargeaud's eyes. From Charybdis he had fallen into Scylla, by marrying his second wife, the mild and poetic Emmeline, with eyes of oceanic azure. That one he had adored immensely at fourteen, with an amour of first adolescence in which he entire delusions of the heart were singing. And that was his only excuse for having, at an age when a man ought to reflect on his creation engendered a child with a consumptive woman: Claude, whose pathological heredity had condemned him, after an apparently strong youth to suffer all the struggles of tuberculosis.

Having grown old, the bitterness of his disappointments was softened when he had put his eye before the kaleidoscope of his family, and he wanted his youngest son to create in his turn, as he had done himself, in ruination and misfortune; forty years of cruel observations had not sufficed to enable him to conceive the fault of his sed. And how many more examples there were around Claude! How many hearths in which the seed, egotistically restricted or stupidly dispersed, was leading the race to calvary!

The Fortins had no children, and her amour was desperate in consequence.

The Servants, the miserly farmers hypnotized by the ambition of social ascension for their daughter Marthe, after having deflected their fecundity, after having bent their backs over the soil for half a century and watered it with their acid sweat in order to perfect the elevation of that only scion had just lost the schoolteacher, Claude had heard, to typhoid fever, because the Chantemesse serum was not yet known;[9] and it was said that when the last spadeful of dirt had fallen on the coffin, the father, on returning to the great fields quivering from his labor saw them now, in their splendid fecundity, so futile to his limbs broken by the catastrophe, that he had fled to the neighboring pond and drowned himself

Not far from them, in the badly maintained lodge of the château, the Grignons had been hiccupping their amour for thirty years, gorging their creative fluid on alcohol. Eighteen children had emerged from the loins of the mother, in what filth and in what atavism! Eight, scythed down at the outset by meningitis, had piled up the misery of their birth in the common grave, but ten still remained, bastardized and deliquescent: ten who would eventually propagate generations corrupted by the vice of their ancestors.

Anatole, the first, limited and incapable of active effort, trailed the stripes of an incapable corporal through reengagements, soiling his tunic with brutal contacts abroad, bringing back under its pleats the evocation of distant ruts, unknown germs destroying races and dissolving primitive peoples with the elements of civilized wounds. In China he had killed as stupidly as he had created in Madagascar.

---

[9] André Chantemesse and Fernand Widal demonstrated in the 1890s that a serum derived from animals vaccinated against typhoid had a curative effect in humans, but his treatment was still in the experimental phase when the present novel was written. Many of the experiments were carried out in Paris hospitals, and Couvreur would have been familiar with them.

Arthur, the second, paltry and narrow-shouldered, had not even been able, because of his complexion, to follow his brother's career. A place as a gas-lighter in a big city had enabled him to live at first, but as industrial genius incessantly substituted for the services of human muscles, the recent invention of a system of electricity illuminating and extinguishing street-lights automatically had dispossessed him of his employment. Now he did odd jobs and looked after Hector Fargeaud's automobile, poorly retributed, alimenting himself on alcohol and crusts of bread. For Fecundity he was a null element; one day or another he would become a charge on the community, occupying a bed in the hospital, where he would die.

The third, Alphonsine, fallen on to the asphalt in Paris, as a practical girl, had commercialized amour, extracting both semen and money. The seed that was the refuse of her industry she cast into the void; the money, the fruit of her labor, she hoarded. She was waiting for her purse to be heavy enough to permit her to live on her income, execrating Venus.

Thus, the first three branches of the family spread out, preventing the sun of life from radiating as far as the fertile ground. Then there were seven other boys and girls, whom alcohol was preparing to follow the path of their elders, whom degeneracy would cast into malady, vice and perhaps crime.

And elsewhere, around Claude manifest in his thought at that precise moment, how many more examples there were of sterile disorder!

Miss Clara Boswett, a morbid androgyne, worn away to the marrow by the lie of her spasms, deceived and mocked in her latest passion, had been taken to a padded cell. Her contortions and howls, along a grille similar to those disposed around wild beasts, would soon clamor the protestations of her disappointed sex organs. Rose, her domestic, had died of wanting to stifle the fecund seed, ready to bloom, and Louis, the instigator of that crime, having got away unscathed from his complicity, was disposed to sin elsewhere, profiting egotistically from laws that, in refusing to research paternity, favored male abomination.

Madame de Berge, the ardent socialite, dry and nervous, whose fortune favored lubricity, in her desire for enjoyment without consequences, in her horror of the infant that might damage her loins, had delivered herself to the skillful and costly surgeon, and emerged from the operation triumphant. But later, nature would set its hand on her again, and would avenge that cowardice, making her suffer for years what Rose, less rich and for an identical result, had suffered in one night.

Thus, Claude had before his eyes, summarized in those various individuals, in the conclusions of their passions or their vices, specimen of every field of human culture, and every fashion of sowing them: active and fortunate seed with the sage Doctor Bouret; avid seed with the Servants; reparative seed with the Duverdons and the Fortins, with Julia the farm-girl; egotistical seed with Madame de Berge and Louis the valet de chambre; vitiated and murderous seed with his father Antonin Fargeaud, his half-brother Hector, the Grignons and their two sons; and sterile seeds with Clara Boswett, Alphonsine Grignon and Rose...but around those, the world was pullulating with other magnificent seeds that were neutralized in cloisters or extinguished in celibacy.

Around them there were sick seeds, corrupting seeds that evil Nature allowed to bloom instead of killing them in embryo, which were allowed to attack the special trunk in order to parasitize and putrefy it. And in order to activate those sproutings, those stirrings and those agonies, to exploit them and subsist in them, there was the syringe of Domesta, the glabrous fecundator, a charlatan elevated on the stupidity of others, also sterile, although supported by the pretty Cyrano. There was the needle of matrons with dirty hands, Madame Poupes with anonymous gestures, abolishing future evolutions with a sting. Above all, there were the scalpels of Caresco, the sublime butcher, who repaired and destroyed with an equal lack of conscience and an equal skill.

There were also the somber vices of prostitutes of both sexes, the entire mercantile horde launched to the destruction of seeds, under the utopian eye of pastors and philosophers, those who strove to explain, regulate and soften a destiny inalienable because that disorder was the very expression of life.

Oh, how unequal the distribution of that seed was, and how necessary it was that nature, in its stupid prodigality, was great nevertheless, in order to pour it out so generously; for having sensed that it was necessary to suspend all the passions, all the joy and all the suffering around the generative instincts; for having made the world gravitate around two creative axes, the phallus of the male and the womb of the female. For, in spite of its stupidity, in spite of its incoherence, the individual with whom it played, the individual whom it launched forth unarmed, prey to all the attacks of destiny, subsisted even so, and got up again, and there were still, in that tormented gulf, partial happinesses, smiles, perfumes, radiances and apotheoses...there were Henriette and Raoul.

That last evocation, so fresh amid the mud, so glorious amid so much shame, finally decided Claude's action. Yes, it was necessary for him to aid, in the feeble measure of his means, the renovation of Humankind. He would have liked to overturn the universe; he could only transcribe the few lines of a testament destining his fortune to the utilization of good. He leaned over the blank paper and wrote, after the date:

Being of sound mind, I charge my friend Raoul...

His thought directed his mind surely. His mind was the image of one of those seas suddenly calmed after a violent storm. Beneath the tranquil transparency of their surface, contrary currents still agitate in their depths. Above those intimate eddies of despair, a great pity floated, as placid as a lake of oil. He saw again clearly the immensity of the atavistic route; he was making a will in order for someone to follow it, in order that some fortunate individuals might find a remedy for the evil of generative incoherence.

Society would be renovated by puericulture, every child having a right to a share of wellbeing. Creches would collect

413

them at a young age, schools would be built that would educate them. In adolescence, a special sexual pedagogy would honor the seed. It would teach the boy on the way to becoming a man the laws of hygiene and salubrity that complete creation. It would inform him of the respect that a person owes to his seed, how to avoid crime and engender healthily. It would teach the woman how her most glorious gesture is the one that offers her breast to a nursling, as well as the sources of fecundity and life.

But Claude's effort had to stop there; all his fortune was employed in it. It was very little for the grandeur of his designs; it was enough for his homeland; it was enormous for future thought. It is sufficient for someone to indicate a road for it to be followed.

Finally, after two hours of toil, which summarized his ideas of ten years, Claude put down his pen and sealed his letter. His blue eyes were shining with an incomparable illumination. He went to a cupboard, opened it, and took out a bottle with a red label. He looked at the deceptive transparency for a long time by the light of the window. But the tears he shed were even more mortal than the clarity of the liquid.

XXVII

When Raoul had put his finger on the doorbell he suddenly started to tremble. The letter that he had found on getting out of bed, and which he was still holding in his hand,
nearly escaped. In order not to drop it, he was obliged to put it
in his pocket.

That letter, read and reread a hundred times during the
rapid journey in a fiacre, summoned him for a final adieu.
What, therefore, had happened to his unfortunate friend? Was
it the precipitate return, the fatigue of the journey and the
change of climate that had resumed the offensive in his disease and provoked a further hemoptysis? Raoul could hardly
believe it; Claude had been too improved on quitting Cannes
for such an abrupt and dangerous occurrence to have been
produced so inopportunely. Why, then, the cry of alarming
urgency, why the terms of the missive: *The denouement is
approaching for your poor companion; come and see me one
more time, and don't allow Henriette to suspect what you will
have understood…*?

The ambiguity of those lines frightened him . He divined
suicide therein. As long as he arrived in time to extract him
from his sinister design and bring him back to the life that he
wanted to flee!

He had rung again, and as the door was slow to open he
shook it with a formidable pressure. He heard behind it, under
the arch, the rapid footsteps of a man coming in the opposite
direction. The bolt was drawn and Louis, the valet de
chambre, finally appeared, pulling the batten.

"What's happened, Louis? What do you know?"

The man was nonplussed, uncomprehending. Then he
pushed him aside abruptly and bounded toward the vestibule.
What he saw there reassured him at first; things bore the imprint of their usual calm. In the open dining room, the table

was being laid for lunch. In the small drawing room he perceived Antonin Fargeaud, who was meditating.

For two hours, since the argument with his son, the old man had been there, in his armchair, stuck in his dolorous reflection. Insensible to his surroundings, to the footsteps resonating on the marble flagstones of the entrance and the return of Henriette from mass, he had concentrated on the grave problem of his responsibility, inexorably denounced by Claude. But he did not seem to be deploring a drama.

Then Raoul sighed with deliverance. If some event threatening the life of his friend had occurred, would not the old man have been the first to be informed? He started to hope that the suicide was simply moral, that Claude was about to depart. He approached cheerfully and pronounced a bonjour in order to be recognized. And as the old man did not reply, he noticed his cold, closed, immensely dolorous attitude.

"Are you suffering, Monsieur Fargeaud?"

"No, my friend," he replied, effortfully, "but I had a conversation this morning with my son that has broken me."

"It's for that reason, then, that Claude has written to me?" Raoul observed, already seized again by his suspicions.

"He's written to you? On what subject?"

"He begged me to come to see him without delay, in order to bid him adieu."

"Adieu? Is Claude going away, then?"

The same frisson of fear that had seized the young man a little while ago took possession of the old man. It was, however, admirable that the invalid had made a sudden resolution and, without wanting to open up to the man whose anger he had just been subjected, was going to a new destination, some precocious spa.

But deep down, Antonin Fargeaud sensed the implausibility of that supposition. Raoul's words had resounded like the toll of a bell sounding the alarm, like one of those mysterious telepathic warnings that reveal distant catastrophes. The spring of his old legs was suddenly released and brought him to his feet.

"Let's go, quickly! I fear a misfortune. Help me, guide me!"

Raoul was already far away before he had finished speaking and held out his arm in order to be conducted.

The young man ran upstairs, hastening toward the familiar bedroom. Having reached the landing he stopped, suffocating, interrogating the silence, seeking revelatory sounds, emissary sobs, the emanation of dolor that gives the proximity of death so much cruel solemnity. He only heard slow and regular footsteps approaching. They were Henriette's.

The young woman went pale on seeing him. Her beautiful dark eyes, widened by a surprise mingled with anguish, interrogated him anxiously. She divined that the presence of the young man at that moment, at a time when the pretext of a illness ought to keep him distant from their grave conversations, had been solicited by her fiancé with a view to a final resolution, and that thought was sufficient to upset her. In addition, the customary serenity of the blond Christ was modified this time by such an expression of dread that, before subscribing to the primary formulae of politeness, she exclaimed: "You, Raoul! You? What's wrong, then?"

"Claude…?" stammered the newcomer. "Is Claude suffering, then?"

Again, he did not wait for a reply. It seemed to him that every second spent away from the man who had summoned him was an eternity stolen from his amity. He ran to the bedroom, which was not locked, and he went in, followed by Henriette.

A body was there, collapsed on the floor, amid the clutter of trunks that had not been unpacked.

Before collapsing Claude must have attempted to hang on to some nearby object, for his right hand was still holding in its clenched fingers a strap that had given way. His face, turned toward the parquet and partly folded toward the torso, could not be seen; they could not tell whether life still animated him, whether the lips were still respiring, or whether the fatal work was already accomplished. That frightful tableau immediately made them gasp, with an incomparable seizure.

The Pravaz syringe of which he had made use had fallen beside him, and a cruel ray of light, reflected by the nickel, gave the little killing machine a sinister appearance; but nothing nearby revealed the poison, the alkaloid that had destroyed so brutally, which Claude must have put away again after having filled the implement.

"Oh my God! Is he dead?" exclaimed Henriette, terrified, her eyes staring.

Without replying to the young woman, Raoul was already kneeling before the unfortunate. He had seized his arms and imprinted a half-turn to him, sustaining the stuff head, which seemed to be united with the trunk. On seeing the livid face and staring eyes, they thought at first that he had indeed been carried away by the irremediable slumber, but soon, a few contractions of the limbs tendered them a glimmer of hope. Claude appeared to be reanimating. Doubtless it was the position that was stifling him, because he started to respire, and a few bubbles of white foam burst on his lips.

"No, he's alive; send for a doctor right away," Raoul commanded, in a breath.

She was about to obey when they were surprised to hear a voice speak, jerkily, seemingly having difficulty fraying a path as far as the taut lips.

"No, I beg you…no stranger, no doctor…he'd arrive too late."

There was still a soul in that body, which seemed annihilated. Raoul and Henriette looked at one another with the same radiance of joy that had once traversed them when they witnessed the first amelioration of their invalid. They said nothing; they waited, suspended above him in an enormous silence, for him to give other signs of his thought. Raoul, still kneeling and sustaining the head, mopped the white face, where droplets of sweat were filtering. Henriette had taken his hand, and was alarmed to find it icy, as if death were already installed there.

Life was, in fact, withdrawing, fleeing the limbs paralyzed by the poison in order to take refuge in the chest animated by accelerated respiratory movements, and to concentrate
above all in the sea-blue eyes with contracted pupils. But the
voice rose again, strangely soft and distant, evocative of reposing regions where the desperate soul had already nearly land-
ed, from which he was about to return momentarily. It stammered through the enamel of barely parted teeth: "Thank you,
Raoul! Thank you Henriette! I thought you'd come together,
and it does me good to know that you're there, both of you, at
the moment when I'm about to leave."

"You're not going to die, Claude. We're going to send
for a doctor, who'll reanimate you after a temporary weakness."

"No! No doctors!" ordered the dying man, sharply. "No
priest either, Henriette," he added, noticing the gesture of his
fiancée, who had just put her hands together. "They'd take
away the few short moments I still have to give you. What I
want to confide to you, you both know, but I'll say it again:
I'm doomed, irremediably doomed. You understand, Raoul!
Don't weep. Be valiant, as two hearts ought to be who love
one another, in the presence of a brother vanquished by destiny."

His tongue was glued by a thick saliva. He made an effort to get rid of it and murmured: "Give me something to
drink…I can no longer speak…"

Henriette held out a glass of water that she had taken
from the dressing-table and slid a little into his mouth, but his
throat remained refractory and he could not swallow; he had to
let it escape along his cheeks. Henriette mopped it up with her
handkerchief, trembling with an emotion that rendered her
clumsy.

"How emotional you are, my poor Henriette!" said
Claude, trying to smile but not succeeding. "You're wrong,
you see; it's very little to go away, when one leaves happy…"

In contradiction with his words, a great frisson seized
him, which revealed the horrible sacrifice. His entire body

undulated, his lips became bloodless, his face was varnished by a sweat of agony. They thought that he was about to expire. Then Raoul laid him in his arms, like a child, surrounding him with his muscles, striving to transfuse him with a little of his warmth. And it seemed that he succeeded, for life was emitted from his grip. Claude overcame that assault again and revived with a new flame.

"Oh, this cold...this cold!" he said. "I didn't believe I'd feel it. It almost made me forget you...my hands can no longer feel, my legs seem detached from me. Come closer, listen to me, time's passing. We're alone, aren't we? No one can hear me? I can no longer see clearly...and my ears are also betraying me..."

Just as he was about to continue, a dolor of a wounded animal, a echo of all that the human heart can feel of the most cruel howled at the other end of the room. At the same time, the tottering mass of Antonin Fargeaud came to collide with the trunk next to the group. He pirouetted and collapsed next to Claude.

"My child! My child!"

The drama increased. The old man had crawled as far as his son in a supreme struggle against the death that was also felling him, an aneurism having suddenly burst in his breast. He clung to him, reached his forehead and applied his lips to it. Their two lividities were confounded. But he was dying. An ultimate spasm of his throat still allowed words to escape: "It's my fault...forgive...child...forgive..."

Then he rolled over. But Claude turned his eyes away from him. His pity, too pressed for time while he was still alive, could no longer linger over the fallen old man. It went toward the resplendent future, still standing, in the person of Raoul and Henriette. He smiled. Was any sunset, sumptuous as it might be, worth as much as the glory of the sun that was about to rise tomorrow? Did any falling oak attain the splendor of the flower that was about to blossom tomorrow?

He smiled; he had resumed his tender charm of an apostle whose face proclaims hope in future spaces. However, he had to hurry, for the rest of his body was extinct; his respiration was diminishing in amplitude, his heart was having difficulty continuing its rhythm; everything was failing save for the eyes and the forehead, aureoled by an immense altruism behind their veil of death.

"You heard," he said, in a precipitate murmur. "You heard my father ask me to forgive? Doesn't it seem frightful, a dying father imploring the pity of his son, also dying? Yes, that might seem abominable... If you knew however how many parents ought to beg their children's pardon for having created them! The world is full of those unconscious criminals, responsible toward the society that they encumber with bad citizens, responsible toward their progeniture, whom they charge with a morbid heredity. Society I won't talk about; it's the first guilty party, since it owes individuals the instruction, the warning and the moral awakening that it doesn't give them. But the children! Those exquisite and frail creatures, who are already condemned when they appear in the daylight. Can you imagine that abomination? Can you imagine that calvary?"

He suspended his breathing again, which, afflicted by the poison, was gasping more and more, only escaping now with an infinite difficulty. But the immensity of his immolation was radiant in his eyes, still enthused by life. The anxiety of Raoul and Henriette espoused their intense light more avidly. They listened to his speech like thirsty people in a desert welcoming the alms of fresh water. He went on:

"I'm at the end; I sense it. I can see myself dying. My hands want to unite yours and seal them over my mortal remains, but I can no longer move, and it's my subsisting thought that must accomplish your union. Come closer...closer, closer to my face. Let my last kiss be common to you; let your lips touch in touching my forehead. Listen! You adore one another; you must marry. Humanity is radiant in you. You have the triumphant seed within you! It's a splendid treasure; it would be impious to allow it to be lost. You'll keep that treasure of life, that hereditary flame, soundly, in order to

421

bequeath it to your children, who will transit it to theirs in their turn. That's the wish of a dying man; may I carry it, granted, to my grave! Respond, Raoul; respond, Henriette. But respond with a sign, for I can no longer hear…respond!"

Raoul, in tears, had already affirmed with his head; but a frightful combat dominated the uncertainty of the young woman. What final torture was she about to cause her unfortunate fiancé, in promising aloud what her heart accepted in a whisper? But at that moment, her gaze encountering that of the dying man, she understood that it was no longer a question of heroism, and that she ought to yield to that magnificent prayer, whose realization would be the supreme joy of a broken soul. Then she consented too, with a nod of the head, and she was dazzled by the radiance that she provoked.

"I no longer regret having lived, now," said Claude. "I thank you…I bless you!"

That was the last intelligible word he pronounced, and they scarcely heard it. His blue eyes clouded over, as if a twilight were attenuating the azure waves of which they bore the reflection. His head inclined gently over Raoul's shoulder. However, his lips were still moving. They sensed that he was continuing to repeat until the end the beautiful song of the amour that awakens eternity.

They stayed for a long time watching him fade away. Then, when he had finished breathing, they leaned over at the same time to kiss him piously. And if the lips of the two lovers did not meet above his forehead, at least their tears traced the same furrow, at least they flowed together like a rain of future fecundity.

Thus life is perpetuated over tombs; thus the generative idea subsists in phenomena that pass.

PART THREE

XXVIII

The August day was hot, but with a good, healthy and beneficent warmth, after the stormy night that had absorbed the electricity of the atmosphere, swept away the miasmas and macadamized the dust of the air. A breath of purity coming from the banks of the Seine caused the verdure to quiver in the garden where Monsieur and Madame Fortin were taking their coffee after the midday meal: a light and vivifying breath evoking exterior splendors, the busy life of the quays and the great arteries of the city; a suggestive breath too, mingling with it as it ran along the river, connecting with the activity of others. The slackness of the two spouses, idly installed in large wicker armchairs, was unconsciously moved by it. Madame Fortin raised her blonde head, which a fortunate digestion was making drowsy, and turned toward her husband,

"What if we were to have the carriage harnessed, my darling? We can take Baby and the nurse. Baby didn't sleep well last night. The fatigue of an excursion will be profitable to his repose. What do you say, Father?"

She no longer called him anything else, now that Julia's child, a boy named Maurice, had been installed in the house, accepted as a real product of the household, cared for with the tenderness of an heir around whom the anxieties, joys and hopes of a hearth gravitate. She loved to salute with that term the generative potency of her husband; she found therein a derivative of the disillusions of her maternity. After the first regrets of having dispossessed the former farm-girl, she had yielded to the unconscious egotism of the rich, who take possession to the detriment of the poor, and the surges of pity for the rival frustrated of her fruit only returned to torment her at rare intervals.

In any case, when she thought about it, she immediately found good arguments to absolve herself. Had not Julia recognized that the child was as much Monsieur Fortin's as her own? In addition, her fear of evil tongues that would reduce her to the level of her mother, the streetwalker, and her fear of being repudiated by Douvard, the schoolmaster, whom she still loved—Douvard, who, knowing that she was a mother thanks to the work of another, would certainly not have wanted her any longer, whereas a round sum offered by Monsieur Fortin would render her desirable to the teacher—had acted on her rudimentary conception of honor and stifled the vague instinct that already stirred her when she felt her child twitching in her loins. She had accepted gratefully the bargain that stole her progeniture while simultaneously assuring her of the consideration of others, wealth and marriage with the man of her choice.

Everything had happened, therefore, as simply as could be. When the childbirth was accomplished in Paris, in secret, in the home of a midwife, Monsieur Fortin had hastened, for fear that he might be refused, to steal from her the parcel of pink flesh before she had hard his first wails, and the separation had not been in the least heart-rending. Now, united with the man who had tried to cast her down in the hay, recaptured by amorous atavism, Julia accepted his caresses ardently, and gave free rein to his bestial impulses, the contacts of which stirred all her fibers. She had already had a child in consequence, and considered it as the first of her true lineage, which would be numerous, since they had the means to raise children, and since it was so good to do so. As for the other, the one she had conceived in Nice, she no longer thought about him; she was reassured as to his fate.

It was with those arguments, deduced from the evidence of the facts, that Madame Fortin put her conscience to sleep. She therefore fed her maternal hunger in all tranquility, and deployed the tender cares, precautions and even the coquetries of a true maman around the cradle subtly introduced to her hearth, only laying the baby down in floods of lace and ribbons in pastel colors. She was like the hens that sit on the eggs of other species, according them the same natural obstinacy as their own. Her instinct was appeased on a object that was, in sum, only half-illusory, since the cherub originated from a man she loved.

She leaned toward her husband with a slightly languid grace, as she did every time she wanted to obtain something.

"That's it, Father, have the carriage harnessed. We'll go as far as Dieppedalle to visit the Duverdons You know that they're due to leave the Château de la Taquainerie today, to make way for the young household?"

"The young household?" asked Monsieur Fortin, who was not up to date.

"Henriette and Raoul are now Monsieur and Madame Fieux. They're getting married today in Paris, in the strictest intimacy. No one has been invited to the wedding except the witnesses, and Julien Duverdon is one of them; he's bringing them back this evening and then leaving immediately, with Rolande, and Jacques, their son…"

She interrupted herself momentarily, for a comparison had been imposed on her mind. She confessed: "He's nice, their little Jacques, but not as nice as our Maurice, is he, Father? Ours weighs twelve pounds; I weighed him his morning."

"Oh, really?" conceded Monsieur Fortin, with an apparent mockery, but fundamentally very proud, as he was every time he heard his work praised.

"We'll also see the monument that Monsieur Raoul has had erected to his friend," the wife continued. "Do you know, Father, that it's already a year and four months since Claude Fargeaud died? How quickly time passes, and how things change! Who would have believed in that marriage, after such a long separation of the two your people, Henriette returned to the convent and Raoul retired here, to Dieppedalle, in order to turn the château upside-down, to create a school there, a creche and a farm, in accordance with the intentions of the testator…!"

Suddenly, she stopped speaking, her blonde face dotted with abrupt patches of redness, almost frightened, by the perception of a faint sound coming from the upper story, one of the windows of which as open.

"I can hear Baby! He's just woken up and I'll wager that the nounou isn't with him!"

She fled, followed by her husband, more heavily, thickened out beneath his creator's laurels. They climbed the staircase and ran to the child, who occupied the room where they had hoped for his advent for such a long time, preparing his layette, his small items of clothing and his toys. Now that he was there they had made it into a veritable little temple, with walls hung with blue silk, with a profusion of things that would only have utility later, with, in the middle, the gilded altar raised on a pedestal: the cradle. The Redeemer was there, wailing at the moment, filling the house with his authoritarian whimpers, his little face all swollen, twisting his plump hands, in which good health described a furrow at the wrist.

"Well, Nounou, didn't you hear him?" cried Madame Fortin, as annoyed as could be, at the appearance of a superb nurse, who was belated in obeying the tyrant's order.

She lifted him out of the cradle herself, with infinite precaution, like a sacred object; she admired him; she noticed with a quasi-pride that he was going to be the portrait of his father. She kissed him greedily on the mouth. It would not have taken much for her to offer him her breast; she was saddened by having to pass him to the mercenary in order for her to offer him hers.

"Hurry up, Nounou, we're going out."

A quarter of an hour later the victoria was ready, and they set forth. Madame Fortin and the nurse, carrying the treasure, occupied the back. Monsieur Fortin, sitting facing them, gazed at all three. The little one, having been fed, had gone back to sleep. A veil of white gauze, thrown over his lace, protected his face, and his adoptive mother was also holding a tiring umbrella over him.

They traversed part of the picturesque town, going along quays bustling with animation. A delightful sunlight made the admirable décor of the cliffs flamboyant. The spouses, concentrated on the child's slumber, saw nothing of that beauty.

They were about to quit the river and veer right toward the woods of Roumare in order to reach the château when the blaring warning of a horn, preceding the appearance of chocolate-colored automobile coming down the hill on which they were already engaged, at great speed, made the carriage stop.

The enormous eight-seater vehicle, the prow of which was constituted by the torso and unkempt head of a gilded naked woman, was only occupied by two people. The one driving was svelte and harmonious, so far as one could judge, beneath the gray overcoat and behind the ugliness of the mask with the eyes of a fantastic animal. The other, small, fat, rotund and glabrous, had not donned a special garment. He was wearing his customary frock-coat and was having great difficulty maintaining his wide-brimmed panama hat. The wind produced by the speed was whipping the folds of his ruffled shirt. The bouncing of his abdomen, echoing the jolts of the course, was visible from afar. Pale with fear, having a terror of speed, he was clinging on to the arm of the seat, and begging his companion to slow down with an avalanche of exclamations.

Domesta was making his first excursion by automobile, with the inseparable Cyrano beside him.

"Get back, coachman! Move aside! You're going to cause an accident!" his reedy little voice cried, at a distance.

By chance, the two vehicles stopped, stuck to one another, just as the machine was about to crush the carriage. The poussah hastened to jump down to the ground. Anger succeeding fear, white with rage, he started heaping Cyrano with insults, whirling his little arms.

"Two hundred an hour! Santa Maria! You've gone mad, son of carrion! You wanted to kill me, swine! Just wait, you'll see, I'll send you back to the gutter! He wanted to kill Domesta, the great Domesta!"

427

Only then did he remember the strangers. Gripped again by his medical dignity, he smoothed the folds of his long frock-coat, expelled with little thrust of his fingers the dust that powdered him, and, removing his hat courteously, unveiled the baldness of his cranium with multiple bumps. Then, sticking out his lips devoid of mucus with an attempted smile, he said:

"Excuse my getting cried away, Signor and Signora. This child is mad, and I'm scolding him. He doesn't know what a great wrong he was about to do humankind, for I'm a great philanthropist, Signor and Signora! I'm Domesta, independent professor of artificial fecundation...the entire universe sings my praises!"

He rummaged in the folds of his garment, and was about extract his portfolio and offer his card when Monsieur Fortin cut off his effect dryly. "No need! I know who you are!"

"That's true by the Madonna! I recognize you too! You're my clients! I have so many! My house is overflowing! Pardon me, Signor! And you too, pretty Signora, pardon me!"

He stopped again, halted before the nurse, before the child, whom his presence caused to cry in fright,

"Ah! The darling! I recognize him too, the pretty darling! Can you ever thank me enough for having given him to you, that child of the syringe? Didn't I tell you that my method was infallible? Is it a boy? A girl? Do you want another? Now I inseminate the sex at will, without increasing the price, and I also give the hair color to order: blond hair, brown hair, red hair, and so pretty, the cherubs! But for that I have to charge more. It's uniquely a question of the date and the moon, anyway, and only I know them. My experiments are irrefutable. I've submitted them to the Global Academy of New Medicine, of which I'm the president. Scientists, nothing but scientists! You must have heard mention of it? All the newspapers have cried miracle!"

He moderated his volubility, suspending his gesture for an explanation. The two streaks of black pencil that replaced his eyebrows, inclining toward the root of the nose, almost joined up.

"I chose six women of different races and complexion, Signor. I would never dare to say the commerce that those women engaged in, for fear of offending the Signora's ears, but I made them the guinea pigs of my experiments. They were all charming, even the African—for there was a black woman, wasn't there, Cyrano?—and they all seemed inapt for reproduction. Well, would you believe it, with those six women, in nine months, after having cared for them, I gave eight children to France! Yes signor, eight…for the African brought three twins into the world, three adorable little twins the color of my automobile…good chocolate, one could have eaten them, isn't that so, Cyrano? And I'm the godfather of all of them. They'll inherit my immense fortune."

He replaced his panama on his head, which he had removed in order to declare the importance of his production, the play of his hat always underlining the effects of his verbiage. Then his little arms circumscribed his back, slanting toward the basques of his frock-coat, where his instruments were clicking. He only pulled out a wad of papers however.

"And people deny my utility in your beautiful country! 'Domesta is a charlatan,' they say. By the blood of Christ, you know that he isn't! I've served you well, you have a little darling there who resembles his mother! Isn't he your joy, the darling? And here, Signor, look at all these letters, all these testimonials. My pockets are full of them. Take them! Read them! I've blacked out the proper names, out of respect for professional secrecy."

After having stood on the footstep of the carriage, which leaned in his direction, he slid his papers insistently into Monsieur Fortin's hand and forced him to cast his eyes upon them.

"This is a letter from a widow without children who, in order to inherit from her husband had need of a scion before the legal lapse of ten months. She wanted it chastely. I gave it to her in nine months and three days, didn't I, Cyrano? She thanks me, poor woman, she adores me she weeps with gratitude. I'm going to have her letter framed."

In the heat of his discourse, he was sweating abundantly. He wiped his brow with a lace handkerchief. Then, pushing another sheet of paper, he resumed:

"And this! Have no fear, Signor, you can look at it. This, with this image, is the birth-announcement of another darling, whose name is Jacques, his baptismal name. He's now a year old, the little darling. By Saint Antoine, it's a funny story. But I'd be wasting my time recounting it to you. It reminds me that the impregnation of the spermatozoon into the ovule can be obtained without the woman's consent. I'm going to frame that one too. Let's pass on to another. This…"

"Yes, I know…*En route!*" Monsieur Fortin ordered the coachman, pushing away he monastic hand of the dwarf, who nearly fell backwards under the impulsion of the carriage pulling away. The rig resumed its course, leaving the fairground performer there, whose language of exotic terms— impregnation, ovule—and reedy invocations of the Madonna, the saints and Heaven reanimated in the memory of the two spouses a ridiculously sad page in their conjugal romance. However, an astonishment still pursued them, that of the second paper presented by Domesta, so similar to the announcement of the birth of little Jacques Duverdon that they had received a year ago, and which had struck them by virtue of the originality of the engraving accompanying the text: a little cherub with angel's wings, an idea of Rolande's.

Madame Fortin could not help confiding her surprise.

"So, Father, they were going for that, the Duverdons, when we met them at Domesta's door?"

"That's very possible, my dear. That charlatan made fools of us, but he might have succeeded with others."

And that success of the fecundator lifted their spirits, attenuating their rancor. But the beauty of the location framed by two valleys, in the gap of which the tower of the château was perceptible, soon dissipated their epic obsession.

After a further turn toward the wooded plain, they found themselves before the gate of the château. Ringing the bell caused Madame Grignon to appear, tottering; but the lodge was empty. The Fortins knew that the children had been taken away from the example of their parents, and that, removed to one of the new buildings of the château, the crèche, efforts were already being made, in accordance with Claude's will, to disengage them from their atavism. It was the little children that it was necessary to attack, if one wanted to remake the race, and not their elders, already enslaved by their habits. The parents had not protested. If they had been robbed of arms they had, on the other hand, been left the facility to get drunk more at their ease.

On foot, Monsieur and Madame Fortin, and the nurse, carrying the child, climbed the shallow slope that led to the habitation via an avenue of plane trees. Having reached the level of the lawn, the green space of which circumscribed the dwelling, they were amazed by the changes that had been effected in a year. One might have thought that a magician's wand had manifested its influence there.

The massive tower still existed, with its air of an old feudal guardian, and the buildings of the last century had also been respected. They already served as the lodgings of the director, the supervisors and the masters, and the refectory, study rooms and dormitories for the pupils. To the right, however, toward the plain, other buildings had surged from the ground, an entire agglomeration designed in accordance with the good sense of hygiene: the crèche, the school and the farm, with large windows hospitable to sunlight and air, and shady courtyards, or rather gardens, in which the adopted unfortunates played most of the time, in obedience to the system prescribed by Claude, who wanted the beast to be cared for before the mind was tormented.

Thirty infants were benefiting thus from the liberality of the benefactor, thirty children that had been extracted from the most wretched origins. They were being allowed to bloom before life had made slaves of them, endowed with a moral

431

health before being armed with a profession. The youngest, those in the cradle, received the cares of the crèche; others, more advanced, learned to read and write, and then to work as they chose, in accordance with their affinities; the adults were employed on the farm or in manual trades. To all of them, work and emulation were indicated as the elements of wellbeing, but without forcing them to it, and Raoul had been very surprised to see them accept as a pleasure what was imposed elsewhere as a chore.

A few black sheep, inevitably, already caught by vice or too tributary to their atavism, had darkened the bright flock, but, supervised very closely, they had been expelled as soon as counsels had remained without effect. Thus, the selection was accomplished very simply, and later, thirty glorious families would emerge from that elite, thirty sowers aware of the respect that was owed to human seed, the source of happiness or woe.

Edified on an isolated mound, dominating the ensemble and emerging from a clump of trees, a funerary stone stood. Madame Fortin noticed it immediately

"The monument to Claude Fargeaud, undoubtedly. Shall we go to see it, Father?"

"Let's go salute Madame Duverdon first," replied the husband, indicating a group they had not perceived before. It was Rolande, who had been masked by a large tree. Sitting in the shade, she was rocking a child asleep in a hammock. They approached, sympathizing with her maternal love, and seduced by the splendor of her tranquil, transformed beauty.

"This is my little Jacques," she said, proudly.

"This is our Maurice," relied Madame Fortin in her turn, no less proudly, so much had she succeeded in imputing to herself that foreign birth.

"And I can confide to you now," Rolande confessed, "that we're reserving a little brother, or sister, for him. I'd prefer a girl, and so would Julien.

She was radiant, and that confession was evidence of her modified life, her healthy acceptance of natural pleasures. As

Madame Fortin's expression darkened slightly with jealousy, she did not insist.

They returned to the château, in order to comment on the transformation and the real interest of the beneficent puericulture.

"It's Raoul who's done everything," said Madame Duverdon. "He's been working for a year on his organization, giving himself to it body and soul, stimulating the architects, putting in the masons, recruiting pupils in advance, beating the region to persuade the parents, and almost always receiving the gracious collaboration of the masters. Doctor Bouret has also harnessed himself to the work, and is continuing it, coming several times a week to teach a course to adults. Both of them have accomplished tours de force, with the result that it was inaugurated last April, a year after Claude's demise, on the anniversary of his death.

Monsieur Fortin's positivism calculated what it must have cost to move so many stones. He was worried by it, and Rolande explained that Claude possessed the heritage of his mother, who had died when he was very young, and had been able to gather, with the accumulated interest, about two millions; but that had not been sufficient. After having elevated the buildings for five hundred thousand francs, it was necessary to ensure the income for the maintenance of the property, to nourish the adopted children, and the salaries of the servants, so many expensive obligations. Fortunately for the enterprise, Claude had inherited a third of Antonin Fargeaud's fortune, it happened that, although deceased at almost the same time, it had been the father who had succumbed before the son.

"Raoul and Henriette, who were present at the drama," she continued, "affirmed that to us, and that was sufficient for Julien and me to believe it We could have contested that priority, but that would have been bad—the work is too beautiful! We therefore ceded the château and twenty thousand francs of income. It might be, alas, that an equal sum will soon increase that acquisition, for the recent news of my brother Hector, interned, as you know, in a sanitarium, is increasingly bad We're the inheritors by law, but we'll renounce that patrimony to the profit of the pupils, the number of whom it will be possible to increase. We have enough for ourselves."

The illumination of her eyes revealed how much she now believed in the race, and how much she would be able to participate herself in its renovation. Maternal enthusiasm, having arrived late in her heart, deflected from the true creative goal, was compensating for a long hostility, making her feel the precious satisfaction of throwing a little manna to the disinherited, of playing providence a little for those whom the clemency of destiny has not favored.

"In sum," she concluded, "this is the last day we shall spend here. Raoul and his wife will soon arrive to take possession of the apartments that we're abandoning, and which are reserved henceforth for her. They've both consecrated themselves to obeying Claude's last will."

"I'd like to go and place flowers on his tomb," Madame Fortin requested.

That same evening, in the fluid calm of the night, two strollers, Raoul and Henriette, headed for that tomb at a slow pace. A troubling grip kept them enlaced, and their breath confounded. They advanced sadly, but their melancholy did not attenuate their ardent desire. Were they not going toward the man who had inspired their passion? Had not Claude, who was lying here, under the stone sealed for four months, in his merciful intelligence, revealed the truth of amour, and how everything has its designation down here, how life engenders death, how subsistence and disappearance are only different phases of the same eternal cycle, and how, finally, each of our disaggregated particles ought, as soon as the last sigh, to rediscover its utility in the existence of others?

And it seemed, in fact, that the vegetation they were approaching had collected a little of the soul of the dear departed, the languid deployment of the plants sent so many intoxicating perfumes to them, and the branches of the trees, extended over their heads, seemed to join together so magnificently to shelter their kisses. Around them, everything was in repose; no more light shone in the windows of the children with closed eyes, no more wing-beats revealed the energy of birds. There was an infinitely mild, infinitely pious tranquility in the magical expansion of the light of the moon, at its apogee.

They climbed the tumulus at the top of which the funerary cone, sitting on a stone slab, surged forth. They had not separated their hands, knowing that they could show to Claude's manes that spectacle of adorable tenderness: two harmonious individuals, united by his sacrifice, coming to salute and thank him before the generative communion.

They knelt down. At first they remained silent, riveted to the marble slab beneath which their friend lay. A ray of moonlight, perforating the trees, surrounded them with a silver aureole. Then Raoul's voice rose up, grave, hoarse and gripping in its emotion.

"Can you see us, Claude? Can you hear us? The brother and sister of your thought are here. They have come to affirm to you that your memory is imperishable in them; they have come to promise you to consecrate to you the existence that you reserved for them so beautifully, to struggle for your last ideas, to make life triumph…the life that you loved for others, which you did not want to keep for yourself…"

That was all he said, for a sob responded to his simple prayer. Henriette had finally divined the secret of the mysterious death that has struck her fiancé so abruptly when everything concluded his resurrection. Poor, dear Claude! She understood him, at that moment, to be so great, so far beyond other men, so superb in his immolation that she truly loved him, that she loved him with an influx of intense dolor. She wept all her regrets, and Raoul had to guide her in order to enable her to follow the path that led back to the château, which they had traveled a little while before.

"Come, my love, come!" he murmured, very quietly

Outside the little wood, the suggestion of the night caught them again. Claude survived in them, but like a distant

435

flame, so soft and so chaste that it could not have anything in common with the feverish turbulence that set them ablaze at that moment. And the evocation of the dead man gradually dissipated as they drew away from his tomb and powerful creation solicited them. Raoul's masculine voice became gradually more tender, and also more imploring, to sing the few words that pressed her toward the work:

"Come, my love, come!"

He led her, fainting, all the way to their abode. He lifted her up in his heroic arms in order to climb the stairs. He only felt the burden in order to increase his desire. And when they had entered, when the closed door left him definitively her master, he hesitated again before the grave moment of the virginal rout. He went to the window and opened it wide.

"Look, Henriette look!" Facing them was an enchantment so vast that their nervousness suddenly calmed down. The moon, entirely full, was inundating that corner of the universe with its pure and suave tranquility. In front of them there was the river, which it caused to shine in little iridescent fractures; there was also the plain, which recoiled as far as the eye could see, all the way to the gigantic circle of hills. It drowned all of it in the same luminous confusion: the islets of the Seine, the trees, the distant steeples of the city, and the white chessboard of the cliffs. But higher up, it disseminated its rays in infinite space, espousing the heavens, with, as a nuptial veil, the blue-tinted radiance of its transparent fluid, spangled with scintillating stars, which seemed to be the jewels of the veil.

"Oh, the night, the night! Look, my Henriette!"

No more darkness in the firmament, no more chaos on the earth. Everything was resplendent with the sovereign light. Its sumptuous joy, limpid and serene, its quivering, pale, bridal joy, spread in sensual effluvia over everything, in shuddering and swooning embraces.

What loving kisses the Moon gave to the immensity, in order that humans could become its bewildered contemplators. Of what magnanimous fecundation was she a particle herself? What smiles of amour and eternity she sent to the crop of

436

stars, her fellows, all emerged from the same womb of fire. And from her, from her great blue-tinted heart, a creative inspiration descended through space, which penetrated the slightest coverts of the earth, transpierced the mystery of woods, searched the plains and the mountains, followed the mirroring of waters, infiltrated the interstices of thatched cottages and palaces, in order to bring to others the divine suggestion of sensuality.

Everywhere, everywhere, her divine light palpitated; everywhere, her marvelous lava flowed, inundating with desires, shuddering with sensuality. And toward her, in order to obey her and to thank her, a concert of adoration made of sighs, whispers, oath and gasps, the hosanna of the fecundating world, the soul of seeds, rose up like the supreme action of grace of vegetables, animals and humans.

"Oh, that infinity! It will never be as infinite as my tenderness, Henriette!"

He had brought her very close to his chest, and he divined that she was profoundly his. His hand ran behind her neck, beneath the aureole of hair, which came undone. As he unfastened her dress, he noticed the electric gleam of her dark eyes, touched by the star. Under the celestial radiance, the dimples in her cheeks, the gracious oval of her chin and her radiant teeth gave her a new, unknown, strangely seductive beauty, almost dolorous in vanquished expectation. Her breasts, soon uncovered, undulated with a great rhythm; and having pressed her against him he sensed their statures weakening under that caress. He undressed her.

Soon, their bewildered flesh touched and writhed with the same creative enthusiasm. Then he carried her to the alcove, and their splendors mingled. And when, the first plaint uttered, she entered into amour, quivering with the glorious gift of the seed, their cries of intoxication celebrated the most sacred act, the first act of races, that of the fecund sowing from which life emerges.